Dear Reader,

Romance and excitement are a given in the city that never sleeps. And Nora Roberts doesn't disappoint with these two classic novels set in the heart of New York City.

Local Hero, which is available for the first time in many years, features the kind of man any woman would want to share Central Park views with! But Hester Wallace isn't just any woman. She's a single mom struggling to start over with her new son. And she wonders if her handsome neighbor Mitch Dempsey could truly be the hero her son believes him to be.

In *Dual Image,* another classic novel being offered once more after several years, New York City is the setting for the love affair between Ariel Kirkwood and Booth DeWitt. She is a beautiful actress playing the role of a lifetime. And he's the man she's falling in love with, despite the fact that Booth is doing everything to fight his powerful feelings.

We hope you enjoy these two tales from the Big Apple!

Happy reading!

The Editors
Silhouette Books

NORA ROBERTS

TRULY Madly MANHATTAN

Silhouette Books

Published by Silhouette Books

America's Publisher of Contemporary Romance

SILHOUETTE BOOKS

TRULY MADLY MANHATTAN

Copyright © 2003 by Harlequin Books S.A.

ISBN 0-373-21803-6

The publisher acknowledges the copyright holder of the individual works as follows:

LOCAL HERO
Copyright © 1988 by Nora Roberts

DUAL IMAGE
Copyright © 1985 by Nora Roberts

Visit Silhouette at www.eHarlequin.com

Printed in U.S.A.

CONTENTS

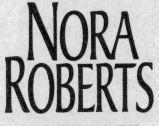

LOCAL HERO

For Dan, with thanks for the idea
and the tons of research material.
And for Jason, for keeping me in tune
with the ten-year-old mind.

Chapter 1

Zark drew a painful breath, knowing it could be his last. The ship was nearly out of oxygen, and he was nearly out of time. A life span could pass in front of the eyes in a matter of seconds. He was grateful that he was alone so no one else could witness his joys and mistakes.

Leilah, it was always Leilah. With each ragged breath he could see her, the clear blue eyes and golden hair of his one and only beloved. As the warning siren inside the cockpit wailed, he could hear Leilah's laughter. Tender, sweet. Then mocking.

"By the red sun, how happy we were together!" The words shuddered out between gasps as he dragged himself over the floor toward the command console. "Lovers, partners, friends."

The pain in his lungs grew worse. It seared through him like dozens of hot knives tipped with poison from the pits of Argenham. He couldn't waste air on useless words. But his thoughts...his thoughts even now were on Leilah.

That she, the only woman he had ever loved, should be the cause of his ultimate destruction! His destruction, and the world's as they knew it. What fiendish twist of fate had caused the freak accident that had turned her from a devoted scientist to a force of evil and hate?

She was his enemy now, the woman who had once been his wife. Who was still his wife, Zark told himself as he painfully pulled himself up to the console. If he lived, and stopped her latest scheme to obliterate civilization on Perth, he would have to go after her. He would have to destroy her. If he had the strength.

Commander Zark, Defender of the Universe, Leader of Perth, hero and husband, pressed a trembling finger to the button.

CONTINUED IN THE NEXT EXCITING ISSUE!

"Damn!" Radley Wallace mumbled the oath, then looked around quickly to be sure his mother hadn't heard. He'd started to swear, mostly in whispers, about six months ago, and wasn't anxious for her to find out. She'd get that look on her face.

But she was busy going through the first boxes the movers had delivered. He was supposed to be putting his books away, but had decided it was time to take a break. He liked breaks best when they included Universal Comics and Commander Zark. His mother liked him to read real books, but they didn't have many pictures. As far as Radley was concerned, Zark had it all over Long John Silver or Huck Finn.

Rolling over on his back, Radley stared at the freshly painted ceiling of his new room. The new apartment was okay. Mostly he liked the view of the park, and having an elevator was cool. But he wasn't looking forward to starting in a new school on Monday.

Mom had told him it would be fine, that he would make new friends and still be able to visit with some of the old ones. She was real good about it, stroking his hair and smiling in that way that made him feel everything was really okay. But she wouldn't be there when all the kids gave him the once-over. He wasn't going to wear that new sweater, either, even if Mom said the color matched his eyes. He wanted to wear one of his old sweatshirts so at least something would be familiar. He figured she'd understand, because Mom always did.

She still looked sad sometimes, though. Radley squirmed up to the pillow with the comic clutched in his hand. He wished she wouldn't feel bad because his father had gone away. It had been a long time now, and he had to think hard to bring a picture of his father to his mind. He never visited, and only phoned a couple of times a year. That was okay. Radley wished he could tell his mother it was okay, but he was afraid she'd get upset and start crying.

He didn't really need a dad when he had her. He'd told her that once, and she'd hugged him so hard he hadn't been able to breathe. Then he'd heard her crying in her room that night. So he hadn't told her that again.

Big people were funny, Radley thought with the wisdom of his almost ten years. But his mom was the best. She hardly ever yelled at him, and was always sorry when she did. And she was pretty. Radley smiled as he began to sleep. He guessed his mom was just about as pretty as Princess Leilah. Even though her hair was brown instead of golden and her eyes were gray instead of cobalt blue.

She'd promised they could have pizza for dinner, too, to celebrate their new apartment. He liked pizza best, next to Commander Zark.

He drifted off to sleep so he, with the help of Zark, could save the universe.

When Hester looked in a short time later, she saw her son, her universe, dreaming with an issue of Universal Comics in his hand. Most of his books, some of which he paged through from time to time, were still in the packing boxes. Another time she would have given him a mild lecture on responsibility when he woke, but she didn't have the heart for it now. He was taking the move so well. Another upheaval in his life.

"This one's going to be good for you, sweetie." Forgetting the mountain of her own unpacking, she sat on the edge of the bed to watch him.

He looked so much like his father. The dark blond hair, the dark eyes and sturdy chin. It was a rare thing now for her to look at her son and think of the man who had been her husband. But today was different. Today was another beginning for them, and beginnings made her think of endings.

Over six years now, she thought, a bit amazed at the passage of time. Radley had been just a toddler when Allan had walked out on them, tired of bills, tired of family, tired of her in particular. That pain had passed, though it had been a long, slow process. But she had never forgiven, and would never forgive, the man for leaving his son without a second glance.

Sometimes she worried that it seemed to mean so little to Radley. Selfishly she was relieved that he had never formed a strong, enduring bond with the man who would leave them behind, yet she often wondered, late at night when everything was quiet, if her little boy held something inside.

When she looked at him, it didn't seem possible. Hester stroked his hair now and turned to look at his view of Central Park. Radley was outgoing, happy and good-natured. She'd worked hard to help him be those things. She never spoke ill of his father, though there had been times, especially in the early years, when the bitterness and anger had simmered very close to the surface. She'd tried to be both mother and father, and most of the time thought she'd succeeded.

She'd read books on baseball so she would know how to coach him. She'd raced beside him, clinging to the back of the seat of his first two-wheeler. When it had been time to let go, she'd forced back the urge to hang on and had cheered as he'd made his wobbly way down the bike path.

She even knew about Commander Zark. With a smile, Hester eased the wrinkled comic book from his fist. Poor, heroic Zark and his misguided wife Leilah. Yes, Hester knew all about Perth's politics and tribulations. Trying to wean Radley from Zark to Dickens or Twain wasn't easy, but neither was raising a child on your own.

"There's time enough," she murmured as she stretched out beside her son. Time enough for real books and for real life. "Oh, Rad, I hope I've done the right thing." She closed her eyes, wishing, as she'd learned to wish rarely, that she had someone to talk to, someone who could advise her or make decisions, right or wrong.

Then, with her arm hooked around her son's waist, she, too, slept.

* * *

The room was dim with dusk when she awoke, groggy and disoriented. The first thing Hester realized was that Radley was no longer curled beside her. Grogginess disappeared in a quick flash of panic she knew was foolish. Radley could be trusted not to leave the apartment without permission. He wasn't a blindly obedient child, but her top ten rules were respected. Rising, she went to find him.

"Hi, Mom." He was in the kitchen, where her homing instinct had taken her first. He held a dripping peanut butter and jelly sandwich in his hands.

"I thought you wanted pizza," she said, noting the good-sized glop of jelly on the counter and the yet-to-be-resealed loaf of bread.

"I do." He took a healthy bite, then grinned. "But I needed something now."

"Don't talk with your mouth full, Rad," she said automatically, even as she bent to kiss him. "You could have woken me if you were hungry."

"That's okay, but I couldn't find the glasses."

She glanced around, seeing that he'd emptied two boxes in his quest. Hester reminded herself that she should have made the kitchen arrangements her first priority. "Well, we can take care of that."

"It was snowing when I woke up."

"Was it?" Hester pushed the hair out of her eyes and straightened to see for herself. "Still is."

"Maybe it'll snow ten feet and there won't be any school on Monday." Radley climbed onto a stool to sit at the kitchen counter.

Along with no first day on the new job, Hester thought, indulging in some wishful thinking of her own for a moment. No new pressures, new responsibilities. "I don't think there's much chance of that." As she washed out glasses, she looked over her shoulder. "Are you really worried about it, Rad?"

"Sort of." He shrugged his shoulders. Monday was still a day away. A lot could happen. Earthquakes, blizzards, an attack from outer space. He concentrated on the last.

He, Captain Radley Wallace of Earth's Special Forces, would protect and shield, would fight to the death, would—

"I could go in with you if you'd like."

"Aw, Mom, the kids would make fun of me." He bit into his sandwich. Grape jelly oozed out the sides. "It won't be so bad. At least that dumb Angela Wiseberry won't be at this school."

She didn't have the heart to tell him there was a dumb Angela Wiseberry at every school. "Tell you what. We'll both go to our new jobs Monday, then convene back here at 1600 for a full report."

His face brightened instantly. There was nothing Radley liked better than a military operation. "Aye, aye, sir."

"Good. Now I'll order the pizza, and while we're waiting we'll put the rest of the dishes away."

"Let the prisoners do it."

"Escaped. All of them."

"Heads will roll," Radley mumbled as he stuffed the last of the sandwich into his mouth.

Mitchell Dempsey II sat at his drawing board without an idea in his head. He sipped cold coffee, hoping it would stimulate his imagination, but his mind remained as blank as the paper in front of him. Blocks happened, he knew, but they rarely happened to him. And not on deadline. Of course, he was going about it backward. Mitch cracked another peanut, then tossed the shell in the direction of the bowl. It hit the side and fell on the floor to join several others. Normally the story line would have come first, then the illustrations. Since he'd been having no luck that way, Mitch had switched in the hope that the change in routine would jog something loose.

It wasn't working, and neither was he.

Closing his eyes, Mitch tried for an out-of-body experience. The old Slim Whitman song on the radio cruised on, but he didn't hear it. He was traveling light-years away; a century was passing. The second millennium, he thought with a smile. He'd been born too soon. Though he didn't think he could blame his parents for having him a hundred years too early.

Nothing came. No solutions, no inspiration. Mitch opened his eyes again and stared at the blank white paper. With an editor like Rich Skinner, he couldn't afford to claim artistic temperament. Famine or plague would barely get you by. Disgusted, Mitch reached for another peanut.

What he needed was a change of scene, a distraction. His life was becoming too settled, too ordinary and, despite the temporary block, too easy. He needed challenge. Pitching the shells, he rose to pace.

He had a long, limber body made solid by the hours he spent each week with weights. As a boy he'd been preposterously skinny, though he'd always eaten like a horse. He hadn't minded the teasing too much until he'd discovered girls. Then, with the quiet determination he'd been born with, Mitch had changed what could be changed. It had taken him a couple of years and a lot of sweat to build himself, but he had. He still didn't take his body for granted, and exercised it as regularly as he did his mind.

His office was littered with books, all read and re-read. He was tempted to pull one out now and bury himself in it. But he was on deadline. The big brown mutt on the floor rolled over on his stomach and watched.

Mitch had named him Taz, after the Tasmanian Devil from the old Warner Brothers cartoons, but Taz was hardly a whirlwind of energy. He yawned now and rubbed his back lazily on the rug. He liked Mitch. Mitch never expected him to do anything that he didn't care to, and hardly ever complained about dog hair on the furniture or an occasional forage into the trash. Mitch had a nice voice, too, low and patient. Taz liked it best when Mitch sat on the floor with him and stroked his heavy brown fur, talking out one of his ideas. Taz could look up into the lean face as if he understood every word.

Taz liked Mitch's face, too. It was kind and strong, and the mouth rarely firmed into a disapproving line. His eyes were pale and dreamy. Mitch's wide, strong hands knew the right places to scratch. Taz was a very contented dog. He yawned and went back to sleep.

When the knock came to the door, the dog stirred enough to thump his tail and make a series of low noises in his throat.

"No, I'm not expecting anyone. You?" Mitch responded. "I'll go see." He stepped on peanut shells in his bare feet and swore, but didn't bother to stoop and pick them up. There was a pile of newspapers to be skirted around, and a bag of clothes that hadn't made it to the laundry. Taz had left one of his bones on the

Aubusson. Mitch simply kicked it into a corner before
he opened the door.

"Pizza delivery."

A scrawny kid of about eighteen was holding a box
that smelled like heaven. Mitch took one long, avari-
cious sniff. "I didn't order any."

"This 406?"

"Yeah, but I didn't order any pizza." He sniffed
again. "Wish I had."

"Wallace?"

"Dempsey."

"Shoot."

Wallace, Mitch thought as the kid shifted from foot
to foot. Wallace was taking over the Henley apartment,
604. He rubbed a hand over his chin and considered.
If Wallace was that leggy brunette he'd seen hauling
in boxes that morning, it might be worth investigating.

"I know the Wallaces," he said, and pulled crumpled bills out of his pocket. "I'll take it on up to
them."

"I don't know, I shouldn't—"

"Worry about a thing," Mitch finished, and added
another bill. Pizza and the new neighbor might be just
the distraction he needed.

The boy counted his tip. "Okay, thanks." For all he
knew, the Wallaces wouldn't be half as generous.

With the box balanced in his hand, Mitch started out.
Then he remembered his keys. He took a moment to
search through his worn jeans before he remembered
he'd tossed them at the gateleg table when he'd come
in the night before. He found them under it, stuck them
in one pocket, found the hole in it and stuck them in
the other. He hoped the pizza had some pepperoni.

"That should be the pizza," Hester announced, but

caught Radley before he could dash to the door. "Let me open it. Remember the rules?"

"Don't open the door unless you know who it is," Radley recited, rolling his eyes behind his mother's back.

Hester put a hand on the knob, but checked the peephole. She frowned a little at the face. She'd have sworn the man was looking straight back at her with amused and very clear blue eyes. His hair was dark and shaggy, as if it hadn't seen a barber or a comb in a little too long. But the face was fascinating, lean and bony and unshaven.

"Mom, are you going to open it?"

"What?" Hester stepped back when she realized she'd been staring at the delivery boy for a good deal longer than necessary.

"I'm starving," Radley reminded her.

"Sorry." Hester opened the door and discovered the fascinating face went with a long, athletic body. And bare feet.

"Did you order pizza?"

"Yes." But it was snowing outside. What was he doing barefoot?

"Good." Before Hester realized his intention, Mitch strolled inside.

"I'll take that," Hester said quickly. "Take this into the kitchen, Radley." She shielded her son with her body and wondered if she'd need a weapon.

"Nice place." Mitch looked casually around at crates and open boxes.

"I'll get your money."

"It's on the house." Mitch smiled at her. Hester wondered if the self-defense course she'd taken two years before would come back to her.

"Radley, take that into the kitchen while I pay the delivery man."

"Neighbor," Mitch corrected. "I'm in 406—you know, two floors down. The pizza got delivered to my place by mistake."

"I see." But for some reason it didn't make her any less nervous. "I'm sorry for the trouble." Hester reached for her purse.

"I took care of it." He wasn't sure whether she looked more likely to lunge or to flee, but he'd been right about her being worth investigating. She was a tall one, he thought, model height, with that same kind of understated body. Her rich, warm brown hair was pulled back from a diamond-shaped face dominated by big gray eyes and a mouth just one size too large.

"Why don't you consider the pizza my version of the welcoming committee?"

"That's really very kind, but I couldn't—"

"Refuse such a neighborly offer?"

Because she was a bit too cool and reserved for his taste, Mitch looked past her to the boy. "Hi, I'm Mitch." This time his smile was answered.

"I'm Rad. We just moved in."

"So I see. From out of town?"

"Uh-uh. We just changed apartments because Mom got a new job and the other was too small. I can see the park from my window."

"Me, too."

"Excuse me, Mr.—?"

"It's Mitch," he repeated with a glance at Hester.

"Yes, well, it's very kind of you to bring this up." As well as being very odd, she thought. "But I don't want to impose on your time."

"You can have a piece," Radley invited. "We never finish it all."

"Rad, I'm sure Mr.—Mitch has things to do."

"Not a thing." He knew his manners, had been taught them painstakingly. Another time, he might even have put them to use and bowed out, but something about the woman's reserve and the child's warmth made him obstinate. "Got a beer?"

"No, I'm sorry, I—"

"We've got soda," Radley piped up. "Mom lets me have one sometimes." There was nothing Radley liked more than company. He gave Mitch a totally ingenuous smile. "Want to see the kitchen?"

"Love to." With something close to a smirk for Hester, Mitch followed the boy.

She stood in the center of the room for a moment, hands on her hips, unsure whether to be exasperated or furious. The last thing she wanted after a day of lugging boxes was company. Especially a stranger's. The only thing to do now was to give him a piece of the damn pizza and blot out her obligation to him.

"We've got a garbage disposal. It makes great noises."

"I bet." Obligingly Mitch leaned over the sink while Radley flipped the switch.

"Rad, don't run that with nothing in it. As you can see, we're a bit disorganized yet." Hester went to the freshly lined cupboard for plates.

"I've been here for five years, and I'm still disorganized."

"We're going to get a kitten." Radley climbed up on a stool, then reached for the napkins his mother had already put in one of her little wicker baskets. "The other place wouldn't allow pets, but we can have one here, can't we, Mom?''

"As soon as we're settled, Rad. Diet or regular?" she asked Mitch.

"Regular's fine. Looks like you've gotten a lot accomplished in one day." The kitchen was neat as a pin. A thriving asparagus fern hung in a macrame holder in the single window. She had less space than he did, which he thought was too bad. She would probably make better use of the kitchen than he. He took another glance around before settling at the counter. Stuck to the refrigerator was a large crayon drawing of a spaceship. "You do that?" Mitch asked Rad.

"Yeah." He picked up the pizza his mother had set on his plate and bit in eagerly—peanut butter and jelly long since forgotten.

"It's good."

"It's supposed to be the Second Millennium, that's Commander Zark's ship."

"I know." Mitch took a healthy bite of his own slice. "You did a good job."

As he plowed through his pizza, Radley took it for granted that Mitch would recognize Zark's name and mode of transportation. As far as he was concerned, everybody did. "I've been trying to do the Defiance, Leilah's ship, but it's harder. Anyway, I think Commander Zark might blow it up in the next issue."

"Think so?" Mitch gave Hester an easy smile as she joined them at the counter.

"I don't know, he's in a pretty tough spot right now."

"He'll get out okay."

"Do you read comic books?" Hester asked. It wasn't until she sat down that she noticed how large his hands were. He might have been dressed with disregard, but his hands were clean and had the look of easy competence.

"All the time."

"I've got the biggest collection of all my friends. Mom got me the very first issue with Commander Zark in it for Christmas. It's ten years old. He was only a captain then. Want to see?"

The boy was a gem, Mitch thought, sweet, bright and unaffected. He'd have to reserve judgment on the mother. "Yeah, I'd like that."

Before Hester could tell him to finish his dinner, Radley was off and running. She sat in silence a moment, wondering what sort of man actually read comic books. Oh, she paged through them from time to time to keep a handle on what her son was consuming, but to actually read them? An adult?

"Terrific kid."

"Yes, he is. It's nice of you to…listen to him talk about his comics."

"Comics are my life," Mitch said, straight-faced.

Her reserve broke down long enough for her to stare at him. Clearing her throat, Hester went back to her meal. "I see."

Mitch put his tongue in his cheek. She was some piece of work, all right, he decided. First meeting or not, he saw no reason to resist egging her on. "I take it you don't."

"Don't what?"

"Read comic books."

"No, I, ah, don't have a lot of time for light reading." She rolled her eyes, unaware that that was where Radley had picked up the habit. "Would you like another piece?"

"Yeah." He helped himself before she could serve him. "You ought to take some time, you know. Comics can be very educational. What's the new job?"

"Oh, I'm in banking. I'm the loan officer for National Trust."

Mitch gave an appreciative whistle. "Big job for someone your age."

Hester stiffened automatically. "I've been in banking since I was sixteen."

Touchy, too, he mused as he licked sauce from his thumb. "That was supposed to be a compliment. I have a feeling you don't take them well." Tough lady, he decided, then thought perhaps she'd had to be. There was no ring on her finger, not even the faintest white mark to show there had been one recently. "I've done some business with banks myself. You know, deposits, withdrawals, returned checks."

She shifted uncomfortably, wondering what was taking Radley so long. There was something unnerving about being alone with this man. Though she had always felt comfortable with eye contact, she was having a difficult time with Mitch. He never looked away for very long.

"I didn't mean to be abrupt."

"No, I don't suppose you did. If I wanted a loan at National Trust, who would I ask for?"

"Mrs. Wallace."

Definitely a tough one. "Mrs. is your first name?"

"Hester," she said, not understanding why she resented giving him that much.

"Hester, then." Mitch offered a hand. "Nice to meet you."

Her lips curved a bit. It was a cautious smile, Mitch thought, but better than none at all. "I'm sorry if I've been rude, but it's been a long day. A long week, really.''

"I hate moving." He waited until she'd unbent enough to put her hand in his. Hers was cool and as slender as the rest of her. "Got anyone to help you?"

"No." She removed her hand, because his was as overwhelming as it looked. "We're doing fine."

"I can see that." *No Help Wanted.* The sign was up and posted in big letters. He'd known a few women like her, so fiercely independent, so suspicious of men in general that they had not only a defensive shield but an arsenal of poisonous darts behind it. A sensible man gave them a wide berth. Too bad, because she was a looker, and the kid was definitely a kick.

"I forgot where I'd packed it." Radley came back in, flushed with the effort. "It's a classic, the dealer even told Mom."

He'd also charged her an arm and a leg for it, Hester thought. But it had meant more to Radley than any of his other presents.

"Mint condition, too." Mitch turned the first page with the care of a jeweler cutting a diamond.

"I always make sure my hands are clean before I read it."

"Good idea." It was amazing that after all this time the pride would still be there. An enormous feeling it was, too, a huge burst of satisfaction.

It was there on the first page. Story and drawings by Mitch Dempsey. Commander Zark was his baby, and in ten years they'd become very close friends.

"It's a great story. It really explains why Commander Zark devoted his life to defending the universe against evil and corruption."

"Because his family had been wiped out by the evil Red Arrow in his search for power."

"Yeah." Radley's face lit up. "But he got even with Red Arrow."

"In issue 73."

Hester put her chin in her hand and stared at the two of them. The man was serious, she realized, not just humoring the child. He was as obsessed by comic books as her nine-year-old son.

Strange, he looked fairly normal; he even spoke well. In fact, sitting next to him had been uncomfortable largely because he was so blatantly masculine, with that tough body, angular face and large hands. Hester shook off her thoughts quickly. She certainly didn't want to lean in that direction toward a neighbor, particularly not one whose mental level seemed to have gotten stuck in adolescence.

Mitch turned a couple of pages. His drawing had improved over a decade. It helped to remind himself of that. But he'd managed to maintain the same purity, the same straightforward images that had come to him ten years ago when he'd been struggling unhappily in commercial art.

"Is he your favorite?" Mitch pointed a blunt fingertip toward a drawing of Zark.

"Oh, sure. I like Three Faces, and the Black Diamond's pretty neat, but Commander Zark's my favorite."

"Mine, too." Mitch ruffled the boy's hair. He hadn't realized when he'd delivered a pizza that he would find the inspiration he'd been struggling for all afternoon.

"You can read this sometime. I'd lend it to you, but—"

"I understand." He closed the book carefully and

handed it back. "You can't lend out a collector's item."

"I'd better put it away."

"Before you know it, you and Rad will be trading issues." Hester stood up to clear the plates.

"That amuses the hell out of you, doesn't it?"

His tone had her glancing over quickly. There wasn't precisely an edge to it, and his eyes were still clear and mild, but...something warned her to take care.

"I didn't mean to insult you. I just find it unusual for a grown man to read comic books as a habit." She stacked the plates in the dishwasher. "I've always thought it was something boys grew out of at a certain age, but I suppose one could consider it, what, a hobby?"

His brow lifted. She was facing him again, that half smile on her lips. Obviously she was trying to make amends. He didn't think she should get off quite that easily. "Comic books are anything but a hobby with me, Mrs. Hester Wallace. I not only read them, I write them."

"Holy cow, really?" Radley stood staring at Mitch as though he'd just been crowned king. "Do you really? Honest? Oh, boy, are you Mitch Dempsey? The real Mitch Dempsey?"

"In the flesh." He tugged on Radley's ear while Hester looked at him as though he'd stepped in from another planet.

"Oh, boy, Mitch Dempsey right here! Mom, this is Commander Zark. None of the kids are going to believe it. Do you believe it, Mom, Commander Zark right here in our kitchen!"

"No," Hester murmured as she continued to stare. "I can't believe it."

Chapter 2

Hester wished she could afford to be a coward. It would be so easy to go back home, pull the covers over her head and hide out until Radley came home from school. No one who saw her would suspect that her stomach was in knots or that her palms were sweaty despite the frigid wind that whipped down the stairs as she emerged from the subway with a crowd of Manhattan's workforce.

If anyone had bothered to look, they would have seen a composed, slightly preoccupied woman in a long red wool coat and white scarf. Fortunately for Hester, the wind tunnel created by the skyscrapers whipped color into cheeks that would have been deadly pale. She had to concentrate on not chewing off her lipstick as she walked the half block to National Trust. And to her first day on the job.

It would only take her ten minutes to get back home, lock herself in and phone the office with some excuse.

She was sick, there'd been a death in the family—preferably hers. She'd been robbed.

Hester clutched her briefcase tighter and kept walking. Big talk, she berated herself. She'd walked Radley to school that morning spouting off cheerful nonsense about how exciting new beginnings were, how much fun it was to start something new. Baloney, she thought, and hoped the little guy wasn't half as scared as she was.

She'd earned the position, Hester reminded herself. She was qualified and competent, with twelve years of experience under her belt. And she was scared right out of her shoes. Taking a deep breath, she walked into National Trust.

Laurence Rosen, the bank manager, checked his watch, gave a nod of approval and strode over to greet her. His dark blue suit was trim and conservative. A woman could have powdered her nose in the reflection from his shiny black shoes. "Right on time, Mrs. Wallace, an excellent beginning. I pride myself on having a staff that makes optimum use of time." He gestured toward the back of the bank, and her office.

"I'm looking forward to getting started, Mr. Rosen," she said, and felt a wave of relief that it was true. She'd always liked the feel of a bank before the doors opened to the public. The cathedral-like quiet, the pregame anticipation.

"Good, good, we'll do our best to keep you busy." He noted with a slight frown that two secretaries were not yet at their desks. In a habitual gesture, he passed a hand over his hair. "Your assistant will be in momentarily. Once you're settled, Mrs. Wallace, I'll expect you to keep close tabs on her comings and goings. Your efficiency depends largely on hers."

"Of course."

Her office was small and dull. She tried not to wish for something airier—or to notice that Rosen was as stuffy as they came. The increase this job would bring to her income would make things better for Radley. That, as always, was the bottom line. She'd make it work, Hester told herself as she took off her coat. She'd make it work well.

Rosen obviously approved of her trim black suit and understated jewelry. There was no room for flashy clothes or behavior in banking. "I trust you looked over the files I gave you."

"I familiarized myself with them over the weekend." She moved behind the desk, knowing it would establish her position. "I believe I understand National Trust's policy and procedure."

"Excellent, excellent. I'll leave you to get organized then. Your first appointment's at—" he turned pages over on her desk calendar "—9:15. If you have any problems, contact me. I'm always around somewhere."

She would have bet on it. "I'm sure everything will be fine, Mr. Rosen. Thank you."

With a final nod, Rosen strode out. The door closed behind him with a quiet click. Alone, Hester let herself slide bonelessly into her chair. She'd gotten past the first hurdle, she told herself. Rosen thought she was competent and suitable. Now all she had to do was be those things. She would be, because too much was riding on it. Not the least of those things was her pride. She hated making a fool of herself. She'd certainly done a good job of that the night before with the new neighbor.

Even hours later, remembering it, her cheeks

warmed. She hadn't meant to insult the man's—even now she couldn't bring herself to call it a profession—his work, then, Hester decided. She certainly hadn't meant to make any personal observations. The problem had been that she hadn't been as much on her guard as usual. The man had thrown her off by inviting himself in and joining them for dinner and charming Radley, all in a matter of minutes. She wasn't used to people popping into her life. And she didn't like it.

Radley loved it. Hester picked up a sharpened pencil with the bank's logo on the side. He'd practically glowed with excitement, and hadn't been able to speak of anything else even after Mitch Dempsey had left.

She could be grateful for one thing. The visit had taken Radley's mind off the new school. Radley had always made friends easily, and if this Mitch was willing to give her son some pleasure, she shouldn't criticize. In any case, the man seemed harmless enough. Hester refused to admit to the uncomfortable thrill she'd experienced when his hand had closed over hers. What possible trouble could come from a man who wrote comic books for a living? She caught herself chewing at her lipstick at the question.

The knock on the door was brief and cheerful. Before she could call out, it was pushed open.

"Good morning, Mrs. Wallace. I'm Kay Lorimar, your assistant. Remember, we met for a few minutes a couple of weeks ago."

"Yes, good morning, Kay." Her assistant was everything Hester had always wanted to be herself: petite, well-rounded, blond, with small delicate features. She folded her hands on the fresh blotter and tried to look authoritative.

"Sorry I'm late." Kay smiled and didn't look the

least bit sorry. "Everything takes longer than you think it does on Monday. Even if I pretend it's Tuesday it doesn't seem to help. I don't know why. Would you like some coffee?"

"No, thank you, I've an appointment in a few minutes."

"Just ring if you change your mind." Kay paused at the door. "This place could sure use some cheering up, it's dark as a dungeon. Mr. Blowfield, that's who you're replacing, he liked things dull—matched him, you know." Her smile was ingenuous, but Hester hesitated to answer it. It would hardly do for her to get a reputation as a gossip the first day on the job. "Anyway, if you decide to do any redecorating, let me know. My roommate's into interior design. He's a real artist."

"Thank you." How was she supposed to run an office with a pert little cheerleader in tow? Hester wondered. One day at a time. "Just send Mr. and Mrs. Browning in when they arrive, Kay."

"Yes, ma'am." She sure was more pleasant to look at than old Blowfield, Kay thought. But it looked as if she had the same soul. "Loan application forms are in the bottom left drawer of the desk, arranged according to type. Legal pads in the right. Bank stationery, top right. The list of current interest rates are in the middle drawer. The Brownings are looking for a loan to remodel their loft as they're expecting a child. He's in electronics, she works part-time at Bloomingdale's. They've been advised what papers to bring with them. I can make copies while they're here."

Hester lifted her brow. "Thank you, Kay," she said, not certain whether to be amused or impressed.

When the door closed again, Hester sat back and

smiled. The office might be dull, but if the morning was any indication, nothing else at National Trust was going to be.

Mitch liked having a window that faced the front of the building. That way, whenever he took a break, he could watch the comings and goings. After five years, he figured he knew every tenant by sight and half of them by name. When things were slow or, better, when he was ahead of the game, he whiled away time by sketching the more interesting of them. If his time stretched further, he made a story line to go with the faces.

He considered it the best of practice because it amused him. Occasionally there was a face interesting enough to warrant special attention. Sometimes it was a cabdriver or a delivery boy. Mitch had learned to look close and quick, then sketch from lingering impressions. Years before, he had sketched faces for a living, if a pitiful one. Now he sketched them for entertainment and was a great deal more satisfied.

He spotted Hester and her son when they were still half a block away. The red coat she wore stood out like a beacon. It certainly made a statement, Mitch mused as he picked up his pencil. He wondered if the coolly distant Mrs. Wallace realized what signals she was sending out. He doubted it.

He didn't need to see her face to draw it. Already there were a half a dozen rough sketches of her tossed on the table in his workroom. Interesting features, he told himself as his pencil began to fly across the pad. Any artist would be compelled to capture them.

The boy was walking along beside her, his face all but obscured by a woolen scarf and hat. Even from this distance, Mitch could see the boy was chattering earnestly. His head was angled up toward his mother. Every now and again she would glance down as if to comment; then the boy would take over again. A few steps away from the building, she stopped. Mitch saw the wind catch at her hair as she tossed her head back and laughed. His fingers went limp on the pencil as he leaned closer to the window. He wanted to be nearer, near enough to hear the laugh, to see if her eyes lit up with it. He imagined they did, but how? Would that subtle, calm gray go silvery or smoky?

She continued to walk, and in seconds was in the building and out of sight.

Mitch stared down at his sketch pad. He had no more than a few lines and contours. He couldn't finish it, he thought as he set the pencil down. He could only see her laughing now, and to capture that on paper he'd need a closer look.

Picking up his keys, he jangled them in his hand. He'd given her the better part of a week. The aloof Mrs. Wallace might consider another neighborly visit out of line, but he didn't. Besides, he liked the kid. Mitch would have gone upstairs to see him before, but he'd been busy fleshing out his story. He owed the kid for that, too, Mitch considered. The little weekend visit had not only crumbled the block, but had given Mitch enough fuel for three issues. Yeah, he owed the kid.

He pushed the keys into his pocket and walked into his workroom. Taz was there, a bone clamped between his paws as he snoozed. "Don't get up," Mitch said mildly. "I'm going out for a while." As he spoke, he ruffled through papers. Taz opened his eyes to half-mast and grumbled. "I don't know how long I'll be." After wracking through his excuse for a filing system,

Mitch found the sketch. Commander Zark in full military regalia, sober-faced, sad-eyed, his gleaming ship at his back. Beneath it was the caption: THE MISSION: Capture Princess Leilah—or DESTROY her!!

Mitch wished briefly that he had the time to ink and color it, but figured the kid would like it as is. With a careless stroke he signed it, then rolled it into a tube.

"Don't wait dinner for me," he instructed Taz.

"I'll get it!" Radley danced to the door. It was Friday, and school was light-years away.

"Ask who it is."

Radley put his hand on the knob and shook his head. He'd been going to ask. Probably. "Who is it?"

"It's Mitch."

"It's Mitch!" Radley shouted, delighted. In the bedroom, Hester scowled and pulled the sweatshirt over her head.

"Hi." Breathless with excitement, Radley opened the door to his latest hero.

"Hi, Rad, how's it going?"

"Fine. I don't have any homework all weekend." He reached out a hand to draw Mitch inside. "I wanted to come down and see you, but Mom said no 'cause you'd be working or something."

"Or something," Mitch muttered. "Look, it's okay with me if you come over. Anytime."

"Really?"

"Really." The kid was irresistible, Mitch thought as he ruffled the boy's hair. Too bad his mother wasn't as friendly. "I thought you might like this." Mitch handed him the rolled sketch.

"Oh, wow." Awestruck, reverent, Radley stared at

the drawing. "Jeez, Commander Zark and the Second Millennium. Can I have it, really? To keep?"

"Yeah."

"I gotta show Mom." Radley turned and dashed toward the bedroom as Hester came out. "Look what Mitch gave me. Isn't it great? He said I could keep it and everything."

"It's terrific." She put a hand on Radley's shoulder as she studied the sketch. The man was certainly talented, Hester decided. Even if he had chosen such an odd way to show it. Her hand remained on Radley's shoulder as she looked over at Mitch. "That was very nice of you."

He liked the way she looked in the pastel sweats, casual, approachable, if not completely relaxed. Her hair was down, too, with the ends just sweeping short of her shoulders. Parted softly on the side and unpinned, it gave her a completely different look.

"I wanted to thank Rad." Mitch forced himself to look away from her face, then smiled at the boy. "You helped me through a block last weekend."

"I did?" Radley's eyes widened. "Honest?"

"Honest. I was stuck, spinning wheels. After I talked to you that night, I went down and everything fell into place. I appreciate it."

"Wow, you're welcome. You could stay for dinner again. We're just having Chinese chicken, and maybe I could help you some more. It's okay, isn't it, Mom? Isn't it?"

Trapped again. And again she caught the gleam of amusement in Mitch's eyes. "Of course."

"Great. I want to go hang this up right away. Can I call Josh, too, and tell him about it? He won't believe it."

"Sure." She barely had time to run a hand over his hair before he was off and running.

"Thanks, Mitch." Radley paused at the turn of the hallway. "Thanks a lot."

Hester found the deep side pockets in her sweats and slipped her hands inside. There was absolutely no reason for the man to make her nervous. So why did he? "That was really very kind of you."

"Maybe, but I haven't done anything that's made me feel that good in a long time." He wasn't completely at ease himself, Mitch discovered, and he tucked his thumbs into the back pockets of his jeans. "You work fast," he commented as he glanced around the living room.

The boxes were gone. Bright, vivid prints hung on the walls and a vase of flowers, fresh as morning, sat near the window, where sheer curtains filtered the light. Pillows were plumped, furniture gleamed. The only signs of confusion were a miniature car wreck and a few plastic men scattered on the carpet. He was glad to see them. It meant she wasn't the type who expected the boy to play only in his room.

"Dali?" He walked over to a lithograph hung over the sofa.

She caught her bottom lip between her teeth as Mitch studied one of her rare extravagances. "I bought that in a little shop on Fifth that's always going out of business."

"Yeah, I know the one. It didn't take you long to put things together here."

"I wanted everything back to normal as soon as possible. The move wasn't easy for Radley."

"And you?" He turned then, catching her off guard with the sudden sharp look.

"Me? I—ah…"

"You know," he began as he crossed over to her, attracted by her simple bafflement. "You're a lot more articulate when you talk about Rad than you are when you talk about Hester."

She stepped back quickly, aware that he would have touched her and totally unsure what her reaction might have been. "I should start dinner."

"Want some help?"

"With what?"

This time she didn't move quickly enough. He cupped her chin in his hand and smiled. "With dinner."

It had been a long time since a man had touched her that way. He had a strong hand with gentle fingers. That had to be the reason her heart leaped up to her throat and pounded there. "Can you cook?"

What incredible eyes she had. So clear, so pale a gray they were almost translucent. For the first time in years he felt the urge to paint, just to see if he could bring those eyes to life on canvas. "I make a hell of a peanut butter sandwich."

She lifted a hand to his wrist, to move his away, she thought. But her fingers lay there lightly a moment, experimenting. "How are you at chopping vegetables?"

"I think I can handle it."

"All right, then." She backed up, amazed that she had allowed the contact to go for so long. "I still don't have any beer, but I do have some wine this time."

"Fine." What the hell were they talking about? Why were they talking at all, when she had a mouth that was made to fit on a man's? A little baffled by his own train of thought, he followed her into the kitchen.

"It's really a simple meal," she began. "But when it's all mixed up, Radley hardly notices he's eating something nutritious. A Twinkie's the true way to his heart."

"My kind of kid."

She smiled a little, more relaxed now that she had her hands full. She set celery and mushrooms on the chopping block. "The trick's in moderation." Hester took the chicken out, then remembered the wine. "I'm willing to concede to Rad's sweet tooth in small doses. He's willing to accept broccoli on the same terms."

"Sounds like a wise arrangement." She opened the wine. Inexpensive, he thought with a glance at the label, but palatable. She filled two glasses, then handed him one. It was silly, but her hands were damp again. It had been some time since she'd shared a bottle of wine or fixed a simple dinner with a man. "To neighbors," he said, and thought she relaxed fractionally as he touched his glass to hers.

"Why don't you sit down while I bone the chicken? Then you can deal with the vegetables."

He didn't sit, but did lean back against the counter. He wasn't willing to give her the distance he was sure she wanted. Not when she smelled so good. She handled the knife like an expert, he noted as he sipped his wine. Impressive. Most of the career women he knew were more experienced in takeouts. "So, how's the new job?"

Hester moved her shoulders. "It's working out well. The manager's a stickler for efficiency, and that trickles down. Rad and I have been having conferences all week so we can compare notes."

Was that what they'd been talking about when they'd walked home today? he wondered. Was that why she'd laughed? "How's Radley taking the new school?"

"Amazingly well." Her lips softened and curved again. He was tempted to touch a fingertip to them to feel the movement. "Whatever happens in Rad's life, he rolls with. He's incredible."

There was a shadow there, a slight one, but he could see it in her eyes. "Divorce is tough," he said, and watched Hester freeze up.

"Yes." She put the boned and cubed chicken in a bowl. "You can chop this while I start the rice."

"Sure." No trespassing, he thought, and let it drop. For now. He'd gone with the law of averages when he'd mentioned divorce, and realized he'd been on the mark. But the mark was still raw. Unless he missed his guess, the divorce had been a lot tougher on her than on Radley. He was also sure that if he wanted to draw her out, it would have to be through the boy. "Rad mentioned that he wanted to come down and visit, but you'd put him off."

Hester handed Mitch an onion before she put a pan on the stove. "I didn't want him disturbing your work."

"We both know what you think of my work."

"I had no intention of offending you the other night," she said stiffly. "It was only that—"

"You can't conceive of a grown man making a living writing comic books."

Hester remained silent as she measured out water. "It's none of my business how you make your living."

"That's right." Mitch took a long sip of wine before he attacked the celery. "In any case, I want you to know that Rad can come see me whenever he likes."

"That's very nice of you, but—"

"No buts, Hester. I like him. And since I'm in the position of calling my own hours, he won't bother me. What do I do with the mushrooms?"

"Slice." She put the lid on the rice before crossing over to show him. "Not too thin. Just make sure…" Her words trailed off when he closed his hand over hers on the knife.

"Like this?" The move was easy. He didn't even have to think about it, but simply shifted until she was trapped between his arms, her back pressed against him. Giving in to the urge, he bent down so that his mouth was close to her ear.

"Yes, that's fine." She stared down at their joined hands and tried to keep her voice even. "It really doesn't matter."

"We aim to please."

"I have to put on the chicken." She turned and found herself in deeper water. It was a mistake to look up at him, to see that slight smile on his lips and that calm, confident look in his eyes. Instinctively she lifted a hand to his chest. Even that was a mistake. She could feel the slow, steady beat of his heart. She couldn't back up, because there was no place to go, and stepping forward was tempting, dangerously so. "Mitch, you're in my way."

He'd seen it. Though it had been free briefly and suppressed quickly, he'd seen the passion come into her eyes. So she could feel and want and wonder. Maybe it was best if they both wondered a little while longer. "I think you're going to find that happening a lot." But he shifted aside and let her pass. "You smell good, Hester, damn good."

That quiet statement did nothing to ease her pulse rate. Humoring Radley or not, she vowed this would be the last time she entertained Mitch Dempsey. Hester turned on the gas under the wok and added peanut oil. "I take it you do your work at home, then. No office?"

He'd let her have it her way for the time being. The minute she'd turned in his arms and looked up at him, he'd known he'd have it his way—have her his way— before too long. "I only have to go a couple of times a week. Some of the writers or artists prefer working in the office. I do better work at home. After I have the story and the sketches, I take them in for editing and inking."

"I see. So you don't do the inking yourself?" she asked, though she'd have been hard-pressed to define what inking was. She'd have to ask Radley.

"Not anymore. We have some real experts in that, and it gives me more time to work on the story. Believe it or not, we shoot for quality, the kind of vocabulary that challenges a kid and a story that entertains."

After adding chicken to the hot oil, Hester took a deep breath. "I really do apologize for anything I said that offended you. I'm sure your work's very important to you, and I know Radley certainly appreciates it."

"Well said, Mrs. Wallace." He slid the vegetable-laden chopping block toward her.

"Josh doesn't believe it." Radley bounced into the room, delighted with himself. "He wants to come over tomorrow and see. Can he? His mom says okay if it's okay with you? Okay, Mom?"

Hester turned from the chicken long enough to give Radley a hug. "Okay, Rad, but it has to be after noon. We have some shopping to do in the morning."

"Thanks. Just wait till he sees. He's gonna go crazy. I'll tell him."

"Dinner's nearly ready. Hurry up and wash your hands."

Radley rolled his eyes at Mitch as he raced from the room again.

"You're a big hit," Hester commented.

"He's nuts about you."

"The feeling's mutual."

"So I noticed." Mitch topped off his wine. "You know, I was curious. I always thought bankers kept bankers' hours. You and Rad don't get home until five or so." When she turned her head to look at him, he merely smiled. "Some of my windows face the front. I like to watch people going in and out."

It gave her an odd and not entirely comfortable feeling to know he'd watched her walk home. Hester dumped the vegetables in and stirred. "I get off at four, but then I have to pick Rad up from the sitter." She glanced over her shoulder again. "He hates it when I call her a sitter. Anyway, she's over by our old place, so it takes awhile. I have to start looking for someone closer."

"A lot of kids his age and younger come home on their own."

Her eyes did go smoky, he noted. All she needed was a touch of anger. Or passion. "Radley isn't going to be a latchkey child. He isn't coming home to an empty house because I have to work."

Mitch set her glass by her elbow. "Coming home to empty can be depressing," he murmured, remembering his own experiences. "He's lucky to have you."

"I'm luckier to have him." Her tone softened. "If you'd get out the plates, I'll dish this up."

Mitch remembered where she kept her plates, white ones with little violet sprigs along the edges. It was odd to realize they pleased him when he'd become so accustomed to disposable plastic. He took them out, then set them beside her. Most things were best done on impulse, he'd always thought. He went with the feeling now.

"I guess it would be a lot easier on Rad if he could come back here after school."

"Oh, yes. I hate having to drag him across town, though he's awfully good about it. It's just so hard to find someone you can trust, and who Radley really likes."

"How about me?"

Hester reached to turn off the gas, but stopped to stare at him. Vegetables and chicken popped in hot oil. "I'm sorry?"

"Rad could stay with me in the afternoons." Again Mitch put a hand over hers, this time to turn off the heat. "He'd only be a couple floors away from his own place."

"With you? No, I couldn't."

"Why not?" The more he thought of it, the more Mitch liked the idea. He and Taz could use the company in the afternoons, and as a bonus he'd be seeing a lot more of the very interesting Mrs. Wallace. "You want references? No criminal record, Hester. Well, there was the case of my motorcycle and the prize roses, but I was only eighteen."

"I didn't mean that—exactly." When he grinned, she began to fuss with the rice. "I mean I couldn't impose that way. I'm sure you're busy."

"Come on, you don't think I do anything all day but doodle. Let's be honest."

"We've already agreed it isn't any of my business," she began.

"Exactly. The point is I'm home in the afternoons, I'm available and I'm willing. Besides, I may even be able to use Rad as a consultant. He's good, you know." Mitch indicated the drawing on the refrigerator. "The kid could use some art lessons."

"I know. I was hoping I'd be able to swing it this summer, but I don't—"

"Want to look a gift horse in the mouth," Mitch finished. "Look, the kid likes me, I like him. And I'll swear to no more than one Twinkie an afternoon."

She laughed then, as he'd seen her laugh a few hours before from his window. It wasn't easy to hold himself back, but something told him if he made a move now, the door would slam in his face and the bolt would slide shut. "I don't know, Mitch. I do appreciate the offer, God knows it would make things easier, but I'm not sure you understand what you're asking for."

"I hasten to point out that I was once a small boy." He wanted to do it, he discovered. It was more than a gesture or impulse; he really wanted to have the kid around. "Look, why don't we put this to a vote and ask Rad?"

"Ask me what?" Radley had run some water over his hands after he'd finished talking to Josh, and figured his mother was too busy to give them a close look.

Mitch picked up his wine, then lifted a brow. My ball, Hester thought. She could have put the child off, but she'd always prided herself on being honest with him. "Mitch was just suggesting that you might like to stay with him after school in the afternoons instead of going over to Mrs. Cohen's."

"Really?" Astonishment and excitement warred until he was bouncing with both. "Really, can I?"

"Well, I wanted to think about it and talk to you before—"

"I'll behave." Radley rushed over to wrap his arms around his mother's waist. "I promise. Mitch is much better than Mrs. Cohen. Lots better. She smells like mothballs and pats me on the head."

"I rest my case," Mitch murmured.

Hester sent Mitch a smoldering look. She wasn't accustomed to being outnumbered or to making a decision without careful thought and consideration. "Now, Radley, you know Mrs. Cohen's very nice. You've been staying with her for over two years."

Radley squeezed harder and played his ace. "If I stayed with Mitch I could come right home. And I'd do my homework first." It was a rash promise, but it was a desperate situation. "You'd get home sooner, too, and everything. Please, Mom, say yes."

She hated to deny him anything, because there were too many things she'd already had to. He was looking up at her now with his cheeks rosy with pleasure. Bending, she kissed him. "All right, Rad, we'll try it and see how it works out."

"It's going to be great." He locked his arms around her neck before he turned to Mitch. "It's going to be just great."

Chapter 3

Mitch liked to sleep late on weekends—whenever he thought of them as weekends. Because he worked in his own home, at his own pace, he often forgot that to the vast majority there was a big difference between Monday mornings and Saturday mornings. This particular Saturday, however, he was spending in bed, largely dead to the world.

He'd been restless the evening before after he'd left Hester's apartment. Too restless to go back to his own alone. On the spur of the moment he'd gone out to the little lounge where the staff of Universal Comics often got together. He'd run into his inker, another artist and one of the staff writers for *The Great Beyond,* Universal's bid for the supernatural market. The music had been loud and none too good, which had been exactly what his mood had called for.

From there he'd been persuaded to attend an all-night horror film festival in Times Square. It had been

past six when he'd come home, a little drunk and with
only enough energy left to strip and tumble into bed—
where he'd promised himself he'd stay for the next
twenty-four hours. When the phone rang eight hours
later, he answered it mostly because it annoyed him.

"Yeah?"

"Mitch?" Hester hesitated. It sounded as though
he'd been asleep. Since it was after two in the afternoon, she dismissed the thought. "It's Hester Wallace.
I'm sorry to bother you."

"What? No, it's all right." He rubbed a hand over
his face, then pushed at the dog, who had shifted to
the middle of the bed. "Damn it, Taz, shove over.
You're breathing all over me."

Taz? Hester thought as both brows lifted. She hadn't
thought that Mitch would have a roommate. She caught
her bottom lip between her teeth. That was something
she should have checked out. For Radley's sake.

"I really am sorry," she continued in a voice that
had cooled dramatically. "Apparently I've caught you
at a bad time."

"No." Give the stupid mutt an inch and he took a
mile, Mitch thought as he hefted the phone and
climbed to the other side of the bed. "What's up?"

"Are you?"

It was the mild disdain in her voice that had him
bristling. That and the fact that it felt as though he'd
eaten a sandbox. "Yeah, I'm up. I'm talking to you,
aren't I?"

"I only called to give you all the numbers and information you need if you watch Radley next week."

"Oh." He pushed the hair out of his eyes and
glanced around, hoping he'd left a glass of watered-

down soda or something close at hand. No luck. "Okay. You want to wait until I get a pencil?"

"Well, I..." He heard her put her hand over the receiver and speak to someone—Radley, he imagined from the quick intensity of the voice. "Actually, if it wouldn't put you out, Radley was hoping we could come by for a minute. He wants to introduce you to his friend. If you're busy, I can just drop the information by later."

Mitch started to tell her to do just that. Not only could he go back to sleep, but he might just be able to wrangle five minutes alone with her. Then he thought of Radley standing beside his mother, looking up at her with those big dark eyes. "Give me ten minutes," he muttered, and hung up before Hester could say a word.

Mitch pulled on jeans, then went into the bath to fill the sink with cold water. He took a deep breath and stuck his face in it. He came up swearing but awake. Five minutes later he was pulling on a sweatshirt and wondering if he'd remembered to wash any socks. All the clothes that had come back from the laundry neatly folded had been dumped on the chair in the corner of the bedroom. He briefly considered pushing his way through them, then let it go when he heard the knock. Taz's tail thumped on the mattress.

"Why don't you pick up this place?" Mitch asked him. "It's a pigsty."

Taz grinned, showing a set of big white teeth, then made a series of growls and groans.

"Excuses. Always excuses. And get out of bed. Don't you know it's after two?" Mitch rubbed a hand over his unshaven chin, then went to open the door.

She looked great, just plain great, with a hand on a

shoulder of each boy and a half smile on her face. Shy?
he thought, a little surprised as he realized it. He had
thought her cool and aloof, but now he believed she
used that to hide an innate shyness, which he found
amazingly sweet.

"Hiya, Rad."

"Hi, Mitch," Radley returned, almost bursting with
importance. "This is my friend Josh Miller. He doesn't
believe you're Commander Zark."

"Is that so?" Mitch looked down at the doubting
Thomas, a skinny towhead about two inches taller than
Rad. "Come on in."

"It's nice of you to put up with this," Hester began.
"We weren't going to have any peace until Rad and
Josh had it settled." The living room looked as though
it had exploded. That was Hester's first thought as
Mitch closed the door behind them. Papers and clothes
and wrappers were everywhere. She imagined there
was furniture, too, but she couldn't have described it.

"Tell Josh you're Commander Zark," Radley insisted.

"I guess you could say that." The notion pleased
him. "I created him, anyway." He looked down again
at Josh, whose pout had gone beyond doubt to true
suspicion. "You two go to school together?"

"Used to." Josh stood close to Hester as he studied
Mitch. "You don't look like Commander Zark."

Mitch rubbed a hand over his chin again. "Rough
night."

"He is too Zark. Hey, look, Mom. Mitch has a
VCR." Radley easily overlooked the clutter and
homed in on the entertainment center. "I'm saving up
my allowance to buy one. I've got seventeen dollars."

"It adds up," Mitch murmured, and flicked a finger

down his nose. "Why don't we go into the office? I'll show you what's cooking in the spring issue."

"Wow."

Taking this as an assent, Mitch led the way.

The office, Hester noted, was big and bright and every bit as chaotic as the living room. She was a creature of order, and it was beyond her how anyone could produce under these conditions. Yet there was a drawing board set up, and tacked to it were sketches and captions.

"You can see Zark's going to have his hands full when Leilah teams up with the Black Moth."

"The Black Moth. Holy cow." Faced with the facts, Josh was duly impressed. Then he remembered his comic book history, and suspicion reared again. "I thought he destroyed the Moth five issues ago."

"The Moth only went into hibernation after Zark bombarded the Zenith with experimental ZT-5. Leilah used her scientific genius to bring him out again."

"Wow." This came from Josh as he stared at the oversized words and drawings. "How come you make this so big? It can't fit in a comic book."

"It has to be reduced."

"I read all about that stuff." Radley gave Josh a superior glance. "I got this book out of the library that gave the history of comic books, all the way back to the 1930s."

"The Stone Age." Mitch smiled as the boys continued to admire his work. Hester was doing some admiring of her own. Beneath the clutter, she was certain there was a genuine, French rococo cupboard. And books. Hundreds of them. Mitch watched her wander the room. And would have gone on watching if Josh hadn't tugged on his arm.

"Please, can I have your autograph?"

Mitch felt foolishly delighted as he stared down at the earnest face. "Sure." Shuffling through papers, he found a blank one and signed it. Then, with a flourish, he added a quick sketch of Zark.

"Neat." Josh folded the paper reverently and slipped it in his back pocket. "My brother's always bragging because he's got an autographed baseball, but this is better."

"Told ya." With a grin, Radley moved closer to Mitch. "And I'm going to be staying with Mitch after school until Mom gets home from work."

"No kidding?"

"All right, guys, we've taken up enough of Mr. Dempsey's time." Hester started to shoo the boys along when Taz strolled into the room.

"Gee whiz, he's really big." Radley started forward, hand out, when Hester caught him.

"Radley, you know better than to go up to a strange dog."

"Your mom's right," Mitch put in. "But in this case it's okay. Taz is harmless."

And enormous, Hester thought, keeping a firm grip on both boys.

Taz, who had a healthy respect for little people, sat in the doorway and eyed them both. Small boys had a tendency to want to play rough and pull ears, which Taz suffered heroically but could do without. Waiting to see which way the wind blew, he sat and thumped his tail.

"He's anything but an aggressive dog," Mitch reassured Hester. He stepped around her and put a hand on Taz's head. Without, Hester noted, having to bend over.

"Does he do tricks?" Radley wanted to know. It was one of his most secret wishes to own a dog. A big one. But he never asked, because he knew they couldn't keep one shut in an apartment all day alone.

"No, all Taz does is talk."

"Talk?" Josh went into a fit of laughter. "Dogs can't talk."

"He means bark," Hester said, relaxing a little.

"No, I mean talk." Mitch gave Taz a couple of friendly pats. "How's it going, Taz?"

In answer, the dog pushed his head hard against Mitch's leg and began to groan and grumble. Eyes wide and sincere, he looked up at his master and howled and hooted until both boys were nearly rolling with laughter.

"He *does* talk." Radley stepped forward, palm up. "He really does." Taz decided Radley didn't look like an ear puller and nuzzled his long snout in the boy's hand. "He likes me. Look, Mom." It was love at first sight as Radley threw his arms around the dog's neck. Automatically Hester started forward.

"He's as gentle as they come, I promise you." Mitch put a hand on Hester's arm. Even though the dog was already grumbling out his woes in Radley's ear and allowing Josh to pet him, Hester wasn't convinced.

"I don't imagine he's used to children."

"He fools around with kids in the park all the time." As if to prove it, Taz rolled over to expose his belly for stroking. "Added to that is the fact that he's bone lazy. He wouldn't work up the energy to bite anything that hadn't been put in a bowl for him. You aren't afraid of dogs, are you?"

"No, of course not." Not really, she added to herself. Because she hated to show a weakness, Hester crouched down to pet the huge head. Unknowingly she hit the perfect spot, and Taz recognized a patsy when he saw one. He shifted to lay a paw on her thigh and, with his dark, sad eyes on hers, began to moan. Laughing, Hester rubbed behind his ears. "You're just a big baby, aren't you?"

"An operator's more like it," Mitch murmured, wondering what sort of trick he'd have to do to get Hester to touch him with such feeling.

"I can play with him every day, can't I, Mitch?"

"Sure." Mitch smiled down at Radley. "Taz loves attention. You guys want to take him for a walk?"

The response was immediate and affirmative. Hester straightened up, looking doubtfully at Taz. "I don't know, Rad."

"Please, Mom, we'll be careful. You already said me and Josh could play in the park for a little while."

"Yes, I know, but Taz is awfully big. I wouldn't want him to get away from you."

"Taz is a firm believer in conserving energy. Why run if strolling gets you to the same place?" Mitch went back into his office, rooted around and came up with Taz's leash. "He doesn't chase cars, other dogs or park police. He will, however, stop at every tree."

With a giggle, Radley took the leash. "Okay, Mom?"

She hesitated, knowing there was a part of her that wanted to keep Radley with her, within arm's reach. And, for his sake, it was something she had to fight. "A half hour." The words were barely out when he and Josh let out a whoop. "You have to get your coats—and gloves."

"We will. Come on, Taz."

The dog gave a huge sigh before gathering himself up. Grumbling only a little, he stationed himself between the two boys as they headed out.

"Why is it every time I see that kid I feel good?"

"You're very kind to him. Well, I should go upstairs and make sure they bundle up."

"I think they can handle it. Why don't you sit down?" He took advantage of her brief hesitation by taking her arm. "Come over by the window. You can watch them go out."

She gave in because she knew how Radley hated to be hovered over. "Oh, I have my office number for you, and the name and number of his doctor and the school." Mitch took the paper and stuck it in his pocket. "If there's any trouble at all, call me. I can be home in ten minutes."

"Relax, Hester. We'll get along fine."

"I want to thank you again. It's the first time since he started school, that Rad's looked forward to a Monday."

"I'm looking forward to it myself."

She looked down, waiting to see the familiar blue cap and coat. "We haven't discussed terms."

"What terms?"

"How much you want for watching him. Mrs. Cohen—"

"Good God, Hester, I don't want you to pay me."

"Don't be ridiculous. Of course I'll pay you."

He put a hand on her shoulder until she'd turned to face him. "I don't need the money, I don't want the money. I made the offer because Rad's a nice kid and I enjoy his company."

"That's very kind of you, but—"

His exasperated sigh cut her off. "Here come the buts again."

"I couldn't possibly let you do it for nothing."

Mitch studied her face. He'd thought her tough at their first meeting, and tough she was—at least on the outside. "Can't you accept a neighborly gesture?"

Her lips curved a bit, but her eyes remained solemn. "I guess not."

"Five bucks a day."

This time the smile reached her eyes. "Thank you."

He caught the ends of her hair between his thumb and forefinger. "You drive a hard bargain, lady."

"So I've been told." Cautiously she took a step away. "Here they come." He hadn't forgotten his gloves, she noted as she leaned closer to the window. Nor had he forgotten that he'd been taught to walk to the corner and cross at the light. "He's in heaven, you know. Rad's always wanted a dog." She touched a hand to the window and continued to watch. "He doesn't mention it because he knows we can't keep one in the apartment when no one's home all day. So he's settled for the promise of a kitten."

Mitch put a hand on her shoulder again, but gently this time. "He doesn't strike me as a deprived child, Hester. There's nothing for you to feel guilty about."

She looked at him then, her eyes wide and just a little sad. Mitch discovered he was just as drawn to that as he had been to her laughter. Without planning to, without knowing he'd needed to, he lifted a hand to her cheek. The pale gray of her irises deepened. Her skin warmed. Hester backed away quickly.

"I'd better go. I'm sure they'll want hot chocolate when they get back in."

"They have to bring Taz back here first," Mitch

reminded her. "Take a break, Hester. Want some coffee?"

"Well, I—"

"Good. Sit down and I'll get it."

Hester stood in the center of the room a moment, a bit amazed at how smoothly he ran things—his way. She was much too used to setting her own rules to accept anyone else's. Still, she told herself it would be rude to leave, that her son would be back soon and that the least she could do after Mitch had been so good to the boy was bear his company for a little while.

She would have been lying if she'd denied that he interested her. In a casual way, of course. There was something about the way he looked at her, so deep and penetrating, while at the same time he appeared to take most of life as a joke. Yet there was nothing funny about the way he touched her.

Hester lifted fingertips to her cheek, where his had been. She would have to take care to avoid too much of that sort of contact. Perhaps, with effort, she could think of Mitch as a friend, as Radley did already. It might not sit well with her to be obliged to him, but she could swallow that. She'd swallowed worse.

He was kind. She let out a little breath as she tried to relax. Experience had given her a very sensitive antenna. She could recognize the kind of man who tried to ingratiate himself with the child to get to the mother. If she was sure of anything, it was that Mitch genuinely liked Radley. That, if nothing else, was a point in his favor.

But she wished he hadn't touched her that way, looked at her that way, made her feel that way.

"It's hot. Probably lousy, but hot." Mitch walked in with two mugs. "Don't you want to sit down?"

Hester smiled at him. "Where?"

Mitch set the mugs down on a stack of papers, then pushed magazines from the sofa. "Here."

"You know..." She stepped over a stack of old newspapers. "Radley's very good at tidying. He'd be glad to help you."

"I function best in controlled confusion."

Hester joined him on the sofa. "I can see the confusion, but not the controlled."

"It's here, believe me. I didn't ask if you wanted anything in the coffee, so I brought it black."

"Black's fine. This table—it's Queen Anne, isn't it?"

"Yeah." Mitch set his bare feet on it, then crossed them at the ankles. "You've got a good eye."

"One would have to under the circumstances." Because he laughed, she smiled as she took her first sip. "I've always loved antiques. I suppose it's the endurance. Not many things last."

"Sure they do. I once had a cold that lasted six weeks." He settled back as she laughed. "When you do that, you get a dimple at the corner of your mouth. Cute."

Hester was immediately self-conscious again. "You have a very natural way with children. Did you come from a large family?"

"No. Only child." He continued to study her, curious about her reaction to the most casual of compliments.

"Really? I wouldn't have guessed it."

"Don't tell me you're of the school who believes only a woman can relate to children?"

"No, not really," she hedged, because that had been her experience thus far. "It's just that you're particularly good with them. No children of your own?" The question came out quickly, amazing and embarrassing her.

"No. I guess I've been too busy being a kid myself to think about raising any."

"That hardly makes you unusual," she said coolly.

He tilted his head as he studied her. "Tossing me in with Rad's father, Hester?"

Something flashed in her eyes. Mitch shook his head as he sipped again. "Damn, Hester, what did the bastard do to you?" She froze instantly. Mitch was quicker. Even as she started to rise, he put a restraining hand on her arm. "Okay, hands off that one until you're ready. I apologize if I hit a sore spot, but I'm curious. I've spent a couple of evenings with Rad now, and he's never mentioned his father."

"I'd appreciate it if you wouldn't ask him any questions."

"Fine." Mitch was capable of being just as snotty. "I didn't intend to grill the kid."

Hester was tempted to get up and excuse herself. That would be the easiest way. But the fact was that she was trusting her son to this man every afternoon. She supposed it would be best if he had some background.

"Rad hasn't seen his father in almost seven years."

"At all?" He couldn't help his surprise. His own family had been undemonstrative and distant, but he never went more than a year without seeing his parents. "Must be rough on the kid."

"They were never close. I think Radley's adjusted very well."

"Hold on. I wasn't criticizing you." He'd placed his hand over hers again, too firmly to be shaken off.

"I know a happy, well-loved boy when I see one. You'd walk through fire for him. Maybe you don't think it shows, but it does."

"There's nothing that's more important to me than Radley." She wanted to relax again, but he was sitting too close, and his hand was still on hers. "I only told you this so that you wouldn't ask him questions that might upset him."

"Does that sort of thing happen often?"

"Sometimes." His fingers were linked with hers now. She couldn't quite figure out how he'd managed it. "A new friend, a new teacher. I really should go."

"How about you?" He touched her cheek gently and turned her face toward him. "How have you adjusted?"

"Just fine. I have Rad, and my work."

"And no relationships?"

She wasn't sure if it was embarrassment or anger, but the sensation was very strong. "That's none of your business."

"If people only talked about what was their business, they wouldn't get very far. You don't strike me as a man-hater, Hester."

She lifted a brow. When pushed, she could play the game by someone else's rules. And she could play it well. "I went through a period of time when I despised men on principle. Actually, it was a very rewarding time of my life. Then, gradually, I came to the opinion that some members of your species weren't lower forms of life."

"Sounds promising."

She smiled again, because he made it easy. "The point is, I don't blame all men for the faults of one."

"You're just cautious."

"If you like."

"The one thing I'm sure I like is your eyes. No, don't look away." Patiently, he turned her face back to his. "They're fabulous—take it from an artist's standpoint."

She had to stop being so jumpy, Hester ordered herself. With an effort, she remained still. "Does that mean they're going to appear in an upcoming issue?"

"They just might." He smiled, appreciating the thought and the fact that though tense, she was able to hold her own. "Poor old Zark deserves to meet someone who understands him. These eyes would."

"I'll take that as a compliment." And run. "The boys will be back in a minute."

"We've got some time yet. Hester, do you ever have fun?"

"What a stupid question. Of course I do."

"Not as Rad's mother, but as Hester." He ran a hand through her hair, captivated.

"I *am* Rad's mother." Though she managed to rise, he stood with her.

"You're also a woman. A gorgeous one." He saw the look in her eyes and ran his thumb along her jawline. "Take my word for it. I'm an honest man. You're one gorgeous bundle of nerves."

"That's silly. I don't have anything to be nervous about." Other than the fact that he was touching her, and his voice was quiet, and the apartment was empty.

"I'll take the shaft out of my heart later," he murmured. He bent to kiss her, then had to catch her when she nearly stumbled over the newspapers. "Take it easy. I'm not going to bite you. This time."

"I have to go." She was as close to panic as she

ever allowed herself to come. "I have a dozen things to do."

"In a minute." He framed her face. She was trembling, he realized. It didn't surprise him. What did was that he wasn't steady himself. "What we have here, Mrs. Wallace, is called attraction, chemistry, lust. It doesn't really matter what label you put on it."

"Maybe not to you."

"Then we'll let you pick the label later." He stroked his thumbs over her cheekbones, gently, soothingly. "I already told you I'm not a maniac. I'll have to remember to get those references."

"Mitch, I told you I appreciate what you're doing for Rad, but I wish you'd—"

"Here and now doesn't concern Rad. This is you and me, Hester. When was the last time you let yourself be alone with a man who wanted you?" He casually brushed his thumb over her lips. Her eyes went to smoke. "When was the last time you let anyone do this?"

His mouth covered hers quickly, with a force that came as a shock. She hadn't been prepared for violence. His hands had been so gentle, his voice so soothing. She hadn't expected this edgy passion. But God, how she'd wanted it. With the same reckless need, she threw her arms around his neck and answered demand for demand.

"Too long," Mitch managed breathlessly when he tore his mouth from hers. "Thank God." Before she could utter more than a moan, he took her mouth again.

He hadn't been sure what he'd find in her—ice, anger, fear. The unrestrained heat came as much of a shock to his system as to hers. Her wide, generous mouth was warm and willing, with all traces of shyness swallowed by passion. She gave more than he would have asked for, and more than he'd been prepared to take.

His head spun, a fascinating and novel sensation he couldn't fully appreciate as he struggled to touch and taste. He dragged his hands through her hair, scattering the two thin silver pins she'd used to pull it back from her face. He wanted it free and wild in his hands, just as he wanted her free and wild in his bed. His plans to go slowly, to test the waters, evaporated in an overwhelming desire to dive in headfirst. Thinking only of this, he slipped his hands under her sweater. The skin there was tender and warm. The silky little concoction she wore was cool and soft. He slid his hands around her waist and up to cup her breasts.

She stiffened, then shuddered. She hadn't known how much she'd wanted to be touched like this. Needed like this. His taste was so dark, so tempting. She'd forgotten what it was like to hunger for such things. It was madness, the sweet release of madness. She heard him murmur her name as he moved his mouth down her throat and back again.

Madness. She understood it. She'd been there before, or thought she had. Though it seemed sweeter now, richer now, she knew she could never go there again.

"Mitch, please." It wasn't easy to resist what he was offering. It surprised Hester how difficult it was to draw away, to put the boundaries back. "We can't do this."

"We are," he pointed out, and drew the flavor from her lips again. "And very well."

"*I* can't." With the small sliver of willpower she had left, she struggled away. "I'm sorry. I should never have let this happen.'' Her cheeks were hot. Hester put her hands to them, then dragged them up through her hair.

His knees were weak. That was something to think about. But for the moment he concentrated on her. "You're taking a lot on yourself, Hester. It seems to be a habit of yours. I kissed you, and you just happened to kiss me back. Since we both enjoyed it, I don't see where apologies are necessary on either side.''

"I should have made myself clear.'' She stepped back, hit the newspapers again, then skirted around them. "I do appreciate what you're doing for Rad—''

"Leave him out of this, for God's sake.''

"I can't.'' Her voice rose, surprising her again. She knew better than to lose control. "I don't expect you to understand, but I can't leave him out of it.'' She took a deep breath, amazed that it did nothing to calm her pulse rate. "I'm not interested in casual sex. I have Rad to think about, and myself.''

"Fair enough.'' He wanted to sit down until he'd recovered, but figured the situation called for an eye-to-eye discussion. "I wasn't feeling too casual about it myself.''

That was what worried her. "Let's just drop it.''

Anger was an amazing stimulant. Mitch stepped forward, and caught her chin in his hand. "Fat chance.''

"I don't want to argue with you. I just think that—'' The knock came as a blessed reprieve. "That's the boys.''

"I know.'' But he didn't release her. "Whatever you're interested in, have time for, room for, might just have to be adjusted.'' He was angry, really angry, Mitch realized. It wasn't like him to lose his temper so quickly. "Life's full of adjustments, Hester." Letting her go, he opened the door.

"It was great." Rosy-cheeked and bright-eyed, Radley tumbled in ahead of Josh and the dog. "We even got Taz to run once, for a minute."

"Amazing." Mitch bent to unclip the leash. Grumbling with exhaustion, Taz walked to a spot by the window, then collapsed.

"You guys must be freezing." Hester kissed Radley's forehead. "It must be time for hot chocolate."

"Yeah!" Radley turned his beaming face to Mitch. "Want some? Mom makes real good hot chocolate."

It was tempting to put her on the spot. Perhaps it was a good thing for both of them that his temper was already fading. "Maybe next time." He pulled Radley's cap over his eyes. "I've got some things to do."

"Thanks a lot for letting us take Taz out. It was really neat, wasn't it, Josh?"

"Yeah. Thanks, Mr. Dempsey."

"Anytime. See you Monday, Rad."

"Okay." The boys fled, laughing and shoving. Mitch looked, but Hester was already gone.

Chapter 4

Mitchell Dempsey II had been born rich, privileged and, according to his parents, with an incorrigible imagination. Maybe that was why he'd taken to Radley so quickly. The boy was far from rich, not even privileged enough to have a set of parents, but his imagination was first-class.

Mitch had always liked crowds as much as one-on-one social situations. He was certainly no stranger to parties, given his mother's affection for entertaining and his own gregarious nature, and no one who knew him would ever have classed him as a loner. In his work, however, he had always preferred the solitary. He worked at home not because he didn't like distractions—he was really fond of them—but because he didn't care to have anyone looking over his shoulder or timing his progress. He'd never considered working any way other than alone. Until Radley.

They made a pact the first day. If Radley finished

his homework, with or without Mitch's dubious help, he could then choose to either play with Taz or give his input into Mitch's latest story line. If Mitch had decided to call it quits for the day, they could entertain themselves with his extensive collection of videotapes or with Radley's growing army of plastic figures.

To Mitch, it was natural—to Radley, fantastic. For the first time in his young life he had a man who was part of his daily routine, one who talked to him and listened to him. He had someone who was not only as willing to spend time to set up a battle or wage a war as his mother was, but someone who understood his military strategy.

By the end of their first week, Mitch was not only a hero, creator of Zark and owner of Taz, but the most solid and dependable person in his life other than his mother. Radley loved, without guards or restrictions.

Mitch saw it, wondered at it and found himself just as captivated. He had told Hester no less than the truth when he'd said that he'd never thought about having children. He'd run his life on his own clock for so long that he'd never considered doing things differently. If he'd known what it was to love a small boy, to find pieces of himself in one, he might have done things differently.

Perhaps it was because of his discoveries that he thought of Radley's father. What kind of man could create something that special and then walk away from it? His own father had been stern and anything but understanding, but he'd been there. Mitch had never questioned the love.

A man didn't get to be thirty-five without knowing several contemporaries who'd been through divorces— many of them bitter. But he also was acquainted with

several who'd managed to call a moratorium with their
ex-wives in order to remain fathers. It was difficult
enough to understand how Radley's father not only
could have walked out, but could have walked away.
After a week in Radley's company, it was all but impossible.

And what of Hester? What kind of man left a woman
to struggle alone to raise a child they had brought into
the world together? How much had she loved him?
That was a thought that dug into his brain too often
for comfort. The results of the experience were obvious. She was tense and overly cautious around men.
Around him, certainly, Mitch thought with a grimace
as he watched Radley sketch. So cautious that she'd
stayed out of his path throughout the week.

Every day between 4:15 and 4:25, he received a polite call. Hester would ask him if everything had gone
well, thank him for watching Radley, then ask him to
send her son upstairs. That afternoon, Radley had
handed him a neatly written check for twenty-five dollars drawn on the account of Hester Gentry Wallace.
It was still crumpled in Mitch's pocket.

Did she really think he was going to quietly step
aside after she'd knocked the wind out of him? He
hadn't forgotten what she'd felt like pressed against
him, inhibitions and caution stripped away for one
brief, stunning moment. He intended to live that moment again, as well as the others his incorrigible imagination had conjured up.

If she did think he'd bow out gracefully, Mrs. Hester
Wallace was in for a big surprise.

"I can't get the retro rockets right," Radley complained. "They never look right."

Mitch set aside his own work, which had stopped

humming along the moment he'd started to think of Hester. "Let's have a look." He took the spare sketch pad he'd lent to Radley. "Hey, not bad." He grinned, foolishly pleased with Radley's attempt at the Defiance. It seemed the few pointers he'd given the kid had taken root. "You're a real natural, Rad."

The boy blushed with pleasure, then frowned again. "But see, the boosters and retros are all wrong. They look stupid."

"Only because you're trying to detail too soon. Look, light strokes, impressions first." He put a hand over the boy's to guide it. "Don't be afraid to make mistakes. That's why they make those big gum erasers."

"You don't make mistakes." Radley caught his tongue between his teeth as he struggled to make his hand move as expertly as Mitch's.

"Sure I do. This is my fifteenth eraser this year."

"You're the best artist in the whole world," Radley said, looking up, his heart in his eyes.

Moved and strangely humbled, Mitch ruffled the boy's hair. "Maybe one of the top twenty, but thanks." When the phone rang, Mitch felt a strange stab of disappointment. The weekend meant something different now—no Radley. For a man who had lived his entire adult life without responsibilities, it was a sobering thought to realize he would miss one. "That should be your mother."

"She said we could go out to the movies tonight 'cause it's Friday and all. You could come with us."

Giving a noncommittal grunt, Mitch answered the phone. "Hi, Hester."

"Mitch, I—everything okay?"

Something in her tone had his brows drawing to-gether. "Just dandy."

"Did Radley give you the check?"

"Yeah. Sorry, I haven't had a chance to cash it yet."

If there was one thing she wasn't in the mood for at the moment, it was sarcasm. "Well, thanks. If you'd send Radley upstairs, I'd appreciate it."

"No problem." He hesitated. "Rough day, Hester?"

She pressed a hand to her throbbing temple. "A bit. Thank you, Mitch."

"Sure." He hung up, still frowning. Turning to Rad-ley, he made the effort to smile. "Time to transfer your equipment, Corporal."

"Sir, yes, sir!" Radley gave a smart salute. The in-tergalactic army he'd left at Mitch's through the week was tossed into his backpack. After a brief search, both of his gloves were located and pushed in on top of the plastic figures. Radley stuffed his coat and hat in before kneeling down to hug Taz. "Bye, Taz. See ya." The dog rumbled a goodbye as he rubbed his snout into Radley's shoulder. "Bye, Mitch." He went to the door, then hesitated. "I guess I'll see you Monday."

"Sure. Hey, maybe I'll just walk up with you. Give your mom a full report."

"Okay!" Radley brightened instantly. "You left your keys in the kitchen. I'll get them." Mitch watched the tornado pass, then swirl back. "I got an A in spell-ing. When I tell Mom, she'll be in a real good mood. We'll probably get sodas."

"Sounds like a good deal to me," Mitch said, and let himself be dragged along.

Hester heard Radley's key in the lock and set down the ice pack. Leaning closer, she checked her face in the bathroom mirror, saw a bruise was already forming, and swore. She'd hoped to be able to tell Radley about the mishap, gloss over it and make it a joke before any battle scars showed. Hester downed two aspirin and prayed the headache would pass.

"Mom! Hey, Mom!"

"Right here, Radley." She winced at her own raised voice, then put on a smile as she walked out to greet him. The smile faded when she saw her son had brought company.

"Mitch came up to report," Radley began as he shrugged out of his backpack.

"What the hell happened to you?" Mitch crossed over to her in two strides. He had her face in his hands and fury in his eyes. "Are you all right?"

"Of course I am." She shot him a quick warning look, then turned to Radley. "I'm fine."

Radley stared up at her, his eyes widening, then his bottom lip trembling as he saw the black-and-blue mark under her eye. "Did you fall down?"

She wanted to lie and say yes, but she'd never lied to him. "Not exactly." She forced a smile, annoyed to have a witness to her explanation. "It seems that there was a man at the subway station who wanted my purse. I wanted it, too."

"You were mugged?" Mitch wasn't sure whether to swear at her or gather her close and check for injuries. Hester's long, withering look didn't give him the chance to do either.

"Sort of." She moved her shoulders to show Radley it was of little consequence. "It wasn't all that exciting, I'm afraid. The subway was crowded. Someone saw what was going on and called security, so the man changed his mind about my purse and ran away."

Radley looked closer. He'd seen a black eye before. Joey Phelps had had a really neat one once. But he'd never seen one on his mother. "Did he hit you?"

"Not really. That part was sort of an accident." An accident that hurt like the devil. "We were having this tug-of-war over my purse, and his elbow shot up. I didn't duck quick enough, that's all."

"Stupid," Mitch muttered loud enough to be heard.

"Did you hit him?"

"Of course not," Hester answered, and thought longingly of her ice pack. "Go put your things away now, Radley."

"But I want to know about—"

"Now," his mother interrupted in a tone she used rarely and to great effect.

"Yes, ma'am," Radley mumbled, and lugged the backpack off the couch.

Hester waited until he'd turned the corner into his room. "I want you to know I don't appreciate your interference."

"You haven't begun to see interference. What the hell's wrong with you? You know better than to fight with a mugger over a purse. What if he'd had a knife?" Even the thought of it had his reliable imagination working overtime.

"He didn't have a knife." Hester felt her knees begin to tremble. The damnedest thing was that the reaction had chosen the most inopportune moment to set in. "And he doesn't have my purse, either."

"Or a black eye. For God's sake, Hester, you could have been seriously hurt, and I doubt there's anything in your purse that would warrant it. Credit cards can be canceled, a compact or a lipstick replaced.''

"I suppose if someone had tried to lift your wallet you'd have given him your blessing.''

"That's different.''

"The hell it is.''

He stopped pacing long enough to give her a long study. Her chin was thrust out, in the same way he'd seen Radley's go a few times. He'd expected the stubbornness, but he had to admit he hadn't expected the ready temper, or his admiration for it. But that was beside the point, he reminded himself as his gaze swept over her bruised cheekbone again.

"Let's just back up a minute. In the first place, you've got no business taking the subway alone.''

She let out what might have been a laugh. "You've got to be kidding.''

The funny thing was, he couldn't remember ever having said anything quite that stupid. It brought his own temper bubbling over. "Take a cab, damn it.''

"I have no intention of taking a cab.''

"Why?''

"In the first place it would be stupid, and in the second I can't afford it.''

Mitch dragged the check out of his pocket and pushed it into her hand. "Now you can afford it, along with a reasonable tip.''

"I have no intention of taking this." She shoved the crumpled check back at him. "Or of taking a taxi when the subway is both inexpensive and convenient. And I have less intention of allowing you to take a small incident and blow it into a major calamity. I don't want Radley upset.''

"Fine, then take a cab. For the kid's sake, if not

your own. Think how it would have been for him if you'd really been hurt.''

The bruise stood out darkly as her cheeks paled. "I don't need you or anyone to lecture me on the welfare of my son."

"No, you do just fine by him. It's when it comes to Hester that you've got a few loose screws." He jammed his hands into his pockets. "Okay, you won't take a cab. At least promise you won't play Sally Courageous the next time some lowlife decides he likes the color of your purse."

Hester brushed at the sleeve of her jacket. "Is that the name of one of your characters?"

"It might be." He told himself to calm down. He didn't have much of a temper as a rule, but when it started to perk, it could come to a boil in seconds. "Look, Hester, did you have your life savings in your bag?"

"Of course not."

"Family heirlooms?"

"No."

"Any microchips vital to national security?"

She let out an exasperated sigh and dropped onto the arm of a chair. "I left them at the office." She pouted as she looked up at him. "Don't give me that disgusting smile now."

"Sorry." He changed it to a grin.

"I just had such a rotten day." Without realizing it, she slipped off her shoe and began to massage her instep. "The first thing this morning, Mr. Rosen went on an efficiency campaign. Then there was the staff meeting, then the idiot settlement clerk, who made a pass at me."

"What idiot settlement clerk?"

"Never mind." Tired, she rubbed her temple. "Just take it that things went from bad to worse until I was ready to bite someone's head off. Then that jerk grabbed my purse, and I just exploded. At least I have the satisfaction of knowing he'll be walking with a limp for a few days."

"Got in a few licks, did you?"

Hester continued to pout as she gingerly touched her eye with her fingertips. "Yeah."

Mitch walked over, then bent down to her level. With a look more of curiosity than sympathy, he examined the damage. "You're going to have a hell of a shiner."

"Really?" Hester touched the bruise again. "I was hoping this was as bad as it would get."

"Not a chance. It's going to be a beaut."

She thought of the stares and the explanations that would be necessary the following week. "Terrific."

"Hurt?"

"Yes."

Mitch touched his lips to the bruise before she could evade him. "Try some ice."

"I've already thought of that."

"I put my things away." Radley stood in the hallway looking down at his shoes. "I had homework, but I already did it."

"That's good. Come here." Radley continued to look at his shoes as he walked to her. Hester put her arms around his neck and squeezed. "Sorry."

"'S okay. I didn't mean to make you mad."

"You didn't make me mad. Mr. Rosen made me mad. That man who wanted my purse made me mad, but not you, baby."

"I could get you a wet cloth the way you do when my head hurts."

"Thanks, but I think I need a hot bath and an ice pack." She gave him another squeeze, then remembered. "Oh, we had a date didn't we? Cheeseburgers and a movie."

"We can watch TV instead."

"Well, why don't we see how I feel in a little while?"

"I got an *A* on my spelling test."

"My hero," Hester said, laughing.

"You know, that hot bath's a good idea. Ice, too." Mitch was already making plans. "Why don't you get started on that while I borrow Rad for a little while."

"But he just got home."

"It'll only take a little while." Mitch took her arm and started to lead her toward the hall. "Put some bubbles in the tub. They're great for the morale. We'll be back in half an hour."

"But where are you going?"

"Just an errand I need to run. Rad can keep me company, can't you, Rad?"

"Sure."

The idea of a thirty-minute soak was too tempting. "No candy, it's too close to dinner."

"Okay, I won't eat any," Mitch promised, and scooted her into the bath. Putting a hand on Radley's shoulder, he marched back into the living room. "Ready to go out on a mission, Corporal?"

Radley's eyes twinkled as he saluted. "Ready and willing, sir."

The combination of ice pack, hot bath and aspirin proved successful. By the time the water had cooled in the tub, Hester's headache was down to dull and manageable. She supposed she owed Mitch for giving her a few minutes to herself, Hester admitted as she pulled on jeans. Along with most of the pain, the shakiness had drained away in the hot water. In fact, when she took the time to examine her bruised eye, she felt downright proud of herself. Mitch had been right, bubbles had been good for the morale.

She pulled a brush through her hair and wondered how disappointed Radley would be if they postponed their trip to the movies. Hot bath or no, the last thing she felt like doing at the moment was braving the cold to sit in a crowded theater. She thought a matinee the next day might satisfy him. It would mean adjusting her schedule a bit, but the idea of a quiet evening at home after the week she'd put in made doing the laundry after dinner a lot more acceptable.

And what a week, Hester thought as she pulled on slippers. Rosen was a tyrant and the settlement clerk was a pest. She'd spent almost as much time during the last five days placating one and discouraging the other as she had processing loans. She wasn't afraid of work, but she did resent having to account for every minute of her time. It was nothing personal; Hester had discovered that within the first eight-hour stretch. Rosen was equally overbearing and fussy with everyone on his staff.

And that fool Cummings. Hester pushed the thought of the overamorous clerk out of her mind and sat on the edge of the bed. She'd gotten through the first two weeks, hadn't she? She touched her cheekbone gingerly. With the scars to prove it. It would be easier now. She wouldn't have the strain of meeting all those

new people. The biggest relief of all was that she didn't
have to worry about Radley.

She'd never admit it to anyone, but she'd waited for
Mitch to call every day that week to tell her Radley
was too much trouble, he'd changed his mind, he was
tired of spending his afternoons with a nine-year-old.
But the fact was that every afternoon when Radley had
come upstairs the boy had been full of stories about
Mitch and Taz and what they'd done.

Mitch had showed him a series of sketches for the
big anniversary issue. They'd taken Taz to the park.
They'd watched the original, uncut, absolutely classic
King Kong on the VCR. Mitch had showed him his
comic book collection, which included the first issues
of *Superman* and *Tales From the Crypt,* which everyone knew, she'd been informed, were practically priceless. And did she know that Mitch had an original,
honest-to-God *Captain Midnight* decoder ring? Wow.

Hester rolled her eyes, then winced when the movement reminded her of the bruise. The man might be
odd, she decided, but he was certainly making Radley
happy. Things would be fine as long as she continued
to think of him as Radley's friend and forgot about
that unexpected and unexplainable connection they'd
made last weekend.

Hester preferred to think about it as a connection
rather than any of the terms Mitch had used. Attraction,
chemistry, lust. No, she didn't care for any of those
words, or for her immediate and unrestrained reaction
to him. She knew what she'd felt. Hester was too honest to deny that for one crazed moment she'd welcomed the sensation of being held and kissed and desired. It wasn't something to be ashamed of. A woman

who'd been alone as long as she had was bound to feel certain stirrings around an attractive man.

Then why didn't she feel any of those stirrings around Cummings?

Don't answer that, she warned herself. Sometimes it was best not to dig too deeply when you really didn't want to know.

Think about dinner, she decided. Poor Radley was going to have to make do with soup and a sandwich instead of his beloved cheeseburger tonight. With a sigh, she rose as she heard the front door open.

"Mom! Mom, come see the surprise."

Hester made sure she was smiling, though she wasn't sure she could take any more surprises that day. "Rad, did you thank Mitch for...oh." He was back, Hester saw, automatically adjusting her sweater. The two of them stood just inside the doorway with identical grins on their faces. Radley carried two paper bags, and Mitch hefted what looked suspiciously like a tape machine with cables dangling.

"What's all this?"

"Dinner and a double feature," Mitch informed her. "Rad said you like chocolate shakes."

"Yes, I do." The aroma finally carried to her. Sniffing, she eyed Radley's bags. "Cheeseburgers?"

"Yeah, and fries. Mitch said we could have double orders. We took Taz for a walk. He's eating his downstairs."

"He's got lousy table manners." Mitch carried the unit over to Hester's television.

"And I helped Mitch unhook the VCR. We got *Raiders of the Lost Ark*. Mitch has millions of movies."

"Rad said you like musical junk."

"Well, yes, I—"

"We got one of them, too." Rad set the bags down to go over and sit with Mitch on the floor. "Mitch said it's pretty funny, so I guess it'll be okay." He put a hand on Mitch's leg and leaned closer to watch the hookup.

"Singin' in the Rain." Handing Radley a cable, Mitch sat back to let him connect it.

"Really?"

He had to smile. There were times she sounded just like the kid. "Yeah. How's the eye?"

"Oh, it's better." Unable to resist, Hester walked over to watch. How odd it seemed to see her son's small hands working with those of a man.

"It's a tight squeeze, but the VCR just about fits under your television stand." Mitch gave Radley's shoulder a quick squeeze before he rose. "Colorful." With a finger under her chin, he turned Hester's face to the side to examine her eye. "Rad and I thought you looked a little beat, so we figured we'd bring the movie to you."

"I was." She touched her hand to his wrist a moment. "Thanks."

"Anytime." He wondered what her reaction, and Radley's, would be if he kissed her right now. Hester must have seen the question in his eyes, because she backed up quickly.

"Well, I guess I'd better get some plates so the food doesn't get cold."

"We've got plenty of napkins." He gestured toward the couch. "Sit down while my assistant and I finish up."

"I did it." Flushed with success, Radley scrambled back on all fours. "It's all hooked up."

Mitch bent to check the connections. "You're a regular mechanic, Corporal."

"We get to watch *Raiders* first, right?"

"That was the deal." Mitch handed him the tape. "You're in charge."

"It looks like I have to thank you again," Hester said when Mitch joined her on the couch.

"What for? I figured to wangle myself in on your date with Rad tonight." He pulled a burger out of the bag. "This is cheaper."

"Most men wouldn't choose to spend a Friday night with a small boy."

"Why not?" He took a healthy bite, and after swallowing continued, "I figure he won't eat half his fries, and I'll get the rest."

Radley took a running leap and plopped onto the couch between them. He gave a contented and very adult sigh as he snuggled down. "This is better than going out. Lots better."

He was right, Hester thought as she relaxed and let herself become caught up in Indiana Jones's adventures. There had been a time when she'd believed life could be that thrilling, romantic, heart-stopping. Circumstances had forced her to set those things aside, but she'd never lost her love of the fantasy of films. For a couple of hours it was possible to close off reality and the pressures that went with it and be innocent again.

Radley was bright-eyed and full of energy as he switched tapes. Hester had no doubt his dreams that night would revolve around lost treasures and heroic deeds. Snuggling against her, he giggled at Donald O'Connor's mugging and pratfalls, but began to nod off soon after Gene Kelly's marvelous dance through the rain.

"Fabulous, isn't it?" Mitch murmured. Radley had shifted so that his head rested against Mitch's chest.

"Absolutely. I never get tired of this movie. When I was a little girl, we'd watch it whenever it came on TV. My father's a big movie buff. You can name almost any film, and he'll tell you who was in it. But his first love was always the musical."

Mitch fell silent again. It took very little to learn how one person felt about another—a mere inflection in their voice, a softening of their expression. Hester's family had been close, as he'd always regretted his hadn't been. His father had never shared Mitch's love of fantasy or film, as he had never shared his father's devotion to business. Though he would never have considered himself a lonely child—his imagination had been company enough—he'd always missed the warmth and affection he'd heard so clearly in Hester's voice when she'd spoken of her father.

When the credits rolled, he turned to her again. "Your parents live in the city?"

"Here? Oh, no." She had to laugh as she tried to picture either of her parents coping with life in New York. "No, I grew up in Rochester, but my parents moved to the Sunbelt almost ten years ago—Fort Worth. Dad's still in banking and my mother has a part-time job in a bookstore. We were all amazed when she went to work. I guess all of us thought she didn't know how to do anything but bake cookies and fold sheets."

"How many's we?"

Hester sighed a little as the screen went blank. She couldn't honestly remember when she'd enjoyed an evening more. "I have a brother and a sister. I'm the oldest. Luke's settled in Rochester with a wife and a new baby on the way, and Julia's in Atlanta. She's a disc jockey."

"No kidding?"

"Wake up, Atlanta, it's 6:00 a.m., time for three hits in a row." She laughed a little as she thought of her sister. "I'd give anything to take Rad down for a visit."

"Miss them?"

"It's just hard thinking how spread out we all are. I know how nice it would be for Rad to have more family close by."

"What about Hester?"

She looked over at him, a bit surprised to see how natural Radley looked dozing in the crook of his arm. "I have Rad."

"And that's enough?"

"More than." She smiled; then, uncurling her legs, she rose. "And speaking of Rad, I'd better take him in to bed."

Mitch picked the boy up and settled him over his shoulder. "I'll carry him."

"Oh, that's all right. I do it all the time."

"I've got him." Radley turned his face into Mitch's neck. What an amazing feeling, he thought, a little shaken by it. "Just show me where."

Telling herself it was silly to feel odd, Hester led him into Radley's bedroom. The bed had been made à la Rad, which meant the *Star Wars* spread was pulled up over rumpled sheets. Mitch narrowly missed stepping on a pint-size robot and a worn rag dog. There was a night-light burning by the dresser, because for all Radley's bravado he was still a bit leery about what might or might not be in the closet.

Mitch laid him down on the bed, then began to help Hester take off the boy's sneakers. "You don't have to bother." Hester untangled a knot in the laces with the ease of experience.

"It's not a bother. Does he use pajamas?" Mitch was already tugging off Radley's jeans. In silence, Hester moved over to Radley's dresser and took out his favorites. Mitch studied the bold imprint of Commander Zark. "Good taste. It always ticked me off they didn't come in my size."

The laugh relaxed her again. Hester bundled the top over Radley's head while Mitch pulled the bottoms over his legs.

"Kid sleeps like a rock."

"I know. He always has. He rarely woke up during the night even as a baby." As a matter of habit, she picked up the rag dog and tucked it in beside him before kissing his cheek. "Don't mention Fido," she murmured. "Radley's a bit sensitive about still sleeping with him."

"I never saw a thing." Then, giving in to the need, he brushed a hand over Radley's hair. "Pretty special, isn't he?"

"Yes, he is."

"So are you." Mitch turned and touched her hair in turn. "Don't close up on me, Hester," he said as she shifted her gaze away from his. "The best way to accept a compliment is to say thank you. Give it a shot."

Embarrassed more by her reaction to him than by his words, she made herself look at him. "Thank you."

"That's a good start. Now let's try it again." He

slipped his arms around her. "I've been thinking about kissing you again for almost a week."

"Mitch, I—"

"Did you forget your line?" She'd lifted her hands to his shoulders to hold him off. But her eyes... He much preferred the message he read in them. "That was another compliment. I don't make a habit of thinking about a woman who goes out of her way to avoid me."

"I haven't been. Exactly."

"That's okay, because I figured it was because you couldn't trust yourself around me."

That had her eyes locking on his again, strong and steady. "You have an amazing ego."

"Thanks. Let's try another angle, then." As he spoke, he moved his hand up and down her spine, lighting little fingers of heat. "Kiss me again, and if the bombs don't go off this time I'll figure I was wrong."

"No." But despite herself she couldn't dredge up the will to push him away. "Radley's—"

"Sleeping like a rock, remember?" He touched his lips, very gently, to the swelling under her eye. "And even if he woke up, I don't think the sight of me kissing his mother would give him nightmares."

She started to speak again, but the words were only a sigh as his mouth met hers. He was patient this time, even...tender. Yet the bombs went off. She would have sworn they shook the floor beneath her as she dug her fingers hard into his shoulders.

It was incredible. Impossible. But the need was there, instant, incendiary. It had never been so strong before, not for anyone. Once, when she'd been very young, she'd had a hint of what true, ripe passion could be. And then it had been over. She had come to believe that, like so many other things, such passions were only temporary. But this—this felt like forever.

He'd thought he knew all there was to know about women. Hester was proving him wrong. Even as he felt himself sliding down that warm, soft tunnel of desire, he warned himself not to move too quickly or take too much. There was a hurricane in her, one he had already realized had been channeled and repressed for a long, long time. The first time he'd held her he'd known he had to be the one to free it. But slowly. Carefully. Whether she knew it or not, she was as vulnerable as the child sleeping beside them.

Then her hands were in his hair, pulling him closer. For one mad moment, he dragged her hard against him and let them both taste of what might be.

"Bombs, Hester." She shuddered as he traced his tongue over her ear. "The city's in shambles."

She believed him. With his mouth hot on hers, she believed him. "I have to think."

"Yeah, maybe you do." But he kissed her again. "Maybe we both do." He ran his hands down her body in one long, possessive stroke. "But I have a feeling we're going to come up with the same answer."

Shaken, she backed away. And stumbled over the robot. The crash didn't penetrate Radley's dreams.

"You know, you run into things every time I kiss you." He was going to have to go now or not at all. "I'll pick up the VCR later."

There was a little breath of relief as she nodded. She'd been afraid he'd ask her to sleep with him, and she wasn't at all sure what her answer would have been. "Thank you for everything."

"Good, you're learning." He stroked a finger down her cheek. "Take care of the eye."

Cowardly or not, Hester stayed by Radley's bed until she heard the front door shut. Then, easing down, she put a hand on her sleeping son's shoulder. "Oh, Rad, what have I gotten into?"

Chapter 5

When the phone rang at 7:25, Mitch had his head
buried under a pillow. He would have ignored it, but
Taz rolled over, stuck his snout against Mitch's cheek
and began to grumble in his ear. Mitch swore and
shoved at the dog, then snatched up the receiver and
dragged it under the pillow.

"What?"

On the other end of the line, Hester bit her lip.
"Mitch, it's Hester."

"So?"

"I guess I woke you up."

"Right."

It was painfully obvious that Mitch Dempsey wasn't
a morning person. "I'm sorry. I know it's early."

"Is that what you called to tell me?"

"No…I guess you haven't looked out the window
yet."

"Honey, I haven't even looked past my eyelids yet."

"It's snowing. We've got about eight inches, and it's not expected to let up until around midday. They're calling for twelve to fifteen inches."

"Who are they?"

Hester switched the phone to her other hand. Her hair was still wet from the shower, and she'd only had a chance to gulp down one cup of coffee. "The National Weather Service."

"Well, thanks for the bulletin."

"Mitch! Don't hang up."

He let out a long sigh, then shifted away from Taz's wet nose. "Is there more news?"

"The schools are closed."

"Whoopee."

She was tempted, very tempted to hang up the phone in his ear. The trouble was, she needed him. "I hate to ask, but I'm not sure I can get Radley all the way over to Mrs. Cohen's. I'd take the day off, but I have back-to-back appointments most of the day. I'm going to try to shift things around and get off early, but—"

"Send him down."

There was the briefest of hesitations. "Are you sure?"

"Did you want me to say no?"

"I don't want to interfere with any plans you had."

"Got any hot coffee?"

"Well, yes, I—"

"Send that, too."

Hester stared at the phone after it clicked in her ear, and tried to remind herself to be grateful.

Radley couldn't have been more pleased. He took Taz for his morning walk, threw snowballs—which the dog, on principle, refused to chase—and rolled in the thick blanket of snow until he was satisfactorily covered.

Since Mitch's supplies didn't run to hot chocolate, Radley raided his mother's supply, then spent the rest of the morning happily involved with Mitch's comic books and his own sketches.

As for Mitch, he found the company appealing rather than distracting. The boy lay sprawled on the floor of his office and, between his reading or sketching, rambled on about whatever struck his fancy. Because he spoke to either Mitch or Taz, and seemed to be content to be answered or not, it suited everyone nicely.

By noon the snow had thinned to occasional flurries, dashing Radley's fantasy about another holiday. In tacit agreement, Mitch pushed away from his drawing board.

"You like tacos?"

"Yeah." Radley turned away from the window. "You know how to make them?"

"Nope. But I know how to buy them. Get your coat, Corporal, we've got places to go."

Radley was struggling into his boots when Mitch walked out with a trio of cardboard tubes. "I've got to stop by the office and drop these off."

Radley's mouth dropped down to his toes. "You mean the place where they make the comics?"

"Yeah." Mitch shrugged into his coat. "I guess I could do it tomorrow if you don't want to bother."

"No, I want to." The boy was up and dragging Mitch's sleeve. "Can we go today? I won't touch anything, I promise. I'll be real quiet, too."

"How can you ask questions if you're quiet?" He pulled the boy's collar up. "Get Taz, will you?"

It was always a bit of a trick, and usually an expensive one, to find a cabdriver who didn't object to a hundred-and-fifty pound dog as a passenger. Once inside, however, Taz sat by the window and morosely watched New York pass by.

"It's a mess out here, isn't it?" The cabbie shot a grin in the rearview mirror, pleased with the tip Mitch had given him in advance. "Don't like the snow myself, but my kids do." He gave a tuneless whistle to accompany the big-band music on his radio. "I guess your boy there wasn't doing any complaining about not going to school. No, sir," the driver continued, without any need for an answer. "Nothing a kid likes better than a day off from school, is there? Even going to the office with your dad's better than school, isn't it, kid?" The cabbie let out a chuckle as he pulled to the curb. The snow there had already turned gray. "Here you go. That's a right nice dog you got there, boy." He gave Mitch his change and continued to whistle as they got out. He had another fare when he pulled away.

"He thought you were my dad," Radley murmured as they walked down the sidewalk.

"Yeah." He started to put a hand on Radley's shoulder, then waited. "Does that bother you?"

The boy looked up, wide-eyed and, for the first time, shy. "No. Does it bother you?"

Mitch bent down so they were at eye level. "Well, maybe it wouldn't if you weren't so ugly."

Radley grinned. As they continued to walk, he slipped his hand into Mitch's. He'd already begun to fantasize about Mitch as his father. He'd done it once before with his second grade teacher, but Mr. Stratham hadn't been nearly as neat as Mitch.

"Is this it?" He stopped as Mitch walked toward a tall, scarred brownstone.

"This is it."

Radley struggled with disappointment. It looked so—ordinary. He'd thought they would at least have the flag of Perth or Ragamond flying. Understanding perfectly, Mitch led him inside.

There was a guard in the lobby who lifted a hand to Mitch and continued to eat his pastrami sandwich. Acknowledging the greeting, Mitch took Radley to an elevator and drew open the iron gate.

"This is pretty neat," Radley decided.

"It's neater when it works." Mitch pushed the button for the fifth floor, which housed the editorial department. "Let's hope for the best."

"Has it ever crashed?" The question was half wary, half hopeful.

"No, but it has been known to go on strike." The car shuddered to a stop on 5. Mitch swung the gate open again. He put a hand on Radley's head. "Welcome to bedlam."

It was precisely that. Radley forgot his disappointment with the exterior in his awe at the fifth floor. There was a reception area of sorts. In any case, there was a desk and a bank of phones manned by a harassed-looking black woman in a Princess Leilah sweatshirt. The walls around her were crammed with posters depicting Universal's most enduring characters: the Human Scorpion, the Velvet Saber, the deadly Black Moth and, of course, Commander Zark.

"How's it going, Lou?"

"Don't ask." She pushed a button on a phone. "I

ask you, is it my fault the deli won't deliver his corned beef?''

"If I put him in a good mood, will you dig up some samples for me?"

"Universal Comics, please hold." The receptionist pushed another button. "You put him in a good mood, you've got my firstborn."

"Just the samples, Lou. Put on your helmet, Corporal. This could be messy." He led Radley down a short hall into the big, brightly lit hub of activity. It was a series of cubicles with a high noise level and a look of chaos. Pinned to the corkboard walls were sketches, rude messages and an occasional photograph. In a corner was a pyramid made of empty soda cans. Someone was tossing wadded-up balls of paper at it.

"Scorpion's never been a joiner. What's his motivation for hooking up with Worldwide Law and Justice?"

A woman with pencils poking out of her wild red hair at dangerous angles shifted in her swivel chair. Her eyes, already huge, were accented by layers of liner and mascara. "Look, let's be real. He can't save the world's water supply on his own. He needs someone like Atlantis."

A man sat across from her, eating an enormous pickle. "They hate each other. Ever since they bumped heads over the Triangular Affair."

"That's the point, dummy. They'll have to put personal feelings aside for the sake of mankind. It's a moral." Glancing over, she caught sight of Mitch. "Hey, Dr. Deadly's poisoned the world's water supply. Scorpion's found an antidote. How's he going to distribute it?"

"Sounds like he'd better mend fences with Atlantis," Mitch replied. "What do you think, Radley?"

For a moment, Rad was so tongue-tied he could only stare. Then, taking a deep breath, he let the words blurt out. "I think they'd make a neat team, 'cause they'd always be fighting and trying to show each other up."

"I'm with you, kid." The redhead held out her hand. "I'm M. J. Jones."

"Wow, really?" He wasn't sure whether he was more impressed with meeting M. J. Jones or with discovering she was a woman. Mitch didn't see the point in mentioning that she was one of the few in the business.

"And this grouch over here is Rob Myers. You bring him as a shield, Mitch?" she asked without giving Rob time to swallow his pickle. They'd been married for six years, and she obviously enjoyed frustrating him.

"Do I need one?"

"If you don't have something terrific in those tubes, I'd advise you to slip back out again." She shoved aside a stack of preliminary sketches. "Maloney just quit, defected to Five Star."

"No kidding?"

"Skinner's been muttering about traitors all morning. And the snow didn't help his mood. So if I were you... Oops, too late." Respecting rats who deserted tyrannically captained ships, M.J. turned away and fell into deep discussion with her husband.

"Dempsey, you were supposed to be in two hours ago."

Mitch gave his editor an ingratiating smile. "My alarm didn't go off. This is Radley Wallace, a friend of mine. Rad, this is Rich Skinner."

Radley stared. Skinner looked exactly like Hank Wheeler, the tanklike and overbearing boss of Joe David, alias the Fly. Later, Mitch would tell him that the resemblance was no accident. Radley switched Taz's leash to his other hand.

"Hello, Mr. Skinner. I really like your comics. They're lots better than Five Star. I hardly ever buy Five Star, because the stories aren't as good."

"Right." Skinner dragged a hand through his thinning hair. "Right," he repeated with more conviction. "Don't waste your allowance on Five Star, kid."

"No, sir."

"Mitch, you know you're not supposed to bring that mutt in here."

"You know how Taz loves you." On cue, Taz lifted his head and howled.

Skinner started to swear, then remembered the boy. "You got something in those tubes, or did you just come by to brighten up my dull day?"

"Why don't you take a look for yourself?"

Grumbling, Skinner took the tubes and marched off. As Mitch started to follow, Radley grabbed at his hand. "Is he really mad?"

"Sure. He likes being mad best."

"Is he going to yell at you like Hank Wheeler yells at the Fly?"

"Maybe."

Radley swallowed and buried his hand in Mitch's. "Okay."

Amused, Mitch led Radley into Skinner's office, where the venetian blinds had been drawn to shut off any view of the snow. Skinner unrolled the contents of the first tube and spread them over his already cluttered desk. He didn't sit, but loomed over them while Taz plopped down on the linoleum and went to sleep.

"Not bad," Skinner announced after he had studied the series of sketches and captions. "Not too bad. This new character, Mirium, you have plans to expand her?"

"I'd like to. I think Zark's ready to have his heart tugged from a different direction. Adds more emotional conflict. He loves his wife, but she's his biggest enemy. Now he runs into this empath and finds himself torn up all over again because he has feelings for her, as well."

"Zark never gets much of a break."

"I think he's the best," Radley piped in, forgetting himself.

Skinner lifted his bushy brows and studied Radley carefully. "You don't think he gets carried away with this honor and duty stuff?"

"Uh-uh." He wasn't sure if he was relieved or disappointed that Skinner wasn't going to yell. "You always know Zark's going to do the right thing. He doesn't have any super powers and stuff, but he's real smart."

Skinner nodded, accepting the opinion. "We'll give your Mirium a shot, Mitch, and see what the reader response is like." He let the papers roll into themselves again. "This is the first time I can remember you being this far ahead of deadline."

"That's because I have an assistant now." Mitch laid a hand on Radley's shoulder.

"Good work, kid. Why don't you take your assistant on a tour?"

It would take Radley weeks to stop talking about his hour at Universal Comics. When they left, he carried a shopping bag full of pencils with Universal's logo, a Mad Matilda mug that had been unearthed from someone's storage locker, a half dozen rejected sketches and a batch of comics fresh off the presses.

"This was the best day in my whole life," Radley said, dancing down the snow-choked sidewalk. "Wait until I show Mom. She won't believe it."

Oddly enough, Mitch had been thinking of Hester himself. He lengthened his stride to keep up with Radley's skipping pace. "Why don't we go by and pay her a visit?"

"Okay." He slipped his hand into Mitch's again. "The bank's not nearly as neat as where you work, though. They don't let anyone play radios or yell at each other, but they have a vault where they keep lots of money—millions of dollars—and they have cameras everywhere so they can see anybody who tries to rob them. Mom's never been in a bank that's been robbed."

Since the statement came out as an apology, Mitch laughed. "We can't all be blessed." He ran a hand over his stomach. He hadn't put anything into it in at least two hours. "Let's grab that taco first."

Inside the staid and unthreatened walls of National Trust, Hester dealt with a stack of paperwork. She enjoyed this part of her job, the organized monotony of it. There was also the challenge of sorting through the facts and figures and translating them into real estate, automobiles, business equipment, stage sets or college funds. Nothing gave her greater pleasure than to be able to stamp a loan with her approval.

She'd had to teach herself not to be softhearted. There were times the facts and figures told you to say no, no matter how earnest the applicant might be. Part of her job was to dictate polite and impersonal letters of refusal. Hester might not have cared for it, but she accepted that responsibility, just as she accepted the occasional irate phone call from the recipient of a loan refusal.

At the moment she was stealing half an hour, with the muffin and coffee that would be her lunch, to put together three loan packages she wanted approved by the board when they met the following day. She had another appointment in fifteen minutes. And, with that and a lack of interruptions, she could just finish. She wasn't particularly pleased when her assistant buzzed through.

"Yes, Kay."

"There's a young man out here to see you, Mrs. Wallace."

"His appointment isn't for fifteen minutes. He'll have to wait."

"No, it isn't Mr. Greenburg. And I don't think he's here for a loan. Are you here for a loan, honey?"

Hester heard the familiar giggle and hurried to the door. "Rad? Is everything all right—oh."

He wasn't alone. Hester realized she'd been foolish to think Radley would have made the trip by himself. Mitch was with him, along with the huge, mild-eyed dog.

"We just ate tacos."

Hester eyed the faint smudge of salsa on Radley's chin. "So I see." She bent to hug him, then glanced up at Mitch. "Is everything okay?"

"Sure. We were just out taking care of a little business and decided to drop by." He took a good long look. She'd covered most of the colorful bruise with makeup. Only a hint of yellow and mauve showed through. "The eye looks better."

"I seem to have passed the crisis."

"That your office?" Without invitation, he strolled over to stick his head inside. "God, how depressing. Maybe you can talk Radley into giving you one of his posters."

"You can have one," Radley agreed immediately. "I got a bunch of them when Mitch took me to Universal. Wow, Mom you should see it. I met M. J. Jones and Rich Skinner and I saw this room where they keep zillions of comics. See what I got." He held up his shopping bag. "For free. They said I could."

Her first feeling was one of discomfort. It seemed her obligation to Mitch grew with each day. Then she looked down at Radley's eager, glowing face. "Sounds like a pretty great morning."

"It was the best ever."

"Yellow alert," Kay murmured. "Rosen at three o'clock."

It didn't take words to show Mitch that Rosen was a force to be reckoned with. He saw Hester's face poker up instantly as she smoothed a hand over her hair to be sure it was in place.

"Good afternoon, Mrs. Wallace." He glanced meaningfully at the dog, who sniffed the toe of his shoe. "Perhaps you've forgotten that pets are not permitted inside the bank."

"No, sir. My son was just—"

"Your son?" Rosen gave Radley a brief nod. "How do you do, young man. Mrs. Wallace, I'm sure you remember that bank policy frowns on personal visits during working hours."

"Mrs. Wallace, I'll just put these papers on your

desk for your signature—when your lunch break is
over." Kay shuffled some forms importantly, then
winked at Radley.

"Thank you, Kay."

Rosen harrumphed. He couldn't argue with a lunch
break, but it was his duty to deal with other infractions
of policy. "About this animal—"

Finding Rosen's tone upsetting, Taz pushed his nose
against Radley's knee and moaned. "He's mine."
Mitch stepped forward, his smile charming, his hand
outstretched. Hester had time to think that with that
look he could sell Florida swampland. "Mitchell
Dempsey II. Hester and I are good friends, very good
friends. She's told me so much about you and your
bank." He gave Rosen's hand a hearty political shake.
"My family has several holdings in New York. Hester's convinced me I should use my influence to have
them transfer to National Trust. You might be familiar
with some of the family companies. Trioptic, D and H
Chemicals, Dempsey Paperworks?"

"Well, of course, of course." Rosen's limp grip on
Mitch's hand tightened. "It's a pleasure to meet you,
a real pleasure."

"Hester persuaded me to come by and see for myself how efficiently National Trust ticked." He definitely had the man's number, Mitch thought. Dollar
signs were already flitting through the pudgy little
brain. "I am impressed. Of course, I could have taken
Hester's word for it." He gave her stiff shoulder an
intimate little squeeze. "She's just a whiz at financial
matters. I can tell you, my father would snatch her up
as a corporate adviser in a minute. You're lucky to
have her."

"Mrs. Wallace is one of our most valued employees."

"I'm glad to hear it. I'll have to bring up National Trust's advantages when I speak with my father."

"I'll be happy to take you on a tour personally. I'm sure you'd like to see the executive offices."

"Nothing I'd like better, but I am a bit pressed for time." If he'd had days stretching out before him, he wouldn't have spent a minute of them touring the stuffy corners of a bank. "Why don't you work up a package I can present at the next board meeting?"

"Delighted." Rosen's face beamed with pleasure. Bringing an account as large and diversified as Dempsey's to National Trust would be quite a coup for the stuffy bank manager.

"Just send it through Hester. You don't mind playing messenger, do you, darling?" Mitch said cheerfully.

"No," she managed.

"Excellent," Rosen said, the excitement evident in his voice. "I'm sure you'll find we can serve all your family's needs. We are the bank to grow with, after all." He patted Taz's head. "Lovely dog," he said and strode off with a new briskness in his step.

"What a fusty old snob," Mitch decided. "How do you stand it?"

"Would you come into my office a moment?" Hester's voice was as stiff as her shoulders. Recognizing the tone, Radley rolled his eyes at Mitch. "Kay, if Mr. Greenburg comes in, please have him wait."

"Yes, ma'am."

Hester led the way into her office, then closed the door and leaned against it. There was a part of her that wanted to laugh, to throw her arms around Mitch and

howl with delight over the way he'd handled Rosen.
There was another part, the part that needed a job, a
regular salary and employee benefits, that cringed.

"How could you do that?"

"Do what?" Mitch took a look around the office.
"The brown carpet has to go. And this paint. What do
you call this?"

"Yuk," Radley ventured as he settled in a chair with
Taz's head in his lap.

"Yeah, that's it. You know, your work area has a
lot to do with your work production. Try that on Rosen."

"I won't be trying anything with Rosen once he
finds out what you did. I'll be fired."

"Don't be silly. I never promised my family would
move their interests to National Trust. Besides, if he
puts together an intriguing enough package, they just
might." He shrugged, indicating it made little difference to him. "If it'll make you happier, I can move
my personal accounts here. A bank's a bank as far as
I'm concerned."

"Damn it." It was very rare for her to swear out
loud and with heat. Radley found the fur on Taz's neck
of primary interest. "Rosen's got corporate dynasty on
his mind, thanks to you. He's going to be furious with
me when he finds out you made all that up."

Mitch tapped a hand on a tidy stack of papers.
"You're obsessively neat, did you know that? And I
didn't make anything up. I could have," he said
thoughtfully. "I'm good at it, but there didn't seem to
be any reason to."

"Would you stop?" Frustrated, she moved to him
to slap his hands away from her work. "All that business about Trioptic and D and H Chemicals." Letting

out a long sigh, she dropped down on the edge of the desk. "I know you did it to try to help me, and I appreciate the thought, but—"

"You do?" With a smile, he fingered the lapel of her suit jacket.

"You mean well, I suppose," Hester murmured.

"Sometimes." He leaned a little closer. "You smell much too good for this office."

"Mitch." She put a hand on his chest and glanced nervously at Radley. The boy had an arm hooked around Taz and was already deeply involved in one of his new comic books.

"Do you really think it would be a traumatic experience if the kid saw me kiss you?"

"No." At his slight movement, she pressed harder. "But that's beside the point."

"What *is* the point?" He took his hand from her jacket to fiddle with the gold triangle at her ear.

"The point is I'm going to have to see Rosen and explain to him that you were just..." What was the word she wanted? "Fantasizing."

"I've done a lot of that," he admitted as he moved his thumb down her jawline. "But I'm damned if I think it's any of his business. Want me to tell you the one about you and me in the life raft on the Indian Ocean?"

"No." This time she had to laugh, though the reaction in her stomach had more to do with heat than humor. Curiosity pricked at her so that she met his eyes, then looked quickly away again. "Why don't you and Rad go home? I have another appointment; then I'll go and explain things to Mr. Rosen."

"You're not mad anymore?"

She shook her head and gave in to the urge to touch

his face. "You were just trying to help. It was sweet of you."

He imagined she'd have taken the same attitude with Radley if he'd tried to wash the dishes and had smashed her violet-edged china on the floor. Telling himself it was a kind of test, he pressed his lips firmly to hers. He felt each layer of reaction—the shock, the tension, the need. When he drew back, he saw more than indulgence in her eyes. The fire flickered briefly, but with intensity.

"Come on, Rad, your mom has to get back to work. If we're not in the apartment when you get home, we're in the park."

"Fine." Unconsciously she pressed her lips together to seal in the warmth. "Thanks."

"Anytime."

"Bye, Rad, I'll be home soon."

"Okay." He lifted his arms to squeeze her neck. "You're not mad at Mitch anymore?"

"No," she answered in the same carrying whisper. "I'm not mad at anyone."

She was smiling when she straightened, but Mitch saw the worried look in her eye. He paused with his hand on the knob. "You're really going to go up to Rosen and tell him I made that business up?"

"I have to." Then, because she felt guilty about launching her earlier attack, she smiled. "Don't worry. I'm sure I can handle him."

"What if I told you I didn't make it up, that my family founded Trioptic forty-seven years ago?"

Hester lifted a brow. "I'd say don't forget your gloves. It's cold out there."

"Okay, but do yourself a favor before you bare your soul to Rosen. Look it up in *Who's Who*."

With her hands in her pockets, Hester walked to her office door. From there she saw Radley reach up to put a gloved hand into Mitch's bare one.

"Your son's adorable," Kay said, offering Hester a file. The little skirmish with Rosen had completely changed her opinion of the reserved Mrs. Wallace.

"Thanks." When Hester smiled, Kay's new opinion was cemented. "And I do appreciate you covering for me that way."

"That's no big deal. I don't see what's wrong with your son dropping by for a minute."

"Bank policy," Hester murmured under her breath, and Kay let out a snort.

"Rosen policy, you mean. Beneath that gruff exterior is a gruff interior. But don't worry about him. I happen to know he considers your work production far superior to your predecessor's. As far as he's concerned, that's the bottom line."

Kay hesitated a moment as Hester nodded and flipped through the file. "It's tough raising a kid on your own. My sister has a little girl, she's just five. I know some nights Annie's just knocked out from wearing all the badges, you know."

"Yes, I do."

"My parents want her to move back home so Mom can watch Sarah while Annie works, but Annie's not sure it's the best thing."

"Sometimes it's hard to know if accepting help's right," Hester murmured, thinking of Mitch. "And sometimes we forget to be grateful that someone's there to offer it." She shook herself and tucked the file under her arm. "Is Mr. Greenburg here?"

"Just came in."

"Fine, send him in, Kay." She started for her office, then stopped. "Oh, and Kay, dig me up a copy of *Who's Who*."

Chapter 6

He was loaded.

Hester was still dazed when she let herself into her apartment. Her downstairs neighbor with the bare feet and the holes in his jeans was an heir to one of the biggest fortunes in the country.

Hester took off her coat and, out of habit, went to the closet to hang it up. The man who spent his days writing the further adventures of Commander Zark came from a family who owned polo ponies and summer houses. Yet he lived on the fourth floor of a very ordinary apartment building in Manhattan.

He was attracted to her. She'd have had to be blind and deaf not to be certain of that, and yet she'd known him for weeks and he hadn't once mentioned his family or his position in an effort to impress her.

Who was he? she wondered. She'd begun to think she had a handle on him, but now he was a stranger all over again.

She had to call him, tell him she was home and to send Radley up. Hester looked at the phone with a feeling of acute embarrassment. She'd lectured him about spinning a tale to Mr. Rosen; then, in her soft-hearted and probably condescending way, she'd forgiven him. It all added up to her doing what she hated most. Making a fool of herself.

Swearing, Hester snatched up the phone. She would have felt much better if she could have rapped Mitchell Dempsey II over the head with it.

She'd dialed half the numbers when she heard Radley's howl of laughter and the sound of stomping feet in the hall outside. She opened the door just as Radley was digging his key out of his pocket.

Both of them were covered with snow. Some that was beginning to melt dripped from Radley's ski cap and boot tops. They looked unmistakably as if they'd been rolling in it.

"Hi, Mom. We've been in the park. We stopped by Mitch's to get my bag, then came on up because we thought you'd be home. Come on out with us."

"I don't think I'm dressed for snow wars."

She smiled and peeled off her son's snow-crusted cap but, Mitch noted, she didn't look up. "So change." He leaned against the doorjamb, ignoring the snow that fell at his feet.

"I built a fort. Please come out and see. I already started a snow warrior, but Mitch said we should check in so you wouldn't worry."

His consideration forced her to look up. "I appreciate that."

He was watching her thoughtfully—too thoughtfully, Hester decided. "Rad says you build a pretty good snow warrior yourself."

"Please, Mom. What if we got a freak heat wave and the snow was all gone tomorrow? It's like the greenhouse effect, you know. I read all about it."

She was trapped and knew it. "All right, I'll change. Why don't you fix Mitch some hot chocolate and warm up?"

"All right!" Radley dropped down on the floor just inside the door. "You have to take off your boots," he told Mitch. "She gets mad if you track up the carpet."

Mitch unbuttoned his coat as Hester walked away. "We wouldn't want to make her mad."

Within fifteen minutes, Hester had changed into corduroys, a bulky sweater and old boots. In place of her red coat was a blue parka that showed some wear. Mitch kept one hand on Taz's leash and the other in his pocket as they walked across to the park. He couldn't say why he enjoyed seeing her dressed casually with Radley's hand joined tight with hers. He couldn't say for certain why he'd wanted to spend this time with her, but it had been he who'd planted the idea of another outing in Radley's head, and he who'd suggested that they go up together to persuade her to come outside.

He liked the winter. Mitch took a deep gulp of cold air as they walked through the soft, deep snow of Central Park. Snow and stinging air had always appealed to him, particularly when the trees were draped in white and there were snow castles to be built.

When he'd been a boy, his family had often wintered in the Caribbean, away from what his mother had termed the "mess and inconvenience." He'd picked up an affection for scuba and white sand, but had never felt that a palm tree replaced a pine at Christmas.

The winters he'd liked best had been spent in his uncle's country home in New Hampshire, where there'd been woods to walk in and hills to sled. Oddly enough, he'd been thinking of going back there for a few weeks—until the Wallaces popped up two floors above, that is. He hadn't realized until today that he'd shuffled those plans to the back of his mind as soon as he'd seen Hester and her son.

Now she was embarrassed, annoyed and uncomfortable. Mitch turned to study her profile. Her cheeks were already rosy with cold, and she'd made certain that Radley walked between them. He wondered if she realized how obvious her strategies were. She didn't use the boy, not in the way some parents used their offspring for their own ambitions or purposes. He respected her for that more than he could have explained. But she had, by putting Radley in the center, relegated Mitch to the level of her son's friend.

And so he was, Mitch thought with a smile. But he'd be damned if he was going to let it stop there.

"There's the fort. See?" Radley tugged on Hester's hand, then let it go to run, too impatient to wait any longer.

"Pretty impressive, huh?" Before she could avoid it, Mitch draped a casual arm over her shoulder. "He's really got a knack."

Hester tried to ignore the warmth and pressure of his arm as she looked at her son's handiwork. The walls of the fort were about two feet high, smooth as stone, with one end sloping nearly a foot higher in the shape of a round tower. They'd made an arched doorway high enough for Radley to crawl through. When Hester reached the fort, she saw him pass through on his hands and knees and pop up inside, his arms held high.

"It's terrific, Rad. I imagine you had a great deal to do with it," she said quietly to Mitch.

"Here and there." Then he smiled, as though he was laughing at himself. "Rad's a better architect than I'll ever be."

"I'm going to finish my snow warrior." Belly down, Rad crawled through the opening again. "Build one, Mom, on the other side of the fort. They'll be the sentries." Rad began to pack and smooth snow on his already half-formed figure. "You help her, Mitch, 'cause I've got a head start."

"Fair's fair." Mitch scooped up a handful of snow. "Any objections to teamwork?"

"No, of course not." Still avoiding giving him a straight look, Hester knelt in the snow. Mitch dropped the handful of snow on her head.

"I figured that was the quickest way to get you to look at me." She glared, then began to push the snow into a mound. "Problem, Mrs. Wallace?"

Seconds ticked by as she pushed at the snow. "I got a copy of *Who's Who*."

"Oh?" Mitch knelt down beside her.

"You were telling the truth."

"I've been known to from time to time." He shoved some more snow on the mound she was forming. "So?"

Hester frowned and punched the snow into shape. "I feel like an idiot."

"I told the truth, and you feel like an idiot." Patiently Mitch smoothed over the base she was making. "Want to explain the correlation?"

"You let me lecture you."

"It's kinda hard to stop you when you get rolling." Hester began to dig out snow with both hands to form the legs. "You let me think you were some poor, eccentric Good Samaritan. I was even going to offer to put patches on your jeans."

"No kidding." Incredibly touched, Mitch caught her chin in his snow-covered glove. "That's sweet."

There was no way she was going to let his charm brush away the discomfort of her embarrassment. "The fact is, you're a rich, eccentric Good Samaritan." She shoved his hand away and began to gather snow for the torso.

"Does this mean you won't patch my jeans?"

Hester's long-suffering breath came out in a white plume. "I don't want to talk about it."

"Yes, you do." Always helpful, Mitch packed on more snow and succeeded in burying her up to the elbows. "Money shouldn't bother you, Hester. You're a banker."

"Money doesn't bother me." She yanked her arms free and tossed two good-sized hunks of snow into his face. Because she had to fight back a giggle, she turned her back. "I just wish the situation had been made clear earlier, that's all."

Mitch wiped the snow from his face, then scooped up more, running his tongue along the inside of his lip. He'd had a lot of experience in forming what he considered the ultimate snowball. "What's the situation, Mrs. Wallace?"

"I wish you'd stop calling me that in that tone of voice." She turned, just in time to get the snowball right between the eyes.

"Sorry." Mitch smiled, then began to brush off her coat. "Must've slipped. About this situation…"

"There is no situation between us." Before she realized it, she'd shoved him hard enough to send him sprawling in the snow. "Excuse me." Her laughter came out in hitches that were difficult to swallow. "I didn't mean to do that. I don't know what it is about you that makes me do things like that." He sat up and continued to stare at her. "I *am* sorry," she repeated. "I think it's best if we just let this other business drop. Now, if I help you up, will you promise not to retaliate?"

"Sure." Mitch held out a gloved hand. The moment he closed it over hers, he yanked her forward. Hester went down, face first. "I don't *always* tell the truth, by the way." Before she could respond, he wrapped his arms around her and began to roll.

"Hey, you're supposed to be building another sentry."

"In a minute," Mitch called to Rad, while Hester tried to catch her breath. "I'm teaching your mom a new game. Like it?" he asked her as he rolled her underneath him again.

"Get off me. I've got snow down my sweater, down my jeans—"

"No use trying to seduce me here. I'm stronger than that."

"You're crazy." She tried to sit up, but he pinned her beneath him.

"Maybe." He licked a trace of snow from her cheek and felt her go utterly still. "But I'm not stupid." His voice had changed. It wasn't the easy, carefree voice of her neighbor now, but the slow, soft tones of a lover. "You feel something for me. You may not like it, but you feel it."

It wasn't the unexpected exercise that had stolen her breath, and she knew it. His eyes were so blue in the lowering sunlight, and his hair glistened with a dusting of snow. And his face was close, temptingly close. Yes, she felt something, she felt something almost from the first minute she saw him, but she wasn't stupid, either.

"If you let go of my arms I'll show you just how I feel."

"Why do I think I wouldn't like it? Never mind." He brushed his lips over hers before she could answer. "Hester, the situation is this. You have feelings for me that have nothing to do with my money, because you didn't know until a few hours ago that I had any to speak of. Some of those feelings don't have anything to do with the fact that I'm fond of your son. They're very personal, as in you and me."

He was right, absolutely and completely right. She could have murdered him for it. "Don't tell me how I feel."

"All right." After he spoke, he surprised her by rising and helping her to her feet. Then he took her in his arms again. "I'll tell you how *I* feel then. I care for you—more than I'd counted on."

She paled beneath her cold-tinted cheeks. There was more than a hint of desperation in her eyes as she shook her head and tried to back away. "Don't say that to me."

"Why not?" He struggled against impatience as he lowered his brow to hers. "You'll have to get used to it. I did."

"I don't want this. I don't want to feel this way."

He tipped her head back, and his eyes were very serious. "We'll have to talk about that."

"No. There's nothing to talk about. This is just getting out of hand."

"It's not out of hand yet." He tangled his fingers in

the tips of her hair, but his eyes never left hers. "I'm almost certain it will be before long, but it isn't yet. You're too smart and too strong for that."

She'd be able to breathe easier in a moment. She was sure of it. She'd be able to breathe easier as soon as she was away from him. "No, I'm not afraid of you." Oddly, she discovered that much was true.

"Then kiss me." His voice was coaxing now, gentle. "It's nearly twilight. Kiss me, once, before the sun goes down."

She found herself leaning into him, lifting her lips up and letting her lashes fall without questioning why it should seem so right, so natural to do as he asked. There would be questions later, though she was certain the answers wouldn't come as easily. For now, she touched her lips to his and found them cool, cool and patient.

The world was all ice and snow, forts and fairylands, but his lips were real. They fit on hers firmly, warming her soft, sensitive skin while the racing of her heart heated her body. There was the rushing whoosh of traffic in the distance, but closer, more intimate, was the whisper of her coat sliding against his as they pressed tighter together.

He wanted to coax, to persuade, and just once to see her lips curve into a smile as he left them. He knew there were times when a man who preferred action and impulse had to go step by step. Especially when the prize at the top was precious.

He hadn't been prepared for her, but he knew he could accept what was happening between them with more ease than she. There were still secrets tucked inside her, hurts that had only partially healed. He knew better than to wish for the power to wipe all that aside.

How she'd lived and what had happened to her were all part of the woman she was. The woman he was very, very close to falling in love with.

So he would take it step by step, Mitch told himself as he placed her away from him. And he would wait.

"That might have cleared up a few points, but I think we still have to talk." He took her hand to keep her close another moment. "Soon."

"I don't know." Had she ever been this confused before? She'd thought she'd left these feelings, these doubts behind her long ago.

"I'll come up or you can come down, but we'll talk."

He was jockeying her into a corner, one she knew she'd be backed into sooner or later. "Not tonight," she said, despising herself for being a coward. "Rad and I have a lot to do."

"Procrastination's not your style."

"It is this time," she murmured, and turned away quickly. "Radley, we have to go in."

"Look, Mom, I just finished, isn't it great?" He stood back to show off his warrior. "You hardly started yours."

"Maybe we'll finish it tomorrow." She walked to him quickly and took him by the hand. "We have to go in and fix dinner now."

"But can't we just—"

"No, it's nearly dark."

"Can Mitch come?"

"No, he can't." She shot a glance over her shoulder as they walked. He was hardly more than a shadow now, standing beside her son's fort. "Not tonight."

Mitch put a hand on his dog's head as Taz whined and started forward. "Nope. Not this time."

* * *

There didn't seem any way of avoiding him, Hester thought as she started down to Mitch's apartment at her son's request. She had to admit it had been foolish of her to try. On the surface, anyone would think that Mitch Dempsey was the solution to many of her problems. He was genuinely fond of Radley, and gave her son both a companion and a safe and convenient place to stay while she worked. His time was flexible, and he was very generous with it.

The truth was, he'd complicated her life. No matter how much she tried to look at him as Radley's friend or her slightly odd neighbor, he brought back feelings she hadn't experienced in almost ten years. Fluttery pulses and warm surges were things Hester had attributed to the very young or the very optimistic. She'd stopped being either when Radley's father had left them.

In all the years that had followed that moment, she'd devoted herself to her son—to making the best possible home for him, to make his life as normal and well balanced as possible. If Hester the woman had gotten lost somewhere in the shuffle, Radley's mother figured it was a fair exchange. Now Mitch Dempsey had come along and made her feel and, worse, had made her wish.

Taking a deep breath, Hester knocked on Mitch's door. Radley's friend's door, she told herself firmly. The only reason she was here was because Radley had been so excited about showing her something. She wasn't here to see Mitch; she wasn't hoping he would reach out and run his fingertips along her cheek as he sometimes did. Hester's skin warmed at the thought of it.

Hester linked her hands together and concentrated

on Radley. She would see whatever it was he was so
anxious for her to see, and then she would get them
both back upstairs to their own apartment—and safety.

Mitch answered the door. He wore a sweatshirt
sporting a decal of a rival super hero across the chest,
and sweatpants with a gaping hole in one knee. There
was a towel slung over his shoulders. He used one end
of it to dry the sweat off his face.

"You haven't been out running in this weather?"
she asked before she'd allowed herself to think, immediately regretting the question and the obvious concern in her voice.

"No." He took her hand to draw her inside. She
smelled like the springtime that was still weeks and
weeks away. Her dark blue suit gave her a look of
uncreased professionalism he found ridiculously sexy.
"Weights," he told her. The fact was, he'd been lifting
weights a great deal since he'd met Hester Wallace.
Mitch considered it the second best way to decrease
tension and rid the body of excess energy.

"Oh." So that explained the strength she'd felt in
his arms. "I didn't realize you went in for that sort of
thing."

"The Mr. Macho routine?" he said, laughing. "No,
I don't, actually. The thing is, if I don't work out regularly, my body turns into a toothpick. It's not a pretty
sight." Because she looked nervous enough to jump
out of her skin, Mitch couldn't resist. He leered and
flexed his arm. "Want to feel my pecs?"

"I'll pass, thanks." Hester kept her hands by her
sides. "Mr. Rosen sent this package." She slipped the
fat bank portfolio out from where she'd held it at her
side. "Just remember, you asked for it."

"So I did." Mitch accepted it, then tossed it on a

pile of magazines on the coffee table. ''Tell him I'll pass it along.''

''And will you?''

He lifted a brow. ''I usually keep my word.''

She was certain of that. It reminded her that he'd said they would talk, and soon. ''Radley called and said there was something he had to show me.''

''He's in the office. Want some coffee?''

It was such a casual offer, so easy and friendly, that she nearly agreed. ''Thanks, but we really can't stay. I had to bring some paperwork home with me.''

''Fine. Just go on in. I need a drink.''

''Mom!'' The minute she stepped into the office, Radley jumped up and grabbed her hands. ''Isn't it great? It's the neatest present I ever got in my life.'' With his hands still locked on hers, Radley dragged her over to a scaled-down drawing board.

It wasn't a toy. Hester could see immediately that it was top-of-the-line equipment, if child-sized. The small swivel stool was worn, but the seat was leather. Radley already had graph paper tacked to the board, and with compass and ruler had begun what appeared to be a set of blueprints.

''Is this Mitch's?''

''It was, but he said I could use it now, for as long as I wanted. See, I'm making the plans for a space station. This is the engine room. And over here and here are the living quarters. It's going to have a green-house, sort of like the one they had in this movie Mitch let me watch. Mitch showed me how to draw things to scale with these squares.''

''I see.'' Pride in her son overshadowed any tension as she crouched down for a better look. ''You catch on fast, Rad. This is wonderful. I wonder if NASA has an opening.''

He chuckled, facedown, as he did when he was both pleased and embarrassed. ''Maybe I could be an engineer.''

''You can be anything you want.'' She pressed a kiss to his temple. ''If you keep drawing like this, I'm going to need an interpreter to know what you're doing. All these tools.'' She picked up a square. ''I guess you know what they're for.''

''Mitch told me. He uses them sometimes when he draws.''

''Oh?'' She turned the square over in her hand. It looked so—professional.

''Even comic art needs a certain discipline,'' Mitch said from the doorway. He held a large glass of orange juice, which was already half-gone. Hester rose. He looked—virile, she realized.

There was a faint vee of dampness down the center of his shirt. His hair had been combed through with no more than his fingers and, not for the first time, he hadn't bothered to shave off the night's growth of beard. Beside her, her son was happily remodeling his blueprint.

Virile, dangerous, nerve-wracking he might be, but a kinder man she'd never met. Concentrating on that, Hester stepped forward. ''I don't know how to thank you.''

''Rad already has.''

She nodded, then laid a hand on Radley's shoulder. ''You finish that up, Rad. I'll be in the other room with Mitch.''

Hester walked into the living room. It was, as she'd come to expect, cluttered and chaotic. Taz nosed around the carpet looking for cookie crumbs. "I thought I knew Rad inside and out," Hester began. "But I didn't know a drawing board would mean so much to him. I guess I would have thought him too young to appreciate it."

"I told you once he had a natural talent."

"I know." She gnawed on her lip. She wished she had accepted the offer of coffee so that she'd have something to do with her hands. "Rad told me that you were giving him some art lessons. You've done more for him than I ever could have expected. Certainly much more than you're obligated to."

He gave her a long, searching look. "It hasn't got anything to do with obligation. Why don't you sit down?"

"No." She linked her hands together, then pulled them apart again. "No, that's all right."

"Would you rather pace?"

It was the ease of his smile that had her unbending another notch. "Maybe later. I just wanted to tell you how grateful I am. Rad's never had..." A father. The words had nearly come out before Hester had swallowed them in a kind of horror. She hadn't meant that, she assured herself. "He's never had anyone to give him so much attention—besides me." She let out a little breath. That was what she'd meant to say. Of course it was. "The drawing board was very generous. Rad said it was yours."

"My father had it made for me when I was about Rad's age. He'd hoped I'd stop sketching monsters and start doing something productive." He said it without bitterness, but with a trace of amusement. Mitch had long since stopped resenting his parents' lack of understanding.

"It must mean a great deal to you for you to have kept it all this time. I know Rad loves it, but shouldn't you keep it for your own children?"

Mitch took a sip of juice and glanced around the apartment. "I don't seem to have any around at the moment."

"But still—"

"Hester, I wouldn't have given it to him if I hadn't wanted him to have it. It's been in storage for years, gathering dust. It gives me a kick to see Rad putting it to use." He finished off the juice, then set the glass down before he crossed to her. "The present's for Rad, with no strings attached to his mother."

"I know that, I didn't mean—"

"No, I don't think you did, exactly." He was watching her now, unsmiling, with that quiet intensity he drew out at unexpected moments. "I doubt if it was even in the front of your mind, but it was milling around in there somewhere."

"I don't think you're using Radley to get to me, if that's what you mean."

"Good." He did as she'd imagined he might, and ran a finger along her jawline. "Because the fact is, Mrs. Wallace, I'd like the kid without you, or you without the kid. It just so happens that in this case, you came as a set."

"That's just it. Radley and I are a unit. What affects him affects me."

Mitch tilted his head as a new thought began to dawn. "I think I'm getting a signal here. You don't think I'm playing pals and buddies with Rad to get Rad's mother between the sheets?"

"Of course not." She drew back sharply, looking

toward the office. "If I had thought that, Radley wouldn't be within ten feet of you."

"But…" He laid his arms on her shoulders, linking his hands loosely behind her neck. "You're wondering if your feelings for me might be residual of Radley's feelings."

"I never said I had feelings for you."

"Yes, you did. And you say it again every time I manage to get this close. No, don't pull away, Hester." He tightened his hands. "Let's be upfront. I want to sleep with you. It has nothing to do with Rad, and less than I figured to do with the primal urge I felt the first time I saw your legs." Her eyes lifted warily to his, but held. "It has to do with the fact that I find you attractive in a lot of ways. You're smart, you're strong and you're stable. It might not sound very romantic, but the fact is, your stability is very alluring. I've never had a lot of it myself."

He brushed his linked hands up the back of her neck. "Now, maybe you're not ready to take a step like this at the moment. But I'd appreciate it if you'd take a straight look at what you want, at what you feel."

"I'm not sure I can. You only have yourself. I have Rad. Whatever I do, whatever decisions I make, ripple down to affect him. I promised myself years ago that he would never be hurt by another one of his parents. I'm going to keep that promise."

He wanted to demand that she tell him about Radley's father then and there, but the boy was just in the next room. "Let me tell you what I believe. You could never make a decision that could hurt Rad. But I do think you could make one that could hurt yourself. I want to be with you, Hester, and I don't think our being together is going to hurt Radley."

"It's all done." Radley streamed out of the office, the graph paper in both hands. Hester immediately started to move away. To prove a point to both of them, Mitch held her where she was. "I want to take it and show Josh tomorrow. Okay?"

Knowing a struggle would be worse than submission, Hester stayed still with Mitch's arms on her shoulders. "Sure you can."

Radley studied them a moment. He'd never seen a man with his arms around his mother, except his grandpa or his uncle. He wondered if this made Mitch like family. "I'm going over to Josh's tomorrow afternoon and I'm staying for a sleepover. We're going to stay up all night."

"Then I'll just have to look after your mom, won't I?"

"I guess." Radley began to roll the graph paper into a tube as Mitch had shown him.

"Radley knows I don't have to be looked after."

Ignoring her, Mitch continued to speak to Radley. "How about if I took your mom on a date?"

"You mean get dressed up and go to a restaurant and stuff?"

"Something like that."

"That'd be okay."

"Good. I'll pick her up at seven."

"I really don't think—"

"Seven's not good?" Mitch interrupted Hester. "All right, seven-thirty, but that's as late as it gets. If I don't eat by eight I get nasty." He gave Hester a quick kiss on the temple before releasing her. "Have a good time at Josh's."

"I will." Radley gathered up his coat and backpack. Then he walked to Mitch and hugged him. The words that had been on the tip of Hester's tongue dried up. "Thanks for the drawing board and everything. It's really neat."

"You're welcome. See you Monday." He waited until Hester was at the door. "Seven-thirty."

She nodded and closed the door quietly behind her.

Chapter 7

She could have made excuses, but the fact was, Hester didn't want to. She knew Mitch had hustled her into this dinner date, but as she crossed the wide leather belt at her waist and secured it, she discovered she didn't mind. In fact, she was relieved that he'd made the decision for her—almost.

The nerves were there. She stood in front of the bureau mirror and took a few long, deep breaths. Yes, there were nerves, but they weren't the stomach-roiling sort she experienced when she went on job interviews. Though she wasn't quite sure where her feelings lay when it came to Mitch Dempsey, she was glad to be certain she wasn't afraid.

Picking up her brush, she studied her reflection as she smoothed her hair. She didn't look nervous, Hester decided. That was another point in her favor. The black wool dress was flattering with its deep cowl neck and nipped-in waist. The red slash of belt accented the line before the skirt flared out. For some reason, red gave her confidence. She considered the bold color another kind of defense for a far-from-bold person.

She fixed oversized scarlet swirls at her ears. Like most of her wardrobe, the dress was practical. It could go to the office, to a PTA meeting or a business lunch. Tonight, she thought with a half smile, it was going on a date.

Hester tried not to dwell on how long it had been since she'd been on a date, but comforted herself with the fact that she knew Mitch well enough to keep up an easy conversation through an evening. An adult evening. As much as she adored Radley, she couldn't help but look forward to it.

When she heard the knock, she gave herself a last quick check, then went to answer. The moment she opened the door, her confidence vanished.

He didn't look like Mitch. Gone were the scruffy jeans and baggy sweatshirts. This man wore a dark suit with a pale blue shirt. And a tie. The top button of the shirt was open, and the tie of dark blue silk was knotted loose and low, but it was still a tie. He was clean-shaven, and though some might have thought he still needed a trim, his hair waved dark and glossy over his ears and the collar of his shirt.

Hester was suddenly and painfully shy.

She looked terrific. Mitch felt a moment's awkwardness himself as he looked at her. Her evening shoes put her to within an inch of his height so that they were eye to eye. It was the wariness in hers that had him relaxing with a smile.

"Looks like I picked the right color." He offered her an armful of red roses.

She knew it was foolish for a woman of her age to

be flustered by something as simple as flowers. But her heart rushed up to her throat as she gathered them to her.

"Did you forget your line again?" he murmured.

"My line?"

"Thank you."

The scent of the roses flowed around her, soft and sweet. "Thank you."

He touched one of the petals. He already knew her skin felt much the same. "Now you're supposed to put them in water."

Feeling a great deal more than foolish, Hester stepped back. "Of course. Come in."

"The apartment feels different without Rad," he commented when Hester went to get a vase.

"I know. Whenever he goes to a sleepover, it takes me hours to get used to the quiet." He'd followed her into the kitchen. Hester busied herself with arranging the roses. I am a grown woman, she reminded herself, and just because I haven't been on a date since high school doesn't mean I don't remember how.

"What do you usually do when you have a free evening?"

"Oh, I read, watch a late movie." She turned with the vase and nearly collided with him. Water sloshed dangerously close to the top of the vase.

"The eye's barely noticeable now." He lifted a fingertip to where the bruise had faded to a shadow.

"It wasn't such a calamity." Her throat had tightened. Grown woman or not, she found herself enormously glad that the vase of roses was between them. "I'll get my coat."

After carrying the roses to the table beside the sofa, Hester went to the closet. She slipped one arm into the sleeve before Mitch came up behind her to help her finish. He made such an ordinary task sensual, she thought as she stared straight ahead. He brushed his hands over her shoulders, lingered, then trailed them down her arms before bringing them up again to gently release her hair from the coat collar.

Hester's hands were balled into fists as she turned her head. "Thank you."

"You're welcome." With his hands on her shoulders, Mitch turned her to face him. "Maybe you'll feel better if we get this out of the way now." He kept his hands where they were and touched his lips, firm and warm, to hers. Hester's rigid hands went lax. There was nothing demanding or passionate in the kiss. It moved her unbearably with its understanding.

"Feel better?" Mitch murmured.

"I'm not sure."

With a laugh, he touched his lips to hers again. "Well, I do." Linking his hand with hers, he walked to the door.

The restaurant was French, subdued and very exclusive. The pale flowered walls glowed in the quiet light and the flicker of candles. Diners murmured their private conversations over linen cloths and crystal stemware. The hustle and bustle of the streets were shut out by beveled glass doors.

"Ah, Monsieur Dempsey, we haven't seen you in some time." The maitre d' stepped forward to greet him.

"You know I always come back for your snails."

With a laugh, the maitre d' waved a waiter aside. "Good evening, *mademoiselle*. I'll take you to your table."

The little booth was candlelit and secluded, a place for hand-holding and intimate secrets. Hester's leg brushed Mitch's as they settled.

"The sommelier will be right with you. Enjoy your evening."

"No need to ask if you've been here before."

"From time to time I get tired of frozen pizza. Would you like champagne?"

"I'd love it."

He ordered a bottle, pleasing the wine steward with the vintage. Hester opened her menu and sighed over the elegant foods. "I'm going to remember this the next time I'm biting into half a tuna sandwich between appointments."

"You like your job?"

"Very much." She wondered if *soufflé de crabe* was what it sounded like. "Rosen can be a pain, but he does push you to be efficient."

"And you like being efficient."

"It's important to me."

"What else is, other than Rad?"

"Security." She looked over at him with a half smile. "I suppose that has to do with Rad. The truth is, anything that's been important to me over the last few years has to do with Rad."

She glanced up as the steward brought the wine and began his routine for Mitch's approval. Hester watched the wine rise in her fluted glass, pale gold and frothy. "To Rad, then," Mitch said as he lifted his glass to touch hers. "And his fascinating mother."

Hester sipped, a bit stunned that anything could taste so good. She'd had champagne before, but like everything that had to do with Mitch, it hadn't been quite like this. "I've never considered myself fascinating."

"A beautiful woman raising a boy on her own in one of the toughest cities in the world fascinates me." He sipped and grinned. "Added to that, you do have terrific legs, Hester."

She laughed, and even when he slipped his hand over hers, felt no embarrassment. "So you said before. They're long, anyway. I was taller than my brother until he was out of high school. It infuriated him, and I had to live down the name Stretch."

"Mine was String."

"String?"

"You know those pictures of the eighty-pound weakling? That was me."

Over the rim of her glass, Hester studied the way he filled out the suit jacket. "I don't believe it."

"One day, if I'm drunk enough, I'll show you pictures."

Mitch ordered in flawless French that had Hester staring. This was the comic-book writer, she thought, who built snow forts and talked to his dog. Catching the look, Mitch lifted a brow. "I spent a couple of summers in Paris during high school."

"Oh." It reminded her forcefully where he'd come from. "You said you didn't have any brothers or sisters. Do your parents live in New York?"

"No." He broke off a hunk of crusty French bread. "My mother zips in from time to time to shop or go to the theater, and my father might come in occasionally on business, but New York isn't their style. They still live most of the year in Newport, where I grew up."

"Oh, Newport. We drove through once when I was a kid. We'd always take these rambling car vacations in the summer." She tucked her hair behind her ear in an unconscious gesture that gave him a tantalizing view of her throat. "I remember the houses, the enormous mansions with the pillars and flowers and ornamental trees. We even took pictures. It was hard to believe anyone really lived there." Then she caught herself up abruptly and glanced over at Mitch's amused face. "You did."

"It's funny. I spent some time with binoculars watching the tourists in the summer. I might have homed in on your family."

"We were the ones in the station wagon with the suitcases strapped to the roof."

"Sure, I remember you." He offered her a piece of bread. "I envied you a great deal."

"Really?" She paused with her butter knife in mid-air. "Why?"

"Because you were going on vacation and eating hot dogs. You were staying in motels with soda machines outside the door and playing car bingo between cities."

"Yes," she murmured. "I suppose that sums it up."

"I'm not pulling poor-little-rich boy," he added when he saw the change in her eyes. "I'm just saying that having a big house isn't necessarily better than having a station wagon." He added more wine to her glass. "In any case, I finished my rebellious money-is-beneath-me stage a long time ago."

"I don't know if I can believe that from someone who lets dust collect on his Louis Quinze."

"That's not rebellion, that's laziness."

"Not to mention sinful," she put in. "It makes me itch for a polishing cloth and lemon oil."

"Any time you want to rub my mahogany, feel free."

She lifted a brow when he smiled at her. "So what did you do during your rebellious stage?"

Her fingertips grazed his. It was one of the few times she'd touched him without coaxing. Mitch lifted his gaze from their hands to her face. "You really want to know?"

"Yes."

"Then we'll make a deal. One slightly abridged life story for another."

It wasn't the wine that was making her reckless, Hester knew, but him. "All right. Yours first."

"We'll start off by saying my parents wanted me to be an architect. It was the only practical and acceptable profession they could see me using my drawing abilities for. The stories I made up didn't really appall them, they merely baffled them—so they were easily ignored. Straight out of high school, I decided to sacrifice my life to art."

Their appetizers were served. Mitch sighed approvingly over his escargots.

"So you came to New York?"

"No, New Orleans. At that time my money was still in trusts, though I doubt I would have used it, in any case. Since I refused to use my parents' financial backing, New Orleans was as close to Paris as I could afford to get. God, I loved it. I starved, but I loved the city. Those dripping, steamy afternoons, the smell of the river. It was my first great adventure. Want one of these? They're incredible."

"No, I—"

"Come on, you'll thank me." He lifted his fork to her lips. Reluctantly, Hester parted them and accepted.

"Oh." The flavor streamed, warm and exotic, over her tongue. "It's not what I expected."

"The best things usually aren't."

She lifted her glass and wondered what Radley's reaction would be when she told him she'd eaten a snail. "So what did you do in New Orleans?"

"I set up an easel in Jackson Square and made my living sketching tourists and selling watercolors. For three years I lived in one room where I baked in the summer and froze in the winter and considered myself one lucky guy."

"What happened?"

"There was a woman. I thought I was crazy about her and vice versa. She modeled for me when I was going through my Matisse period. You should have seen me then. My hair was about your length, and I wore it pulled back and fastened with a leather thong. I even had a gold earring in my left ear."

"You wore an earring?"

"Don't smirk, they're very fashionable now. I was ahead of my time." Appetizers were cleared away to make room for green salads. "Anyway, we were going to play house in my miserable little room. One night, when I'd had a little too much wine, I told her about my parents and how they'd never understood my artistic drive. She got absolutely furious."

"She was angry with your parents?"

"You are sweet," he said unexpectedly, and kissed her hand. "No, she was angry with me. I was rich and hadn't told her. I had piles of money and expected her to be satisfied with one filthy little room in the Quarter where she had to cook red beans and rice on a hot plate. The funny thing was she really cared for me when she'd thought I was poor, but when she found out I wasn't, and that I didn't intend to use what was available to me—and, by association, to her—she was infuriated. We had one hell of a fight, where she let me know what she really thought of me and my work.''

Hester could picture him, young, idealistic and struggling. ''People say things they don't mean when they're angry.''

He lifted her hand and kissed her fingers. ''Yes, very sweet.'' His hand remained on hers as he continued. ''Anyway, she left and gave me the opportunity to take stock of myself. For three years I'd been living day to day, telling myself I was a great artist whose time was coming. The truth was I wasn't a great artist. I was a clever one, but I'd never be a great one. So I left New Orleans for New York and commercial art. I was good; I worked fast tucked in my little cubicle and generally made the client happy—and I was miserable. But my credentials there got me a spot at Universal, originally as an inker, then as an artist. And then—'' he lifted his glass in salute ''—there was Zark. The rest is history.''

''You're happy.'' She turned her hand under his so their palms met. ''It shows. Not everyone is as content with themselves as you are, as at ease with himself and what he does.''

''It took me awhile.''

''And your parents; have you reconciled with them?''

''We came to the mutual understanding that we'd never understand each other. But we're family. I have my stock portfolio, so they can tell their friends the comic-book business is something that amuses me. Which is true enough.''

Mitch ordered another bottle of champagne with the main course. ''Now it's your turn.''

She smiled and let the delicate soufflé melt on her tongue. "Oh, I don't have anything so exotic as an artist's garret in New Orleans. I had a very average childhood with a very average family. Board games on Saturday nights, pot roast on Sundays. Dad had a good job, Mom stayed home and kept the house. We loved each other very much, but didn't always get along. My sister was very outgoing, head cheerleader, that sort of thing. I was miserably shy."

"You're still shy," Mitch murmured as he wound his fingers around hers.

"I didn't think it showed."

"In a very appealing way. What about Rad's father?" He felt her hand stiffen in his. "I've wanted to ask, Hester, but we don't have to talk about it now if it upsets you."

She drew her hand from his to reach for her glass. The champagne was cold and crisp. "It was a long time ago. We met in high school. Radley looks a great deal like his father, so you can understand that he was very attractive. He was also just a little wild, and I found that magnetic."

She moved her shoulders a little, restlessly, but was determined to finish what she'd started. "I really was painfully shy and a bit withdrawn, so he seemed like something exciting to me, even a little larger than life. I fell desperately in love with him the first time he noticed me; it was as simple as that. In any case, we went together for two years and were married a few weeks after graduation. I wasn't quite eighteen and was absolutely sure that marriage was going to be one adventure after another."

"And it wasn't?" he asked when she paused.

"For a while it was. We were young, so it never

seemed terribly important that Allan moved from one job to another, or quit altogether for weeks at a time. Once he sold the living room set that my parents had given us as a wedding present so that we could take a trip to Jamaica. It seemed impetuous and romantic, and at that time we didn't have any responsibilities except to ourselves. Then I got pregnant.''

She paused again and, looking back, remembered her own excitement and wonder and fear at the idea of carrying a child. "I was thrilled. Allan got a tremendous kick out of it and started buying strollers and high chairs on credit. Money was tight, but we were optimistic, even when I had to cut down to part-time work toward the end of my pregnancy and then take maternity leave after Radley was born. He was beautiful.'' She laughed a little. "I know all mothers say that about their babies, but he was honestly the most beautiful, the most precious thing I'd ever seen. He changed my life. He didn't change Allan's.''

She toyed with the stem of her glass and tried to work out in her mind what she hadn't allowed herself to think about for a very long time. "I couldn't understand it at the time, but Allan resented having the burden of responsibility. He hated it that we couldn't just stroll out of the apartment and go to the movies or go dancing whenever we chose. He was still unbelievably reckless with money, and because of Rad I had to compensate.''

"In other words," Mitch said quietly, "you grew up.''

"Yes.'' It surprised her that he saw that so quickly, and it relieved her that he seemed to understand. "Allan wanted to go back to the way things were, but we weren't children anymore. As I look back, I can see that he was jealous of Radley, but at the time I just wanted him to grow up, to be a father, to take charge. At twenty he was still the sixteen-year-old boy I'd known in high school, but I wasn't the same girl. I was a mother. I'd gone back to work because I'd thought the extra income would ease some of the strain. One day I'd come home after picking Radley up at the sitter's, and Allan was gone. He'd left a note saying he just couldn't handle being tied down any longer.''

"Did you know he was leaving?"

"No, I honestly didn't. In all probability it was done on impulse, the way Allan did most things. It would never have occurred to him that it was desertion, to him it would've meant moving on. He thought he was being fair by taking only half the money, but he left all the bills. I had to get another part-time job in the evenings. I hated that, leaving Rad with a sitter and not seeing him. That six months was the worst time of my life.''

Her eyes darkened a moment; then she shook her head and pushed it all back into the past. "After a while I'd straightened things out enough to quit the second job. About that time, Allan called. It was the first I'd heard from him since he'd left. He was very amiable, as if we'd been nothing more than passing acquaintances. He told me he was heading up to Alaska to work. After he hung up, I called a lawyer and got a very simple divorce.''

"It must have been difficult for you." Difficult? he thought—he couldn't even imagine what kind of hell it had been. "You could have gone home to your parents.''

"No. I was angry for a long, long time. The anger made me determined to stay right here in New York and make it work for me and Radley. By the time the anger had died down, I was making it work.''

''He's never come back to see Rad?''

''No, never.''

''His loss.'' He cupped her chin, then leaned over to kiss her lightly. ''His very great loss.''

She found it easy to lift a hand to his cheek. ''The same can be said about that woman in New Orleans.''

''Thanks.'' He nibbled her lips again, enjoying the faint hint of champagne. ''Dessert?''

''Hmmm?''

He felt a wild thrill of triumph at her soft, distracted sigh. ''Let's skip it.'' Moving back only slightly, he signaled the waiter for the check, then handed Hester the last of the champagne. ''I think we should walk awhile.''

The air was biting, almost as exhilarating as the wine. Yet the wine warmed her, making her feel as though she could walk for miles without feeling the wind. She didn't object to Mitch's arm around her shoulders or to the fact that he set the direction. She didn't care where they walked as long as the feelings that stirred inside her didn't fade.

She knew what it was like to fall in love—to be in love. Time slowed down. Everything around you went quickly, but not in a blur. Colors were brighter, sounds sharper, and even in midwinter you could smell flowers. She had been there once before, had felt this intensely once before, but had thought she would never find that place again. Even as a part of her mind struggled to remind her that this couldn't be love—or certainly shouldn't be—she simply ignored it. Tonight she was just a woman.

There were skaters at Rockefeller Center, swirling

around and around the ice as the music flowed. Hester watched them, tucked in the warmth of Mitch's arms. His cheek rested on her hair, and she could feel the strong, steady rhythm of his heart.

"Sometimes I bring Rad here on Sundays to skate or just to watch like this. It seems different tonight." She turned her head, and her lips were barely a whisper from his. "Everything seems different tonight."

If she looked at him like that again, Mitch knew he'd break his vow to give her enough time to clear her head and would bundle her into the nearest cab so that he could have her home and in bed before the look broke. Calling on willpower, he shifted her so he could brush his lips over her temple. "Things look different at night, especially after champagne." He relaxed again, her head against his shoulder. "It's a nice difference. Not necessarily steeped in reality, but nice. You can get enough reality from nine to five."

"Not you." Unaware of the tug-of-war she was causing inside him, she turned in his arms. "You make fantasies from nine to five, or whatever hours you choose."

"You should hear the one I'm making up now." He drew another deep breath. "Let's walk some more, and you can tell me about one of yours."

"A fantasy?" Her stride matched his easily. "Mine isn't nearly as earth-shaking as yours, I imagine. It's just a house."

"A house." He walked toward the Park, hoping they'd both be a little steadier on their feet by the time they reached home. "What kind of house?"

"A country house, one of those big old farmhouses with shutters at the windows and porches all around. Lots of windows so you could look at the woods—

there would have to be woods. Inside there would be high ceilings and big fireplaces. Outside would be a garden with wisteria climbing on a trellis." She felt the sting of winter on her cheeks, but could almost smell the summer.

"You'd be able to hear the bees hum in it all summer long. There'd be a big yard for Radley, and he could have a dog. I'd have a swing on the porch so I could sit outside in the evening and watch him catch lightning bugs in a jar." She laughed and let her head rest on his shoulder. "I told you it wasn't earth-shaking."

"I like it." He liked it so well he could picture it, white shuttered and hip roofed, with a barn off in the distance. "But you need a stream so Rad could fish."

She closed her eyes a moment, then shook her head. "As much as I love him, I don't think I could bait a hook. Build a tree house maybe, or throw a curveball, but no worms."

"You throw a curveball?"

She tilted her head and smiled. "Right in the strike zone. I helped coach Little League last year."

"The woman's full of surprises. You wear shorts in the dugout?"

"You're obsessed with my legs."

"For a start."

He steered her into their building and toward the elevators. "I haven't had an evening like this in a very long time."

"Neither have I."

She drew back far enough to study him as they began the ride to her floor. "I've wondered about that, about the fact that you don't seem to be involved with anyone."

He touched her chin with his fingertip. "Aren't I?"

She heard the warning signal, but wasn't quite sure what to do about it. "I mean, I haven't noticed you dating or spending any time with women."

Amused, he flicked the finger down her throat. "Do I look like a monk?"

"No." Embarrassed and more than a little unsettled, she looked away. "No, of course not."

"The fact is, Hester, after you've had your share of wild oats, you lose your taste for them. Spending time with a woman just because you don't want to be alone isn't very satisfying."

"From the stories I hear around the office from the single women, there are plenty of men who disagree with you."

He shrugged as they stepped off the elevator. "It's obvious you haven't played the singles scene." Her brows drew together as she dug for her key. "That was a compliment, but my point is it gets to be a strain or a bore—"

"And this is the age of the meaningful relationship."

"You say that like a cynic. Terribly uncharacteristic, Hester." He leaned against the jamb as she opened the door. "In any case, I'm not big on catchphrases. Are you going to ask me in?"

She hesitated. The walk had cleared her head enough for the doubts to seep through. But along with the doubts was the echo of the way she'd felt when they'd stood together in the cold. The echo was stronger. "All right. Would you like some coffee?"

"No." He shrugged out of his coat as he watched her.

"It's no trouble. It'll only take a minute."

He caught her hands. "I don't want coffee, Hester. I want you." He slipped her coat from her shoulders. "And I want you so bad it makes me jumpy."

She didn't back away, but stood, waiting. "I don't know what to say. I'm out of practice."

"I know." For the first time his own nerves were evident as he dragged a hand through his hair. "That's given me some bad moments. I don't want to seduce you." Then he laughed and walked a few paces away. "The hell I don't."

"I knew—I tried to tell myself I didn't, but I knew when I went out with you tonight that we'd come back here like this." She pressed a hand to her stomach, surprised that it was tied in knots. "I think I was hoping you'd just sort of sweep me away so I wouldn't have to make a decision."

He turned to her. "That's a cop-out, Hester."

"I know." She couldn't look at him then, wasn't certain she dared. "I've never been with anyone but Rad's father. The truth is, I've never wanted to be."

"And now?" He only wanted a word, one word.

She pressed her lips together. "It's been so long, Mitch. I'm frightened."

"Would it help if I told you I am, too?"

"I don't know."

"Hester." He crossed to her to lay his hands on her shoulders. "Look at me." When she did, her eyes were wide and achingly clear. "I want you to be sure, because I don't want regrets in the morning. Tell me what you want."

It seemed her life was a series of decisions. There was no one to tell her which was right or which was wrong. As always, she reminded herself that once the

decision was made, she alone would deal with the consequences and accept the responsibility.

"Stay with me tonight," she whispered. "I want
you."

Chapter 8

He cupped her face in his hands and felt her tremble. He touched his lips to hers and heard her sigh. It was a moment he knew he would always remember. Her acceptance, her desire, her vulnerability.

The apartment was silent. He would have given her music. The scent of the roses she'd put in a vase was pale next to the fragrance of the garden he imagined for her. The lamp burned brightly. He wouldn't have chosen the secrets of the dark, but rather the mystery of candlelight.

How could he explain to her that there was nothing ordinary, nothing casual in what they were about to give each other? How could he make her understand that he had been waiting all his life for a moment like this? He wasn't certain he could choose the right words, or that the words he did choose would reach her.

So he would show her.

With his lips still lingering on hers, he swept her up into his arms. Though he heard her quick intake of breath, she wrapped her arms around him.

"Mitch—"

"I'm not much of a white knight." He looked at her, half smiling, half questioning. "But for tonight we can pretend."

He looked heroic and strong and incredibly, impossibly sweet. Whatever doubts had remained slipped quietly away. "I don't need a white knight."

"Tonight I need to give you one." He kissed her once more before he carried her into the bedroom.

There was a part of him that needed, ached with that need, so much so that he wanted to lay her down on the bed and cover her with his body. There were times that love ran swiftly, even violently. He understood that and knew that she would, too. But he set her down on the floor beside the bed and touched only her hand.

He drew away just a little. "The light."

"But—"

"I want to see you, Hester."

It was foolish to be shy. It was wrong, she knew, to want to have this moment pass in the dark, anonymously. She reached for the bedside lamp and turned the switch.

The light bathed them, capturing them both standing hand in hand and eye to eye. The quick panic returned, pounding in her head and her heart. Then he touched her and quieted it. He drew off her earrings and set them on the bedside table so that the metal clicked quietly against the wood. She felt a rush of heat, as though with that one simple, intimate move he had already undressed her.

He reached for her belt, then paused when her hands fluttered nervously to his. "I won't hurt you."

"No." She believed him and let her hands drop away. He unhooked her belt to let it slide to the floor. When he lowered his lips to hers again, she slipped her arms around his waist and let the power guide her.

This was what she wanted. She couldn't lie to herself or make excuses. For tonight, she wanted to think only as a woman, to be thought of only as a woman. To be desired, enjoyed, wondered over. When their lips parted, their eyes met. And she smiled.

"I've been waiting for that." He touched a finger to her lips, overcome with a pleasure that was so purely emotional even he couldn't describe it.

"For what?"

"For you to smile at me when I kiss you." He brought his hand to her face. "Let's try it again."

This time the kiss went deeper, edging closer to those uncharted territories. She lifted her hands to his shoulders, then slid them around to encircle his neck. He felt her fingers touch the skin there, shyly at first, then with more confidence.

"Still afraid?"

"No." Then she smiled again. "Yes, a little. I'm not—" she looked away, and he once more brought her face back to his.

"What?"

"I'm not sure what to do. What you like."

He wasn't stunned by her words so much as humbled. He'd said he'd cared for her, and that was true. But now his heart, which had been teetering on the edge, fell over into love.

"Hester, you leave me speechless." He drew her

against him, hard, and just held her there. "Tonight, just do what seems right. I think we'll be fine."

He began by kissing her hair, drawing in the scent that had so appealed to him. The mood was already set, seduction on either side unnecessary. He felt her heart begin to race against his; then she turned her head and found his lips with her own.

His hands weren't steady as he drew down the long zipper at her back. He knew it was an imperfect world, but needed badly to give her one perfect night. No one would ever have called him a selfish man, but it was a fact that he'd never before put someone else's needs so entirely before his own.

He drew the wool from her shoulders, down her arms. She wore a simple chemise beneath it, plain white without frills or lace. No fantasy of silk or satin could have excited him more.

"You're lovely." He pressed a kiss to one shoulder, then the other. "Absolutely lovely."

She wanted to be. It had been so long since she'd felt the need to be any more than presentable. When she saw his eyes, she felt lovely. Gathering her courage together, she began to undress him in turn.

He knew it wasn't easy for her. She drew his jacket off, then began to unknot his tie before she was able to lift her gaze to his again. He could feel her fingers tremble lightly against him as she unbuttoned his shirt.

"You're lovely, too," she murmured. The last, the only man she had ever touched this way had been little more than a boy. Mitch's muscles were subtle but hard, and though his chest was smooth, it was that of a man. Her movements were slow, from shyness rather than a knowledge of arousal. His stomach muscles quivered as she reached for the hook of his slacks.

"You're driving me crazy."

She drew her hands back automatically. "I'm sorry."

"No." He tried to laugh, but it sounded like a groan. "I like it."

Her fingers trembled all the more as she slid his slacks over his hips. Lean hips, with the muscles long and hard. She felt a surge that was both fascination and delight as she brought her hands to them. Then she was against him, and the shock of flesh against flesh vibrated through her.

He was fighting every instinct that pushed him to move quickly, to take quickly. Her shy hands and wondering eyes had taken him to the brink and he had to claw his way back. She sensed a war going on inside him, felt the rigidity of his muscles and heard the raggedness of his breathing.

"Mitch?"

"Just a minute." He buried his face in her hair. The battle for control was hard won. He felt weakened by it, weakened and stunned. When he found the soft, sensitive skin of her neck, he concentrated on that alone.

She strained against him, turning her head instinctively to give him freer access. It seemed as though a veil had floated down over her eyes so that the room, which had become so familiar to her, was hazy. She could feel her blood begin to pound where his lips rubbed and nibbled; then it was throbbing hot, close to the skin, softening it, sensitizing it. Her moan sounded primitive in her own ears. Then it was she who was drawing him down to the bed.

He'd wanted another minute before he let his body spread over hers. There were explosions bombarding

his system, from head to heart to loins. He knew he
had to calm them before they shattered his senses. But
her hands were moving over him, her hips straining
upward. With an effort, Mitch rolled so that they were
side by side.

He brought his lips down on her, and for a moment
all the needs, the fantasies, the darker desires centered
there. Her mouth was moist and hot, pounding into his
brain how she would be when he filled her. He was
already dragging the thin barrier of her chemise aside
so that she gasped when her breasts met him unencum-
bered. As his lips closed over the first firm point, he
heard her cry out his name.

This was abandonment. She'd been sure she'd never
wanted it, but now, as her body went fluid in her movements against his, she thought she might never want
anything else. The feelings of flesh against flesh, growing hot and damp, were new and exhilarating. As were
the avid seeking of mouths and the tastes they found
and drew in. His murmurs to her were hot and inco-
herent, but she responded. The light played over his
hands as he showed her how a touch could make the
soul soar.

She was naked, but the shyness was gone. She
wanted him to touch and taste and look his fill, just as
she was driven to. His body was a fascination of muscle and taut skin. She hadn't known until now that to
touch another, to please another, could bring on such
wild waves of passion. He cupped a hand over her, and
the passion contracted into a ball of flame in her center
that abruptly, almost violently, burst. Gasping for
breath, she reached for him.

He'd never had a woman respond so utterly. Watching her rise and peak had given him a delirious thrust

of pleasure. He wanted badly to take her up and over again and again, until she was limp and mindless. But his control was slipping, and she was calling for him.

His body covered hers, and he filled her.

He couldn't have said how long they moved together—minutes, hours. But he would never forget how her eyes had opened and stared into his.

He was a little shaken as he lay with her on top of the crumpled spread with drops of freezing rain striking the windows. He turned his head toward the hiss and wondered idly how long it had been going on. As far as he could remember, he'd never been so involved with a woman that the outside world, and all its sights and sounds, had simply ceased to exist.

He turned away again and drew Hester against him. His body was cooling rapidly, but he had no desire to move. "You're quiet," he murmured.

Her eyes were closed. She wasn't ready to open them again. "I don't know what to say."

"How about 'Wow'?"

She was surprised she could laugh after such intensity. "Okay. Wow."

"Try for more enthusiasm. How about 'Fantastic, incredible, earth-shattering?'"

She opened her eyes now and looked into his. "How about beautiful?"

He caught her hand in his and kissed it. "Yeah, that'll do." When he propped himself up on his elbow to look down at her, she shifted. "Too late to be shy now," he told her. Then he ran a hand, light and possessively, down her body. "You know, I was right about your legs. I don't suppose I could talk you into putting on a pair of shorts and those little socks that stop at the ankles.''

''I beg your pardon?''

Her tone had him gathering her to him and covering her face with kisses. ''I have a thing about long legs in shorts and socks. I drive myself crazy watching women jog in the park in the summer. When they color-coordinate them, I'm finished.''

''You're crazy.''

''Come on, Hester, don't you have some secret turn-on? Men in muscle shirts, in tuxedos with black tie and studs undone?''

''Don't be silly.''

''Why not?''

Why not, indeed, she thought, catching her bottom lip between her teeth. ''Well, there is something about jeans riding low on the hips with the snap undone.''

''I'll never snap my jeans again as long as I live.''

She laughed again. ''That doesn't mean I'm going to start wearing shorts and socks.''

''That's okay. I get excited when I see you in a business suit.''

''You do not.''

''Oh, yes, I do.'' He rolled her on top of him and began to play with her hair. ''Those slim lapels and high-collar blouses. And you always wear your hair up.'' With it caught in his hands, he lifted it on top of her head. It wasn't the same look at all, but one that still succeeded in making his mouth dry. ''The efficient and dependable Mrs. Wallace. Every time I see you dressed that way I imagine how fascinating it would be to peel off those professional clothes and take out those tidy little pins.'' He let her hair slide down through his fingers.

Thoughtful, Hester rested her cheek against his cheek. "You're a strange man, Mitch."

"More than likely."

"You depend so much on your imagination, on what it might be, on fantasies and make-believe. With me it's facts and figures, profit and loss, what is or what isn't."

"Are you talking about our jobs or our personalities?"

"Isn't one really the same as the other?"

"No. I'm not Commander Zark, Hester."

She shifted, lulled by the rhythm of his heart. "I suppose what I mean is that the artist in you, the writer in you, thrives on imagination or possibilities. I guess the banker in me looks for checks and balances."

He was silent for a moment, stroking her hair. Didn't she realize how much more there was to her? This was the woman who fantasized about a home in the country, the one who threw a curveball, the one who had just taken a man of flesh and blood and turned him into a puddle of need.

"I don't want to get overly philosophical, but why do you think you chose to deal with loans? Do you get the same feeling when you turn down an application as you do when you approve one?"

"No, of course not."

"Of course not," he repeated. "Because when you approve one, you've had a hand in the possibilities. I have no doubt that you play by the book, that's part of your charm, but I'd wager you get a great deal of personal satisfaction by being able to say, 'Okay, buy your home, start your business, expand.'"

She lifted her head. "You seem to understand me

very well.'' No one else had, she realized with a jolt. Ever.

"I've been giving you a great deal of thought.'' He drew her to him, wondering if she could feel how well their bodies fit. "A very great deal. In fact, I haven't thought about another woman since I delivered your pizza.''

She smiled at that, and would have settled against him again, but he held her back. "Hester...'' It was one of the few times in his life he'd ever felt self-conscious. She was looking at him expectantly, even patiently, while he struggled for the right words. "The thing is, I don't want to think about another woman, or be with another woman—this way.'' He struggled again, then swore. "Damn, I feel like I'm back in high school.''

Her smile was cautious. "Are you going to ask me to go steady?''

It wasn't exactly what he'd had in mind, but he could see by the look in her eyes that he'd better go slowly. "I could probably find my class ring if you want.''

She looked down at her hand, which was resting so naturally on his heart. Was it foolish to be so moved? If not, it was certainly dangerous. "Maybe we can just leave it that there's no one else I want to be with this way, either.''

He started to speak, then stopped himself. She needed time to be sure that was true, didn't she? There had only been one other man in her life, and she'd been no more than a girl then. To be fair, he had to give her room to be certain. But he didn't want to be fair. No, Mitch Dempsey was no self-sacrificing Commander Zark.

"All right." He'd devised and won enough wars to know how to plan strategy. He'd win Hester before she realized there'd been a battle.

Drawing her down to him, he closed his mouth over hers and began the first siege.

It was an odd and rather wonderful feeling to wake up in the morning beside a lover—even one who nudged you over to the edge of the mattress. Hester opened her eyes and, lying very still, savored it.

His face was buried against the back of her neck, and his arm was wrapped tightly around her waist—which was fortunate, as without it she would have rolled onto the floor. Hester shifted slightly and experienced the arousing sensation of having her sleep-warmed skin rub cozily against his.

She'd never had a lover. A husband, yes, but her wedding night, her first initiation into womanhood, had been nothing like the night she'd just shared with Mitch. Was it fair to compare them? she wondered. Would she be human if she didn't?

That first night so long ago had been frenzied, complicated by her nerves and her husband's hurry. Last night the passion had built layer by layer, as though there'd been all the time in the world to enjoy it. She'd never known that making love could be so liberating. In truth, she hadn't known a man could sincerely want to give pleasure as much as he desired to take it.

She snuggled into the pillow and watched the thin winter light come through the windows. Would things be different this morning? Would there be an awkwardness between them or, worse, a casualness that would diminish the depth of what they'd shared? The simple fact was she didn't know what it was like to have a lover—or to be one.

She was putting too much emphasis on one evening, she told herself, sighing. How could she not, when the evening had been so special?

Hester touched a hand to his, let it linger a moment, then shifted to rise. Mitch's arm clamped down.

"Going somewhere?"

She tried to turn over, but discovered his legs had pinned her. "It's almost nine."

"So?" His fingers spread out lazily to stroke.

"I have to get up. I need to pick Rad up in a couple of hours."

"Hmmm." He watched his little dream bubble of a morning in bed with her deflate, then reconstructed it to fit two hours. "You feel so good." He released his hold, but only so he could turn her around so they were face-to-face. "Look good, too," he decided as he studied her face through half-closed eyes. "And taste—" he touched his lips to hers, and there was nothing awkward, nothing casual "—wonderful. Imagine this." He ran a hand down her flank. "We're on an island—the South Seas, let's say. The ship was wrecked a week ago, and we're the only survivors." His eyes closed as he pressed a kiss to her forehead. "We've been living on fruit and the fish I cleverly catch with my pointed stick."

"Who cleans them?"

"This is a fantasy, you don't worry about details like that. Last night there was a storm—a big, busting tropical storm—and we had to huddle together for warmth and safety under the lean-to I built."

"You built?" Her lips curved against his. "Do I do anything useful?"

"You can do all you want in your own fantasy. Now shut up." He snuggled closer and could almost smell the salt air. "It's morning, and the storm washed everything clean. There are gulls swooping down near the surf. We're lying together on an old blanket."

"Which you heroically salvaged from the wreck."

"Now you're catching on. When we wake up, we discover we'd tangled together during the night, drawn together despite ourselves. The sun's hot; it's already warmed our half-naked bodies. Still dazed with sleep, already aroused, we come together. And then…" His lips hovered a breath away from hers. Hester let her eyes close as she found herself caught up in the picture he painted. "And then a wild boar attacks, and I have to wrestle him."

"Half-naked and unarmed?"

"That's right. I'm badly bitten, but I kill him with my bare hands."

Hester opened her eyes again to narrow slits. "And while you're doing that, I put the blanket over my head and whimper."

"Okay." Mitch kissed the tip of her nose. "But afterward you're very, very grateful that I saved your life."

"Poor, defenseless female that I am."

"That's the ticket. You're so grateful you tear the rags of your skirt to make bandages for my wounds, and then…" He paused for impact. "You make me coffee."

Hester drew back, not certain whether to be amazed or amused. "You went through that whole scenario so I'd offer to make you coffee?"

"Not just coffee, morning coffee, the first cup of coffee. Life's blood."

"I'd have made it even without the story."

"Yeah, but did you like the story?"

She combed the hair away from her face as she considered. "Next time I get to catch the fish."

"Deal."

She rose and, though she knew it was foolish, wished that she'd had her robe within arm's reach. Going to the closet, she slipped it on with her back still to him. "Do you want some breakfast?"

He was sitting up, rubbing his hands over his face when she turned. "Breakfast? You mean likes eggs or something? Hot food?" The only time he managed a hot breakfast was when he had the energy to drag himself to the corner diner. "Mrs. Wallace, for a hot breakfast you can have the crown jewels of Perth."

"All that for bacon and eggs?"

"Bacon, too? God, what a woman."

She laughed, sure he was joking. "Go ahead and get a shower if you want. It won't take long."

He hadn't been joking. Mitch watched her walk from the room and shook his head. He didn't expect a woman to offer to cook for him, or for one to offer as though he had a right to expect it. But this, he remembered, was the woman who would have sewed patches on his jeans because she'd thought he couldn't afford new ones.

Mitch climbed out of bed, then slowly, thoughtfully ran a hand through his hair. The aloof and professional Hester Wallace was a very warm and special woman, and he had no intention of letting her get away.

She was stirring eggs in a skillet when he came into the kitchen. Bacon was draining on a rack, and coffee was already hot. He stood in the doorway a moment, more than a little surprised that such a simple domestic scene would affect him so strongly. Her robe was flannel and covered her from neck to ankle, but to him Hester had never looked more alluring. He hadn't realized he'd been looking for this—the morning smells, the morning sounds of the Sunday news on the radio on the counter, the morning sights of the woman who'd shared his night moving competently in the kitchen.

As a child, Sunday mornings had been almost formal affairs—brunch at eleven, served by a uniformed member of the staff. Orange juice in Waterford, shirred eggs on Wedgewood. He'd been taught to spread the Irish linen on his lap and make polite conversation. In later years, Sunday mornings had meant a bleary-eyed search through the cupboards or a dash down to the nearest diner.

He felt foolish, but he wanted to tell Hester that the simple meal at her kitchen counter meant as much to him as the long night in her bed. Crossing to her, he wrapped his arms around her waist and pressed a kiss to her neck.

Strange how a touch could speed up the heart rate and warm the blood. Absorbing the sensation, she leaned back against him. "It's almost done. You didn't say how you liked your eggs, so you've got them scrambled with a little dill and cheese."

She could have offered him cardboard and told him to eat it with a plastic fork. Mitch turned her to face him and kissed her long and hard. "Thanks."

He'd flustered her again. Hester turned to the eggs in time to prevent them from burning. "Why don't you sit down?" She poured coffee into a mug and handed it to him. "With your life's blood."

He finished half the mug before he sat. "Hester, you know what I said about your legs?"

She glanced over as she heaped eggs on a plate. "Yes?"

"Your coffee's almost as good as they are. Tremendous qualities in a woman."

"Thanks." She set the plate in front of him before moving to the toaster.

"Aren't you eating any of this?"

"No, just toast."

Mitch looked down at the pile of golden eggs and crisp bacon. "Hester, I didn't expect you to fix me all this when you aren't eating."

"It's all right." She arranged a stack of toast on a plate. "I do it for Rad all the time."

He covered her hand with his as she sat beside him. "I appreciate it."

"It's only a couple of eggs," she said, embarrassed. "You should eat them before they get cold."

"The woman's a marvel," Mitch commented as he obliged her. "She raises an interesting and well-balanced son, holds down a demanding job, and cooks." Mitch bit into a piece of bacon. "Want to get married?"

She laughed and added more coffee to both mugs. "If it only takes scrambled eggs to get you to propose, I'm surprised you don't have three or four wives hidden in the closet."

He hadn't been joking. She would have seen it in his eyes if she'd looked at him, but she was busy spreading butter on toast. Mitch watched her competent, ringless hands a moment. It had been a stupid way to propose and a useless way to make her see he was serious. It was also too soon, he admitted as he scooped up another forkful of eggs.

The trick would be first to get her used to having him around, then to have her trust him enough to believe he would stay around. Then there was the big one, he mused as he lifted his cup. She had to need him. She wouldn't ever need him for the roof over her head or the food in her cupboards. She was much too self-sufficient for that, and he admired it. In time, she might come to need him for emotional support and companionship. It would be a start.

The courting of Hester would have to be both complex and subtle. He wasn't certain he knew exactly how to go about it, but he was more than ready to start. Today was as good a time as any.

"Got any plans for later?"

"I've got to pick up Rad around noon." She lingered over her toast, realizing it had been years since she had shared adult company over breakfast and that it had an appeal all its own. "Then I promised that I'd take him and Josh to a matinee. *The Moon of Andromeda.*"

"Yeah? Terrific movie. The special effects are tremendous."

"You've seen it?" She felt a twinge of disappointment. She'd been wondering if he might be willing to come along.

"Twice. There's a scene between the mad scientist and the sane scientist that'll knock you out. And there's this mutant that looks like a carp. Fantastic."

"A carp." Hester sipped her coffee. "Sounds wonderful."

"A cinematic treat for the eyes. Can I tag along?"

"You just said you've seen it twice already."

"So? The only movies I see once are dogs. Besides, I'd like to see Rad's reaction to the laser battle in deep space."

"Is it gory?"

"Nothing Rad can't handle."

"I wasn't asking for him."

With a laugh, Mitch took her hand. "I'll be there to protect you. How about it? I'll spring for the popcorn." He brought her hand up to his lips. "Buttered."

"How could I pass up a deal like that?"

"Good. Look, I'll give you a hand with the dishes, then I've got to go down and take Taz out before his bladder causes us both embarrassment."

"Go on ahead. There isn't that much, and Taz is probably moaning at the door by this time."

"Okay." He stood with her. "But next time I cook."

Hester gathered up the plates. "Peanut butter and jelly?"

"I can do better than that if it impresses you."

She smiled and reached for his empty mug. "You don't have to impress me."

He caught her face in his hands while she stood with her hands full of dishes. "Yes, I do." He nibbled at her lips, then abruptly deepened the kiss until they were both breathless. She was forced to swallow when he released her.

"That's a good start."

He was smiling as he brushed his lips over her forehead. "I'll be up in an hour."

Hester stood where she was until she heard the door close, then quietly set the dishes down again. How in the world had it happened? she wondered. She'd fallen in love with the man. He'd be gone only an hour, yet she wanted him back already.

Taking a deep breath, she sat down again. She had to keep herself from overreacting, from taking this, as she took too many other things, too seriously. He was fun, he was kind, but he wasn't permanent. There was nothing permanent but her and Radley. She'd promised herself years ago that she would never forget that again. Now, more than ever, she had to remember it.

at least whispered, but he had waited before, and Tanner had not noticed. ...

It had been enough, he was about to...

...from frames, from corner to corner, take his characters and carry a series this way, he had

...was left. Remember, Cornelius? Don't let...

...leaning back and she might up... another...

...and imagining to pre hope... more on as

Chapter 9

"Rich, you know I hate business discussions before noon."

Mitch sat in Skinner's office with Taz snoozing at his feet. Though it was after ten and he'd been up working for a couple of hours, he hadn't been ready to venture out and talk shop. He'd had to leave his characters on the drawing board in a hell of a predicament, and Mitch imagined they resented being left dangling as much as he resented leaving them.

"If you're going to give me a raise, that's fine by me, but you could've waited until after lunch."

"You're not getting a raise." Skinner ignored the phone that rang on his desk. "You're already overpaid."

"Well, if I'm fired, you could definitely have waited a couple of hours."

"You're not fired." Skinner drew his brows together

until they met above his nose. "But if you keep bringing that hound in here, I could change my mind."

"I made Taz my agent. Anything you say to me you can say in front of him."

Skinner sat back in his chair and folded hands that were swollen at the knuckles from years of nervous cracking. "You know, Dempsey, someone who didn't know you so well would think you were joking. The problem is, I happen to know you're crazy."

"That's why we get along so well, right? Listen, Rich, I've got Mirium trapped in a roomful of wounded rebels from Zirial. Being an empath, she's not feeling too good herself. Why don't we wrap this up so I can get back and take her to the crisis point?"

"Rebels from Zirial," Skinner mused. "You aren't thinking of bringing back Nimrod the Sorceror?"

"It's crossed my mind, and I could get back and figure out what he's got up his invisible sleeve if you'd tell me why you dragged me in here."

"You work here," Skinner pointed out.

"That's no excuse."

Skinner puffed out his cheeks and let the subject drop. "You know Two Moon Pictures has been negotiating with Universal for the rights to product Zark as a full-length film?"

"Sure. That's been going on a year, a year and a half now." Since the wheeling and dealing didn't interest him, Mitch stretched out a leg and began to massage Taz's flank with his foot. "The last thing you told me was that the alfalfa sprouts from L.A. couldn't get out of their hot tubs long enough to close the deal." Mitch grinned. "You've got a real way with words, Rich."

"The deal closed yesterday," Rich said flatly. "Two Moon wants to go with Zark."

Mitch's grin faded. "You're serious?"

"I'm always serious," Rich said, studying Mitch's reaction. "I thought you'd be a little more enthusiastic. Your baby's going to be a movie star."

"To tell you the truth, I don't know how I feel." Pushing himself out of the chair, Mitch began to pace Rich's cramped office. As he passed the window, he pulled open the blinds to let in slants of hard winter light. "Zark's always been personal. I don't know how I feel about him going Hollywood."

"You got a kick out of when B.C. Toys made the dolls."

"Action figures," Mitch corrected automatically. "I guess that's because they stayed pretty true to the theme." It was silly, he knew. Zark didn't belong to him. He'd created him, true, but Zark belonged to Universal, just like all the other heroes and villains of the staff's fertile imaginations. If, like Maloney, Mitch decided to move on, Zark would stay behind, the responsibility of someone else's imagination. "Did we retain any creative leeway?"

"Afraid they're going to exploit your firstborn?"

"Maybe."

"Listen, Two Moon bought the rights to Zark because he has potential at the box office—the way he is. It wouldn't be smart businesswise to change him. Let's look at the bottom line—comics are big business. A hundred and thirty million a year isn't something to shrug off. The business is thriving now the way it hasn't since the forties, and even though it's bound to level off, it's going to stay hot. Those jokers on the coast might dress funny, but they know a winner when they see one. Still, if you're worried, you could take their offer.''

"What offer?"

"They want you to write the screenplay."

Mitch stopped where he was. "Me? I don't write movies."

"You write Zark; apparently that's enough for the producers. Our publishers aren't stupid, either. Stingy," he added with a glance at his worn linoleum, "but not stupid. They wanted the script to come from in-house, and there's a clause in the contract that says we have a shot. Two Moon agreed to accept a treatment from you first. If it doesn't pan out, they still want you on the project as a creative consultant."

"Creative consultant." Mitch rolled the title around on his tongue.

"If I were you, Dempsey, I'd get myself a two-legged agent."

"I just might. Look, I'm going to have to think about it. How long are they giving me?"

"Nobody mentioned a time frame. I don't think the possibility of your saying no occurred to them. But then, they don't know you like I do."

"I need a couple of days. There's someone I have to talk to."

Skinner waited until he'd started out. "Mitch, opportunity doesn't often kick down your door this way."

"Just let me make sure I'm at home first. I'll be in touch."

When it rains it pours, Mitch thought as he and Taz walked. It had started off as a fairly normal, even ordinary new year. He'd planned to dig his heels in a bit and get ahead of schedule so that he could take three or four weeks off to ski, drink brandy and kick up some snow on his uncle's farm. He'd figured on meeting one or two attractive women on the slopes to make the evenings interesting. He'd thought to sketch a little, sleep a lot and cruise the lodges. Very simple.

Then, within weeks, everything had changed. In Hester he'd found everything he'd ever wanted in his personal life, but he'd only begun to convince her that he was everything she'd ever wanted in hers. Now he was being offered one of the biggest opportunities of his professional life, but he couldn't think of one without considering the other.

In truth, he'd never been able to draw a hard line of demarcation between his professional and personal lives. He was the same man whether he was having a couple of drinks with friends or burning the midnight oil with Zark. If he'd changed at all, it had been Hester and Radley who had caused it. Since he'd fallen for them, he wanted the strings he'd always avoided, the responsibilities he'd always blithely shrugged off.

So he went to her first.

Mitch strolled into the bank with his ears tingling from the cold. The long walk had given him time to think through everything Skinner had told him, and to feel the first twinges of excitement. Zark, in Technicolor, in stereophonic sound, in Panavision.

Mitch stopped at Kay's desk. "She had lunch yet?"

Kay rolled back from her terminal. "Nope."

"Anybody with her now?"

"Not a soul."

"Good. When's her next appointment?"

Kay ran her finger down the appointment book. "Two-fifteen."

"She'll be back. If Rosen stops by, tell him I took Mrs. Wallace to lunch to discuss some refinancing."

"Yes, sir."

She was working on a long column of figures when Mitch opened the door. She moved her fingers quickly over the adding machine, which clicked as it spewed out a stream of tape. "Kay, I'm going to need Lorimar's construction estimate. And would you mind ordering me a sandwich? Anything as long as it's quick. I'd like to have these figures upstairs by the end of the day. Oh, and I'll need the barter exchange transactions on the Duberry account. Look up the 1099."

Mitch shut the door at his back. "God, all this bank talk excites me."

"Mitch." Hester glanced up with the last of the figures still rolling through her head. "What are you doing here?"

"Breaking you out, and we have to move fast. Taz'll distract the guards." He was already taking her coat from the rack behind the door. "Let's go. Just keep your head down and look natural."

"Mitch, I've got—"

"To eat Chinese take-out and make love with me. In whatever order you like. Here, button up."

"I've only half-finished with these figures."

"They won't run away." He buttoned her coat, then closed his hands over her collar. "Hester, do you know how long it's been since we had an hour alone? Four days."

"I know. I'm sorry, things have been busy."

"Busy." He nodded toward her desk. "No one's going to argue with you there, but you've also been holding me off."

"No, I haven't." The truth was she'd been holding

herself off, trying to prove to herself that she didn't need him as badly as it seemed. It hadn't been working as well as she'd hoped. There was tangible proof of that now as she stood facing him with her heart beating fast. "Mitch, I explained how I felt about…being with you with Radley in the apartment."

"And I'm not arguing that point, either." Though he would have liked to. "But Rad's in school and you have a constitutional right to a lunch hour. Come with me, Hester." He let his brow rest on hers. "I need you."

She couldn't resist or refuse or pretend she didn't want to be with him. Knowing she might regret it later, she turned her back on her work. "I'd settle for a peanut butter and jelly. I'm not very hungry."

"You got it."

Fifteen minutes later, they were walking into Mitch's apartment. As usual, his curtains were open wide so that the sun poured through. It was warm, Hester thought as she slipped out of her coat. She imagined he kept the thermostat up so that he could be comfortable in his bare feet and short-sleeved sweat-shirts. Hester stood with her coat in her hands and wondered what to do next.

"Here, let me take that." Mitch tossed her coat care-lessly over a chair. "Nice suit, Mrs. Wallace," he mur-mured, fingering the lapel of the dark blue pin-stripe.

She put a hand over his, once again afraid that things were moving too fast. "I feel…"

"Decadent?"

Once again, it was the humor in his eyes that relaxed her. "More like I've just climbed out my bedroom window at midnight."

"Did you ever?"

"No. I thought about it a lot, but I could never figure out what I was supposed to do once I climbed down."

"That's why I'm nuts about you." He kissed her cautious smile and felt her lips soften and give under his. "Climb out the bedroom window to me, Hester. I'll show you what to do." Then his hands were in her hair, and her control scattered as quickly as the pins.

She wanted him. Perhaps it had a great deal to do with madness, but oh, how she wanted him. In the long nights since they'd been together like this, she'd thought of him, of how he touched her, where he touched her, and now his hands were there, just as she remembered. This time she moved faster than he, pulling his sweater up over his head to feast on the warm, taut flesh beneath. Her teeth nipped into his lip, insisting, inciting, until he was dragging the jacket from her and fumbling with the buttons that ranged down the back of her blouse.

His touch wasn't as gentle when he found her, nor was he as patient. But she had long since thrown caution aside. Now, pressed hard against him, she gripped passion with both hands. Whether it was day or night no longer mattered. She was where she wanted to be, where, no matter how she struggled to pretend otherwise, she needed to be.

Madness, yes, it was madness. She wondered how she'd lived so long without it.

He unfastened her skirt so that it flowed over her hips and onto the floor. With a groan of satisfaction he pressed his mouth to her throat. Four days? Had it only been four days? It seemed like years since he had had her close and alone. She was as hot and as desperate against him as he'd dreamed she would be. He could savor the feel of her even as desire clamped inside his gut and swam in his head. He wanted to spend hours touching, being touched, but the intensity of the moment, the lack of time and her urgent murmurs made it impossible.

"The bedroom," she managed as he pulled the thin straps of her lingerie over her shoulders.

"No, here. Right here." He fastened his mouth on hers and pulled her to the floor.

He would have given her more. Even though his own system was straining toward the breaking point, he would have given her more, but she was wrapped around him. Before he could catch his breath, her hands were on his hips, guiding her to him. She dug her fingers into his flesh as she murmured his name, and whole galaxies seemed to explode inside his head.

When she could think again, Hester stared at the dust motes that danced in a beam of sunlight. She was lying on a priceless Aubusson with Mitch's head pillowed between her breasts. It was the middle of the day, she had a pile of paperwork on her desk, and she'd just spent the better part of her lunch making love on the floor. She couldn't remember ever being more content.

She hadn't known life could be like this—an adventure, a carnival. For years she hadn't believed there was room for the madness of love and lovemaking in a world that revolved around responsibilities. Now, just now, she was beginning to realize she could have both. For how long, she couldn't be sure. Perhaps one day would be enough. She combed her fingers through his hair.

"I'm glad you came to take me to lunch."

"If this is any indication, we're going to have to make it a habit. Still want that sandwich?"

"Uh-uh. I don't need anything." But you. Hester sighed, realizing she was going to have to accept that. "I'm going to have to get back."

"You don't have an appointment until after two. I checked. Your barter exchange transactions can wait a few more minutes, can't they?"

"I suppose."

"Come on." He was up and pulling her to her feet.

"Where?"

"We'll have a quick shower, then I need to talk to you."

Hester accepted his offer of a robe and tried not to worry about what he had to say. She understood Mitch well enough to know he was full of surprises. The trouble was, she wasn't certain she was ready for another. Shoulders tense, she sat beside him on the couch and waited.

"You look like you're waiting for the blindfold and your last cigarette."

Hester shook back her still damp hair and tried to smile. "No, it's just that you sounded so serious."

"I've told you before, I have my serious moments." He shoved magazines off the table with his foot. "I had some news today, and I haven't decided how I feel about it. I wanted to see what you thought."

"Your family?" she began, instantly concerned.

"No." He took her hand. "I guess I'm making it sound like bad news, and it's not. At least I don't think it is. A production company in Hollywood just cut a deal with Universal to make a movie out of Zark."

Hester stared at him a moment, then blinked. "A movie. Well, that's wonderful. Isn't it? I mean, I know he's very popular in comics, but a movie would be even bigger. You should be thrilled, and very proud that your work can translate that way.''

"I just don't know if they can pull it off, if they can bring him to the screen with the right tone, the right emotion. Don't look at me that way.''

"Mitch, I know how you feel about Zark. At least I think I do. He's your creation, and he's important to you.''

"He's real to me,'' Mitch corrected. "Up here,'' he said, tapping his temple. "And, as corny as it might sound, in here.'' He touched a hand to his heart. "He made a difference in my life, made a difference in how I looked at myself and my work. I don't want to see them screw him up and make him into some cardboard hero or, worse, into something infallible and perfect.''

Hester was silent a moment. She began to understand that giving birth to an idea might be as life-altering as giving birth to a child. "Let me ask you something: why did you create him?''

"I wanted to make a hero—a very human one—with flaws and vulnerabilities, and I guess with high standards. Someone kids could relate to because he was just flesh and blood, but powerful enough inside to fight back. Kids don't have a hell of a lot of choices, you know. I remember when I was young I wanted to be able to say 'no, I don't want to, I don't like that.' When I read, I could see there were possibilities, ways out. That's what I wanted Zark to be.''

"Do you think you succeeded?''

"Yeah. On a personal level, I succeeded when I came up with the first issue. Professionally, Zark has pushed Universal to the top. He translates into millions of dollars a year for the business.''

"Do you resent that?''

"No, why should I?"

"Then you shouldn't resent seeing him take the next step."

Mitch fell silent, thinking. He might have known Hester would see things more clearly and be able to cut through everything to the most practical level. Wasn't that just one more reason he needed her?

"They offered to let me do the screenplay."

"What?" She was sitting straight up now, eyes wide. "Oh, Mitch, that's wonderful. I'm so proud of you."

He continued to play with her fingers. "I haven't done it yet."

"Don't you think you can?"

"I'm not sure."

She started to speak, then caught herself. After a moment, she spoke carefully. "Strange, if anyone had asked, I would have said you were the most self-confident man I'd ever met. Added to that, I'd have said that you'd be much too selfish with Zark to let anyone else write him."

"There's a difference between writing a story line for a comic series and writing a screenplay for a major motion picture."

"So?"

He had to laugh. "Tossing my own words back at me, aren't you?"

"You can write, I'd be the first to say that you have a very fluid imagination, and you know your character better than anyone else. I don't see the problem."

"Screwing up is the problem. Anyway, if I don't do the script, they want me as creative consultant."

"I can't tell you what to do, Mitch."

"But?"

She leaned forward, putting her hands on his shoulders. "Write the script, Mitch. You'll hate yourself if you don't try. There aren't any guarantees, but if you don't take the risk, there's no reward either."

He lifted a hand to hers and held it firmly as he watched her. "Do you really feel that way?"

"Yes, I do. I also believe in you." She leaned closer and touched her mouth to his.

"Marry me, Hester."

With her lips still on his, she froze. Slowly, very slowly, she drew away. "What?"

"Marry me." He took her hands in his to hold them still. "I love you."

"Don't. Please don't do this."

"Don't what? Don't love you?" He tightened his grip as she struggled to pull away. "It's a great deal too late for that, and I think you know it. I'm not lying when I tell you that I've never felt about anyone the way I feel about you. I want to spend my life with you."

"I can't." Her voice was breathless. It seemed each word she pushed out seared the back of her throat. "I can't marry you. I don't want to marry anyone. You don't understand what you're asking."

"Just because I haven't been there doesn't mean I don't know." He'd expected surprise, even some resistance. But he could see now he'd totally miscalculated. There was out-and-out fear in her eyes and full panic in her voice. "Hester, I'm not Allan and we both know you're not the same woman you were when you were married to him."

"It doesn't matter. I'm not going through that again, and I won't put Radley through it." She pulled away and started to dress. "You're not being reasonable."

"*I'm* not?" Struggling for calm, he walked behind her and began to do up her buttons. Her back went rigid. "You're the one who's basing her feelings now on something that happened years ago."

"I don't want to talk about it."

"Maybe not, and maybe now's not the best time, but you're going to have to." Though she resisted, he turned her around. "We're going to have to."

She wanted to get away, far enough that she could bury everything that had been said. But for the moment she had to face it. "Mitch, we've known each other for a matter of weeks, and we've just begun to be able to accept what's happening between us."

"What *is* happening?" he demanded. "Aren't you the one who said at the beginning that you weren't interested in casual sex?"

She paled a bit, then turned away to pick up her suit jacket. "There wasn't anything casual about it."

"No, there wasn't, not for either of us. You understand that?"

"Yes, but—"

"Hester, I said I loved you. Now I want to know how you feel about me."

"I don't know." She let out a gasp when he grabbed her shoulders again. "I tell you I don't know. I think I love you. Today. You're asking me to risk everything I've done, the life I've built for myself and Rad, over an emotion I already know can change overnight."

"Love doesn't change overnight," he corrected. "It can be killed or it can be nurtured. That's up to the people involved. I want a commitment from you, a family, and I want to give those things back to you."

"Mitch, this is all happening too fast, much too fast for both of us."

"Damn it, Hester, I'm thirty-five years old, not some kid with hot pants and no brains. I don't want to marry you so I can have convenient sex and a hot breakfast, but because I know we could have something together, something real, something important."

"You don't know what marriage is like, you're only imagining."

"And you're only remembering a bad one. Hester, look at me. Look at me," he demanded again. "When the hell are you going to stop using Radley's father as a yardstick?"

"He's the only one I've got." She shook him off again and tried to catch her breath. "Mitch, I'm flattered that you want me."

"The hell with that."

"Please." She dragged a hand through her hair. "I do care about you, and the only thing I'm really sure of is that I don't want to lose you."

"Marriage isn't the end of a relationship, Hester."

"I can't think about marriage. I'm sorry." The panic flowed in and out of her voice until she was forced to stop and calm it. "If you don't want to see me anymore, I'll try to understand. But I'd rather…I hope we can just let things go on the way they are."

He dug his hands into his pockets. He had a habit of pushing too far too fast, and knew it. But he hated to waste the time he could already imagine them having together. "For how long, Hester?"

"For as long as it lasts." She closed her eyes. "That sounds hard. I don't mean it to. You mean a great deal to me, more than I thought anyone ever would again."

Mitch brushed a finger over her cheek and brought it away wet. "A low blow," he murmured, studying the tear.

"I'm sorry. I don't mean to do this. I had no idea that you were thinking along these lines."

"I can see that." He gave a self-deprecating laugh. "In three dimensions."

"I've hurt you. I can't tell you how much I regret that."

"Don't. I asked for it. The truth is, I hadn't planned on asking you to marry me for at least a week."

She started to touch his hand, then stopped. "Mitch, can we just forget all this, go on as we were?"

He reached out and straightened the collar of her jacket. "I'm afraid not. I've made up my mind, Hester. That's something I try to do only once or twice a year. Once I've done it, there's no turning back." His gaze came up to hers with that rush of intensity she felt to the bone. "I'm going to marry you, sooner or later. If it has to be later, that's fine. I'll just give you some time to get used to it."

"Mitch, I won't change my mind. It wouldn't be fair if I let you think I would. It isn't a matter of a whim, but of a promise I made to myself."

"Some promises are best broken."

She shook her head. "I don't know what else to say. I just wish—"

He pressed his finger to her lips. "We'll talk about it later. I'll take you back to work."

"No, don't bother. Really," she said when he started to argue. "I'd like some time to think, anyway. Being with you makes that difficult."

"That's a good start." He took her chin in his hand and studied her face. "You look fine, but next time don't cry when I ask you to marry me. It's hell on the ego." He kissed her before she could speak. "See you later, Mrs. Wallace. Thanks for lunch."

A little dazed, she walked out into the hall. "I'll call you later."

"Do that. I'll be around."

He closed the door, then turned to lean back against it. Hurt? He rubbed a spot just under his heart. Damn right it hurt. If anyone had told him that being in love could cause the heart to twist, he'd have continued to avoid it. He'd had a twinge when his long-ago love in New Orleans had deserted him. It hadn't prepared him for this sledgehammer blow. What could possibly have?

But he wasn't giving up. What he had to do was figure out a plan of attack—subtle, clever and irresistible. Mitch glanced down at Taz consideringly.

"Where do you think Hester would like to go on our honeymoon?"

The dog grumbled, then rolled over on his back.

"No," Mitch decided. "Bermuda's overdone. Never mind, I'll come up with something."

Chapter 10

"Radley, you and your friends have to tone down the volume on the war, please." Hester took the measuring tape from around her neck and stretched it out over the wall space. Perfect, she thought with a satisfied nod. Then she took the pencil from behind her ear to mark two Xs where the nails would go.

The little glass shelves she would hang were a present to herself, one that was completely unnecessary and pleased her a great deal. She didn't consider the act of hanging them herself a show of competence or independence, but simply one more of the ordinary chores she'd been doing on her own for years. With a hammer in one hand, she lined up the first nail. She'd given it two good whacks when someone knocked on the door.

"Just a minute." She gave the nail a final smack. From Radley's bedroom came the sounds of antiaircraft and whistling missiles. Hester took the second nail out of her mouth and stuck it in her pocket. "Rad,

we're going to be arrested for disturbing the peace.''
She opened the door to Mitch. "Hi."

The pleasure showed instantly, gratifying him. It had
been two days since he'd seen her, since he'd told her
he loved her and wanted to marry her. In two days
he'd done a lot of hard thinking, and could only hope
that, despite herself, Hester had done some thinking,
too.

"Doing some remodeling?" he asked with a nod at
the hammer.

"Just hanging a shelf." She wrapped both hands
around the handle of the hammer, feeling like a teenager. "Come in."

He glanced toward Radley's room as she shut the
door. It sounded as though a major air strike was in
progress. "You didn't mention you were opening a
playground."

"It's been a lifelong dream of mine. Rad, they've
just signed a treaty—hold your fire!" With a cautious
smile for Mitch, she waved him toward a chair. "Radley has Josh over today, and Ernie—Ernie lives upstairs and goes to school with Rad."

"Sure, the Bitterman kid. I know him. Nice," he
commented as he looked at the shelves.

"They're a present for completing a successful
month at National Trust." Hester ran a finger along a
beveled edge. She really did want this more than a new
outfit.

"You're on the reward program?"

"Self-reward."

"The best kind. Want me to finish that for you?"

"Oh?" She glanced down at the hammer. "Oh, no,
thanks. I can do it. Why don't you sit down? I'll get
you some coffee."

"You hang the shelf, I'll get the coffee." He kissed the tip of her nose. "And relax, will you?"

"Mitch." He'd taken only two steps away when she reached for his arm. "I'm awfully glad to see you. I was afraid, well, that you were angry."

"Angry?" He gave her a baffled look. "About what?"

"About..." She trailed off as he continued to stare at her in a half interested, half curious way that made her wonder if she'd imagined everything he'd said. "Nothing." She dug the nail out of her pocket. "Help yourself to the coffee."

"Thanks." He grinned at the back of her head. He'd done exactly what he'd set out to do—confuse her. Now she'd be thinking about him, about what had been said between them. The more she thought about it, the closer she'd be to seeing reason.

Whistling between his teeth, he strolled into the kitchen while Hester banged in the second nail.

He *had* asked her to marry him. She remembered everything he'd said, everything she'd said in return. And she knew that he'd been angry and hurt. Hadn't she spent two days regretting that she'd had to cause that? Now he strolled in as though nothing had happened.

Hester set down the hammer, then lifted the shelves. Maybe he'd cooled off enough to be relieved that she'd said no. That could be it, she decided, wondering why the idea didn't ease her mind as much as it should have.

"You made cookies." Mitch came in carrying two mugs, with a plate of fresh cookies balanced on top of one.

"This morning." She smiled over her shoulder as she adjusted the shelves.

"You want to bring that up a little on the right." He sat on the arm of a chair, then set her mug down so his hands would be free for the chocolate-chip cookies. "Terrific," he decided after the first bite. "And, if I say so myself, I'm an expert."

"I'm glad they pass." With her mind on her shelves, Hester stepped back to admire them.

"It's important. I don't know if I could marry a woman who made lousy cookies." He picked up a second one and examined it. "Yeah, maybe I could," he said as Hester turned slowly to stare at him. "But it would be tough." He devoured the second one and smiled at her. "Luckily, it won't have to be an issue."

"Mitch." Before she could work out what to say, Radley came barreling in, his two friends behind him.

"Mitch!" Delighted with the company, Radley screeched to a halt beside him so that Mitch's arm went naturally around his shoulders. "We just had the neatest battle. We're the only survivors."

"Hungry work. Have a cookie."

Radley took one and shoved it into his mouth. "We've got to go up to Ernie's and get more weapons." He reached for another cookie, then caught his mother's eye. "You didn't bring Taz up."

"He stayed up late watching a movie. He's sleeping in today."

"Okay." Radley accepted this before turning to his mother. "Is it okay if we go up to Ernie's for a while?"

"Sure. Just don't go outside unless you let me know."

"We won't. You guys go ahead. I gotta get something."

He raced back to the bedroom while his friends trooped to the door.

"I'm glad he's making some new friends," Hester commented as she reached for her mug. "He was worried about it."

"Radley's not the kind of kid who has trouble making friends."

"No, he's not."

"He's also fortunate to have a mother who lets them come around and bakes cookies for them." He took another sip of coffee. His mother's cook had baked little cakes. He thought Hester would understand it wasn't quite the same thing. "Of course, once we're married we'll have to give him some brothers and sisters. What are you going to put on the shelf?"

"Useless things," she murmured, staring at him. "Mitch, I don't want to fight, but I think we should clear this up."

"Clear what up? Oh, I meant to tell you I started on the script. It's going pretty well."

"I'm glad." And confused. "Really, that's wonderful, but I think we should talk about this business first."

"Sure, what business was that?"

She opened her mouth, and was once more interrupted by her son. When Radley came in, Hester walked away to put a small china cat on the bottom shelf.

"I made something for you in school." Embarrassed, Radley held his hands behind his back.

"Yeah?" Mitch set his coffee down. "Do I get to see it?"

"It's Valentine's Day, you know." After a moment's hesitation, he handed Mitch a card fashioned out of construction paper and blue ribbon. "I made Mom this heart with lace stuff, but I thought the ribbon was better for guys." Radley shuffled his feet. "It opens."

Not certain he could trust his voice, Mitch opened the card. Radley had used his very best block printing.

"To my best friend, Mitch. I love you, Radley." He had to clear his throat, and hoped he wouldn't make a fool out of himself. "It's great. I, ah, nobody ever made me a card before."

"Really?" Embarrassment faded with surprise. "I make them for Mom all the time. She says she likes them better than the ones you buy."

"I like this one a lot better," Mitch told him. He wasn't sure boys that were nearly ten tolerated being kissed, but he ran a hand over Radley's hair and kissed him anyway. "Thanks."

"You're welcome. See ya."

"Yeah." Mitch heard the door slam as he stared down at the little folded piece of construction paper.

"I didn't know he'd made it," Hester said quietly. "I guess he wanted to keep it a secret."

"He did a nice job." At the moment, he didn't have the capacity to explain what the paper and ribbon meant to him. Rising, he walked to the window with the card in his hands. "I'm crazy about him."

"I know." She moistened her lips. She did know it. If she'd ever doubted the extent of Mitch's feelings for her son, she'd just seen full proof of it. It only made things more difficult. "In just a few weeks, you've done so much for him. I know neither one of us have the right to expect you to be there, but I want you to know it means a lot that you are.''

He had to clamp down on a surge of fury. He didn't want her gratitude, but one hell of a lot more. Keep cool, Dempsey, he warned himself. ''The best advice I can give you is to get used to it, Hester.''

''That's exactly what I can't do.'' Driven, she went to him. ''Mitch, I do care for you, but I'm not going to depend on you. I can't afford to expect or anticipate or rely.''

''So you've said.'' He set the card down carefully on the table. ''I'm not arguing.''

''What were you saying before—''

''What did I say?''

''About when we were married.''

''Did I say that?'' He smiled at her as he wound her hair around his finger. ''I don't know what I could have been thinking of.''

''Mitch, I have a feeling you're trying to throw me off guard.''

''Is it working?''

Treat it lightly, she told herself. If he wanted to make a game of it, she'd oblige him. ''Only to the point that it confirms what I've always thought about you. You're a very strange man.''

''In what context?''

''Okay, to begin with, you talk to your dog.''

''He talks back, so that doesn't count. Try again.'' With her hair still wound around his finger, he tugged her a bit closer. Whether she realized it or not, they were talking about their relationship, and she was relaxed.

''You write comic books for a living. And you read them.''

"Being a woman with banking experience, you should understand the importance of a good investment. Do you know what the double issue of my *Defenders of Perth* is worth to a collector? Modesty prevents me from naming figures."

"I bet it does."

He acknowledged this with a slight nod. "And, Mrs. Wallace, I'd be happy to debate the value of literature in any form with you. Did I mention that I was captain of the debating team in high school?"

"No." She had her hands on his chest, once again drawn to the tough, disciplined body beneath the tattered sweater. "There's also the fact that you haven't thrown out a newspaper or magazine in five years."

"I'm saving up for the big paper drive of the second millennium. Conservation is my middle name."

"You also have an answer for everything."

"There's only one I want from you. Did I mention that I fell for your eyes right after I fell for your legs?"

"No, you didn't." Her lips curved just a little. "I never told you that the first time I saw you, through the peephole, I stared at you for a long time."

"I know." He grinned back at her. "If you look in those things right, you can see a shadow."

"Oh," she said, and could think of nothing else to say.

"You know, Mrs. Wallace, those kids could come running back in here anytime. Do you mind if we stop talking for a few minutes?"

"No." She slipped her arms around him. "I don't mind at all."

She didn't want to admit even to herself that she felt safe, protected, with his arms around her. But she did. She didn't want to accept that she'd been afraid of losing him, terrified of the hole he would have left in her life. But the fear had been very real. It faded now as she lifted her lips to his.

She couldn't think about tomorrow or the future Mitch sketched so easily with talk of marriage and family. She'd been taught that marriage was forever, but she'd learned that it was a promise easily made and easily broken. There would be no more broken promises in her life, no more broken vows.

Feelings might rush through her, bringing with them longings and silver-dusted dreams. Her heart might be lost to him, but her will was still her own. Even as her hands gripped him tighter, pulled him closer, Hester told herself it was that will that would save them both unhappiness later.

"I love you, Hester." He murmured the words against her mouth, knowing she might not want to hear them but that it was something he had to say. If he said it enough, she might begin to believe the words and, more, the meaning behind them.

He wanted forever from her—forever for her—not just a moment like this, stolen in the sunlight that poured through the window, or other moments, taken in the shadows. Only once before had he wanted anything with something close to this intensity. That had been something abstract, something nebulous called art. The time had eventually come when he'd been forced to admit that dream would never be within reach.

But Hester was here in his arms. He could hold her like this and taste the sweet, warm longings that stirred in her. She wasn't a dream, but a woman he loved and wanted and would have. If keeping her meant playing games until the layers of her resistance were washed away, then he'd play.

He lifted his hands to her face, twining his fingers into her hair. "I guess the kids will be coming back."

"Probably." Her lips sought his again. Had she ever felt this sense of urgency before? "I wish we had more time."

"Do you?"

Her eyes were half-closed as he drew away. "Yes."

"Let me come back tonight."

"Oh, Mitch." She stepped into his arms to rest her head on his shoulder. For the first time in a decade, she found the mother and the woman at war. "I want you. You know that, don't you?"

Her heart was still pumping hard and fast against his. "I think I figured it out."

"I wish we could be together tonight, but there's Rad."

"I know how you feel about me staying here with Rad in the next room. Hester…" He ran his hands up her arms to rest them on her shoulders. "Why not be honest with him, tell him we care about each other and want to be together?"

"Mitch, he's only a baby."

"No, he's not. No, wait," he continued before she could speak again. "I'm not saying we should make it seem casual or careless, but that we should let Radley know how we feel about each other, and when two grown people feel this strongly about each other they need to show it."

It seemed so simple when he said it, so logical, so natural. Gathering her thoughts, she stepped back. "Mitch, Rad loves you, and he loves with the innocence and lack of restriction of a child."

"I love him, too."

She looked into his eyes and nodded. "Yes, I think you do, and if it's true, I hope you'll understand. I'm afraid that if I bring Radley into this at this point he'll come to depend on you even more than he already does. He'd come to look at you as..."

"As a father," Mitch finished. "You don't want a father in his life, do you, Hester?"

"That's not fair." Her eyes, usually so calm and clear, turned to smoke.

"Maybe not, but if I were you I'd give it some hard thought."

"There's no reason to say cruel things because I won't have sex with you when my son's sleeping in the next room."

He caught her by the shirt so fast she could only stare. She'd seen him annoyed, pushed close to the edge, but never furious. "Damn you, do you think that's all I'm talking about? If all I wanted was sex, I could go downstairs and pick up the phone. Sex is easy, Hester. All it takes is two people and a little spare time."

"I'm sorry." She closed her eyes, knowing she'd never said or done anything in her life she'd been more ashamed of. "That was stupid, Mitch, I just keep feeling as though my back's against the wall. I need some time, please."

"So do I. But the time I need is with you." He dropped his hands and stuck them in his pockets. "I'm pressuring you. I know it and I'm not going to stop, because I believe in us."

"I wish I could, also, honestly I do, but there's too much at stake for me."

And for himself, Mitch thought, but was calm

enough now to hold off. "We'll let it ride for a while. Are you and Rad up to hitting a few arcades at Times Square tonight?"

"Sure. He'd love it." She stepped toward him again. "So would I."

"You say that now, but you won't after I humiliate you with my superior skill."

"I love you."

He let out a long breath, fighting back the urge to grab her again and refuse to let go. "You going to let me know when you're comfortable with that?"

"You'll be the first."

He picked up the card Radley had made him. "Tell Rad I'll see him later."

"I will." He was halfway to the door when she started after him. "Mitch, why don't you come to dinner tomorrow? I'll fix a pot roast."

He tilted his head. "The kind with the little potatoes and carrots all around?"

"Sure."

"And biscuits?"

She smiled. "If you want."

"Sounds great, but I'm tied up."

"Oh." She struggled with the need to ask how, but reminded herself she didn't have the right.

Mitch smiled, selfishly pleased to see her disappointment. "Can I have a rain check?"

"Sure." She tried to answer the smile. "I guess Radley told you about his birthday next week," she said when Mitch reached the door.

"Only five or six times." He paused, his hand on the knob.

"He's having a party next Saturday afternoon. I know he'd like you to come if you can."

"I'll be there. Look, why don't we take off about seven? I'll bring the quarters."

"We'll be ready." He wasn't going to kiss her goodbye, she thought. "Mitch, I—"

"I almost forgot." Casually he reached in his back pocket and pulled out a small box.

"What is it?"

"It's Valentine's Day, isn't it?" He put it in her hand. "So this is a Valentine's Day present."

"A Valentine's Day present," she repeated dumbly.

"Yeah, tradition, remember? I thought about candy, but I figured you'd spend a whole lot of time making sure Radley didn't eat too much of it. But look, if you'd rather have candy, I'll just take this back and—"

"No." She pulled the box out of his reach, then laughed. "I don't even know what it is."

"You'd probably find out if you open the box."

Flipping the lid, she saw the thin gold chain that held a heart no bigger than her thumbnail. It glittered with the diamonds that formed it. "Oh, Mitch, it's gorgeous."

"Something told me it'd be a bigger hit with you than candy. Candy would have made you think about oral hygiene."

"I'm not that bad," she countered, then lifted the heart out of the box. "Mitch, it's really beautiful, I love it, but it's too—"

"Conventional, I know," he interrupted as he took it from her. "But I'm just that kind of guy."

"You are?"

"Just turn around and let me hook it for you."

She obeyed, lifting one hand up under her hair. "I do love it, but I don't expect you to buy me expensive presents."

"Um-hmm." His brows were drawn together as he worked the clasp. "I didn't expect bacon and eggs, but you seemed to get a kick out of fixing them." The clasp secured, he turned her around to face him. "I get a kick out of seeing you wear my heart around your neck."

"Thank you." She touched a finger to the heart. "I didn't buy you any candy, either, but maybe I can give you something else."

She was smiling when she kissed him, gently, teasingly, with a power that surprised them both. It took only an instant, an instant to be lost, to need, to imagine. His back was to the door as he moved his hands from her face to her hair to her shoulders, then to her hips to mold her even more truly against him. The fire burned, hot and fast, so that even when she drew away he felt singed by it. With his eyes on hers, Mitch let out a very long, very slow breath.

"I guess those kids will be coming back."

"Any minute."

"Uh-huh." He kissed her lightly on the brow before he turned and opened the door. "See you later."

He would go down to get Taz, Mitch thought as he started down the hall. Then he was going for a walk. A long one.

True to his word Mitch's pockets were filled with quarters. The arcades were packed with people and echoed with the pings and whistles and machine-gun sound effects of the games. Hester stood to the side as Mitch and Radley used their combined talents to save the world from intergalactic wars.

"Nice shooting, Corporal." Mitch slapped the boy's

shoulder as a Phaser II rocket disintegrated in a flash of colored light.

"It's your turn." Radley relinquished the controls to his superior officer. "Watch out for the sensor missiles."

"Don't worry. I'm a veteran."

"We're going to beat the high score." Radley tore his eyes away from the screen long enough to look at his mother. "Then we can put our initials up. Isn't this a neat place? It's got everything."

Everything, Hester thought, including some seamy-looking characters in leather and tattoos. The machine behind her let out a high-pitched scream. "Just stay close, okay?"

"Okay, Corporal, we're only seven hundred points away from the high score. Keep your eyes peeled for nuclear satellites."

"Aye, aye, sir." Radley clenched his jaw and took the controls.

"Good reflexes," Mitch said to Hester as he watched Radley control his ship with one hand and fire surface-to-air missiles with the other.

"Josh has one of those home video games. Rad loves to go over and play things like this." She caught her bottom lip between her teeth as Radley's ship barely missed annihilation. "I can never figure out how he can tell what's going on. Oh, look, he's passed the high score."

They continued to watch in tense silence as Radley fought bravely to the last man. As a finale, the screen exploded in brilliant fireworks of sound and light.

"A new record." Mitch hoisted Radley in the air. "This calls for a field promotion. Sergeant, inscribe your initials."

"But you got more points than I did."

"Who's counting? Go ahead."

Face flushed with pride, Radley clicked the button that ran through the alphabet. R.A.W. A for Allan, Mitch thought, and said nothing.

"My initials spell raw, and backward they spell war—pretty neat, huh?"

"Pretty neat," Mitch agreed. "Want to give it a shot, Hester?"

"No, thanks. I'll just watch."

"Mom doesn't like to play," Radley confided. "Her palms sweat."

"Your palms sweat?" Mitch repeated with a grin.

Hester sent a telling look in Radley's direction. "It's the pressure. I can't take being responsible for the fate of the world. I know it's a game," she said before Mitch could respond. "But I get, well, caught up."

"You're terrific, Mrs. Wallace." He kissed her as Radley looked on and considered.

It made him feel funny to see Mitch kiss his mother. He wasn't sure if it was a good funny or a bad funny. Then Mitch dropped a hand to his shoulder. It always made Radley feel nice when Mitch put his hand there.

"Okay, what'll it be next, the Amazon jungles, medieval times, a search for the killer shark?"

"I like the one with the ninja. I saw a ninja movie at Josh's once—well, almost did. Josh's mom turned it off because one of the women was taking her clothes off and stuff."

"Oh, yeah?" Mitch stifled a laugh as Hester's mouth dropped open. "What was the name?"

"Never mind." Hester gripped Radley's hand. "I'm sure Josh's parents just made a mistake."

"Josh's father thought it was about throwing stars

and kung fu. Josh's mom got mad and made him take it back to the video place and get something else. But I still like ninjas.''

"Let's see if we can find a free machine.'' Mitch fell into step beside Hester. "I don't think he was marked for life.''

"I'd still like to know what 'and stuff' means.''

"Me, too.'' He swung an arm around her shoulders to steer her through a clutch of teenagers. "Maybe we could rent it.''

"I'll pass, thanks.''

"You don't want to see *Naked Ninjas from Naga-saki?*'' When she turned around to stare at him, Mitch held out both hands, palms up. "I made it up. I swear.''

"Hmmm.''

"Here's one. Can I play this one?''

Mitch continued to grin at Hester as he dug out quarters.

The time passed so that Hester almost stopped hearing the noise from both machines and people. To placate Radley she played a few of the less intense games, ones that didn't deal with world domination or universal destruction. But for the most part she watched him, pleased to see him enjoying what was for him a real night on the town.

They must look like a family, she thought as Radley and Mitch bent over the controls in a head-to-head duel. She wished she still believed in such things. But to her, families and lifetime commitments were as fanciful as the machines that spewed out color and light around them.

Day-to-day, Hester thought with a little sigh. That was all she could afford to believe in now. In a few hours she would tuck Radley in bed and go to her room alone. That was the only way to make sure they were both safe. She heard Mitch laugh and shout encouragement to Radley, and looked away. It was the only way, she told herself again. No matter how much she wanted or was tempted to believe again, she couldn't risk it.

"How about the pinball machines?" Mitch suggested.

"They're okay." Though they rang with wild colors and lights, Radley didn't find them terribly exciting. "Mom likes them though."

"Are you any good?"

Hester pushed aside her uneasy thoughts. "Not bad."

"Care to go one-on-one?" He jingled the quarters in his pockets.

Though she'd never considered herself highly competitive, she was swayed by his smug look. "All right."

She'd always had a touch for pinball, a light enough, quick enough touch to have beaten her brother nine times out of ten. Though these machines were electronic and more sophisticated than the ones she'd played in her youth, she didn't doubt she could make a good showing.

"I could give you a handicap," Mitch suggested as he pushed coins into the slot.

"Funny, I was just going to say the same thing to you." With a smile, Hester took the controls.

It had something to do with black magic and white knights. Hester tuned out the sounds and concentrated on keeping the ball in play. Her timing was sharp.

Mitch stood behind her with his hands tucked in his back pockets and nodded as she sent the ball spinning.

He liked the way she leaned into the machine, her lips slightly parted, her eyes narrowed and alert. Now and then she would catch her tongue between her teeth and push her body forward as if to follow the ball on its quick, erratic course.

The little silver ball rammed into rubber, sending bells ringing and lights flashing. By the time her first ball dropped, she'd already racked up an impressive score.

"Not bad for an amateur," Mitch commented with a wink at Radley.

"I'm just warming up." With a smile, she stepped back.

Radley watched the progress of the ball as Mitch took control. But he had to stand on his toes to get the full effect. It was pretty neat when the ball got hung up in the top of the machine where the bumpers sent it vibrating back and forth in a blur. He glanced behind him at the rows of other machines and wished he'd thought to ask for another quarter before they'd started to play. But if he couldn't play, he could watch. He edged away to get a closer look at a nearby game.

"Looks like I'm ahead by a hundred," Mitch said as he stepped aside for Hester.

"I didn't want to blow you away with the first ball. It seemed rude." She pulled back the plunger and let the ball rip.

This time she had the feel and the rhythm down pat. She didn't let the ball rest as she set it right, then left, then up the middle where it streaked through a tunnel and crashed into a lighted dragon. It took her back to her childhood, when her wants had been simple and her dreams still gilt-edged. As the machine rocked with noise, she laughed and threw herself into the competition.

Her score flashed higher and higher with enough fanfare to draw a small crowd. Before her second ball dropped, people were choosing up sides.

Mitch took position. Unlike Hester, he didn't block out the sounds and lights, but used them to pump the adrenaline. He nearly lost the ball, causing indrawn breaths behind him, but caught it on the tip of his flipper to shoot it hard into a corner. This time he finished fifty points behind her.

The third and final turn brought more people. Hester thought she heard someone placing bets before she tuned them out and put all her concentration on the ball and her timing. She was nearly exhausted before she backed away again.

"You're going to need a miracle, Mitch."

"Don't get cocky." He flicked his wrists like a concert pianist and earned a few hoots and cheers from the crowd.

Hester had to admit as she watched his technique that he played brilliantly. He took chances that could have cost him his last ball, but turned them into triumph. He stood spread-legged and relaxed, but she saw in his eyes that kind of deep concentration that she'd come to expect from him, but had yet to become used to. His hair fell over his forehead, as careless as he was. There was a slight smile on his face that struck her as both pleased and reckless.

She found herself watching him rather than the ball as she toyed with the little diamond heart she'd worn over a plain black turtleneck.

This was the kind of man women dreamed about

and made heroes of. This was the kind of man a woman could come to lean upon if she wasn't careful. With a man like him, a woman could have years of laughter. The defenses around her heart weakened a bit with her sigh.

The ball was lost in the dragon's cave with a series of roars.

"She got you by ten points," someone in the crowd pointed out. "Ten points, buddy."

"Got yourself a free game," someone else said, giving Hester a friendly slap on the back.

Mitch shook his head as he wiped his hands on the thighs of his jeans. "About that handicap—" he began.

"Too late." Ridiculously pleased with herself, Hester hooked her thumbs in her belt loops and studied her score. "Superior reflexes. It's all in the wrist."

"How about a rematch?"

"I don't want to humiliate you again." She turned, intending to offer Radley the free game. "Rad, why don't you...Rad?" She nudged her way through the few lingering onlookers. "Radley?" A little splinter of panic shot straight up her spine. "He's not here."

"He was here a minute ago." Mitch put a hand on her arm and scanned what he could see of the room.

"I wasn't paying any attention." She brought a hand up to her throat, where the fear had already lodged, and began to walk quickly. "I know better than to take my eyes off him in a place like this."

"Stop." He kept his voice calm, but her fear had already transferred itself to him. He knew how easy it was to whisk one small boy away in a crowd. You couldn't pour your milk in the morning without being aware of it. "He's just wandering around the machines.

We'll find him. I'll go around this way, you go down here.''

She nodded and spun away without a word. They were six or seven deep at some of the machines. Hester stopped at each one, searching for a small blond boy in a blue sweater. She called for him over the noise and clatter of machines.

When she passed the big glass doors and looked outside to the lights and crowded sidewalks of Times Square, her heart turned over in her breast. He hadn't gone outside, she told herself. Radley would never do something so expressly forbidden. Unless someone had taken him, or…

Gripping her hands together tightly, she turned away. She wouldn't think like that. But the room was so big, filled with so many people, all strangers. And the noise, the noise was more deafening than she'd remembered. How could she have heard him if he'd called out for her?

She started down the next row, calling. Once she heard a young boy laugh and spun around. But it wasn't Radley. She'd covered half the room, and ten minutes was gone, when she thought she would have to call the police. She quickened her pace and tried to look everywhere at once as she went from row to row.

There was so much noise, and the lights were so bright. Maybe she should double back—she might have missed him. Maybe he was waiting for her now by that damn pinball machine, wondering where she'd gone. He might be afraid. He could be calling for her. He could be…

Then she saw him, hoisted in Mitch's arms. Hester shoved two people aside as she ran for them. ''Radley!'' She threw her arms around both of them and buried her face in his hair.

"He'd gone over to watch someone play," Mitch began as he stroked a hand up and down her back. "He ran into someone he knew from school."

"It was Ricky Nesbit, Mom. He was with his big brother, and they lent me a quarter. We went to play a game. I didn't know it was so far away."

"Radley." She struggled with the tears and kept her voice firm. "You know the rules about staying with me. This is a big place with a lot of people. I have to be able to trust you not to wander away."

"I didn't mean to; it was just that Ricky said it would just take a minute. I was coming right back."

"Rules have reasons, Radley, and we've been through them."

"But, Mom—"

"Rad." Mitch shifted the boy in his arms. "You scared your mother and me."

"I'm sorry," His eyes clouded up. "I didn't mean to make you scared."

"Don't do it again." Her voice softened as she kissed his cheek. "Next time it's solitary confinement. You're all I've got, Rad." She hugged him again. Her eyes were closed so that she didn't see the change in Mitch's expression. "I can't let anything happen to you."

"I won't do it again."

All she had, Mitch thought as he set the boy down. Was she still so stubborn that she couldn't admit, even to herself, that she had someone else now, too? He jammed his hands into his pockets and tried to force back both anger and hurt. She was going to have to make room in her life soon, very soon, or he'd damn well make it for her.

Chapter 11

He wasn't sure if he was doing more harm than good by staying out of Hester's way for a few days, but Mitch needed time himself. It wasn't his style to dissect and analyze, but to feel and act. However, he'd never felt quite this strongly before or acted quite so rashly.

When possible, he buried himself in work and in the fantasies he could control. When it wasn't, he stayed alone in his rooms, with old movies flickering on the television or music blaring through the stereo. He continued to work on the screenplay he didn't know if he could write, in the hope that the challenge of it would stop him from marching two floors up and demanding that Hester Wallace came to her senses.

She wanted him, yet she didn't want him. She opened to him, yet kept the most precious part of her closed. She trusted him, yet didn't believe in him enough to share her life with him.

You're all I've got, Rad. And all she wanted? Mitch was forced to ask himself the question. How could such a bright, giving woman base the rest of her life on a mistake she'd made over ten years before?

The helplessness of it infuriated him. Even when he'd hit bottom in New Orleans, he hadn't been helpless. He'd faced his limitations, accepted them, and had channeled his talents differently. Had the time come for him to face and accept his limitations with Hester?

He spent hours thinking about it, considering compromises and then rejecting them. Could he do as she asked and leave things as they were? They would be lovers, with no promises between them and no talk of a future. They could have a relationship as long as there was no hint of permanency or bonds. No, he couldn't do as she asked. Now that he had found the only woman he wanted in his life, he couldn't accept her either part-time or partway.

It was something of a shock to discover he was such an advocate of marriage. He couldn't say that he'd seen very many that had been made in heaven. His parents had been well suited—the same tastes, the same class, the same outlook—but he couldn't remember ever witnessing any passion between them. Affection and loyalty, yes, and a united front against their son's ambitions, but they lacked the spark and simmer that added excitement.

He asked himself if it was only passion he felt for Hester, but knew the answer already. Even as he sat alone he could imagine them twenty years in the future, sitting on the porch swing she'd described. He could see them growing older together, filing away memories and traditions.

He wasn't going to lose that. However long it took,

however many walls he had to scale, he wasn't going to lose that.

Mitch dragged a hand through his hair, then gathered up the boxes he needed to lug upstairs.

She was afraid he wasn't coming. There had been some subtle change in Mitch since the night they'd gone to Times Square. He'd been strangely distant on the phone, and though she'd invited him up more than once, he'd always made an excuse.

She was losing him. Hester poured punch into paper cups and reminded herself that she'd known it was only temporary. He had the right to live his own life, to go his own way. She could hardly expect him to tolerate the distance she felt she had to put between them or to understand the lack of time and attention she could give him because of Radley and her job. All she could hope was that he would remain a friend.

Oh, God, she missed him. She missed having him to talk to, to laugh with, even to lean on—though she could only allow herself to lean a little. Hester set the pitcher on the counter and took a deep breath. It couldn't matter, she couldn't *let* it matter now. There were ten excited and noisy boys in the other room. Her responsibility, she reminded herself. She couldn't stand here listing her regrets when she had obligations.

As she carried the tray of drinks into the living room, two boys shot by her. Three more were wrestling on the floor, while the others shouted to be heard over the record player. Hester had already noted that one of Radley's newest friends wore a silver earring and spoke knowledgeably about girls. She set the tray down and glanced quickly at the ceiling.

Give me a few more years of comic books and erector sets. Please, I'm just not ready for the rest of it yet.

"Drink break," she said out loud. "Michael, why don't you let Ernie out of that headlock now and have some punch? Rad, set down the kitten. They get cranky if they're handled too much."

With reluctance, Radley set the little bundle of black-and-white fur in a padded basket. "He's really neat. I like him the best." He snatched a drink off the tray as several other hands reached out. "I really like my watch, too." He held it out, pushing a button that sent it from time mode to the first in a series of miniature video games.

"Just make sure you don't play with it when you should be paying attention in school."

Several boys groaned and elbowed Radley. Hester had just about convinced them to settle down with one of Radley's board games when the knock sounded at the door.

"I'll get it!" Radley hopped up and raced for the door. He had one more birthday wish. When he opened the door, it came true. "Mitch! I knew you'd come. Mom said you'd probably gotten real busy, but I knew you'd come. I got a kitten. I named him Zark. Want to see?"

"As soon as I get rid of some of these boxes." Even arms as well tuned as his were beginning to feel the strain. Mitch set them on the sofa and turned, only to have Zark's namesake shoved into his hands. The kitten purred and arched under a stroking finger. "Cute. We'll have to take him down and introduce him to Taz."

"Won't Taz eat him?"

"You've got to be kidding." Mitch tucked the kitten under his arm and looked at Hester. "Hi."

"Hi." He needed a shave, his sweater had a hole in the seam, and he looked wonderful. "We were afraid you wouldn't make it."

"I said I'd be here." Lazily he scratched between the kitten's ears. "I keep my promises."

"I got this watch, too." Radley held up his wrist. "It tells the time and the date and stuff, then you can play Dive Bomb and Scrimmage."

"Oh, yeah, Dive Bomb?" Mitch sat on the arm of the couch and watched Radley send the little dots spinning. "Never have to be bored on a long subway ride again, right?"

"Or at the dentist's office. You want to play?"

"Later. I'm sorry I'm late. I got hung up in the store."

"That's okay. We didn't have the cake yet 'cause I wanted to wait. It's chocolate."

"Great. Aren't you going to ask for your present?"

"I'm not supposed to." He sneaked a look at his mother, who was busy keeping some of his friends from wrestling again. "Did you really get me something?"

"Nah." Laughing at Radley's expression, he ruffled his hair. "Sure I did. It's right there on the couch."

"Which one?"

"All of them."

Radley's eyes grew big as saucers. "All of them?"

"They all sort of go together. Why don't you open that one first?"

Because of the lack of time and materials, Mitch hadn't wrapped the boxes. He'd barely had enough forethought to put tape over the name brand and model, but buying presents for young boys was a new experience, and one he'd enjoyed immensely. Radley began to pry open the heavy cardboard with assistance from his more curious friends.

"Wow, a PC." Josh craned his head over Radley's shoulder. "Robert Sawyer's got one just like it. You can play all kinds of things on it."

"A computer." Radley stared in amazement at the open box, then turned to Mitch. "Is it for me, really? To keep?"

"Sure you can keep it; it's a present. I was hoping you'd let me play with it sometime."

"You can play with it anytime, anytime you want." He threw his arms around Mitch's neck, forgetting to be embarrassed because his friends were watching. "Thanks. Can we hook it up right now?"

"I thought you'd never ask."

"Rad, you'll have to clear off the desk in your room. Hold it," Hester added when a flood of young bodies started by. "That doesn't mean shoving everything on the floor, okay? You take care of it properly, and Mitch and I will bring this in."

They streaked away with war whoops that warned her she'd be finding surprises under Radley's bed and under the rug for some time. She'd worry about that later. Now she crossed the room to stand beside Mitch.

"That was a terribly generous thing to do."

"He's bright. A kid that bright deserves one of these."

"Yes." She looked at the boxes yet to be opened. There'd be a monitor, disk drives, software. "I've wanted to get him one, but haven't been able to swing it."

"I didn't mean that as a criticism, Hester."

"I know you didn't." She gnawed at her lip in a gesture that told him her nerves were working at her. "I also know this isn't the time to talk; and that we have to. But before we take this in to Rad, I want to tell you how glad I am that you're here."

"It's where I want to be." He ran a thumb along her jawline. "You're going to have to start believing that."

She took his hand and turned her lips into his palm. "You might not feel the same way after you spend the next hour or so with ten fifth-graders." She smiled as the first minor crash sounded from Radley's bedroom. "'Once more unto the breach'?"

The crash was followed by several young voices raised in passionate argument. "How about, 'Lay on, MacDuff'?"

"Whatever." Drawing a deep breath, Hester lifted the first box.

It was over. The last birthday guest had been dragged away by his parents. A strange and wonderful silence lay over the living room. Hester sat in a chair, her eyes half-closed, while Mitch lay sprawled on the couch with his closed completely. In the silence Hester could hear the occasional click of Radley's new computer, and the mewing of Zark, who sat in his lap. With a contented sigh, she surveyed the living room.

It was in shambles. Paper cups and plates were strewn everywhere. The remains of potato chips and pretzels were in bowls, with a good portion of them crushed into the carpet. Scraps of wrapping paper were scattered among the toys the boys had decided worthy of attention. She didn't want to dwell on what the kitchen looked like.

Mitch opened one eye and looked at her. "Did we win?"

"Absolutely." Reluctantly, Hester dragged herself up. "It was a brilliant victory. Want a pillow?"

"No." Taking her hand, he flipped her down on top of him.

"Mitch, Radley is—"

"Playing with his computer," he finished, then nuzzled her bottom lip. "I'm betting he breaks down and puts some of the educational software in before it's over."

"It was pretty clever of you to mix those in."

"I'm a pretty clever kind of guy." He shifted her until she fit into the curve of his shoulder. "Besides, I figured I'd win you over with the machine's practicality, and Rad and I could play the games."

"I'm surprised you don't have one of your own."

"Actually…it seemed like such a good idea when I went in for Rad's that I picked up two. To balance my household accounts," he said when Hester looked up at him. "And modernize my filing system."

"You don't have a filing system."

"See?" He settled his cheek on her hair. "Hester, do you know what one of the ten greatest boons to civilization is?"

"The microwave oven?"

"The afternoon nap. This is a great sofa you've got here."

"It needs reupholstering."

"You can't see that when you're lying on it." He tucked his arm around her waist. "Sleep with me awhile."

"I really have to clean up." But she found it easy to close her eyes.

"Why? Expecting company?"

"No. But don't you have to go down and take Taz out?"

"I slipped Ernie a couple of bucks to walk him."

Hester snuggled into his shoulder. "You are clever."

"That's what I've been trying to tell you."

"I haven't even thought about dinner," she murmured as her mind began to drift.

"Let 'em eat cake."

With a quiet laugh, she slipped into sleep beside him.

Radley wandered in a few moments later, the kitten curled in his arms. He'd wanted to tell them about his latest score. Standing at the foot of the sofa, he scratched the kitten's ears and studied his mom and Mitch thoughtfully. Sometimes when he had a bad dream or wasn't feeling very good, his mom would sleep with him. It always made him feel better. Maybe sleeping with Mitch made his mom feel better.

He wondered if Mitch loved his mom. It made his stomach feel funny to think about it. He wanted Mitch to stay and be his friend. If they got married, did that mean Mitch would go away? He would have to ask, Radley decided. His mom always told him the truth. Shifting the kitten to one arm, he lifted the bowl of chips and carried it into his room.

It was nearly dark when she awoke. Hester opened her eyes and looked directly into Mitch's. She blinked, trying to orient herself. Then he kissed her, and she remembered everything.

"We must have slept for an hour," she murmured.

"Closer to two. How do you feel?"

"Groggy. I always feel groggy if I sleep during the day." She stretched her shoulders and heard Radley giggling in his room. "He must still be at that computer. I don't think I've ever seen him happier."

"And you?"

"Yes." She traced his lips with her fingertip. "I'm happy."

"If you're groggy and happy, this might be the perfect time for me to ask you to marry me again."

"Mitch."

"No? Okay, I'll wait until I can get you drunk. Any more of that cake left?"

"A little. You're not angry?"

Mitch combed his fingers through his hair as he sat up. "About what?"

Hester put her hands on his shoulders, then rested her cheek on his. "I'm sorry I can't give you what you want."

He tightened his arms around her; then with an effort, he relaxed. "Good. That means you're close to changing your mind. I'd like a double-ring ceremony."

"Mitch!"

"What?"

She drew back and, because she didn't trust his smile, shook her head. "Nothing. I think it's best to say nothing. Go ahead and help yourself to the cake. I'm going to get started in here."

Mitch glanced around the room, which looked to be in pretty good shape by his standards. "You really want to clean this up tonight?"

"You don't expect me to leave this mess until the morning," she began, then stopped herself. "Forget I said that. I forgot who I was talking to."

Mitch narrowed his eyes suspiciously. "Are you accusing me of being sloppy?"

"Not at all. I'm sure there's a lot to be said for living in a 'junkyard' decor with a touch of 'paper drive' thrown in. It's uniquely you." She began to gather up paper plates. "It probably comes from having maids as a child."

"Actually, it comes from never being able to mess up a room. My mother couldn't stand disorder." He'd always been fond of it, Mitch mused, but there was something to be said for watching Hester tidy up. "For my tenth birthday, she hired a magician. We sat in little folding chairs—the boys in suits, the girls in organdy dresses—and watched the performance. Then we were served a light lunch on the terrace. There were enough servants around so that when it was over there wasn't a crumb to be picked up. I guess I'm overcompensating."

"Maybe a little." She kissed both of his cheeks. What an odd man he was, she thought, so calm and easygoing on one hand, so driven by demons on the other. She strongly believed that childhood affected adulthood, even to old age. It was the strength of that belief that made her so fiercely determined to do the best she could by Radley. "You're entitled to your dust and clutter, Mitch. Don't let anyone take it away from you."

He kissed her cheek in return. "I guess you're entitled to your neat and tidy. Where's your vacuum?"

She drew back, brow lifted. "Do you know what one is?"

"Cute. Very cute." He pinched her, hard, just under the ribs. Hester jumped back with a squeal. "Ah, ticklish, huh?"

"Cut it out," she warned, holding out the stack of paper plates like a shield. "I wouldn't want to hurt you."

"Come on." He crouched like a wrestler. "Two falls out of three."

"I'm warning you." Wary of the gleam in his eye, she backed up as he advanced. "I'll get violent."

"Promise?" He lunged, gripping her under the waist. In reflex, Hester lifted her arms. The plates, dripping with cake and ice cream, caught him full in the face. "Oh, God." Her own scream of laughter had her falling backward into a chair. She opened her mouth to speak, but only doubled up again.

Very slowly Mitch wiped a hand over his cheek, then studied the smear of chocolate. Watching, Hester let out another peal of laughter and held her sides helplessly.

"What's going on?" Radley came into the living room staring at his mother, who could do nothing but point. Shifting his gaze, Radley stared in turn at Mitch. "Jeez." Radley rolled his eyes and began to giggle. "Mike's little sister gets food all over her face like that. She's almost two."

The control Hester had been scratching for slipped out of her grip. Choking with laughter, she pulled Radley against her. "It was—it was an accident," she managed, then collapsed again.

"It was a deliberate sneak attack," Mitch corrected. "And it calls for immediate retribution."

"Oh, please." Hester held out a hand, knowing she was too weak to defend herself. "I'm sorry. I swear. It was a reflex, that's all."

"So's this." He came closer, and though she ducked behind Radley, Mitch merely sandwiched the giggling boy between them. And he kissed her, her mouth, her nose, her cheeks, while she squirmed and laughed and struggled. When he was finished, he'd transferred a satisfactory amount of chocolate to her face. Radley took one look at his mother and slipped, cackling, to the floor.

"Maniac," she accused as she wiped chocolate from her chin with the back of her hand.

"You look beautiful in chocolate, Hester."

It took more than an hour to put everything to rights again. By popular vote, they ended up sharing a pizza as they once had before, then spending the rest of the evening trying out Radley's birthday treasures. When he began to nod over the keyboard, Hester nudged him into bed.

"Quite a day." Hester set the kitten in his basket at the foot of Radley's bed, then stepped out into the hall.

"I'd say it's a birthday he'll remember."

"So will I." She reached up to rub at a slight stiffness at the base of her neck. "Would you like some wine?"

"I'll get it." He turned her toward the living room. "Go sit down."

"Thanks." Hester sat on the couch, stretched out her legs and slipped off her shoes. It was definitely a day she would remember. Sometime during it, she'd come to realize that she could also have a night to remember.

"Here you go." Mitch handed her a glass of wine, then slipped onto the sofa beside her. Holding his own glass up, he shifted her so that she rested against him.

"This is nice." With a sigh, she brought the wine to her lips.

"Very nice." He bent to brush his lips over her neck. "I told you this was a great sofa."

"Sometimes I forget what it's like to relax like this. Everything's done, Radley's happy and tucked into bed, tomorrow's Sunday and there's nothing urgent to think about."

"No restless urge to go out dancing or carousing?"

"No." She stretched her shoulders. "You?"

"I'm happy right here."

"Then stay." She pressed her lips together a moment. "Stay tonight."

He was silent. His hand stopped its easy massage of her neck, then began again, slowly. "Are you sure that's what you want?"

"Yes." She drew a deep breath before she turned to look at him. "I've missed you. I wish I knew what was right and what was wrong, what was best for all of us, but I know I've missed you. Will you stay?"

"I'm not going anywhere."

She settled back against him, content. For a long time they sat just as they were, half dreaming, in silence, with lamplight glowing behind them.

"Are you still working on the script?" she asked at length.

"Mmm-hmm." He could get used to this, he thought, very used to having Hester snuggled beside him in the late evening with the lamplight dim and the scent of her hair teasing his senses. "You were right. I'd have hated myself if I hadn't tried to write it. I guess I had to get past the nerves."

"Nerves?" She smiled over her shoulder. "You?"

"I've been known to have them, when something's either unfamiliar or important. They were stretched pretty thin the first time I made love with you."

Hearing it not only surprised her but made the memory of it all the sweeter. "They didn't show."

"Take my word for it." He stroked the outside of her thigh, lightly and with a casualness that was its own kind of seduction. "I was afraid that I'd make the wrong move and screw up something that was more important than anything else in my life."

"You didn't make any wrong moves, and you make me feel very special."

When she rose, it felt natural to hold out a hand to him, to have his close over hers. She switched off lights as they walked to the bedroom.

Mitch closed the door. Hester turned down the bed. He knew it could be like this every night, for all the years they had left. She was on the edge of believing it. He knew it, he could see it in her eyes when he crossed to her. Her eyes remained on his while she unbuttoned her blouse.

They undressed in silence, but the air had already started to hum. Though nerves had relaxed, anticipation was edgier than ever. Now they knew what they could bring to each other. They slipped into bed together and turned to each other.

It felt so right, just the way his arms slipped around her to bring her close. Just the way their bodies met, merging warmth to warmth. She knew the feel of him now, the firmness, the strength. She knew how easily hers fit against it. She tipped her head back and, with her eyes still on his, offered her mouth.

Kissing him was like sliding down a cool river toward churning white water.

The sound of pleasure came deep in his throat as she pressed against him. The shyness was still there, but without the reserve and hesitation. Now there was only sweetness and an offering.

It was like this each time they came together. Exhilarating, stunning and right. He cupped the back of her head in his hand as she leaned over him. The light zing of the wine hadn't completely faded from her tongue. He tasted it, and her, as she explored his mouth. He sensed a boldness growing in her that hadn't been there before, a new confidence that caused her to come to him with her own demands and needs.

Her heart was open, he thought as her lips raced over his throat. And Hester was free. He'd wanted this for her—for them. With something like a laugh, he rolled over her and began to drive her toward madness.

She couldn't get enough of him. She took her hands, her mouth, over him quickly, almost fiercely, but found it impossible to assuage the greed. How could she have known a man could feel so good, so exciting? How could she have known that the scent of his skin would make her head reel and her desires sharpen? Just her name murmured in his voice aroused her.

Locked together, they tumbled over the sheets, tangling in the blanket, shoving it aside because the need for its warmth was long past. He moved as quickly as she, discovering new secrets to delight and torment her. She heard him gasp out her name as she ranged kisses over his chest. She felt his body tense and arch as she moved her hands lower.

Perhaps the power had always been there inside her, but Hester was certain it had been born in her that night. The power to arouse a man past the civilized, and perhaps past the wise. Wise or not, she gloried in it when he trapped her beneath him and let desire rule.

His mouth was hot and hungry as it raced over her.

Demands, promises, pleas swirled through her head, but she couldn't speak. Even her breath was trapped as he drove her up and up. She caught him close, as though he were a lifeline in a sea that raged.

Then they both went under.

Chapter 12

The sky was cloudy and threatening snow. Half dozing, Hester turned away from the window to reach for Mitch. The bed beside her was rumpled but empty.

Had he left her during the night? she wondered as she ran her hand over the sheets where he'd slept. Her first reaction was disappointment. It would have been so sweet to have had him there to turn to in the morning. Then she drew her hand back and cupped it under her cheek.

Perhaps it was best that he'd gone. She couldn't be sure how Radley would feel. If Mitch was there to reach out to, she knew it would only become more difficult to keep herself from doing so again and again. No one knew how hard and painfully she'd worked to stop herself from needing anyone. Now, after all the years of struggling, she'd just begun to see real progress. She'd made a good home for Radley in a good neighborhood and had a strong, well-paying job. Security, stability.

She couldn't risk those things again for the emotional morass that came with depending on someone else. But she was already beginning to depend on him, Hester thought as she pushed back the blankets. No matter how much her head told her it was best that he wasn't here, she was sorry he wasn't. She *was* sorry, sorrier than he could ever know, that she was strong enough to stand apart from him.

Hester slipped on her robe and went to see if Radley wanted breakfast.

She found them together, hunched over the keyboard of Radley's computer while graphics exploded on the screen. "This thing's defective," Mitch insisted. "That was a dead-on shot."

"You missed by a mile."

"I'm going to tell your mother you need glasses. Look, this is definite interference. How am I supposed to concentrate when this stupid cat's chewing on my toes?"

"Poor sportsmanship," Radley said soberly as Mitch's last man was obliterated.

"Poor sportsmanship! I'll show you poor sportsmanship." With that he snatched Radley up and held him upside down. "Now is this machine defective, or what?"

"No." Giggling, Radley braced his hands on the floor. "Maybe *you* need glasses."

"I'm going to have to drop you on your head. You really leave me no choice. Oh, hi, Hester." With his arm hooked around Radley's legs, he smiled at her.

"Hi, Mom!" Though his cheeks were turning pink,

Radley was delighted with his upside-down position. "I beat Mitch three times. But he's not really mad."

"Says who?" Mitch flipped the boy upright, then dropped him lightly on the bed. "I've been humiliated."

"I destroyed him," Radley said with satisfaction.

"I can't believe I slept through it." She offered them both a cautious smile. It didn't seem as though Radley was anything but delighted to find Mitch here. As for herself, she wasn't having an easy time keeping the pleasure down, either. "I suppose after three major battles you'd both like some breakfast."

"We already ate." Radley leaned over the bed to reach for the kitten. "I showed Mitch how to make French toast. He said it was real good."

"That was before you cheated."

"I did not." Radley rolled on his back and let the kitten creep up his stomach. "Mitch washed the pan, and I dried it. We were going to fix you some, but you just kept on sleeping."

The idea of the two men in her life fiddling in the kitchen while she slept left her flustered. "I guess I didn't expect anyone to be up so early."

"Hester." Mitch stepped closer to swing an arm over her shoulders. "I hate to break this to you, but it's after eleven."

"Eleven?"

"Yeah. How about lunch?"

"Well, I..."

"You think about it. I guess I should go down and take care of Taz."

"I'll do it." Radley was up and bouncing. "I can give him his food and take him for a walk and everything. I know how, you showed me."

"It's okay with me. Hester?"

She was having trouble just keeping up. "All right. But you'll have to bundle up."

"I will." He was already reaching for his coat. "Can I bring Taz back with me? He hasn't met Zark yet."

Hester glanced at the tiny ball of fur, thinking of Taz's big white teeth. "I don't know if Taz would care for Zark."

"He loves cats," Mitch assured her as he picked up Radley's ski cap off the floor. "In a purely noncannibalistic way." He reached in his pocket for his keys.

"Be careful," she called as Radley rushed by, jingling Mitch's keys. The front door slammed with a vengeance.

"Good morning," Mitch said, and turned her into his arms.

"Good morning. You could have woken me up."

"It was tempting." He ran his hands up the back of her robe. "Actually, I was going to make some coffee and bring you in a cup. Then Radley came in. Before I knew it, I was up to my wrists in egg batter."

"He, ah, didn't wonder what you were doing here?"

"No." Knowing exactly how her mind was working, he kissed the tip of her nose. Then, shifting her to his side, he began to walk with her to the kitchen. "He came in while I was boiling water and asked if I was fixing breakfast. After a brief consultation, we decided he was the better qualified of the two. There's some coffee left, but I think you'd be better off pouring it out and starting again."

"I'm sure it's fine."

"I love an optimist."

She almost managed a smile as she reached in the refrigerator for the milk. "I thought you'd gone."

"Would you rather I had?"

She shook her head but didn't look at him. "Mitch, it's so hard. It just keeps getting harder."

"What does?"

"Trying not to want you here like this all the time."

"Say the word and I'll move in, bag and dog."

"I wish I could. I really wish I could. Mitch, when I walked into Rad's bedroom this morning and saw the two of you together, something just clicked. I stood there thinking this is the way it could be for us."

"That's the way it *will* be for us, Hester."

"You're so sure." With a small laugh, she turned to lean her palms on the counter. "You're so absolutely sure, and have been almost from the beginning. Maybe that's one of the things that frightens me."

"A light went on for me when I saw you, Hester." He came closer to put his hands on her shoulders. "I haven't gone through my life knowing exactly what I wanted, and I can't claim that everything always goes the way I'd planned, but with you I'm sure." He pressed his lips to her hair. "Do you love me, Hester?"

"Yes." With a long sigh, she shut her eyes. "Yes, I love you."

"Then marry me." Gently he turned her around to face him. "I won't ask you to change anything but your name."

She wanted to believe him, to believe it was possible to start a new life just once more. Her heart was thudding hard against her ribs as she wrapped her arms around him. *Take the chance,* it seemed to be telling her. *Don't throw love away.* Her fingers tensed against him. "Mitch, I—" When the phone rang, Hester let out a pent-up breath. "I'm sorry."

"So am I," he muttered, but released her.

Her legs were still unsteady as she picked up the receiver to the wall phone. "Hello." The giddiness fled, and with it all the blossoming pleasure. "Allan."

Mitch looked around quickly. Her eyes were as flat as her voice. She'd already twisted the phone cord around her hand as if she wanted to anchor herself. "Fine," she said. "We're both fine. Florida? I thought you were in San Diego."

So he'd moved again, Hester thought as she listened to the familiar voice, restless as ever. She listened with the cold patience of experience as he told her how wonderful, how terrific, how incredibly he was doing.

"Rad isn't here at the moment," she told him, though Allan hadn't asked. "If you want to wish him a happy birthday, I can have him call you back." There was a pause, and Mitch saw her eyes change and the anger come. "Yesterday." She set her teeth, then took a long breath through them. "He's ten, Allan. Radley was ten yesterday. Yes, I'm sure it's difficult for you to imagine."

She fell silent again, listening. The dull anger lodged itself in her throat, and when she spoke again, her voice was hollow. "Congratulations. Hard feelings?" She didn't care for the sound of her own laugh. "No, Allan, there are no feelings whatsoever. All right, then, good luck. I'm sorry, that's as enthusiastic as it gets. I'll tell Radley you called."

She hung up, careful to bolt down the need to slam down the receiver. Slowly she unwound the cord which was biting into her hand.

"You okay?"

She nodded and walked to the stove to pour coffee she didn't want. "He called to tell me he's getting married again. He thought I'd be interested."

"Does it matter?"

"No." She sipped it black and welcomed the bitterness. "What he does stopped mattering years ago. He didn't know it was Radley's birthday." The anger came bubbling to the surface no matter how hard she tried to keep it submerged. "He didn't even know how old he was." She slammed the cup down so that coffee sloshed over the sides. "Radley stopped being real for him the minute he walked out the door. All he had to do was shut it behind him."

"What difference does it make now?"

"He's Radley's father."

"No." His own anger sprang out. "That's something you've got to work out of your system, something you've got to start accepting. The only part he played in Rad's life was biological. There's no trick to that, and no automatic bond of loyalty comes with it."

"He has a responsibility."

"He doesn't want it, Hester." Struggling for patience, he took her hands. "He's cut himself off from Rad completely. No one's going to call that admirable, and it's obvious it wasn't done for the boy's sake. But would you rather have him strolling in and out of Radley's life at his own whim, leaving the kid confused and hurting?"

"No, but I—"

"You want him to care, and he doesn't care." Though her hands remained in his, he felt the change. "You're pulling back from me."

It was true. She could regret it, but she couldn't stop it. "I don't want to."

"But you are." This time, it was he who pulled away. "It only took a phone call."

"Mitch, please try to understand."

"I've been trying to understand." There was an edge to his voice now that she hadn't heard before. "The man left you, and it hurt, but it's been over a long time."

"It's not the hurt," she began, then dragged a hand through her hair. "Or maybe it is, partly. I don't want to go through that ever again, the fear, the emptiness. I loved him. You have to understand that maybe I was young, maybe I was stupid, but I loved him."

"I've always understood that," he said, though he didn't like to hear it. "A woman like you doesn't make promises lightly."

"No, when I make them I mean to keep them. I wanted to keep this one." She picked up the coffee again, wrapping both hands around the cup to keep them warm. "I can't tell you how badly I wanted to keep my marriage together, how hard I tried. I gave up part of myself when I married Allan. He told me we were going to move to New York, we were going to do things in a big way, and I went. Leaving my home, my family and friends was the most terrifying thing I'd ever done, but I went because he wanted it. Almost everything I did during our marriage I did because he wanted it. And because it was easier to go along than to refuse. I built my life around his. Then, at the age of twenty, I discovered I didn't have a life at all."

"So you made one, for yourself and for Radley. That's something to be proud of."

"I am. It's taken me eight years, eight years to feel I'm really on solid ground again. Now there's you."

"Now there's me," he said slowly, watching her. "And you just can't get past the idea that I'll pull the rug out from under you again."

"I don't want to be that woman again." She said the words desperately, searching for the answers even as she struggled to give them to him. "A woman who focuses all her needs and goals around someone else. If I found myself alone this time, I'm not sure I could stand up again."

"Listen to yourself. You'd rather be alone now than risk the fact that things might not work out for the next fifty years? Take a good look at me, Hester, I'm not Allan Wallace. I'm not asking you to bury yourself to make me happy. It's the woman you are today who I love, the woman you are today who I want to spend my life with."

"People change, Mitch."

"And they can change together." He drew a deep breath. "Or they can change separately. Why don't you let me know when you make up your mind what you want to do?"

She opened her mouth, then closed it again when he walked away. She didn't have the right to call him back.

He shouldn't complain, Mitch thought as he sat at his new keyboard and toyed with the next scene in his script. The work was going better than he'd expected— and faster. It was becoming easy for him to bury himself in Zark's problems and let his own stew.

At this point, Zark was waiting by Leilah's bedside, praying that she would survive the freak accident that had left her beauty intact but her brain damaged. Of course, when she awoke she would be a stranger. His wife of two years would become his greatest enemy, her mind as brilliant as ever but warped and evil. All his plans and dreams would be shattered forever. Whole galaxies would be in peril.

"You think you've got problems?" Mitch muttered. "Things aren't exactly bouncing along for me, either."

Eyes narrowed, he studied the screen. The atmosphere was good, he thought as he tipped back. Mitch didn't have any problem imagining a twenty-third-century hospital room. He didn't have any trouble imagining Zark's distress or the madness brewing in Leilah's unconscious brain. What he did have trouble imagining was his life without Hester.

"Stupid." The dog at his feet yawned in agreement. "What I should do is go down to that damn bank and drag her out. She'd love that, wouldn't she?" he said with a laugh as he pushed away from the machine and stretched. "I could beg." Mitch rolled that around in his mind and found it uncomfortable. "I could, but we'd probably both be sorry. There's not much left after reasoning, and I've tried that. What would Zark do?"

Mitch rocked back on his heels and closed his eyes. Would Zark, hero and saint, back off? Would Zark, defender of right and justice, bow out gracefully? Nope, Mitch decided. When it came to love, Zark was a patsy. Leilah kept kicking astrodust in his face, but he was still determined to win her back.

At least Hester hadn't tried to poison him with nerve gas. Leilah had pulled that and more, but Zark was still nuts about her.

Mitch studied the poster of Zark he'd tacked to the wall for inspiration. We're in the same boat, buddy, but I'm not going to pull out the oars and start rowing, either. And Hester's going to find herself in some turbulent waters.

He glanced at the clock on his desk, but remembered it had stopped two days before. He was pretty sure he'd sent his watch to the laundry along with his socks. Because he wanted to see how much time he had before Hester was due home, he walked into the living room. There, on the table, was an old mantel clock that Mitch was fond enough of to remember to wind. Just as he glanced at it, he heard Radley at the door.

"Right on time," Mitch said when he swung the door open. "How cold is it?" He grazed his knuckles down Radley's cheek in a routine they'd developed. "Forty-three degrees."

"It's sunny," Radley said, dragging off his backpack.

"Shooting for the park, are you?" Mitch waited until Radley had folded his coat neatly over the arm of the sofa. "Maybe I can handle it after I fortify myself. Mrs. Jablanski next door made cookies. She feels sorry for me because no one's fixing me hot meals, so I copped a dozen."

"What kind?"

"Peanut butter."

"All right!" Radley was already streaking into the kitchen. He liked the ebony wood and smoked glass table Mitch had set by the wall. Mostly because Mitch didn't mind if the glass got smeared with fingerprints. He settled down, content with milk and cookies and Mitch's company. "We have to do a dumb state project," he said with his mouth full. "I got Rhode Island. It's the smallest state. I wanted Texas."

"Rhode Island." Mitch smiled and munched on a cookie. "Is that so bad?"

"Nobody cares about Rhode Island. I mean, they've got the Alamo and stuff in Texas."

"Well, maybe I can give you a hand with it. I was born there."

"In Rhode Island? Honest?" The tiny state took on a new interest.

"Yeah. How long do you have?"

"Six weeks," Radley said with a shrug as he reached for another cookie. "We've got to do illustrations, which is okay, but we've got to do junk like manufacturing and natural resources, too. How come you moved away?"

He started to make some easy remark, then decided to honor Hester's code of honesty. "I didn't get along with my parents very well. We're better friends now."

"Sometimes people go away and don't come back."

The boy spoke so matter-of-factly that Mitch found himself responding the same way. "I know."

"I used to worry that Mom would go away. She didn't."

"She loves you." Mitch ran a hand along the boy's hair.

"Are you going to marry her?"

Mitch paused in midstroke. "Well, I..." Just how did he handle this one? "I guess I've been thinking about it." Feeling ridiculously nervous, he rose to heat up his coffee. "Actually, I've been thinking about it a lot. How would you feel if I did?"

"Would you live with us all the time?"

"That's the idea." He poured the coffee, then sat down beside Radley again. "Would that bother you?"

Radley looked at him with dark and suddenly inscrutable eyes. "One of my friends' moms got married again. Kevin says since they did his stepfather isn't his friend anymore.''

''Do you think if I married your mom I'd stop being your friend?'' He caught Radley's chin in his hand. ''I'm not your friend because of your mom, but because of you. I can promise that won't change when I'm your stepfather.''

''You wouldn't be my stepfather. I don't want one of those.'' Radley's chin trembled in Mitch's hand. ''I want a real one. Real ones don't go away.''

Mitch slipped his hands under Radley's arms and lifted him onto his lap. ''You're right. Real ones don't.'' Out of the mouth of babes, he thought, and nuzzled Radley against him. ''You know, I haven't had much practice being a father. Are you going to get mad at me if I mess up once in a while?''

Radley shook his head and burrowed closer. ''Can we tell Mom?''

Mitch managed a laugh. ''Yeah, good idea. Get your coat, Sergeant, we're going on a very important mission.''

Hester was up to her elbows in numbers. For some reason, she was having a great deal of trouble adding two and two. It didn't seem terribly important anymore. That, she knew, was a sure sign of trouble. She went through files, calculated and assessed, then closed them again with no feeling at all.

His fault, she told herself. It was Mitch's fault that she was only going through the motions, and thinking about going through the same motions day after day for the next twenty years. He'd made her question herself. He'd made her deal with the pain and anger she'd tried to bury. He'd made her want what she'd once sworn never to want again.

And now what? She propped her elbows on the stack of files and stared into space. She was in love, more deeply and more richly in love than she'd ever been before. The man she was in love with was exciting, kind and committed, and he was offering her a new beginning.

That was what she was afraid of, Hester admitted. That was what she kept heading away from. She hadn't fully understood before that she had blamed herself, not Allan, all these years. She had looked on the breakup of her marriage as a personal mistake, a private failure. Rather than risk another failure, she was turning away her first true hope.

She said it was because of Radley, but that was only partly true. Just as the divorce had been a private failure, making a full commitment to Mitch had been a private fear.

He'd been right, she told herself. He'd been right about so many things all along. She wasn't the same woman who had loved and married Allan Wallace. She wasn't even the same woman who had struggled for a handhold when she'd found herself alone with a small child.

When was she going to stop punishing herself? Now, Hester decided, picking up the phone. Right now. Her hand was steady as she dialed Mitch's number, but her heart wasn't. She caught her bottom lip between her teeth and listened to the phone ring—and ring.

"Oh, Mitch, won't we ever get the timing right?" She hung up the receiver and promised herself she wouldn't lose her courage. In an hour she would go home and tell him she was ready for that new beginning.

At Kay's buzz, Hester picked up the receiver again. "Yes, Kay."

"Mrs. Wallace, there's someone here to see you about a loan."

With a frown, Hester checked her calendar. "I don't have anything scheduled."

"I thought you could fit him in."

"All right, but buzz me in twenty minutes. I've got to clear some things up before I leave."

"Yes, ma'am."

Hester tidied her desk and was preparing to rise when Mitch walked in. "Mitch? I was just... What are you doing here? Rad?"

"He's waiting with Taz in the lobby."

"Kay said I had someone waiting to see me."

"That's me." He stepped up to the desk and set down a briefcase.

She started to reach for his hand, but his face seemed so set. "Mitch, you didn't have to say you'd come to apply for a loan."

"That's just what I'm doing."

She smiled and settled back. "Don't be silly."

"Mrs. Wallace, you *are* the loan officer at this bank?"

"Mitch, really, this isn't necessary."

"I'd hate to tell Rosen you sent me to a competitor." He flipped open the briefcase. "I've brought the financial information usual in these cases. I assume you have the necessary forms for a mortgage application?"

"Of course, but—"

"Then why don't you get one out?"

"All right, then." If he wanted to play games, she'd

oblige him. "So you're interested in securing a mortgage. Are you purchasing the property for investment
purposes, for rental or for a business?"

"No, it's purely personal."

"I see. Do you have a contract of sale?"

"Right here." It pleased him to see her mouth drop
open.

Taking the papers from him, Hester studied them.
"This is real."

"Of course it's real. I put a bid on the place a couple
of weeks ago." He scratched at his chin as if thinking
back. "Let's see, that would have been the day I had
to forgo pot roast. You haven't offered it again."

"You bought a house?" She scanned the papers
again. "In Connecticut?"

"They accepted my offer. The papers just came
through. I believe the bank will want to get its own
appraisal. There is a fee for that, isn't there?"

"What? Oh, yes, I'll fill out the papers."

"Fine. In the meantime, I do have some snapshots
and a blueprint." He slipped them out of the briefcase
and placed them on her desk. "You might want to look
them over."

"I don't understand."

"You might begin to if you look at the pictures."

She lifted them and stared at her fantasy house. It
was big and sprawling, with porches all around and
tall, wide windows. Snow mantled the evergreens beside the steps and lay stark and white on the roof.

"There are a couple of outbuildings you can't see.
A barn, a henhouse—both unoccupied at the moment.
The lot is about five acres, with woods and a stream.
The real estate agent claims the fishing's good. The
roof needs some work and the gutters have to be re-

placed, and inside it could use some paint or paper and a little help with the plumbing. But it's sound." He watched her as he spoke. She didn't look up at him, but continued to stare, mesmerized by the snapshots. "The house has been standing for a hundred and fifty years. I figure it'll hold up a while longer."

"It's lovely." Tears pricked the back of her eyes, but she blinked them away. "Really lovely."

"Is that from the bank's point of view?"

She shook her head. He wasn't going to make it easy. And he shouldn't, she admitted to herself. She'd already made it difficult enough for both of them. "I didn't know you were thinking of relocating. What about your work?"

"I can set up my drawing board in Connecticut just as easily as I can here. It's a reasonable commute, and I don't exactly spend a lot of time in the office."

"That's true." She picked up a pen, but rather than writing down the necessary information only ran it through her fingers.

"I'm told there's a bank in town. Nothing along the lines of National Trust, but a small independent bank. Seems to me someone with experience could get a good position there."

"I've always preferred small banks." There was a lump in her throat that had to be swallowed. "Small towns."

"They've got a couple of good schools. The elementary school is next to a farm. I'm told sometimes the cows get over the fence and into the playground."

"Looks like you've covered everything."

"I think so."

She stared down at the pictures, wondering how he could have found what she'd always wanted and how she could have been lucky enough that he would have cared. "Are you doing this for me?"

"No." He waited until she looked at him. "I'm doing it for us."

Her eyes filled again. "I don't deserve you."

"I know." Then he took both her hands and lifted her to her feet. "So you'd be pretty stupid to turn down such a good deal."

"I'd hate to think I was stupid." She drew her hands away to come around the desk to him. "I need to tell you something, but I'd like you to kiss me first."

"Is that the way you get loans around here?" Taking her by the lapels, he dragged her against him. "I'm going to have to report you, Mrs. Wallace. Later."

He closed his mouth over hers and felt the give, the strength and the acceptance. With a quiet sound of pleasure, he slipped his hands up to her face and felt the slow, lovely curve of her lips as she smiled.

"Does this mean I get the loan?"

"We'll talk business in a minute." She held on just a little longer, then drew away. "Before you came in, I'd been sitting here. Actually, I'd been sitting here for the last couple of days, not getting anything done because I was thinking of you."

"Go on, I think I'm going to like this story."

"When I wasn't thinking about you, I was thinking about myself and the last dozen years of my life I've put a lot of energy into *not* thinking about it, so it wasn't easy."

She kept his hand in hers, but took another step away. "I realize that what happened to me and Allan was destined to happen. If I'd been smarter, or stronger, I would have been able to admit a long time ago that what we had could only be temporary. Maybe if he hadn't left the way he did..." She trailed off, shaking her head. "It doesn't matter now. That's the point I had to come to, that it just doesn't matter. Mitch, I don't want to live the rest of my life wondering if you and I could have made it work. I'd rather spend the rest of my life *trying* to make it work. Before you came in today with all of this, I'd decided to ask you if you still wanted to marry me."

"The answer to that is yes, with a couple of stipulations."

She'd already started to move into his arms, but drew back. "Stipulations?"

"Yeah, you're a banker, you know about stipulations, right?"

"Yes, but I don't look at this as a transaction."

"You better hear me out, because it's a big one." He ran his hands up her arms, then dropped them to his side. "I want to be Rad's father."

"If we were married, you would be."

"I believe stepfather's the term used in that case. Rad and I agreed we didn't go for it."

"Agreed?" She spoke carefully, on guard again. "You discussed this with Rad?"

"Yeah, I discussed it with Rad. He brought it up, but I'd have wanted to talk to him, anyway. He asked me this afternoon if I was going to marry you. Did you want me to lie to him?"

"No." She paused a moment, then shook her head. "No, of course not. What did he say?"

"Basically he wanted to know if I'd still be his friend, because he'd heard sometimes stepfathers change a bit once their foot's in the door. Once we'd gotten past that hurdle, he told me he didn't want me as a stepfather."

"Oh, Mitch." She sank down on the edge of the desk.

"He wants a real father, Hester, because real fathers don't go away." Her eyes darkened very slowly before she closed them.

"I see."

"The way I look at it, you've got another decision to make. Are you going to let me adopt him?" Her eyes shot open again with quick surprise. "You've decided to share yourself. I want to know if you're going to share Rad, all the way. I don't see a problem with me being his father emotionally. I just want you to know that I want it legally. I don't think there'd be a problem with your ex-husband."

"No, I'm sure there wouldn't be."

"And I don't think there'd be a problem with Rad. So is there a problem with you?"

Hester rose from the desk to pace a few steps away. "I don't know what to say to you. I can't come up with the right words."

"Pick some."

She turned back with a deep breath. "I guess the best I can come up with is that Radley's going to have a terrific father, in every way. And I love you very, very much."

"Those'll do." He caught her to him with relief. "Those'll do just fine." Then he was kissing her again, fast and desperate. With her arms around him, she laughed. "Does this mean you're going to approve the loan?"

"I'm sorry, I have to turn you down."

"What?"

"I would, however, approve a joint application from

you and your wife.'' She caught his face in her hands. ''Our house, our commitment.''

''Those are terms I can live with—'' he touched her lips with his ''—for the next hundred years or so.'' He swung her around in one quick circle. ''Let's go tell Rad.'' With their hands linked, they started out. ''Say, Hester, how do you feel about honeymooning in Disneyland?''

She laughed and walked through the door with him. ''I'd love it. I'd absolutely love it.''

* * * * *

DUAL IMAGE

Chapter 1

Balancing a bag of groceries in one arm, Amanda let herself into the house. She radiated happiness. From outside came the sound of birds singing in the spring sunshine. The gold of her wedding ring caught the light. As a newlywed of three months, she was anxious to prepare a special, intimate dinner as a surprise for Cameron. Her demanding hours at the hospital and clinic often made it impossible for her to cook, and as a new bride she found pleasure in it. This afternoon, with two appointments unexpectedly canceled, she intended to fix something fancy, time-consuming and memorable. Something that went well with candlelight and wine.

As she entered the kitchen she was humming, a rare outward show of emotion for she was a reserved woman. With a satisfied smile, she drew a bottle of Cameron's favorite Bordeaux from the bag. As she studied the label, a smile lingered on her face while she remembered the first time they'd shared a bottle. He'd been so romantic, so attentive, so much what she'd needed at that point in her life.

A glance at her watch told her she had four full hours before her husband was expected home. Time enough to prepare an elaborate meal, light the candles and set out the crystal.

First, she decided, she was going upstairs to get out of her practical suit and shoes. There was a silk caftan upstairs, sheer, in misty shades of blue. Tonight, she wouldn't be a psychiatrist, but a woman, a woman very much in love.

The house was scrupulously neat and tastefully decorated. Such things came naturally to Amanda. As she walked toward the stairs, she glanced at a vase of Baccarat crystal and wished fleetingly she'd remembered fresh flowers. Perhaps she'd call the florist and have something extravagant delivered. Her hand trailed lightly over the polished banister as she started up. Her eyes, usually serious or intent, were dreamy. Carelessly, she pushed open the bedroom door.

Her smile froze. Utter shock replaced it. As she stood in the doorway, all color seemed to drain out of her cheeks. Her eyes grew huge before pain filled them. Out of her mouth came one anguished word.

"Cameron."

The couple in bed, locked in a passionate embrace, sprang apart. The man, smoothly handsome, his sleek hair disheveled, stared up in disbelief. The woman—feline, sultry, stunning—smiled very, very slowly. You could almost hear her purr.

"Vikki." Amanda looked at her sister with anguished eyes.

"You're home early." There was a hint, only a suspicion of a laugh in her sister's voice.

Cameron put a few more inches between himself and his sister-in-law. "Amanda, I..."

In one split second, Amanda's face contorted. With her eyes locked on the couple in bed, she reached in her jacket pocket and drew out a small, lethal revolver. The lovers stared at it in astonishment, and in silence. Coolly, she aimed and fired. A puff of confetti burst out.

"Ariel!"

Dr. Amanda Lane Jamison, better known as Ariel Kirkwood, turned to her harassed director as the couple in bed and members of the television crew dissolved into laughter.

"Sorry, Neal, I couldn't help myself. Amanda's *always* the victim," she said dramatically while her eyes danced. "Just think what it might do for the ratings if she lost her cool just once and murdered someone."

"Look, Ariel—"

"Or even just seriously injured them," she went on rapidly. "And who," she continued, flinging her hand toward the bed, "deserves it more than her spineless husband and scheming sister?"

At the hoots and applause of the crew, Ariel took a bow, then reluctantly turned over her weapon to her director when he held out his hand.

"You," he said with a long-suffering sigh, "are a certified loony, and have been since I've known you."

"I appreciate that, Neal."

"This time the tape's going to be running," he warned and tried not to grin. "Let's see if we can shoot this scene before lunch."

Agreeably, Ariel went down to the first floor of the

set. She stood patiently while her hair and make-up were touched up. Amanda was always perfection. Organized, meticulous, calm—all the things Ariel herself wasn't. She'd played the character for just over five years on the popular daytime soap opera "Our Lives, Our Loves."

In those five years, Amanda had graduated with honors from college, had earned her degree in psychiatric medicine and had gone on to become a respected therapist. Her recent marriage to Cameron Jamison appeared to be made in heaven. But, of course, he was a weak opportunist who'd married her for her money and social position, while lusting after her sister—and half the female population of the fictional town of Trader's Bend.

Amanda was about to be confronted with the truth. The story line had been leading up to this revelation for six weeks, and the letters from viewers had poured in. Both they and Ariel thought it was about time Amanda found out about her louse of a husband.

Ariel liked Amanda, respected her integrity and poise. When the cameras rolled, Ariel *was* Amanda. While in her personal life she would much prefer a day at an amusement park to an evening at the ballet, she understood all the nuances of the woman she portrayed.

When this scene was aired, viewers would see a neat, slender woman with pale blond hair sleeked back into a sophisticated knot. The face was porcelain, stunning, with an icy kind of beauty that sent out signals of restrained sexuality. Class. Style.

Lake-blue eyes, high curved cheekbones, added to the look of polished elegance. A perfectly shaped mouth tended toward serious smiles. Finely arched brows that were shades darker than the delicate blond of her hair accented luxurious lashes. A flawless beauty, perfectly composed—that was Amanda.

Ariel waited for her cue and wondered vaguely if she'd turned off her coffeepot that morning.

They ran through the scene again, from cue to cut, then a second time when it was discovered that Vikki's strapless bathing suit could be seen when she shifted in bed. Then came reaction shots—the camera zoomed in close on Amanda's pale, shocked face and held for several long, dramatic seconds.

"Lunch."

Response was immediate. The lovers bounded out of either side of the bed. In his bathing trunks, J.T. Brown, Ariel's on-screen husband, took her by the shoulders and gave her a long hard kiss. "Look, sweetie," he began, staying in character, "I'll explain about all this later. Trust me. I gotta call my agent."

"Wimp," Ariel called after him with a very un-Amandalike grin before she hooked her arm through that of Stella Powell, her series sister. "Pull something over that suit, Stella. I can't face the commissary food today."

Stella tossed back her tousled mass of auburn hair. "You buying?"

"Always sponging off your sister," Ariel mumbled. "Okay, I'll spring, but hurry up. I'm starving."

On her way to her dressing room, Ariel walked off the set, then through two more—the fifth floor of Doctors Hospital and the living room of the Lanes, Trader Bend's leading family. It was tempting to shed her costume and take down her hair, but it would only mean fooling with wardrobe and makeup after lunch. Instead, she just grabbed her purse, an outsize hobo bag that looked a bit incongruous with Amanda's elegant business suit. She was already thinking about a thick slice of baklava soaked in honey.

"Come on, Stella." Ariel stuck her head in the adjoining dressing room as Stella zipped up a pair of snug jeans. "My stomach's on overtime."

"It always is," her coworker returned as she pulled on a bulky sweatshirt. "Where to?"

"The Greek deli around the corner." More than ready, Ariel started down the hall in her characteristically long, swinging gait while Stella hurried to keep up. It wasn't that Ariel rushed from place to place, but simply that she wanted to see what was next.

"My diet," Stella began.

"Have a salad," Ariel told her without mercy. She turned her head to give Stella a quick up-and-down glance. "You know, if you weren't always wearing those skimpy outfits on camera, you wouldn't have to starve yourself."

Stella grinned as they came to the street door. "Jealous."

"Yeah. I'm always elegant and *always* proper. You have all the fun." Stepping outside, Ariel took a deep breath of New York. She loved it—had always loved it in a way usually reserved for tourists. Ariel had lived on the long thin island of Manhattan all of her life, and yet it remained an adventure to her. The sights, the smells, the sounds.

It was brisk for mid-April, and threatening to rain. The air was damp and smelled of exhaust. The streets and sidewalks were clogged with lunchtime traffic—everyone hurrying, everyone with important business to attend to. A pedestrian swore and banged a fist on the hood of a cab that had clipped too close to the curb. A woman with spiked orange hair hustled by in black leather boots. Somone had written something uncomplimentary on a poster for a hot Broadway play. But Ariel saw a street vendor selling daffodils.

She bought two bunches and handed one to Stella.

"You can never pass up anything, can you?" Stella mumbled, but buried her face in the yellow blooms.

"Think of all I'd miss," Ariel countered. "Besides, it's spring."

Stella shivered and looked up at the leaden sky. "Sure."

"Eat." Ariel grabbed her arm and pulled her along. "You always get cranky when you miss meals."

The deli was packed with people and aromas. Spices and honey. Beer and oil. Always a creature of the senses, Ariel drew in the mingled scents before she worked her way to the counter. She had an uncanny way of getting where she was going through a throng without using her elbows or stepping on toes. While she moved, she watched and listened. She wouldn't want to miss a scent, or the texture of a voice, or the clashing colors of food. As she looked behind the glass-fronted counter, she could already taste the things there.

"Cottage cheese, a slice of pineapple and coffee—black," Stella said with a sigh. Ariel sent her a brief, pitying look.

"Greek salad, a hunk of that lamb on a hard roll and a slice of baklava. Coffee, cream and sugar."

"You're disgusting," Stella told her. "You never gain an ounce."

"I know." Ariel moved down the counter to the cashier. "It's a matter of mental control and clean living." Ignoring Stella's rude snort she paid the bill then made her way through the crowded deli toward an empty table. She and a bull of a man reached it simultaneously. Ariel simply held her tray and sent him a stunning smile. The man straightened his shoulders, sucked in his stomach and gave way.

"Thanks," Stella acknowledged and dismissed him at the same time, knowing if she didn't Ariel would invite him to join them and upset any chance of a private conversation. The woman, Stella thought, needed a keeper.

Ariel did all the things a woman alone should know better than to do. She talked to strangers, walked alone at night and answered her door without the security chain attached. It wasn't that she was daring or careless, but simply that she believed in the best of people. And somehow, in a bit more than twenty-five years of living, she'd never been disillusioned. Stella marveled at her, even while she worried about her.

"The gun was one of your best stunts all season," Stella remarked as she poked at her cottage cheese. "I thought Neal was going to scream."

"He needs to relax," Ariel said with her mouth full. "He's been on edge ever since he broke up with that dancer. How about you? Are you still seeing Cliff?"

"Yeah." Stella lifted her shoulder. "I don't know why, it's not going anywhere."

"Where do you want it to go?" Ariel countered. "If you have a goal in mind, just go for it."

With a half laugh, Stella began to eat. "Not everyone plunges through life like you, Ariel. It always amazes me that you've never been seriously involved."

"Simple." Ariel speared a fork into her salad then

chewed slowly. "I've never met anyone who made my knees tremble. As soon as I do, that'll be it."

"Just like that?"

"Why not? Life isn't as complicated as most people make it." She added a dash of pepper to the lamb. "Are you in love with Cliff?"

Stell frowned—not because of the question, she was used to Ariel's directness. But because of the answer. "I don't know. Maybe."

"Then you're not," Ariel said easily. "Love's a very definite emotion. Sure you don't want any of this lamb?"

Stella didn't bother to answer the question. "If you've never been in love, how do you know?"

"I've never been to Turkey, but I'm sure it's there."

With a laugh, Stella picked up her coffee. "Damn, Ariel, you've always got an answer. Tell me about the script."

"Oh, God." Ariel put down her fork, and leaning her elbows on the table, folded her hands. "It's the best thing I've ever read. I want that part. I'm going to get that part," she added with something that was apart from confidence. It was simple fact. "I swear, I've been waiting for the character of Rae to come along. She's heartless," Ariel continued, resting her chin on her folded hands. "Complex, selfish, cold, insecure. A part like that..." She trailed off with a shake of her head. "And the story," she added on a long breath as her mind jumped from one aspect to the next. "It's nearly as cold and heartless as she is, but it gets to you."

"Booth DeWitt," Stella mused. "It's rumored that he based the character of Rae on his ex-wife."

"He didn't gloss it over either. If he's telling it

straight, she put him through hell. In any case,'' she said, as she began to eat again, ''it's the best piece of work that's come my way. I'm going to read for it in a couple of days.''

''TV movie,'' Stella said thoughtfully. ''Quality television with DeWitt writing and Marshell producing. You'd have our own producer at your feet if you got it. Boy, what a boost for the ratings.''

''He's already playing politics.'' With a small frown, Ariel broke off a chunk of baklava. ''He got me an invitation to a party tonight at Marshell's condo. DeWitt's supposed to be there. From what I hear, he's got the last say on casting.''

''He's got a reputation for wanting to push his own buttons,'' Stella agreed. ''So why the frown?''

''Politics're like rain in April—you know it's got to happen, but it's messy and annoying.'' Then she shrugged the thought away as she did anything unavoidable. In the end, from what she knew of Booth DeWitt, she'd earn the part on her own merit. If there was one thing Ariel had an abundance of, it was confidence. She'd always needed it.

Unlike Amanda, the character she played on the soap, Ariel hadn't grown up financially secure. There'd been a great deal more love than money in her home. She'd never regretted it, or the struggle to make ends meet. She'd been sixteen when her mother had died and her father had gone into a state of shock that had lasted nearly a year. It had never occurred to her that she was too young to take on the responsibilities of running a home and raising two younger siblings. There'd been no one else to do it. She'd sold powder and perfume in a department store to pay her way through college, while managing the family home and taking any bit part that came her way.

They'd been busy, difficult years, and perhaps that itself had given her the surplus of energy and drive she had today. And the sense that whatever had to be done, could be done.

"Amanda."

Ariel glanced up to see a small, middle-aged woman carrying a take-out bag that smelled strongly of garlic. Because she was called by her character's name almost as often as she was by her own, she smiled and held out her hand. "Hello."

"I'm Dorra Wineberger and I wanted to tell you you're just as beautiful as you are on TV."

"Thank you, Dorra. You enjoy the show?"

"I wouldn't miss it, not one single episode." She beamed at Ariel then leaned closer. "You're wonderful, dear, and so kind and patient. I just feel someone ought to tell you that Cameron—he's not good for you. The best thing for you to do is send him packing before he gets his hands on your money. He's already pawned your diamond earrings. And this one..." Dorra folded her lips and glared at Stella. "Why you bother with this one, after all the trouble she's caused you... If it hadn't been for her, you and Griff would be married like you should be." She sent Stella an affronted glare. "I know you've got your eyes on your sister's husband, Vikki."

Stella struggled with a grin and, playing the role, tossed her head and slanted her eyes. "Men are interested in me," she drawled. "And why not?"

Dorra shook her head and turned back to Ariel. "Go back to Griff," she advised kindly. "He loves you, he always has."

Ariel returned the quick squeeze of hand. "Thanks for caring."

Both women watched Dorra walk away before they turned back to each other. "Everyone loves Dr. Amanda," Vikki said with a grin. "She's practically sacred."

"And everyone loves to hate Vikki." With a chuckle, Ariel finished off her coffee. "You're so rotten."

"Yeah." Stella gave a contented sigh. "I know." She chewed her pineapple slowly, with a wistful look at Ariel's plate. "Anyway, it always strikes me as kind of weird when people get me confused with Vikki."

"It just means you're doing your job," Ariel corrected. "If you go into people's homes every day and don't draw emotion out of them, you better look for another line of work. Nuclear physics, log rolling. Speaking of work," she added with a glance at her watch.

"I know... Hey, are you going to eat the rest of that?"

Laughing, Ariel handed her the baklava as they rose.

It was well after nine when Ariel paid off the cab in front of P.B. Marshell's building on Madison Avenue. She wasn't concerned with being late because she wasn't aware of the time. She'd never missed a cue or a call in her life, but when it wasn't directly concerned with work, time was something to be enjoyed or ignored.

She overtipped the cabbie, stuffed her change in her bag without counting it, then walked through the light drizzle into the lobby. She decided it smelled like a funeral parlor. Too many flowers, too much polish. After giving her name at the security desk, she slipped into an elevator and pushed the Penthouse button. It didn't occur to her to be nervous at the prospect of entering P.B. Marshell's domain. A party to Ariel was a party. She hoped he served champagne. She had a hankering for it.

The door was opened by a stiff-backed, stone-faced man in a dark suit who asked Ariel's name in a discreet British accent. When she smiled, he accepted her offered hand before he realized it. Ariel walked past the butler, leaving him with the impression of vitality and sex—a combination that left him disconcerted for several minutes. She lifted a glass of champagne from a tray, and spotting her agent, crossed the room to her.

Booth saw Ariel's entrance. For an instant, he was reminded of his ex-wife. The coloring, the bone structure. Then the impression was gone, and he was looking at a young woman with casually curling hair that flowed past her shoulders. It seemed misted with fine drops of rain. A stunning face, he decided. But the look of an ice goddess vanished the moment she laughed. Then there was energy and verve.

Unusual, he thought, as vaguely interested in her as he was in the drink he held. He let his eyes skim down her and decided she'd be slim under the casual pleated pants and boxy blouse. Then again, if she was, she would have exploited her figure rather than underplaying it. From what Booth knew of women, they accented whatever charms at their disposal and concealed the flaws. He'd come to accept this as a part of their innate dishonesty.

He gave Ariel one last glance as she rose on her toes to kiss the latest rage in an off-Broadway production. God, he hated these long, crowded pseudo-parties.

"...If we cast the female lead."

Booth turned back to P.B. Marshell and lifted his glass. "Hmmm?"

Too used to Booth's lapses of attention to be annoyed, Marshell backtracked. "We can get this into production and wrapped in time for the fall sweeps if we cast the female lead. That's virtually all that's holding us back now."

"I'm not worried about the fall sweeps," Booth returned dryly.

"The network is."

"Pat, we'll cast Rae when we find Rae."

Marshell frowned into his Scotch, then drank it. At two hundred fifty pounds, he needed several glasses to feel any effect. "You've already turned down three top names."

"I turned down three actresses who weren't suitable," Booth corrected. He drank from his own glass as a man who knew liquor and maintained a cautious relationship with it. "I'll know Rae when I see her." His lips moved into a cool smile. "Who'd know better?"

A free, easy laugh had Marshell glancing across the room. For a moment his eyes narrowed in concentration. "Ariel Kirkwood," he told Booth, gesturing with his empty glass. "The network execs would like to push her your way."

"An actress." Booth studied Ariel again. He wouldn't have pegged her as such. Her entrance had caught his attention simply because it hadn't been an *entrance*. There was something completely unselfconscious about her that was rare in the profession. She'd been at the party long enough to have wangled an introduction to him and Marshell, yet she seemed content to stay across the room sipping champagne and flirting with an up-and-coming actor.

She stood easily, in a relaxed manner that wasn't a pose but would photograph beautifully. She made an unattractive face at the actor. The contrast of the ice-goddess looks and the freewheeling manner piqued his curiosity.

"Introduce me," Booth said simply and started across the room.

Ariel couldn't fault Marshell's taste. The condo was stylishly decorated in elegant golds and creams. The carpet was thick, the walls lacquered. She recognized the signed lithograph behind her. It was a room she knew Amanda would understand and appreciate. Ariel enjoyed visiting it. She'd never have lived there. She laughed up at Tony as he reminisced about the improvisation class they'd taken together a few years before.

"And you started using gutter language to make sure everyone was awake," she reminded him and tugged on the goatee he wore for his current part.

"It worked. What cause is it this week, Ariel?"

Her brows lifted as she sipped her champagne. "I don't have weekly causes."

"Biweekly," he corrected. "Friends of Seals, Save the Mongoose. Come on, what are you into now?"

She shook her head. "There's something that's taking up a lot of my time right now. I can't really talk about it."

Tony's grin faded. He knew that tone. "Important?"

"Vital."

"Well, Tony." Marshell clapped the young actor on the back. "Glad to see you could make it."

Though it was very subtly done, Tony came to attention. "It was nice that you were having this on a

night when the theater's dark, Mr. Marshell. Do you
know Ariel Kirkwood?'' He laid a hand on her shoulder. ''We go back a long way.''

''I've heard good things about you.'' Marshell extended his hand.

''Thank you.'' Ariel left her hand in his a moment
as she sorted her impressions. Successful—fond of
food from the bulk of him—amiable when he chose to
be. Shrewd. She liked the combination. ''You make
excellent films, Mr. Marshell.''

''Thank you,'' he returned and paused, expecting
her to do some campaigning. When she left it at that,
he turned to Booth. ''Booth DeWitt, Ariel Kirkwood
and Tony Lazarus.''

''I've seen your play,'' Booth told Tony. ''You
know your character very well.'' He shifted his gaze
to Ariel. ''Ms. Kirkwood.''

Disconcerting eyes, she thought, so clear and direct
a green in such a remote face. He gave off signals of
aloofness, traces of bitterness, waves of intelligence.
Obviously he didn't concern himself overmuch with
trends or fashion. His hair was thick and dark and a
bit long for the current style. Yet she thought it suited
his face. She thought the face belonged to the nine-
teenth century. Lean and scholarly with a touch of rug-
gedness and a harshness in the mouth that kept it from
being smooth.

His voice was deep and appealing, but he spoke with
a clipped quality that indicated impatience. He had the
eyes of an observer, she thought. And the air of a man
who wouldn't tolerate interference or intimacies. She
wasn't certain she'd like him, but she did know she
admired his work.

''Mr. DeWitt.'' Her palm touched his. Strength—

she'd expected that. It was in his build, long, rangy—
and in his face. Distance—she'd expected that as well.
"I enjoyed *The Final Bell*. It was my favorite film of
last year."

He passed this off as he studied her face. She exuded
sex, in her scent, in her looks—not flagrant or elusive,
but light and free. "I don't believe I'm familiar with
your work."

"Ariel plays Dr. Amanda Lane Jamison on 'Our
Lives, Our Loves,'" Tony put in.

Good God, a soap opera, Booth thought. Ariel
caught the faint disdain on his face. It was something
else she'd expected. "Do you have a moral objection
to entertainment, Mr. DeWitt?" she said easily as she
sipped champagne. "Or are you just an artistic snob?"
She smiled as she spoke, the quick, dashing smile that
took any sting from the words.

Beside her, Tony cleared his throat. "Excuse me a
minute," he said and exited stage left. Marshell mumbled something about freshening his drink.

When they were alone, Booth continued to study her
face. She was laughing at him. He couldn't remember
the last time anyone had had the courage, or the oc-
casion, to do so. He wasn't certain if he was annoyed
or intrigued. But at the moment he wasn't what he'd
been for the past hour. Bored.

"I haven't any moral objections to soap operas, Ms.
Kirkwood."

"Oh." She sipped her champagne. A sliver of sap-
phire on her finger winked in the light and seemed to
reflect in her eyes. "A snob then. Well, everyone's
entitled. Perhaps there's something else we can talk
about. How do you feel about the current administra-
tion's foreign policy?"

"Ambivalent," he murmured. "What sort of character do you play?"

"A sterling one." Her eyes continued to dance. "How do you feel about the space program?"

"I'm more concerned about the planet I'm on. How long have you been on the show?"

"Five years." She beamed a smile at someone across the room and raised her hand.

He looked at her again, carefully, and for the first time since he'd come into the party, he smiled. It did something attractive to his face, though it didn't make him quite as approachable as it indicated. "You don't want to talk about your work, do you?"

"Not particularly." Ariel returned his smile with her own open one. Something stirred faintly in him that he'd thought safely dormant. "Not with someone who considers it garbage. In a moment, you'd ask me if I'd ever considered doing any serious work, then I'd probably get nasty. My agent tells me I'm supposed to charm you."

Booth could feel the friendliness radiating from her and distrusted it. "Is that what you're doing?"

"I'm on my own time," Ariel returned. "Besides—" she finished off her champagne "—you aren't the type to be charmed."

"You're perceptive," Booth acknowledged. "Are you a good actress?"

"Yes, I am. It would hardly be worth doing something if you weren't good at it. What about sports?" She twirled her empty glass. "Do you think the Yankees stand a chance this year?"

"If they tighten up the infield." Not your usual type, he decided. Any other actress up for a prime part in one of his scripts would've been flooding him with compliments and mentioning every job she'd ever had in front of the camera. "Ariel..." Booth plucked a fresh glass of champagne from a passing waiter and handed it to her. "The name suits you. A wise choice."

She felt a pull, a quick, definite pull, that seemed to come simply from the way he's said her name. "I'll tell my mother you said so."

"It's not a stage name?"

"No. My mother was reading *The Tempest* when she went into labor. She was very superstitious. I could have been Prospero if I'd been a boy." With a little shudder, she sipped. "Well, Booth," she began, deciding she'd been formal long enough. "Shouldn't we just come out with the fact that we both know I'll be reading for the part of Rae in a couple of days? I intend to have it."

He nodded in acknowledgment. Though she was refreshingly direct, this was more what he'd expected. "Then I'll be frank enough to tell you that you're not the type I'm looking for."

She lifted a brow without any show of discomfort. "Oh? Why?"

"For one thing, you're too young."

She laughed—a free, breezy sound that seemed completely unaffected. He didn't trust that either. "I think my line is I can be older."

"Maybe. But Rae's a tough lady. Hard as a rock." He lifted his own drink but never took his eyes off her. "You've got too many soft points. They show in your face."

"Because this is me. And I've yet to play myself in front of a camera." She paused a moment as the idea worked around in her head. "I don't think I'd care to."

"Is any actress ever herself?"

Her eyes came back to his. He was watching her again with that steady intenseness most would have found unnerving. Though the pull came again, Ariel accepted the look because it was part of him. "You don't care for us much as a breed, do you?"

"No." For some reason he didn't question, Booth felt compelled to test her. He lifted a strand of her hair. Soft—surprisingly soft. "You're a beautiful woman," he murmured.

Ariel tilted her head as she studied him. His eyes had lost nothing of their directness. She might have felt pleasure in the compliment if she hadn't recognized it as calculated. Instead she felt disappointment. "And?"

His brows drew together. "And?"

"That line usually leads to another. As a writer I'm sure you have several tucked away."

He let his fingers brush over her neck. She felt the strength in them, and the carelessness of the gesture. "Which one would you like?"

"I'd prefer one you meant," Ariel told him evenly. "But since I wouldn't get it, why don't we skip the whole thing? You know, your character, Phil, is narrow-minded, cool-blooded and rude. I believe you portrayed yourself very well." She lifted her glass one last time and decided it was a shame that he thought so little of women, or perhaps of people in general. "Good night, Booth."

When she walked away, Booth stood looking after her for several moments before he started to laugh. At the time, it didn't occur to him that it was the first easy laugh he'd had in almost two years. It didn't even occur to him that he was laughing at himself.

No, she wasn't his Rae, he mused, but she was good. She was very, very good. He was going to remember Ariel Kirkwood.

Chapter 2

Booth stood by the wide expanse of window in Marshell's office and watched New York hustle by. From that height, he felt removed from it, and the rush and energy radiating up from the streets and sidewalks. He was satisfied to be separate. Connections equaled involvement.

None of the actresses they'd auditioned in the past two weeks came close to what he was after. He knew what he wanted for the part of Rae—who better?

When he'd first started the script it had been an impulse—therapy, he mused with a grim smile. Cheaper than a psychiatrist and a lot more satisfying. He'd never expected to do any more than finish it, purge his system and toss it in a drawer. That was before he'd realized it was the best work he'd ever done. Perhaps anger was the tenth Muse. In any case, he was first and foremost a writer. However painful it was to expose himself and his mistakes to the public, there was no tossing his finest work in a drawer. And since he was going to have it performed, he was going to have it performed well.

He'd thought it would be difficult to cast the part of Phil, the character who was essentially himself. And yet that had been surprisingly simple. The core of the story wasn't Phil, but Rae, a devastatingly accurate mirror of his ex-wife, Elizabeth Hunter. A superb actress, a gracious celebrity—a woman without a single genuine emotion.

Their marriage had started with a whirlwind and ended in disaster. Booth didn't consider himself blameless, though he placed most of the blame on his own gullibility. He'd believed in her image, fallen hard for the perfection of face and body. He could have forgiven the faults, the flaws soon discovered. But he could never, would never, forgive being used. And yet, Booth was still far from sure whether he blamed Liz for using him, or himself for allowing it to happen.

Either way, the tempestuous five-year marriage had given him grist for a clean, hard story that was going to be an elaborate television movie. And more, it had given him a firm distrust of women, particularly actresses. Two years before, when the break had finally come, he'd promised himself that he'd never become involved with another woman who could play roles that well. Honesty, if it truly existed, was what he'd look for when he was ready.

His thoughts came back to Ariel. Perhaps she was centered in his mind because of her surface resemblance to Liz, but he wasn't certain. There was no similarity in mannerisms, voice cadence or style of dress. And the biggest contrast seemed to be in personality. She hadn't put herself out to charm him or to hold his attention. And she'd done both. Perhaps she'd simply used a different angle on an old game.

While he hadn't trusted it, he'd enjoyed her lack of artifice. The breezy laugh, the unaffected gestures, the candid looks. It had been a long time since a woman had lingered in his mind. A pity, Booth mused, that she was unsuitable for the part. He could have used the distraction. Instinct told him that Ariel Kirkwood would be nothing if she wasn't a distraction.

"I'm still leaning toward this Julie Newman." Chuck Tyler, the director, tossed an eight-by-ten glossy on Marshell's desk. "A lot of camera presence and her first reading was very good."

With the photo in one hand, Marshell tipped back in his deep leather chair. The sun at his back streamed over both the glossy and the gold he wore on either hand. "An impressive list of credits too."

"No." Booth didn't bother to turn around, but stood watching the traffic stream. For some odd reason he visualized himself on his boat in Long Island Sound, sailing out to sea. "She lacks the elegance. Too much vulnerability."

"She can act, Booth," Marshell said with a now familiar show of impatience.

"She's not the one."

Marshell automatically reached in his pocket for the cigars he'd given up a month before. He swore lightly under his breath. "And we're running out of time and options."

Booth gave an unconcerned shrug. Yes, he'd like to be sailing, stripped to the waist with the sun on his back and the water so blue it hurt the eyes. He'd like to be alone.

When the buzzer on his desk rang, Marshell heaved

a sigh and leaned forward to answer. "Ms. Kirkwood's here for her reading, Mr. Marshell."

With a grunt, Marshell flipped open the portfolio Ariel's agent had sent him, then passed it to Chuck. "Send her in."

"Kirkwood," Chuck mused, frowning over Ariel's publicity shot. "Kirkwood... Oh, yeah, I saw her last summer in an off-Broadway production of *Streetcar*."

Vaguely interested, Booth looked over his shoulder. "Stella?"

"Blanche," Chuck corrected, skimming over her list of credits.

"Blanche DuBois?" Booth gave a short laugh as he turned completely around. "She's fifteen to twenty years too young for that part."

Chuck merely lifted his eyes. "She was good," he said simply. "Very good. And from what I'm told, she's very good on the soap. I don't have to tell you how many of our top stars started that way."

"No, you don't." Booth sat negligently on the arm of a chair. "But if she's stuck with the same part for five years, she's either not good enough for a major film or major theater, or she's completely without ambition. Because she's an actress, I'd have to go with the former."

"Keep sharpening your cynicism," Marshell said dryly. "It's good for you."

Booth's grin flashed—that rare one that came and went so quickly it left the onlooker dazzled and unsure why. Ariel caught a glimpse of it as she entered the room. It went a long way toward convincing her to change her initial opinion of him. It passed through her mind, almost as quickly as Booth's grin, that perhaps he had some redeeming personal qualities after all. She was always ready to believe it.

"Ms. Kirkwood." Marshell heaved his bulk from the chair and extended his hand.

"Mr. Marshell, nice to see you again." She took a brief scan of the room, her gaze lingering only fleetingly on Booth as he remained seated on the arm of the chair. "Your office is just as impressive as your home."

Booth waited while she was introduced to Chuck. She'd dressed very simply, he noticed. Deceptively so if you considered the bold scarves she'd twisted at the waist of the demure blue dress. Violets and emeralds and wild pinks. A daring combination, and stunningly effective. Her hair was loose again, giving her an air of youth and freedom he would never equate with the character she wanted to portray. Absently, he took out a cigarette and lit it.

"Booth." Ariel gave him an easy smile before her gaze flicked over the cigarette. "They'll kill you."

He took a drag and let out a lazy stream of smoke. "Eventually." She wore the same carelessly sexy scent he'd noticed the night of the party. Booth wondered why it was that it suited her while contrasting at the same time. She fascinated. It seemed to be something she did effortlessly. "I'm going to cue you," he continued and reached for a copy of the script. "We'll use the confrontation scene in the third act. You're familiar with it?"

All business, Ariel noted curiously. Does he ever relax? Does he ever choose to? Though she was rarely tense herself, she recognized tension in him and wondered why he was nervous. What nerves she felt herself were confined to a tiny roiling knot in the center of her stomach. She always acknowledged it and knew, if anything, it would help to push her through the reading.

"I'm familiar with it," she told him, accepting another copy of the script.

Booth took a last drag on his cigarette then put it out. "Do you want a lead in?"

"No." Now her palms were damp. Good. Ariel knew better than to want to be relaxed when twinges of emotions would sharpen her skills. Taking deep, quiet breaths she flipped through the bound script until she found the right scene. It wasn't a simple one. It stabbed at the core of the character—selfish ambition and icy sex. She took a minute.

Booth watched her. She looked more like the guileless ingenue than the calculating leading lady, he mused and was almost sorry there wasn't a part for her in the film. Then she looked up and pinned him with a cold, bloodless smile that completely stunned him.

"You always were a fool, Phil, but a successful one and so rarely boring, it's hardly worth mentioning."

The tone, the mannerisms, even the expression was so accurate, he couldn't respond. For a moment, he completely lost Ariel in the character and the woman he'd fashioned her after. He felt a twist in his stomach, not of attraction or even admiration, but of anger— totally unexpected and vilely real. Booth didn't have to look at the script to remember the line.

"You're so transparent, Rae. It amazes me that you could deceive anyone into believing in you."

Ariel laughed, rather beautifully, so that all three men felt a chill race up their spine. "I make my living at deception. Everyone wants illusions, so did you. And that's what you got."

With a long, lazy stretch, she ran a hand through her hair, then let it fall, pale gold in the late-morning sunlight. It was one of Liz Hunter's patented gestures. "I acted my way out of that miserable backwater town in Missouri where I had the misfortune to be born, and I've acted my way right up to the top. You were a great help." She walked over to him with the small, cool smile still on her lips, in her eyes. With an eloquent gesture, she brushed her hand down his cheek. "And you were compensated. Very, very well."

Phil grabbed her wrist and tossed it aside. Ariel merely lifted a brow at the violence of the movement. "Sooner or later you're going to slip," he threatened.

She tilted her head and spoke very softly. "Darling, I never slip."

Slowly, Booth rose. The expression on his face might have had any woman trembling, would have had any woman making some defensive move. Ariel merely looked up at him with the same coldly amused expression. It was he who had to force himself to calm.

"Very good, Ariel Kirkwood." Booth tossed the script aside.

She grinned, because every instinct told her she'd won. With the long expelled breath, she could almost feel Rae drain out of her. "Thanks. It's a tremendous part," she added as her stomach unknotted. "Really a tremendous part."

"You've done your research," Marshell murmured from behind his desk. Because he knew Elizabeth Hunter, Ariel's five-minute read had left him uncomfortable and impressed. And he knew Booth. There was little doubt in his mind as to what Rae's creator was feeling. "You'll be available for a callback?"

"Of course."

"I saw your Blanche DuBois, Ms. Kirkwood," Chuck put in. "I was very impressed then, and now."

She flashed him an unaffected smile though she was aware Booth was still staring at her. If he was moved, she thought, then the reading had gone better than she could have hoped. "It was my biggest challenge, up until now." She wanted to get out, walk, breathe the air, savor the almost-victory while she could. "Well, thank you." She pushed her hair from shoulder as she scanned the three men again. "I'll look forward to hearing from you."

Ariel walked toward the elevator too frightened to believe she was right, too terrified to believe she was wrong. Up until that moment, she hadn't let herself dwell on just how much she wanted the part, and just what it could mean in her life.

She wasn't without ambition, but she had chosen acting and had continued with it for the love of it. And the challenge. Playing the part of Rae would hand her all three needs on a silver platter. As she stepped into the elevator, her palms were dry and her heart was pounding. She didn't hear Booth approach.

"I'd like to talk to you." He stepped in with her and punched the button for the lobby.

"Okay." A long sigh escaped as she leaned back against the side of the car. "God, I'm glad that's over. I'm starving. Nothing makes me hungrier than a reading."

He tried to relate the woman who was smiling at him with eyes warm and alive with the woman who had just exchanged lines with him. He couldn't. She was a better actress than he'd given her credit for, and therefore, more dangerous. "It was an excellent reading."

She eyed him curiously. "Why do I feel I've just been insulted?"

After the doors slid open Booth stood for a moment, then nodded. "I think I said before that you were perceptive."

Her slim heels clicked over the tile as she crossed the lobby with him. Booth noticed a few heads turn, both male and female, to look after her. She was either unaware or unconcerned. "Why are you on daytime TV?"

Ariel slanted him a look before she began to walk north. "Because it's a good part on a well-written, entertaining show. That's number one. Number two is that it's steady work. When actors are between jobs, they wait tables, wash cars, sell toasters and generally get depressed. While I might not mind the first three too much, I hate the fourth. Have you ever seen the show?"

"No."

"Then you shouldn't turn your nose up." She stopped by a sidewalk vendor and drew in the scent of hot pretzels. "Want one?"

"No," Booth said again and tucked his hands in his pockets. Sexuality, sensuality—both seemed to pour out of her as she stood next to a portable pretzel stand on a crowded sidewalk. He continued to watch her as she took the first generous bite.

"I could live off them," she told him with her mouth full and her eyes laughing. "Good nutrition's so admirable and so hard to live with. I like to ignore it for long stretches of time. Let's walk," she suggested. "I have to when I'm keyed up. What do you do?"

"When?"

"When you're keyed up," Ariel explained.

"Write." He matched her casually swinging pace while the bulk of pedestrian traffic bustled by them.

"And when you're not keyed up you write," Ariel added as she took another bite of her pretzel. "Have you always been so serious?"

"It's steady work," he countered and she laughed.

"Very quick. I didn't think I'd like you, but you've got a nice sense of cautious humor." Ariel stopped at another vendor and bought a bunch of spring violets. She closed her eyes and breathed deep. "Wonderful," she murmured. "I always think spring's the best until summer. Then I'm in love with the heat until fall. Then fall's the best until winter." Laughing, she looked over the blooms into his eyes. "And I also tend to ramble when I'm keyed up."

When she lowered the flowers, Booth took her wrist, not with the same violence as he had during the reading, but with the same intensity. "Who are you?" he demanded. "Who the hell are you?"

Her smile faded but she didn't draw away. "Ariel Kirkwood. I can be a lot of other people when there's a stage or a camera, but when it's over, that's who I am. That's all I am. Are you looking for complications?"

"I don't have to look for them—they're always there."

"Strange, I rarely run into any." She studied him, all frank eyes and creamy beauty. Booth didn't care for the stir it brought him. "Come with me," she invited, then took his hand before he'd thought to object.

"Where?"

She threw back her head and pointed up the magnificently sheer surface of the Empire State Building.

"To the top." Laughing, she pulled him inside. "All the way to the top."

Booth looked around impatiently as she bought tickets for the observation deck. "Why?"

"Does there always have to be a reason?" She slipped the violets into the twisted scarves at her waist, then tucked her arm through his. "I love things like this. Ellis Island, the Staten Island ferry, Central Park. What's the use of living in New York if you don't enjoy it? When's the last time you did this?" Her shoulder rested against his upper arm as they crowded into an elevator.

"I think I was ten." Even with the press of bodies and mingling scents he could smell her, wild and sweet.

"Oh." Ariel laughed up at him. "You grew up. Too bad."

Booth said nothing for a moment as he studied her. She seemed to always be laughing—at him or at some private joke she was content to keep to herself. Was she really that easy with herself and her life? Was anyone? Then he asked, "Don't we all?"

"Of course not. We all get older, but the rest is a personal choice." They herded off one elevator and onto another that would take them to the top.

This was a man she could enjoy, Ariel mused as she stood beside Booth. She could enjoy that serious, high-minded streak and the dry, almost reluctant humor. Still, there was the part in the film to think of. Ariel would have to be very careful to keep her feelings for one separate from her feelings for the other. But then, she'd never been a person who'd had any trouble separating the woman and the actress.

For now, the reading was over and the afternoon was

free. Her mood was light, and there was a man with her who'd be fascinating to explore. The day could hardly offer anything more.

The souvenir stands were crowded with people— different countries, different voices. Ariel decided she'd buy something foolish on her way out. She caught Booth looking around him with his eyes slightly narrowed. An observer, she thought with a slight nod of approval. She was one herself, though perhaps on a different level. He'd dissect, analyze and file. She just enjoyed the show.

"Come on outside," she invited and took his hand in a characteristic gesture. "It's wonderful." Pushing open the heavy door, Ariel welcomed the first slap of wind with a laugh. With her hand still firmly gripping Booth's, she hurried to the wall to take in New York.

She never saw it as a toy board as many did from that height, but as something real enough to touch and smell from any distance. It never failed to excite and fascinate her. Ariel rarely asked more of anything or anyone. When she was here, she always believed she could accomplish whatever she needed to.

"I love heights." She leaned out as far as she could and felt the frantic current of air swirl around her. "Staggering heights. And wind. If I could, I'd come here every day. I'd never get tired of it."

Though it was normally an intimacy he would have shunned, Booth allowed his hand to stay in hers. Her skin was smooth and elegant; her face was flushed in the brisk air while her hair blew wildly. The eyes, he thought, the eyes were too alive, too full of everything. A woman like this would demand spectacular emotions from everyone she touched. The stir he felt wasn't as easily suppressed this time. Deliberately, he looked away from her and down.

"Why not the World Trade Center?" he asked and let his gaze skim over the island he lived on.

Ariel shook her head. "It doesn't have the same feeling as this, nothing does. Just like there's only one Eiffel Tower, one Grand Canyon and one Olivier." She didn't bother to brush her hair back from her face as she tilted toward him. "They're all spectacular and unique. What do you like, Booth?"

A family walked by laughing, the mother holding her skirts, the father carrying a toddler. He watched them pause nearby and look over the wall. "In what way?"

"In any way," Ariel told him. "If you could've spent today doing anything you wanted, what would you have done?"

"Gone sailing," he said, remembering that moment in Marshell's office. "I'd've been sailing on the Sound."

Interest flickered in her eyes as it seemed every emotion or thought she had did. "You have a boat?"

"Yes. I don't have much time for it."

Don't take much time for it, she corrected silently. "A solitary pursuit. That's admirable." She turned, leaning back against the wall so that she could watch the people circle the deck. The wind plastered her dress against her, revealing the slenderness, the elegance of woman. "I don't often like to be solitary," she murmured. "I need people, the contacts, the contrasts. I don't have to know them. I just like knowing they're there."

"Is that why you act?" They were face-to-face now, their bodies casually close—as if they were friends. It struck Booth as odd, but he had no desire to back away. "So you can have an audience?"

Her expression become thoughtful, but when she smiled, it was easy. "You're a very cynical man."

"That's the second time today that's been mentioned."

"It's all right. It probably comes in handy with your writing. Yes, I act for an audience," she continued. "I won't deny my own ego, but I think I act for myself first." She lifted her face so that the air could race over it. "It's a marvelous profession. How else can you be so many people? A princess, a tramp, a victim, a loser. You write to be read, but don't you first write to express yourself?"

"Yes." He felt something odd, almost unfamiliar—a loosening of muscles, an easing of thought. It took him a moment to realize he was relaxing, and only a moment longer to draw back. When you relaxed, you got burned. That much he was certain of. "But then writers have egos that nearly rival actors'."

Ariel made a sound that was somewhere between a sigh and an expulsion of air. "She really put you through the mill, didn't she?"

His eyes frosted, his voice chilled. "That's none of your business."

"You're wrong." Though she felt a twinge of regret when she sensed his withdrawal, Ariel went on. "If I'm going to play Rae, it's very much my business. Booth..." She laid a hand on his arm, wishing she understood him well enough to get past the wall of reserve, the waves of bitterness. "If you'd wanted to keep this part of your life private, you wouldn't have written it out."

"It's a story," he said flatly. "I don't put myself on display."

"In most cases, no," she agreed. "I've always felt a certain sense of distance in your work, though it's always excellent. And for someone so successful, you kept a fairly low profile, even when you were married to Liz Hunter. But you've let something out in this script. It's too late to pull it back now."

"I've written a story about two people who are totally unsuited to each other, who used each other. The man is a bit of an idealist, and just gullible enough to fall for an exquisite face. Before the story ends, he learns that appearances mean little and that trust and loyalty are illusions. The woman is cold, ambitious and gifted, but she'll never be satisfied with her own talents. She's a vampire in the pure sense of the word, and she sucks him dry. There may be similarities between the story and actuality, but my life is still my life."

"No trespassing." Ariel turned to look back down into the city, the world she understood. "All right, the signs are posted." She listened to the sound of the wind, the sound of voices. Someone reeked of a drugstore cologne. An empty bag of potato chips skimmed and rustled along the concrete. "I'm not a very good businesswoman. I won't apologize for my life-style or my personality, but I will do my best to keep our conversations very professional."

She took a deep breath and turned back to him. Some of the warmth had left her eyes, and he felt a momentary regret. "I'm a good actress, an excellent craftsman. I've known since the first moment I picked up the script that I could play Rae. And I'm astute enough to know how well my reading went."

"No, you're not a fool." Even with the regret, Booth felt more comfortable on this level. He understood her now—an actress in search of that prime part. "I wouldn't have said you were what I was looking for—until this afternoon. No one's come even close to the core of that character before you."

She felt the tickling dryness down in her throat, the sudden lurch of her heart rate. "And?" she managed.

"And I want you to come back and read with Jack Rohrer; he's cast as Phil. If the chemistry's there, you've got the part."

Ariel took a deep breath. She leaned against the sturdy observation glass and tried to take it calmly. She'd told him she'd be professional. No good, she realized as the pleasure bubbled up inside her. It simply wasn't any use. With a shout of laughter, she threw her arms around his neck and clung. The touching was vital, the sharing essential.

Ariel Kirkwood—the skinny dreamer from West 185th Street—was going to star in a DeWitt script, a P.B. Marshell production opposite Jack Rohrer. Would life never stop amazing her? As she clung to Booth, Ariel dearly hoped it wouldn't.

His hands had come to her waist in reflex, but he left them there as her laughter warmed his ear. He found it odd that he was sharply reminded of two things—his young niece's boundless pleasure when he'd given her an elaborate dollhouse one Christmas, and the first time, as a man, he'd ever held a woman. The softness was there—that unique strength and give only a woman's body has. The childlike pleasure was there—with the innocence only the young possess.

He could have held her. It moved in him to do so, just to hold something soft and sweet and without shadows. She fit so well against him. The curve of cheek against his, the alignment of bodies. She fit too well, so that he stood perfectly still and drew her no closer.

Something drifted through her pleasure and excitement. He smelt of soap—solid—as his body felt. There was nothing casual about him, nothing easy. He was all intensity and intellect. The strength drew her; his reserve drew her. He was a man who would be there to pick you up, however reluctantly, if you stumbled. Who would demand that you keep pace with him, and who would expect you to give him exactly the amount of room he wanted when he wanted it. He was a man whom a woman who ran on her emotions and her senses would do well to avoid. She wished almost painfully that his arms would come around her, even while she knew they wouldn't.

Ariel drew away but kept their faces close so that she might have a hint of what it would be like to have that serious, unsmiling mouth lowered to hers. She was breathless, and her eyes made no secret of her attraction or her surprise in feeling it.

"I'm sorry," she said quietly. "Physical displays come naturally to me. I have a feeling you don't care for them."

Had there ever been a woman he'd wanted to kiss more than this one? Almost, almost, he could taste the mouth inches from his own. Nearly, very nearly, he could feel its texture against his own. When he spoke, his voice was indifferent, his eyes remote. "There's a time and a place."

Ariel let out a long breath and decided she'd set herself up for a backhanded slap. "You're a tough man, Booth DeWitt," she murmured.

"I'm a realist, Ariel." He took out a cigarette, cupping his lighter against the wind with hands that amazed him because they weren't steady.

"What a hard thing to be." Consciously, she relaxed—shoulder muscles, stomach muscles, hands. A moment's awareness didn't equal trouble. She'd felt it before; it was a blessing and a curse in a woman like herself. Ariel didn't understand indifference to people or to things. Everything you saw, touched, heard, triggered some emotion. "But then, you're stuck with it." More at ease, she smiled at him. "I'm going to enjoy working with you, Booth, though I know it's not going to be a picnic. I'm going to give your script my very best shot, and we'll both benefit."

He nodded as the smoke whipped up and away. "I don't accept anything less than the best."

"Fine, you won't be disappointed." It was in her nature to reach out and touch, to add something personal. But one slap was enough for one day.

"Good."

With a laugh, she shook her head. "You're attractive, Booth. I haven't the least idea why because I don't think you're a very nice person."

He blew out another stream of smoke and watched her lazily. "I'm not," he agreed.

"In any case, we'll give each other what's needed professionally."

Then because she rarely resisted impulses of any kind, she kissed his cheek before thrusting the violets at him and walking away. Booth stood in the wind on top of New York with a handful of spring flowers and stared after her.

Chapter 3

Booth had been on and around sets most of his professional life. There were eighteenth-century drawing rooms, twentieth-century bedrooms, bars and restaurants and department stores. Spaceships and log cabins. With props and backdrops and ingenuity, anything could be created.

When you came to the bottom line, one set was the same as another—technicians, lights, cameras, booms, miles of cable. It was an industry of illusion and image. What looked glamorous outside the business was ultimately only a job, and often a tedious and exacting one. Long hours, lengthy delays, lights that made a studio into a furnace, bitter coffee.

From the outset of his career, he'd never been content to be isolated with his typewriter and ideas. He'd insisted from his very first screenplay on being involved with the production end. He understood the practicality and the creativity of the right camera angle, the proper lighting. It appealed to the realistic part of him. Still, he had the ability to see the set and the people while blocking out the crowding equipment. To watch as an outsider, to see as a viewer. This appealed to the dreamer he'd always kept under strict control.

Booth wasn't sure what had motivated him to visit the set of "Our Lives, Our Loves." He knew that the script he was currently working on had hit a snag, and that he wanted to see Ariel again. Perhaps it was the scent of violets that continued to drift to him as he tried to work. Twice he'd started to throw them away...but he hadn't. Part of him, deep, long repressed, needed such things, however much he disliked acknowledging it.

So he had come to see Ariel, telling himself he simply wanted to watch her work before he committed himself to choosing her for the part of Rae. It was logical, practical. It was something he'd tried very hard to resist.

Ariel sat at the kitchen table with her bare feet propped in a chair while Jack Shapiro, who played Griff Martin, Amanda's college sweetheart, mulled over a hand of solitaire. On another part of the soundstage, her television parents were discussing their offspring. After they'd finished, she and Jack would tape their scene.

"Black six on the red seven," she mumbled, earning herself a glare from Jack.

"Solitaire," he reminded her. "As in alone."

"It's an antisocial game."

"You think headphones are antisocial."

"They are." Smiling sweetly, she moved the six herself.

"Why don't you go call the Committee for the Sal-

vation of Three-legged Land Mammals? They probably want you at their next luncheon.''

The timing wasn't quite right, she decided, to ask
him to contribute to the Homes for Kittens fund she
was currently involved with. ''Don't get snotty,'' she
said mildly. ''You're supposed to adore me.''

''Should've had my head examined after you threw
me over for Cameron.''

''It's your own fault for not explaining what you
were doing alone in that hotel room with Vikki.''

Jack sniffed and turned over another card. ''You
should've trusted me. A man has his pride.''

''Now I'm stuck in a disastrous marriage *and* I
might be pregnant.''

Glancing up, he grinned. ''Great for the ratings. Did
you see them posted this week? We're up a whole
point.''

She leaned her elbows on the table. ''Wait until
things start heating up between Amanda and Griff
again.'' She put a black ten on the jack of diamonds.
''Sizzle, spark, smolder.''

He smacked her hand. ''You're a great smolderer.''
Unable to resist, he leered. ''I haven't kissed you in
six months.''

''Then when you get your chance, big guy, make it
good. Amanda's no pushover.'' Rising, she strolled
away for a last-minute check with make-up.

The hospital set had already been prepared for the
brief but intense meeting between the former lovers,
Amanda and Griff. Some subtle dark smudges were
added under her eyes to give the appearance of a sleepless night. The rest of her make-up gave her a slight
pallor.

By the time the cameras rolled, Amanda was in her

office, going through her patient files. She seemed very calm, very much in control. Her expression was totally serene. Abruptly, she slammed the drawer back in the cabinet and whirled around to pace. When the tape was edited, it would flash back to her discovery of her husband and sister. Amanda grabbed a china cup from her desk and hurled it against the wall. With the back of her hand to her mouth, she stared at the broken pieces. The knock at her office door had her balling her fists and making a visible struggle for control. Deliberately, she walked around her desk and sat down.

"Come in."

The camera focused on Jack as Dr. Griff Martin, rough-and-ready looks, rough-and-ready temper— Amanda's first and only lover before her marriage. Ariel knew what the director would expect in a reaction shot later, but now, with the tape running on Jack's entrance, she screwed up her face and stuck out her tongue. Jack gave her one of his character's patented lengthy looks designed to make the female heart flutter.

"Amanda, have you got a minute?"

When the lens was focused on her again, her face was properly composed with just a hint of strain beneath the serenity. "Of course, Griff." For a subtle sign of nerves, she gripped her hands together on the desktop.

"I've got a case of wife beating," he began in the clipped, almost surly tone of his character. Both Amanda and several million female viewers had found his diamond-in-the-rough style irresistible. "I need your help."

They went through the scene, laying the groundwork for a story line that would throw them together again and again over the next few weeks, building the sexual tension. When the camera was briefly at Jack's back he crossed his eyes at Ariel and bared his teeth. As she went back to her patient file, she made certain she walked over his foot. Neither of them lost the rhythm of the scene.

"You look tired." As Griff, Jack started to touch her shoulder, then stopped himself. Frustration radiated from his eyes. "Is everything all right?"

Amanda turned and gave him a soulful eye-locking look. Her mouth trembled open, then closed again. Slowly, she turned back to the file and shut the drawer quietly. "Everything's fine. I have a heavy workload right now. And I have a patient due in a few minutes."

"I'll get out of here then." He started for the door and paused. With his hand on the knob, he stared at her. "Mandy..."

Amanda kept her back to him. The camera came in close as she shut her eyes and fought for control. "I'll see your patient tomorrow, Griff." There was the faintest of tremors in her voice.

He waited five humming seconds. "Yeah, fine."

When she heard the door close, Amanda pressed her hands to her face.

"Cut."

"I'm going to get you for that," Jack said as he pushed the prop door open again. "I think you broke one of my toes."

Ariel fluttered her lashes at him. "You're such a baby."

"All right, children," the director said mildly. "Let's get the reaction shots."

Agreeably, Ariel moved behind Amanda's desk again. It was then she saw Booth. Surprise and pleasure showed on her face, though his expression wasn't welcoming. He was frowning at her, his arms crossed over a casual black sweater. He didn't return her smile, nor did she expect him to. Booth DeWitt wasn't a man who smiled often or easily. It only made her more determined to nudge him into it.

She'd thought about him—surprisingly often. At the moment, she had enough on her mind, both personally and professionally, yet she'd found herself wondering about Booth DeWitt and what went on inside that aloof exterior. She'd seen flashes of something warm, something approachable. For Ariel, it was enough to make her dig for more.

And there'd been that pull—the pull she remembered with perfect clarity. She wanted to feel it again, to enjoy it, to understand it.

She finished the taping and had an hour before she and Stella would play out their confrontation scene on the Lane living-room set. "Jerry, I found a kitten for your daughter," she told one of the technicians as she rose. "It's a little calico, I can bring it in on Friday."

"Been to the pound again," Jack said with a sigh. Ignoring him, Ariel stepped over some cable and walked to Booth.

"Hi, want some coffee?"

"All right."

"I keep a Mr. Coffee in my dressing room. The stuff at the commissary's poison." She led the way, not bothering to ask why he was there. Her door was open, as she usually left it. Walking in, she went directly to the coffee maker. "You have to make do with powdered milk."

"Black's fine."

Her dressing room was chaos. Clothes, magazines, pamphlets were tossed over all available space. Her dressing table was littered with jars and bottles and framed photographs of the cast. It smelled of fresh flowers, make-up and dust.

On the wall was a calendar that read February though it was midway through April. An electric clock was unplugged and stuck on 7:05. Booth counted three and one-half pairs of shoes on the floor.

In the midst of it, Ariel stood in a raw-silk suit the color of apricots with her hair pale and glowing in a sophisticated knot. She smelled like a woman should at sunset—soft, with a hint of anticipation. As the coffee began to drip, she turned back to him.

"I'm glad to see you again."

The simplicity of the statement made Booth almost believe it. Cautiously, he kept half the room between them as he watched her. "The taping was interesting. You're very good, Ariel. You milked that five-minute scene for everything there was."

Again she had the impression more of criticism than flattery. "It's important in a soap. You're working in little capsules. Some people only tune in a couple times a week. Then there are those who turn it on as a whim. You hope to grab them."

"Your character." He eyed the suit, approving the subdued style. "I'd say she's a very controlled professional woman who's currently going through some personal crisis. There were a lot of sexual sparks bouncing around between her and the young doctor."

"Very good." With a smile, Ariel picked up two cups, mismatched. "That's neatly tied up. Want some M & M's? I keep a stash in my drawer."

"No. Do you always play around on set when you're not on camera?"

She stirred powdered milk into her coffee, added a

generous spoon of sugar, then handed Booth his. "Jack and I have a running contest on who can make who blow their lines. Actually, it makes us sharper and lowers the tension level." Carelessly, she took magazines from a chair and left them stacked on the floor. "Sit down."

"How many pages of dialogue do you have to learn a week?"

"Varies," she said and sipped. "We run about eighty-five pages of script a day now that we've gone to an hour. Some days I might have twenty or thirty where my character's involved. But for the most part, I tape about three days a week—we don't do a lot of takes." Opening the drawer on her dressing table, she took a handful of candies and began to eat them one at a time. "I'm told it's the closest thing to live TV you can get."

Watching her, he drank. "You really enjoy it."

"Yes, I've been very comfortable with Amanda. Which is why I want to do other things as well. Ruts are monotonous places, but so easy to stay in."

He glanced around the room. "I can't imagine you in one."

Ariel laughed and sat on the edge of her dressing table. "A great compliment. You're frugal with them." Something in his aloof, cool expression made her smile. "Would you like to have dinner?" she asked on impulse.

For an instant surprise flickered over his face—the first time she'd seen it. "It's a bit early for dinner," he said mildly.

"I like the way you do that," she said with a nod. "Conversations with you are never boring. If you're free tonight, I could pick you up at seven."

She was asking him for a date, he thought, very simply, very smoothly, in a manner more friendly than flirtatious. As he had often since the first time he'd met her, Booth wondered what made her tick. "All right, seven." Reaching in his pocket, he pulled out a note pad and scrawled on it. "Here's the address."

Taking it, Ariel scanned the words with a small sound of approval. "Mmmm, you've got a great view of the park." She looked up and grinned in the way that always made him think she'd just enjoyed a little private joke. "I'm a sucker for views."

"I've gathered that already."

Booth walked over to set down his mug and stood close enough so that his legs brushed hers. She didn't back away but watched him with clear, curious eyes. There was something deadly in that face, she thought. Something any woman would recognize and a wary one would retreat from. Fascinated, she counted the beat of her own rapid pulse.

"I'll let you get back to work."

With the slightest move on his part, the contact was broken. Ariel stayed exactly where she was. "I'm glad you stopped by," she said, though she was no longer sure it was precisely the truth.

With a nod, he was gone. Ariel sat on the edge of her cluttered dressing table and wondered if for the first time in her life she'd bitten off more than she could chew.

Because the sun was setting and it was a huge red ball, Ariel paid off the cab two blocks from Booth's apartment building. She wanted some time to think about a phone call she'd received about Scott, her brother's child.

Poor little guy, she thought. So vulnerable, so grown-up. She wondered how much longer it would be before the courts decided his fate. Because she wanted him with her so badly, Ariel refused to believe anything else would happen. Her brother's son, so suddenly orphaned, so miserably unhappy with his maternal grandparents.

They didn't want him, she reflected. Not really. There was such a world of difference between love and duty. Once everything was arranged, she'd be able to give him the kind of easy, unfettered childhood she'd had—with the financial advantages she hadn't known.

She wouldn't think of the complications now. To think of them would make her start doubting the outcome, and she couldn't bear it. She and her lawyers were taking all the possible steps.

Because she wanted no publicity to touch her nephew, Ariel had kept the entire matter to herself—something she rarely did. Perhaps because she had no one to speak to about it, she worried. Every day she told herself Scott would be with her permanently before the end of summer. As long as she kept telling herself, she was able to believe it. Now it was evening, and there was no more she could do.

It was only a little past seven o'clock when she pushed the button of the elevator for Booth's floor in the sleek building on Park Avenue. She'd already set aside that one flash of nerves she felt about him and had decided to enjoy the evening. The idea that he'd been able to make her nervous at all was intriguing enough.

She liked men, the basic personality differences between them and women. Of her closest friends, many were men, in and out of the business. The key word remained friends—she was very cautious about lovers. She ran on emotion, and knowing it, had always been careful of physical relationships.

She was a romantic, unashamedly. Ariel had never doubted that there was one great love waiting for everyone. She had no intention of settling for less— with hearts and flowers and skyrockets included. When she found the right man, she'd know. Whether it was tomorrow or twenty years from tomorrow didn't matter, as long as she found him. In the meantime, she filled her life with work, her friends and her causes. Ariel Kirkwood simply didn't believe in boredom.

She approved of the quiet, carpeted hallway as she strolled down to Booth's apartment. It was wainscoted and elegant. But as she lifted her hand to press the button on his door, she felt that odd flutter of nerves again.

Inside, Booth was standing by the high wide window that looked out over Central Park. He was thinking of her, had been thinking of her for most of the day. And he didn't care for it.

Twice, he'd nearly called to cancel the dinner, telling himself he had work to do. Telling himself he didn't have the time or the inclination to spend an evening with an actress he hardly knew. But he hadn't canceled because he could still see the way her eyes warmed, the way her whole face moved when she smiled.

A professional trick. Liz had had a bagful of them, and unless his perception was very, very wrong, this woman was as skilled an actress as Liz Hunter. That's what he told himself, and yet... And yet he hadn't canceled.

When the buzzer rang, Booth looked over his shoulder at the closed door. It was simply an evening, he decided. A few hours out of the day in which he could study the woman being considered for a major part in an important film. He had little doubt that she would make a pitch for the part before the night was over. With a shrug, Booth walked to the door. That was the business, and she was entitled.

Then, when he opened the door, she smiled at him. He realized he wanted her with an intensity he hadn't felt in years. "Hi. You look nice," she said.

The struggle with desire only made him more remote, made his voice more scrupulously polite. "Come in."

Ariel walked through the door then studied the room with open curiosity. Neat. Her first impression was one of meticulous order. Style. Who could fault a gleaming mix of Chippendale and Hepplewhite? The colors were muted, easy on the eyes. The furniture was arranged in such a way to give a sense of balance. She could smell neither dust nor polish. It was as though the room was perpetually clean and rarely lived in. Somehow, she didn't think it really suited that harsh, nineteenth-century face. No, there was too much formality here for a man who looked like Booth, for a man who moved like him.

Though she felt no sense of welcome, she could appreciate the rather stationary beauty and respect the organized taste.

"A very fastidious man," she murmured, then walked over to study his view of the city.

She wore a dress with yards of skirt and whirls of color. Booth wondered if that was why he suddenly felt life jump into the room. He preferred the quiet, the settled, even the isolated. Yet somehow, for the first time, he felt the appeal of having warmth in his home.

"I was right about this," Ariel said and put her hands into the deep pockets of her skirt. "It's lovely. Where do you work?"

"I have an office set up in another room."

"I'd probably have put my desk right here." Laughing she turned to him so that the mix of colors in her dress seemed to vibrate. "Then again, I wouldn't get much work done." His eyes were very dark and very steady—his face so expressionless he might have been thinking of anything or nothing. "Do you stare at everyone that way?"

"I suppose I do. Would you like a drink?"

"Yes, some dry vermouth if you have it." She wandered over to a cherrywood breakfront and studied his collection of Waterford. No one chose something so lovely, or so capable of catching light and fire if they lacked warmth. Where was his, she wondered. Buried so deep that he'd forgotten it, or simply dormant from lack of use?

Booth paused beside her and offered a glass. "You like crystal?"

"I like beautiful things."

What woman didn't? he thought brittlely. A Russian lynx, a pear-shaped diamond. Yes, women liked beautiful things, particularly when someone else was providing them. He'd already done more than his share of that.

"I watched your show today," Booth began, deciding to give her the opening for her pitch and see what she did with it. "You come across very well as the competent psychiatrist."

"I like Amanda." Ariel sipped her vermouth.

"She's a very stable woman with little hints of vulnerability and passion. I like seeing how subtle I can make them without hiding them completely. What did you think of the show?"

"A mass of complication and intrigue. I was surprised that the bulk of the plots didn't concern fatal diseases and bed hopping."

"You're out of step." She smiled over the rim. "Of course, every soap has some of those elements, but we've done a lot of expanding. Murder, politics, social issues, even science fiction. We do quite a bit of location shooting now in the race for ratings." She drank again. This time it was an opal, milky blue, that gleamed on her hand. "Last year we shot in Greece and Venice. I've never eaten so much in my life. Griff and Amanda had a lover's rendezvous in Venice that was sabotaged. You must've noticed Stella—she plays my sister Vikki."

"The barracuda." Booth nodded. "I recognized the type."

"Oh, Vikki's that all right. Plotting, scheming, being generally nasty. Stella has a marvelous time with her. Vikki's had a dozen affairs, broken up three marriages, destroyed a senator's career. Just last month she pawned our mother's emerald brooch to pay off gambling debts." With a sigh, Ariel drank again. "She has all the fun."

Booth's grin flashed, lingering in his eyes as they met Ariel's. "Are you talking about Stella or Vikki?"

"Both, I suppose. I wondered if I'd be able to do that."

"What?"

"Make you smile. You don't very often, you know."

"No?"

"No." She felt the tug again, sharp and very physical. Indulging herself, she let her gaze lower briefly to his mouth and enjoyed the sensation it brought to her own. "I guess you're too busy picking up parts of people and filing them away."

Finishing off his drink, he set the glass aside. "Is that what I do?"

"Always. It's natural, I suppose, in your line of work, but I decided I was going to pull one out of you before the evening was over." He was still watching her, and though the smile was only a hint now, it was still lurking. It suited him, she thought, that trace of amusement—a cautious, even reluctant amusement. And again, she felt the tug of attraction. With her brows slightly drawn together, she stepped closer. It wasn't something she could or would walk away from.

"Aren't you curious?" she asked quietly, then went on when he didn't answer. "The thing is, I'm not certain I can go through the evening wondering what it would be like."

She put one hand on his shoulder and leaned forward just until their lips touched. There was no pressure, no demand on either side, and yet she felt that slightest of contacts through her whole system. There was a twinge deep inside her, a soft rushing sound in her ears. The mouth against hers was warmer than she'd expected and its taste more potent. Their bodies weren't touching, and the kiss remained a mere meeting of lips. Ariel felt herself open and was mildly surprised. Then, she felt her knees tremble and was stunned.

Slowly, she backed up, unaware that her eyes were wide with shock. Desire had ripped through him at the taste of her mouth, but Booth knew how to conceal his emotions. He wanted her—in the part of Rae and in his bed. To his thinking it wouldn't be long before she offered him one to ensure the other. He'd been much younger when Liz had lured him into bed for a part. He was older now and knew the game. And somehow, he felt Ariel would be more honest in her playing.

"Well..." Ariel let out a long breath while her mind raced. She wished she had five minutes alone to think this through. Somehow she'd always expected she'd fall in love in the blink of an eye, but she wasn't idealistic enough to believe it would be handed back to her. She needed to work out her next move. "And now that the pressure's off—" she set her glass aside "—why don't we go eat?"

Before she could step away, Booth took her arm. If they were going to play out the scene, he wanted to do it then and there. "What do you want?"

There was none of the quiet warmth in his voice that she'd felt in the kiss. Ariel looked into his eyes and saw nothing but a reflection of herself. An unwise man to love, she thought. And, of course, she should have expected that was what would happen to her when the time came. "To go to dinner," she told him.

"I've given you the opportunity to mention the part, you haven't. Why?"

"That's business. This isn't."

He gave a quick laugh. "In this business, it's all business," he countered. "You want to play Rae."

"I wouldn't have read for it if I didn't want it. And once I finish the next reading I'll have it." It frustrated her that she couldn't read him. "Booth, why don't you tell me what you're getting at? It'd be easier for both of us."

He inclined his head, and with his hand on her arm

drew her an inch closer. "Just how much are you willing to do for it?"

His meaning was like a slap in the face. Outrage didn't come, but a piercing hurt that made her face pale and her eyes darken. "I'm willing to give the very best performance I'm capable of." Jerking out of his hold, she started for the door.

"Ariel..." He hadn't expected to call her back, but the look in her eyes had made him feel foul. When she didn't pause, he was going across the room before he could stop himself. "Ariel." Taking her arm again, he turned her around.

The hurt radiating from her was so sharp and real he couldn't convince himself not to believe it. The strength of the need to draw her against him was almost painful. "I'll apologize for that."

She stared at him, wishing it was in her to tell him to go to hell. "I'll accept it," she said instead, "since I'm sure you don't make a habit of apologizing for anything. She took a few pieces out of you, didn't she?"

His hand dropped away from her arm. "I don't discuss my private life."

"Maybe that's part of the problem. Is it women in general, or just actresses you detest?"

His eyes narrowed so that she could only see a glint of the anger. It wasn't necessary to see what you could feel. "Don't push me."

"I doubt anyone could." Though she felt the anger was a promising sign, Ariel didn't feel capable of dealing with it, or her own feelings at the moment. "It's a pity," she continued as she turned for the door again. "When whatever's frozen inside you thaws, I think you'll be a remarkable man. In the meantime, I'll stay out of your way.'' She opened the door, then turned back. ''About the part, Booth, please deal with my agent.'' Quietly, she closed the door behind her.

Chapter 4

"No, Scott, if you eat any more cotton candy your teeth're going to fall right out. And then—" Ariel hauled her nephew up for one fierce hug "—you'd be stuck with stuff like smashed bananas and strained spinach."

"Popcorn," he demanded, grinning at her.

"Bottomless pit." She nuzzled into his neck and let the love flow over her.

Sunday was precious, not only because of the sunshine and balmy spring temperatures, not only because there were hours and hours of leisure time left to her, but because she had the afternoon to spend with the most important person in her life.

He even smells like his father, Ariel thought and wondered if it were possible to inherit a scent. Still holding him, with his sturdy legs wrapped around her waist, she studied his face.

Essentially, it was like looking in a mirror. There'd

only been ten months between Ariel and her brother, Jeremy, and they'd often been taken for twins. Scott had pale curling hair, clear blue eyes, and a face that promised to be lean and rather elegant once it had fined down from childhood. At the moment, it was sticky with pink spun sugar. Ariel kissed him firmly and tasted the sweetness.

"Yum-yum," she murmured, kissing him again when he giggled.

"What about your teeth?"

Arching a brow, she shifted his weight to a more comfortable position. "It doesn't count when it's secondhand."

He gave her a crooked smile that promised to be a heart,breaker in another decade. "How come?"

"It's scientific," Ariel claimed. "Probably the sugar evaporates after being exposed to air and skin."

"You're making that up," he told her with great approval.

Struggling with a smile, she tossed her long smooth braid behind her back. "Who me?"

"You're the best at making up."

"That's my job," she answered primly. "Let's go look at the bears."

"They better have big ones," Scott stated as he wriggled down. "*Great* big ones."

"I hear they're enormous," she told him. "Maybe even big enough to climb right out of the cages."

"Yeah?" His eyes lit up at the idea. Ariel could almost see him writing out the scenario in his mind. The escape, the panic and screams of the crowd and his ultimate heroism in driving the giant, drooling bears back behind the bars. Then, of course, his humbleness in accepting the gratitude of the zookeepers. "Let's go!"

Ariel allowed herself to be dragged along at Scott's dashing pace, winding through the stream of people who'd come to spend their day at the Bronx Zoo. This she could give him, she thought. The fun, the preciousness of childhood. It was such a short time, so concentrated. So many years were passed as an adult—with obligations, responsibilities, worries, timetables. She wanted to give him the freedom, to show him what boundaries you could leap over and the ones you had to respect. Most of all, she wanted to give him love.

She loved and wanted him, not only for the memories he brought back of her brother, but for himself—his uniqueness and odd stability. Though she was a woman who ran her life on a staggered routine that wasn't a routine at all, who enjoyed coming and going on the impulse of the moment, she'd always needed stability—someone to care for, to nurture, to give her back some portion of the emotion she spent. There was nothing like a child, with its innocence and lack of restrictions, to give and take of love. Even now, while he raced and laughed and pointed, caught up in the day and the animals, Scott was feeding her.

If Ariel had believed Scott was happy living with his grandparents, she could have accepted it. But she knew that they were smothering all the specialness that radiated from him.

They weren't unkind people, she mused, but simply set in their thinking. A child was to be formed along certain lines, and that was that. A child was a duty, a solemn one. While she understood the duty, it was joy that came first. They would raise him to be responsible, polite and well-read. And they'd forget the wonder of it.

Perhaps it would have been easier if Scott's grandparents hadn't disapproved of Ariel's brother so strongly—or if Scott hadn't been conceived in youthful defiance and passion...and out of wedlock. Marriage and Scott's birth hadn't eased over the strain in the relationship, nor had the tragic and sudden accident that had taken her brother and young sister-in-law. Scott's grandparents would look at the boy and be reminded that their daughter had married against their wishes and was dead. Ariel looked at him and saw life at its best.

He needs me, she thought, and ruffled his hair as he stood staring wide-eyed at a lumbering bear. Even when her heart wasn't involved, she'd never been able to resist a need. With Scott, her heart had been lost the first time she'd seen him—red and scrawny behind a hospital glass wall.

And she understood that she needed him. To have someone receive her love was vital. She thought of Booth.

He needed her, too, she thought, as a small secret smile touched her lips. Though he didn't know it. A man like that needed the ease that love could bring to his life, and the laughter. And she wanted to give it to him.

Why? Leaning against the barrier, Ariel shook her head. She had no solid reason, and that was enough to convince her it was right. When you could dissect something and find all the answers, you could find all the wrong ones. She trusted instincts and emotions much more than she trusted the intellect. She loved—quickly, unwisely and completely. When she thought about it, Ariel decided she should never have expected it to be otherwise.

If she told him now, he'd think she was lying or insane. She could hardly blame him. It wouldn't be easy to win the confidence of a man as wary or as cynical as Booth DeWitt. With a smile, Ariel nibbled on some of Scott's popcorn. Challenges kept the excitement in life, after all. Whether Booth realized it or not, she was about to add some excitement to his.

"Why're you laughing, Ariel?"

She grinned down at Scott, then scooped him up. He laughed as he always did at her quick, physical shows of affection. "Because I'm happy. Aren't you? It's a happy day."

"I'm always happy with you." His arms went tight around her neck. "Can't I stay with you? Can't I live at your house—all the time?"

She buried her face in the curve of his shoulder—a tender place—knowing she couldn't tell him how hard she was trying to give him that. "We have today," she said instead. "All day."

Holding him, she could smell the scent of his soap and shampoo, the scent of roasted popcorn, the hot, pungent scent of the sun. With another laugh, she set her nephew down. Today, she told herself, that was what she'd show him.

"Let's go see the snakes. I like to watch them slither."

Booth couldn't understand why she kept crowding his mind. He should have been able to push Ariel into a corner of his brain and keep her there while he worked. Instead, she kept filling it.

He could have accepted it if he'd been able to keep

her in her slot—the actress he was all but certain would play his Rae. He could have rationalized his obsession if it had remained a professional one. But Booth kept seeing her as she'd been on top of New York, with her hair blowing frantically and her eyes filled with the wonder of it. That woman had nothing in common with the character of Rae.

And he could see her as she'd looked in his apartment. Vital, fresh—with energy and integrity shimmering from her. He could remember her hurt when he'd been deliberately cruel, and his own guilt—a sensation he'd sworn he'd never feel again. He hardly knew her, and yet she was drawing things out of him he'd promised himself he wouldn't feel again. He was perceptive enough to know she was a woman who could draw out more. For that reason, he'd decided to keep a safe, professional distance between them.

Still, as Booth watched Ariel talk with Jack Rohrer before the reading, he couldn't keep the established lines firmly in place. Was it because she was beautiful and he had always been susceptible to beauty? Was it because she was just unique enough to catch the attention and hold it?

As a writer he couldn't suppress his fascination with the unusual. But he got something from her—some feeling of absolute stability despite the fact that she dressed somewhere between a Gypsy and a teenager. He'd already asked her who she was and had been far from satisfied with her answer. Perhaps, just perhaps he should find out for himself.

"They look good together," Marshell murmured.

The sound Booth made might have been agreement or disinterest, but he didn't take his eyes from Ariel. If he hadn't remembered her first reading so well, he'd have sworn he was making a mistake even considering her for the part. Her smile was much too open, her gestures too fluid. You could look at her and feel the warmth. He found it disconcerting to realize she made him nervous.

Desire. Yes, he felt desire. Booth weighed and measured it. Strong, hard and very nearly urgent—and that with only a look. Of course, she was a woman a man had to want. He wasn't worried about the desire, or even his interest, but about the niggling sensation that something was being slipped out of him without his knowledge and against his will.

Pulling out a cigarette, he watched her through the blue-tinted smoke. It might be worth his while, both as a man and as a writer, to see how many faces she could wear, and how easily she wore them. He sat on the edge of Marshell's desk.

"Let's get started."

At the brief, quiet order, Ariel turned her head and met Booth's gaze. *He's different today,* she thought, but couldn't quite pigeonhole the reason. He still looked at her with that intrusive, serious stare that bordered on the brooding. The distance was still there; she was sensitive enough to recognize the wall he kept erected between himself and the rest of the world. But there was something...

Ariel smiled at him. When he didn't respond, she picked up her copy of the script. She was going to give the best damn reading of her career. For herself—and for some odd reason, for Booth.

"All right, I'd like you to start at the top of the scene where they've come home from the party." Absently Booth tapped his cigarette in a gold-etched ashtray.

Behind him, Marshell nibbled on a stomach mint. "Do you want to read it over first?"

Ariel glanced up from the script. *He still thinks I'm going to blow it,* she realized, and was grateful for the hard knot in her stomach. "It isn't necessary," she told him, then turned to Jack.

For the second time, Booth witnessed the transformation. How was it that even her eyes seemed to go paler, icier when she spoke as Rae? He could feel the old sexual pull and intellecutal abhorrence his ex-wife had always brought to him. With the cigarette smoldering between his fingertips, Booth listened to Rae's scorn and Phil's anger—and remembered all too clearly.

A vampire. He'd called her that and accurately. Bloodless, heartless, alluring. Ariel slipped into the character as if it were a second skin. Booth knew he should admire her for it, even be grateful that she'd made his search for the right actress end. But her chameleon skill annoyed him.

The chemistry was right. Ariel and Jack hurled their lines at each other while the anger and sexual sparks flew. There wasn't any escaping it and no logical reason to try. Without knowing why, Booth was certain that giving Ariel the part was good professional judgment and a serious personal error. He'd just have to deal with the latter as he went.

"That'll do."

The moment Booth cut the scene, Ariel threw her head back and let out breathless laughter. The release—the sudden absence of tension—was tremendous. It would always be that way, she realized, with a part as tough and as cold as this one.

"Oh God, she's so utterly hateful, so completely

self-consumed.'' Eyes alight, face flushed, she whirled to Booth. ''You despise her, and yet she pulls you in. Even when you see the knife she's going to slide under your ribs, it's hard to step away.''

''Yes.'' Watching the scene had disturbed him more than he'd expected. Rising, Booth left his hands in his pockets. ''I want you for the part. We'll contact your agent and negotiate the details.''

She sighed, but the smile lingered around her mouth. ''I can see I've overwhelmed you,'' Ariel said dryly. ''But the bottom line is the part. You won't regret it. Mr. Marshell, Jack, it'll be a pleasure working with you.''

''Ariel...'' Marshell rose and accepted her offered hand. It had been a long time since he'd watched a scene that had left him as shaken as this one. ''Unless I miss my guess—and I never do—you're going to hit it big with this.''

She flashed him a grin and felt like flying. ''I don't suppose I'll complain. Thank you.''

Booth had her elbow before she could turn around, and before he'd realized he intended to touch her. He wanted to vent fury on something, someone, but reasoned it away. ''I'll walk you out.''

Feeling the tension in his fingers, she had to resist the urge to soothe it. This wasn't a man who'd appreciate stroking. ''All right.''

They followed the same route they'd taken the week before, but this time in silence. Ariel sensed he needed it. When they came to the street door, she waited for him to say whatever he intended to say.

''Are you free?'' he asked her.

A bit puzzled, she tilted her head.

"For an early dinner," he elaborated. "I feel I owe you a meal."

"Well." She brushed the hair back from her face. His invitation, such as it was, pleased her—something she took no trouble to hide. "Technically that's the other way around. Why do you want to have dinner with me?"

Just looking at her—the laughing eyes, the generous mouth—pulled him in two directions. Get closer before you lose it. Back off before it's too late. "I'm not completely sure."

"Good enough." She took his hand and lifted her free one for a cab. "Do you like grilled pork chops?"

"Yes."

She laughed over her shoulder before pulling him into the cab. "An excellent start." After giving the driver an address in Greenwich Village, she settled back. "I think the next move is to have a conversation without a word, one single word, that has to do with business. We might just make it in each other's company for more than an hour."

"All right." Booth nodded. He'd made the decision to get to know her and get to know her he would. "But we'll steer away from politics, too."

"Deal."

"How long have you lived in New York?"

"I was born here. A native." She grinned and crossed her legs. "You're not. I read somewhere that you're from Philadelphia and very top-drawer. Lots of influential relatives." She didn't even glance around when the cab skidded and swerved. "Are you happy in New York?"

He'd never thought about equating it with happiness, but now that he did, the answer came easily. "Yes. I need the demands and the movement for long periods of time.''

"And then you need to go away," she finished. "And be alone—on your boat."

Before he could be uncomfortable with her accuracy, he'd accepted it. "That's right. I relax when I'm sailing and I like to relax alone."

"I paint," she told him. "Terrible paintings." With a laugh, she rolled her eyes. "But it helps me work the kinks out when I get them. I keep threatening people with an original Kirkwood as a Christmas present, but I haven't the heart to do it."

"I'd like to see one," he murmured.

"The problem seems to be that I splatter my mood on the canvas. Here we are." Ariel hopped out of the cab and stood on the curb.

Booth glanced around at the tiny storefronts. "Where're we going?"

"To the market." In her easy manner, she hooked her arm through his. "I don't have any pork chops at home."

He looked down at her. "Home?"

"Most of the time I'd rather cook than eat out. And tonight I'm too wired to deal with a restaurant. I have to be busy."

"Wired?" After studying her profile, Booth shook his head. His hair was dark in the lowering sun, and the movement sent it settling carelessly around his face. A contrast, Ariel mused, to the rather formal exterior. "I'd have said you look remarkably calm."

"Uh-uh. But I'm trying to save the full explosion until after my agent calls and tells me everything's carved in granite. Don't worry—" she smiled up at him "—I'm a fair cook."

If a man judged only by that porcelain face, he'd never have believed she'd know one end of the stove from the other. But Booth knew about surfaces. Maybe, just maybe, there'd be a surprise under hers. Despite all the warnings he'd given himself, he smiled. "Only fair?"

Her eyes lit in appreciation. "I hate to brag, but actually, I'm terrific." She steered him into a small, cluttered market that smelled heavily of garlic and pepper, and began a haphazard selection for the evening meal. "How're the avocados today, Mr. Stanislowski?"

"The best." The grocer looked over her head to study Booth out of the corner of his eye. "Only the best for you, Ariel."

"I'll have two then, but you pick them out." She poked at a head of romaine. "How did Monica do on her history quiz?"

"Ninety-two percent." His chest swelled a bit under his apron, but he continued to speculate on the dark, brooding man who'd come in with Ariel.

"Terrific. I need four really nice center-cut chops." While he selected them, she studied the mushrooms, well aware that he was bursting with curiosity over Booth. "You know, Mr. Stanislowski, Monica would love a kitten."

As he started to weigh the meat, the grocer sent her an exasperated glance. "Now, Ariel..."

"She's certainly old enough to care for one on her own," Ariel continued and pinched a tomato. "It'd be company for her, and a responsibility. And she did get ninety-two on that quiz." Looking over, she sent him a dashing, irresistible smile. He flushed and shifted his feet.

"Maybe if you were to bring one by, we could think about it."

"I will." Still smiling, she reached for her wallet. "How much do I owe you?"

"That was smoothly done," Booth murmured when they stepped outside. "And it's the second time I've heard you palming off a kitten. Did your cat have a litter?"

"No, I just happen to know about a number of homeless kittens." She tilted her face toward him. "If you're interested..."

"No." The answer was firm and brief as he took the bag from her.

Ariel merely smiled and decided she could work on him later. Now, she breathed in the scent of spices and baking from the open doorways. Some children raced along the sidewalk, laughing. A few old men sat out on the stoops to gossip. After the dinner hour, Ariel knew other members of the family would come out to talk and exchange news and enjoy the spring weather. Through a screened window she heard some muted snatches of *Beethoven's Ninth,* and farther down the pulse of top-forty rock.

Two years before, Ariel had moved to the Village for the neighborhood feel, and had never been disappointed. She could sit outside and listen to the elderly reminisce, watch the children play, hear about the latest teenage heartthrob or the newest baby. It had been exactly what she'd needed when her family had gone its separate ways.

"Hi, Mr. Miller, Mr. Zimmerman."

The two old men who sat on the steps of the converted brownstone eyed Booth before they looked at

Ariel. "Don't think you should give that Cameron another chance," Mr. Miller told her.

"Boot him out." Mr. Zimmerman gave a wheeze that might have been a chuckle. "Get yourself a man with backbone."

"Is that an offer?" She kissed his cheek before climbing the rest of the steps.

"I'll have a dance at the block party," he called after her.

Ariel winked over her shoulder. "Mr. Zimmerman, you can have as many as you want." As they started up the inside steps, Ariel began to fish in her bag for her keys. "I'm crazy about him," she told Booth. "He's a retired music instructor and still teaches a few kids on the side. He sits on the stoop so he can watch the women go by." She located the keys attached to a large, plastic, grinning sun. "He's a leg man."

Automatically, Booth glanced over his shoulder. "He told you?"

"You just have to watch the direction his eyes take when a skirt passes."

"Yours included?"

Her eyes danced. "I fit into the category of niece. He thinks I should be married and raising large quantities of babies."

She fit a single key into a single lock, something Booth thought almost unprecedented for New York, then pushed open the door. He'd been expecting the unusual. And he wasn't disappointed.

The focal point of the living room was a long oversize hammock swinging from brass ceiling hooks. One end of it was piled with pillows and beside it was a washstand holding one thick candle, three-quarters burned down.

There was color—he'd known there'd be an abundance of it—and a style that was undefinable.

The sofa was a long, curved French antique upholstered with faded rose brocade, while a long wicker trunk served as a coffee table. As in Ariel's dressing room, the entire area was cluttered with books, papers and scents. He caught the fragrance of candle wax, potpourri and fresh flowers. Bunches of spring blossoms were spilling from a collection of vases that ran from dime-store pottery to Meissen.

There was an umbrella stand in the shape of a stork that was filled with ostrich and peacock feathers. A pair of boxing gloves hung in the corner behind the door.

"I guess you'd class as a featherweight," Booth mused.

Ariel followed his gaze and smiled. "They were my brother's. He boxed in high school. Want a drink?" Before he could answer, she took the bag from him, then headed down a hallway.

"A little Scotch and water." When he turned, his attention and his senses were struck by a wall of paintings. They were hers, of course. Who else would paint with that kind of kinetic energy, verve and disregard for rules? There were splotches of color, lines of it, zigzags. Moving closer, Booth decided that while he wouldn't call them terrible, he wasn't quite sure what he'd call them. Vivid, eccentric, disturbing. Certainly they weren't paintings to relax by. They showed both flair and heedlessness, and whether she'd intended them to or not they suited the room to perfection.

As he continued to study the paintings, three cats came into the room. Two were hardly more than kittens, coal-black and amber-eyed. They dashed around his legs once before they made a beeline for the kitchen. The other was a huge tiger who managed to walk with stiff dignity on three legs. Booth could hear Ariel laugh and say something to the two cats who had found her. The tiger watched Booth with quiet patience.

"Scotch and water." Ariel came back in, barefoot, carrying two glasses.

Booth accepted the glass, then gestured with it. "Those must be some kinks you work out."

Ariel glanced toward her paintings. "Looks like it, doesn't it? Saves money on a therapist—though I shouldn't say that since I play the role of one."

"You've quite a place here."

"I learned I thrive on confusion." Laughing up at him, she sipped. "You've met Butch, I see." She bent and slid one hand over the tiger's back. He arched, letting out a grumble of a purr. "Keats and Shelley were the rude ones. They're having their dinner."

"I see." Booth glanced down to see Butch rub against Ariel's leg before he waddled over to the sofa and leaped onto a cushion. "Don't you find it difficult tending three cats in a city apartment while dealing with a demanding profession?"

She only smiled. "No. I'm going to start the grill."

Booth lifted a brow. "Where?"

"Why, on the terrace." Ariel walked over and slid open a door. Outside was a postage-stamp balcony more along the lines of a window ledge. On it she'd crammed pots of geraniums and a tiny charcoal grill.

"The terrace," Booth murmured over her shoulder. Only an incurable optimist or a hopeless dreamer would have termed it so. He found himself grateful she had. Laughing, he leaned against the doorjamb.

After straightening from the grill, Ariel stared at

him. The sound of his laughter whispered along her skin and eased her mind. "Well, well. That's very nice. Do you know that's the first time since I've met you that you've laughed and meant it?"

Booth shrugged and sipped at his Scotch. "I suppose I'm out of practice."

"We'll soon fix that," Ariel said. She smiled, holding her hand out, palm up. "Got a match?"

Booth reached in his pocket, but something—perhaps the humor in her eyes—changed his mind. Stepping forward, he took her shoulders and lowered his mouth to hers.

He'd caught her off guard. Ariel hadn't expected him to do anything on impulse, and he'd given no sign of his intention. Before she had time to prepare, the power of the kiss whipped through her, touching the emotion, the senses, then taking over.

It wasn't a mere touching of lips this time, but a hard, thorough demand that had her wrapped in his arms and trapped against the side of the door. She reached up to take his face in her hands as she gave, unquestioningly, what he sought from her.

There was no gradual smoldering, no experimentation, but a leap of flame so intense and quick it seemed they were already lovers. She felt the instant intimacy and understood it. Her heart was already his, she couldn't deny him her body.

He felt the need churn and was relieved. It had been long, too long, since he'd more than indifferently wanted a woman. There was nothing indifferent about the passion he felt now. It was hard and clear, like the wind that buffeted him when he sailed. It spelled freedom. Drawing her closer, Booth absorbed it.

He could smell her—that warm, teasing fragrance

that seemed to pulse out of her skin. How often had that scent come to him when he'd only thought of her? He remembered her taste. Alluring, giving and again warm. And the feel of her body—slender, soft, with still more warmth. It was that that touched every aspect of her, that promised to fill him. He needed it, though he'd gone for years without knowing it. Perhaps he needed her.

And it was that that had him pulling back when he wanted more and more of what she had an abundance of.

Her eyes opened slowly when her mouth was free. Ariel looked directly, unblinkingly at him. This time she saw more than a reflection of self. She saw longings and caution and a glimpse of emotion that stirred her.

"I've wanted you to do that," she murmured.

Booth forced himself to level, forced himself to think past the senses she sent swimming. "I haven't got anything for you."

That hurt, but Ariel knew love wasn't painless. "I think you're wrong. But then, I have a tendency to rush into things. You don't." She took a deep breath and a step back. "Why don't you light this and I'll go make a salad?" Without waiting for his answer she turned and walked into the kitchen.

Steady, she ordered herself. She knew she had to be steady to deal with Booth and the feelings he brought to her. He wasn't a man who would accept a flood of emotion all at once, or the demands that went with it. If she wanted him in her life, she'd have to tread carefully, and at his pace.

He wasn't nearly as hard and cool as he tried to be, Ariel mused. With a half smile, she began to wash the fresh vegetables. She could tell from his laugh, and from those flickers of amusement in his eyes. And, of course, she was certain she couldn't have fallen in love with a man without a sense of humor. It pleased her to be able to draw it out of him. The more they were together, the easier it was. She wondered if he knew. Humming, she began to slice avocado.

Booth watched her from the doorway. A smile lingered on her lips, and her eyes held that light he was growing too used to. She used the kitchen knife with the careless confidence of one who was accustomed to domestic chores. In one easy movement she tossed her hair behind her back.

Why should such a simple scene hold so much appeal for him, he wondered. Just looking at her standing at the sink, her hands full, the water running—he could feel himself relaxing. What was it about her that made him want to put his feet up and his head back? At that moment, he could see himself going to her to wrap his arms around her waist and nuzzle. He must be going mad.

She knew he was there. Her senses were keen, and sharper still where Booth was involved. Keeping her back to him, she continued preparing the salad. "Have any trouble lighting it?"

He lifted a brow. "No."

"Well, it doesn't take long to heat up. Hungry?"

"A bit." He crossed the room to her. He wouldn't touch her, but he'd get just a little closer.

Smiling she held up a thin slice of avocado, offering him a bite. Ariel could see the wariness in his eyes as he allowed her to feed him. "I'm never a bit hungry," she told him, finishing off the slice herself. "I'm always starving."

He'd told himself he wouldn't touch her, yet he found that the back of his hand was sliding over the side of her face. "Your skin," he murmured. "It's beautiful. It looks like porcelain, feels like satin." His gaze skimmed over her face, over her mouth before it locked on hers. "I should never have touched you."

Her heart was pounding. Gentleness. That was unexpected and would undermine her completely. "Why?"

"It leads to more." His fingers ran slowly down the length of her hair before he dropped his hands. "I haven't any more. You want something from me," he murmured.

Her breath trembled out. She'd never realized what a strain it was to hold in your emotions. She'd never tried. "Yes, I do. For now, just some companionship at dinner. That should be easy."

When she started to turn back to the sink, Booth stopped her. "Nothing about this is going to be easy. If I continue to see you, like this, I'm going to take you to bed."

It would be easy, so easy, just to go into his arms. But he'd never accept the generosity, and she'd never survive the emptiness. "Booth, I'm a grown woman. If I go to bed with you, it's my choice."

He nodded. "Perhaps. I just want to make sure I have one." He turned and left her alone in the room.

Ariel took a deep breath. She wasn't going to have it, she decided. No, not any of it. He'd simply have to learn how to cope without the moodiness and tension. Lifting the platter of chops, she went back into the living room.

"Lighten up, DeWitt," she ordered and caught a glimpse of surprise on his face as she went to the grill.

"I have to deal with melodrama and misery in every episode. I don't let it into my personal life. Fix yourself another drink, sit down and relax." Ariel set the chops on the grill, added some freshly ground pepper, then walked to the stereo. She switched on jazz, bluesy and mellow.

When she turned around he was still standing, looking at her. "I mean it," she told him. "I have a firm policy about worrying about what complications might come up. They're going to happen if you think about it or if you don't. So why waste your time?"

"Is it that easy for you?"

"Not always. Sometimes I have to work at it."

Thoughtfully, he drew out a cigarette. "We won't be good together," he said after he'd lit it. "I don't want anyone in my life."

"Anyone?" She shook her head. "You're too intelligent to believe a person can live without anyone. Don't you need friendship, companionship, love?"

Blowing out a stream of smoke, he tried to ignore the twinge the question brought him. He'd spent more than two years convincing himself he didn't. Why should he just now, so suddenly, realize the fruitlessness of it? "Each one of those things requires something in return that I no longer want to give."

"Want to give." Her gaze was thoughtful, her mouth unsmiling. "At least you're honest in your phrasing. The more I'm around you, the more I realize you never lie to anyone—but yourself."

"You haven't been around me enough to know who or what I am." He crushed out his cigarette and thrust his hands in his pockets. "And you're much better off that way."

"I or you?" she countered, then shook her head

when he didn't answer. "You're letting her make a victim out of you," Ariel murmured. "I'm surprised."

His eyes narrowed; the green frosted. "Don't open closets unless you know what's inside, Ariel."

"Too safe." She preferred the simple anger she felt from him now. With a half laugh, she crossed to him and put her hands on his upper arms. "There's no fun in life without risks. I can't function without fun." Her fingers squeezed, gently. "Look, I enjoy being with you. Is that all right?"

"I'm not sure." She was pulling him in again, with the lightest of touches. "I'm not sure it is for either of us."

"Do yourself a favor," she suggested. "Don't worry about it for a few days and see what happens." Rising on her toes, she brushed his mouth in a gesture that was both friendly and intimate. "Why don't you fix those drinks?" she added, grinning. "Because I'm burning the chops."

Chapter 5

"No, Griff, I won't discuss my marriage." Amanda picked up a delft-blue watering can and meticulously tended the plants in her office window. The sun, a product of the sweltering stage lights, poured through the glass.

"Amanda, you can't keep secrets in small towns. It's already common knowledge that you and Cameron aren't living together any longer."

Beneath the trim, tailored jacket, her shoulders stiffened. "Common knowledge or not, it's my business." Keeping her back to him, she examined a bloom on an African violet.

"You're losing weight, there are shadows under your eyes. Dammit, Mandy, I can't stand to see you this way."

She waited a beat, then turned slowly. "I'm fine. I'm capable of handling what needs to be handled."

Griff gave a short laugh. "Who'd know that better than I do?"

Something flared in her eyes, but her voice was cool and final. "I'm busy, Griff."

"Let me help you," he said with sudden, characteristic passion. "It's all I've ever wanted to do."

"Help?" Her voice chilled as she set down the can. "I don't need any help. Do you think I should confide in you, trust you after what you did to me?" As she tilted her head, the tiny sapphires in her ears glinted. She shifted on her mark. "The only difference between you and Cameron is that I let you tear up my life. I won't make the same mistake again."

Fury burst from him as he grabbed her arm. "You never asked me what Vikki was doing in my room. Not then, and not in all these months. You bounced back quick, Mandy, and ended up with another man's ring on your finger."

"It's still there," she said quietly. "So you'd better take your hands off me."

"Do you think that's going to stop me now that I know you don't love him?" Passion, rage, desire—all emanated from his eyes, his voice, his body. "I can look at you and see it," he went on before she could deny it. "I know what's inside you like no one else does. So handle it." He dragged his hands through her hair and dislodged pins. The camera dollied closer. "And handle this."

Pulling her against him, Griff crushed her mouth with his. She nearly tore away. Nearly. For a heartbeat, she was still. Amanda lifted her hands to his shoulders to push away, but clung instead. A soft, muffled moan escaped as passion flared. For a moment, they were locked together as they'd once been. Then, he dragged her away, keeping his hands tight on her arms. Desire and anger sparked between them. His tangible, hers restrained.

"You're not going to back away from me this time," he told her. "I'll wait, but I won't wait long. You come to me, Mandy. That's where you belong."

Releasing her, Griff stormed out of the office. Amanda lifted an unsteady hand to her lips and stared at the closed door.

"Cut."

Ariel marched around the prop wall of her office. "You ate those onions on purpose."

Jack tugged on her disheveled hair. "Just for you, sweetie."

"Swine."

"God, I love it when you call me names." Dramatically, Jack gathered her in his arms and bent her backward in an exaggerated dip. "Let me take you to bed and show you the true meaning of passion."

"Not until you chew a roll of breath mints, fella." Giving him a firm push, Ariel freed herself, then turned to her director. The furnace of stage lights had already been dimmed. "Neal, if that's it for today, I've got an appointment across town."

"Take off. See you at seven on Monday."

In the dressing room, Ariel stripped Amanda's elegant facade away and replaced it with slim cotton pants and a billowy, tailored man's shirt. After slipping on flat shoes she left the studio and went outside. There was a small group of fans waiting, hoping that someone recognizable would appear. They clustered around Amanda, autograph books in hand, as they chattered about the show and tossed questions.

"Are you going to go back with Griff?"

Ariel looked over at the sparkling-eyed teenager and grinned. "I don't know...he's awfully hard to resist."

"He's super! I mean his eyes are just so *green*." She tucked her gum into the corner of her mouth and sighed. "I'd die if he looked at me the way he looks at you."

Ariel thought of another pair of green eyes and nearly sighed herself. "We'll have to wait to see what develops, won't we? I'm glad you like the show." Easing away from the crowd, she hailed a cab. The minute she gave the address, she slumped back against the seat.

She wasn't sure why she felt so tired. She supposed it was the prospect of the meeting that made her so bone-weary. True, she hadn't been sleeping as well as was her habit, but she'd gone through wakeful phases before without any strain.

Booth. If Booth were the only thing on her mind, she could have dealt with it well enough. She hoped she would. But there was Scott.

The idea of confronting his grandparents didn't frighten her, but it did weary her. Ariel had spoken with them before. There was no reason to believe this session would be any different.

She remembered the way Scott had beamed and glowed at the zoo. Such a simple thing. Such a vital thing. The way he'd clung to her—it tore at her heart. If there were just some other way...

Closing her eyes, she sighed. She didn't believe there would be another way, not even with all her natural optimism. In the end, they'd come to a complicated, painful custody suit with Scott caught in the middle.

What was best? What was right? Ariel wanted someone to tell her, to advise and comfort her. But for the first time in her life she felt it impossible to confide in anyone. The more private she kept this affair, the less chance there was of Scott being hurt by it. She would just have to follow her instincts, and hope.

With her mind on a dozen other things, Ariel paid the cabbie and walked into the sleek steel building that housed her lawyers' offices. On the way from the lobby to the thirtieth floor, she gathered all her confidence together. This would be perhaps the last time she'd have the opportunity to speak with Scott's grandparents on an informal basis. She needed to give it her best shot.

The little tremor in her stomach wasn't so different from stage fright. Comfortable with it, Ariel walked into Bigby, Liebowitz and Feirson.

"Good afternoon, Ms. Kirkwood." The receptionist beamed a smile at Ariel and wondered if she could get away with a similar outfit. Not slim enough, she decided wistfully. Instead of looking dashing, she'd just look frumpy. "Mr. Bigby's expecting you."

"Hello, Marlene. How's the puppy working out?"

"Oh, he's so smart. My husband couldn't believe that a mutt could learn so many tricks. I really want to thank you for arranging it for me."

"I'm glad he's got a good home." She caught herself lacing her fingers together—a rare outward sign of tension. Deliberately Ariel dropped her hands to her sides as the receptionist rang through.

"Ms. Kirkwood's here, Mr. Bigby. Yes, sir." She rose as she replaced the receiver. "I'll take you back. If you have time before you leave, Ms. Kirkwood, my sister'd love your autograph. She never misses your show."

"I'd be happy to." Ariel's fingers groped for each other and she restrained them. *Save the nerves for later,* she told herself, *when you can afford them.* For once, she'd apply some of Amanda's steady calm to her personal life.

"Well, Ariel." The spindly, bearded man behind the massive desk rose as she entered. The room carried a vague scent of peppermint and polish. "Right on time."

"I never miss a cue." Ariel crossed the plush carpet with both hands extended. "You look good, Charlie."

"I feel good since you talked me into giving up smoking. Six months," he said with a grin. "Three days and—" he checked his watch "—four and a half hours."

She squeezed his hands. "Keep counting."

"We've got about fifteen minutes before the Andersons are due. Want some coffee?"

"Oh, yeah." On the words, Ariel sunk into a creamy leather chair.

Bigby pushed his intercom. "Would you bring some coffee back, Marlene? So..." He set down the receiver and folded his neat, ringless hands. "How're you holding up?"

"I'm a wreck, Charlie." She stretched out her legs and ordered herself to relax. First the toes, then the ankles, then all the way up. "You're practically the only one I can talk to about this. I'm not used to holding things in."

"If things go well you won't have to much longer."

She sent him a level look. "What chance do we have?"

"A fair one."

With a small sigh, Ariel shook her head. "Not good enough."

After a brief knock, Marlene entered with the coffee tray. "Cream and sugar, Ms. Kirkwood?"

"Yes, thank you." Ariel accepted the cup then immediately rose and began to pace. Maybe if she could turn some of the nerves to energy she wouldn't burst. Maybe. "Charlie, Scott needs me."

And you need him, he thought as he watched her. "Ariel, you're a responsible member of your community with a good reputation. You have a steady job with an excellent income, though it can and will be argued that it's not necessarily stable. You put your brother through college and have some sort of an involvement with every charity known to man." He saw her smile at that and was pleased. "You're young, but not a child. The Andersons are both in their midsixties. That should have some bearing on the outcome, and you'll have the emotion on your side."

"God, I hate to think of there being sides," she murmured. "There're sides in arguments, in wars. This can't be a war, Charlie. He's just a child."

"As difficult as it is, you're going to have to think practically about this."

With a nod, she sipped uninterestedly at her coffee. Practical. "But I'm single, and I'm an actress."

"There're pros and cons. This last-ditch meeting was your idea," he continued. "I don't like to see you get churned up this way."

"I have to try just once more before we find ourselves in court. The idea that Scotty might have to testify..."

"Just an easy talk with the judge in chambers, Ariel. It's not traumatic, I promise you."

"Not to you, maybe not to him, but to me..." She whirled around, her eyes dark with passion. "I'd give it up, Charlie. I swear I'd give it up this minute if I could believe he'd be happy with them. But when he looks at me..." Breaking off, she shook her head. Both hands were clenched on the coffee cup and she concentrated on relaxing them. "I know I'm being emotional about this, but it's the only way I've ever been able to judge what was right and what was wrong. If I look at it practically, I know they'll feed him and shelter him and educate him. But nurturing..." She turned to stare out of the window. "I keep coming back to the nurturing. Am I doing the best for him, Charlie? I just want to be sure."

For a moment, he sat fondling the gold pen on his desk. She asked hard questions. In the law, it wasn't a matter of best, but of justice. The two weren't always synonymous. "Ariel, you know the boy. At the risk of sounding very unlawyerlike, I say you have to do what your heart tells you."

Smiling, she turned back. "You say the right things. That's all I've ever been able to do." For a moment, she hesitated, then plunged. Since she was here for advice, she'd go all the way with it. "Charlie, if I told you I'd fallen in love with a man who thinks relationships are to be avoided at all costs and actresses are the least trustworthy individuals on the planet, what would you say?"

"I'd say it was typical of you. How long do you figure it'll take you to change his mind?"

Laughing, she dragged a hand through her hair. "Always the right thing," she said again.

"Sit down and drink your coffee, Ariel," he advised. "You're the one who says if something's meant to happen, it happens."

"When have I ever said anything so trite?" she demanded but did as he said. "All right, Charlie." She heaved a long sigh. "Do you want to give me the lecture on what I should expect and what I shouldn't say?"

"For what good it'll do." He toyed with the edge of Ariel's file. "You'll meet the Andersons' lawyer, Basil Ford. He's very painstaking and very conservative. I've dealt with him before."

"Did you win?"

Bigby grinned at her as he leaned back in his chair. "I'd say we're about even. Since this is a voluntary, informal meeting, there won't be that much for either Ford or me to do. But if he asks you a question you shouldn't answer, I'll take care of it." Meticulously, Bigby settled the English bone-china cup back in its saucer. "Otherwise, say what you want, but don't elaborate more than necessary. Above all, don't lose your temper or your grip. If you want to yell or cry, wait until they've gone."

"You've gotten to know me very well," she murmured. "All right, I'll be calm and lucid." When the buzzer sounded on his desk, Ariel balled her hands into fists.

"Yes, Marlene, bring them in. And we'll need more coffee." He looked across at Ariel, measuring the strain in her eyes against the strength. "It's a discussion," he reminded her. "It's doubtful anything will be decided here today."

She nodded and concentrated on relaxing her hands.

When the door opened, Bigby rose, all joviality. "Basil, good to see you." He stretched his hand out to meet that of the erect, gray-suited man with thinning hair. "Mr. and Ms. Anderson, please have a seat. We'll have coffee in a moment. Basil Ford, Ariel Kirkwood."

Ariel nearly let out a tense giggle at the cocktail introduction. "Hello, Mr. Ford." She found his handshake firm and his gaze formidable.

"Ms. Kirkwood." He sat smoothly with his briefcase by his side.

"Hello, Mr. Anderson, Ms. Anderson."

Ariel received a nod from the woman and a brief formal handshake from her husband. Attractive people. Solid people. She'd always felt that from them—along with their rigidity. Both stood straight, a product of their military training. Anderson had retired from active service as a full colonel ten years before, and in her youth, his wife had been an Army nurse.

They'd met during the war, had served together and married. You could sense their closeness—the intimacy of thoughts and values. Perhaps, Ariel mused, that was why they had trouble seeing anyone else's viewpoint.

Together, the Andersons sat on a cushy two-seater sofa. Both were conservatively dressed: her iron-gray hair was skimmed back and his snowy white was cropped close. Feeling the waves of their disapproval, Ariel bit back a sigh. Instinct and experience told her she'd never get through to them on an emotional level.

While coffee was served, Bigby steered the conversation into generalities. The Andersons answered politely and ignored Ariel as much as possible. Because they spoke around her, she took care not to ask them any direct questions. She'd antagonize them soon enough.

She recognized the signal when Bigby sat behind his desk and folded his hands on the surface.

"I believe we can all agree that we have one mutual concern," he began. "Scott's welfare."

"That's why we're here," Ford said easily.

Bigby skimmed his gaze over Ford and concentrated on the Andersons. "Since that's the case, an informal meeting like this where we can exchange points of view and options should be to everyone's benefit."

"Naturally, my clients' main concern is their grandchild's well-being." Ford spoke in his beautiful orator's voice before he sipped his coffee. "Ms. Kirkwood's interest is understood, of course. As to the matter of custody, there's no question as to the rights and capability of Mr. and Ms. Anderson."

"Nor of Ms. Kirkwood's," Bigby put in mildly. "But it isn't rights and capabilities we're discussing today. It's the child himself. I'd like to make it clear that at this point, we're not questioning your intentions or your ability to raise the child." He spoke to the Andersons again, skillfully bypassing his colleague. "The issue is what's best for Scott as an individual."

"My grandson," Anderson began in his deep, raspy voice, "belongs where he is. He's well-fed, well-dressed and well-disciplined. His upbringing will have a sense of order. He'll be sent to the best schools available."

"What about well-loved?" Ariel blurted out before she could stop herself. "What money can't buy..." Leaning forward she focused her attention on Scott's grandmother. "Will he be well-loved?"

"An abstract question, Ms. Kirkwood," Ford put in briskly. "If we could—"

"No, it isn't," Ariel interrupted, sparing him a

glance before she turned back to the Andersons. "There's nothing more solid than love. Nothing more easily given or withheld. Will you hold him at night if he's frightened of shadows? Will you understand how important it is to pretend that he's protecting you? Will you always listen when he needs to talk?"

"He won't be coddled if that's what you mean." Anderson set down his coffee and rested a hand on one knee. "A child's values are molded early. These fantasies—that you encourage—aren't healthy. I have no intention of allowing my grandson to live in a dream-world."

"A dreamworld." Ariel stared at him and saw a solid rock wall of resistance. "Mr. Anderson, Scott has a beautiful imagination. He's full of life, and visions."

"Visions." Anderson's lips thinned. "Visions will do nothing but make him look for what isn't there, expect what he can't have. The boy needs a firm basis in reality. In what *is*. You make your living from pretending, Ms. Kirkwood. My grandson won't live his life in a storybook."

"There're twenty-four hours in every day, Mr. Anderson. Isn't there enough reality in that so we can put a small portion of time aside for wishing? All children need to believe in wishes, especially Scott after so much has been taken away from him. Please..." Her gaze shifted to the stiff-backed woman on the sofa. "You've known grief. Scott lost the two people in the world who meant love and security and normality. All of those things have to be given back to him."

"By you?" Ms. Anderson sat very still, her eyes remained very level. In them Ariel saw remnants of pain. "My daughter's child will be raised by me."

"Ms. Kirkwood." Ford interrupted smoothly, then

crossed his legs. "To touch on more practical matters, I'm aware that you currently have a key role in a— daytime drama, I believe is the word. This equals a regular job with a steady income. But to be down-to-earth for a moment, it's habitual for these things to change. How would you support a child if your income was interrupted?"

"My income won't be interrupted." Bigby caught her eye, so with an effort Ariel held on to her temper. "I'm under contract. I'm also signed to do a film with P.B. Marshell." Noticing the flicker of speculation, Ariel blessed fate for throwing the part her way.

"That's very impressive," Ford told her. "However, I'm sure you'd be the first to admit that your profession is renowned for its ups and downs."

"If we're talking financial stablity, Mr. Ford, I assure you that I'm capable of giving Scott all the material requirements necessary. If my career should take a downswing, I'd simply supplement it. I've experience in both the retail and the restaurant business." A half smile teased her mouth as she thought of her days selling perfume and powder, and waiting tables. Oh, yes, experience was the right word. "But I can't believe any of us would put a bank statement first when we're discussing a child." It was said calmly, with only a hint of disdain.

"I'm sure we all agree that the child's monetary well-being is of primary importance," Bigby put in. The subtle tone of his voice was his warning to Ariel. "There's no question that both the Andersons and my client are capable of providing Scott with food, shelter, education, etc."

"There's also the matter of marital status." Ford stroked a long finger down the side of his nose. "As a single woman, a single professional woman, Ms. Kirkwood, just how much time would you be able to spare for Scott?''

"Whatever he needs," Ariel said simply. "I recognize my priorities, Mr. Ford."

"Perhaps." He nodded, resting a hand on the arm of his chair. "And perhaps you haven't thought this through completely. Having never raised a child, you might not be fully aware of the time involved. You have an active social life, Ms. Kirkwood."

His words and tone were mild, his meaning clear. Any other time, in any other place, she would have been amused. "Not as active as it reads in print, Mr. Ford."

Again, he nodded. "You're also a young woman, attractive. I'm sure it's reasonable to assume that marriage is highly likely at some time in the future. Have you considered how a potential husband might feel about the responsibility of raising someone else's child?''

"No." Her fingers laced together. "If I loved a man enough to marry him, he'd accept Scott as part of me, of my life. Otherwise, he wouldn't be the kind of man I'd love."

"If you had to make a choice—"

"Basil." Bigby held up a hand, and though he smiled, his eyes were hard. "We shouldn't get bogged down in this sort of speculation. No one expects us to solve this custody issue here today. What we want is to get a clear picture of everyone's feelings. What your clients and mine want for Scott."

"His well-being," Anderson said tersely.

"His happiness," Ariel murmured. "I want to believe they're the same thing."

"You're no different from your brother." Anderson's voice was sharp and low, like the final snap of a whip. "Happiness. He preached happiness at all costs to my daughter until she tossed aside all her responsibilities, her education, her values. Pregnant at eighteen, married to a penniless student who put more effort into flying a kite than keeping a decent job."

Ariel's mouth trembled open as the pain struck. No, she wouldn't waste her breath defending her brother. He needed no defense. "They loved each other," she said instead.

"Loved each other." Color rose in Anderson's cheeks, the first and only sign of emotion Ariel had seen from him. "Can you honestly believe that's enough?"

"Yes. They were happy together. They had a beautiful child together. They had dreams together." Ariel swallowed as the urge to weep pounded at her. "Some people never have that much."

"Barbara would still be alive if we'd kept her away from him."

Ariel looked over at the older woman and saw more than pain now. The strong, bony hands shook slightly, the voice broke. It was a combination of grief and fury which Ariel recognized and understood. "Jeremy's gone too, Ms. Anderson," she said quietly. "But Scott's here."

"He killed my daughter." The woman's eyes glowed against a skin gone abruptly pale.

"Oh, no." Ariel reached out, shocked by the words, drawn by the pain. "Ms. Anderson, Jeremy adored Barbara. He'd never have done anything to hurt her."

"He took her up in that plane. Barbara had no business being up in one of those small planes. She wouldn't have been if he hadn't taken her.''

"Ms. Anderson, I know how you feel—''

She jerked away from Ariel's offer of comfort, her breath suddenly coming fast and shallow. "Don't you tell me you know how I feel. She was my only child. My only child.'' Rising, she sent Ariel an icy stare that shimmered with tears. "I won't discuss Barbara with you, or Barbara's son.'' She walked from the office in quick, controlled steps that were silent on the carpet.

"I won't have you upsetting my wife.'' Mr. Anderson stood, erect and unyielding. "We've known nothing but misery since the first time we heard the name Kirkwood.''

Though her knees had begun to shake, Ariel rose to face him. "Scott's name is Kirkwood, Mr. Anderson.''

Without a word, he turned and strode out of the room.

"My clients are understandably emotional on this issue.'' Ford's voice was so calm Ariel barely heard it. With the slightest nod of agreement, she wandered to stare out the window.

She didn't register the subdued conversation the attorneys carried on behind her. Instead, she concentrated on the flow of traffic she could see but not quite hear from thirty floors below. She wanted to be down there, surrounded by cars and buses and people.

Strange how she'd nearly convinced herself she was resigned to her brother's death. Now, the helpless anger washed over her again until she could have screamed with it. Screamed just one word. *Why?*

"Ariel.'' Bigby put a hand on her shoulder and repeated her name before Ariel turned her head. Ford and his clients had left. "Come sit down.''

She lifted a hand to his. "No, I'm all right."

"Like hell you are."

With a half laugh, she rested her forehead against the glass. "I will be in a minute. Why is it, Charlie, I never believe how hard or how ugly things can be until they happen? And even then—even then I can't quite understand it."

"Because you look for the best. It's a beautiful talent of yours."

"Or an escape mechanism," she murmured.

"Don't start coming down on yourself, Ariel." His voice was sharper then he'd intended, but he had the satisfaction of seeing her shoulders straighten. "Another of your talents is being able to pull in other people's emotions. Don't do it with the Andersons."

Letting out a long sigh, she continued to stare down to the street. "They're hurting. I wish there was a way we could share the grief instead of hurling it at one other. But there's nothing I can do about them," she whispered and closed her eyes briefly, tightly. "Charlie, Scott doesn't belong with them. He's all I care about. Not once, not one single time did either of them call him by name. He was always the boy, or my grandchild, never Scott. It's as though they can't give him his own identity, maybe because it's too close to Jeremy's." For an extra moment she rested her palms against the window ledge. "I only want what's right for Scott—even if it's not me."

"It's going to go to court, Ariel, and it's going to be very, very hard on you."

"You've explained all that before. It doesn't matter."

"I can't give you any guarantees on the outcome."

She moistened her lips and turned to face him. "I

understand that too. I have to believe that whatever happens will be what's best for Scott. If I lose, I was meant to lose."

"At the risk of being completely unprofessional—" he touched the tips of her hair "—what about what's best for you?"

With a smile, she cupped his face in her hand and kissed his cheek. "I'm a survivor, Charlie, and a whole hell of a lot tougher than I look. Let's worry about Scott."

He was capable of worrying about more than one thing at a time—and she was still pale, her eyes still a bit too bright. "Let me buy you a drink."

Ariel rubbed her knuckles against his beard. "I'm fine," she said definitely. "And you're busy." Turning, she picked up her purse. Her stomach was quivering. All she wanted to do was to get out in the air and clear her head. "I just need to walk for a bit," she said half to herself. "After I think it all the way through again I'll feel better."

At the door she paused and looked back. Bigby was still standing by the window, a frown of concern on his face. "Can you tell me we have a chance of winning?"

"Yes, I can tell you that. I wish I could tell you more."

Shaking her head, Ariel pulled open the door. "It's enough. It has to be enough."

Chapter 6

Booth considered taking everything he'd written that day and ditching it. That's what sensible people did with garbage. Leaning back in his chair, he scowled at the half-typed sheet staring back at him, and at the stack of completed pages beside his machine. Then again, tomorrow it might not seem quite so much like garbage and he could salvage something.

He couldn't remember the last time he'd hit a wall like this in his work. It was like carving words into granite—slow, laborious, and the finished product was never perfectly clear and sharp. You got sweaty, your muscles and eyes ached, and you barely made a dent. He'd given the script ten hours that day, and perhaps half of that with his full concentration. It was out of character. It was frustrating.

It was Ariel.

What the hell was he going to do about it? Booth ran his hands over his face with a weariness that came from lack of production rather than lack of energy. There'd never been a woman he couldn't block out of his mind for long periods of time—even Liz at the height of their disastrous marriage. But this woman... With a sound of annoyance, Booth pushed away from the typewriter. This woman was breaking all the rules. His rules—the ones he'd formed for personal survival.

The worst of it was he just wanted to be with her. Just to see her smile, hear her laugh, listen to her talk about something that didn't have to make sense.

And the hardest of it was the desire. It shifted and rippled continually under the surface of his thoughts. He had the blessing-curse of a writer's imagination. No effort was needed for Booth to feel the way her skin would heat under his hands, the way her mouth would give and take. And it took no effort to project mentally how she could foul up his life.

Because they'd be working together, he could only avoid her so much. Making love with her was inevitable—so inevitable he knew he'd have to weigh the consequences. But for now, with his rooms quiet around him and thoughts of Ariel crowding his mind, Booth couldn't think beyond having her. Prices always had to be paid.... Who would know that better than he?

Glancing down at his work, Booth admitted that he was already paying. His writing was suffering because he couldn't control his concentration. His pace, usually smooth, was erratic and choppy. What he was producing lacked the polish so integral to his style.

Too often, he caught himself staring into space—something writers do habitually. But it wasn't his characters who worked in his mind. Too often, he found himself awake before dawn after a restless night. But it wasn't his plot that kept him from sleep.

It was Ariel.

He thought of her too much, too exclusively for comfort. And he was a man who hoarded his comfort. His work was always, had always been, of paramount importance to him. He intended it to continue to be. Yet he was allowing someone to interfere, intrude.

Allowing? Booth shook his head as he lit a cigarette. He was a man of words, of shades of meanings, and knew that wasn't the proper one. He hadn't allowed Ariel into his mind—she'd invaded it.

The smoke seared his throat. Too many cigarettes, he admitted as he took another drag. Too many long days and nights. He was pushing it—and there were moments, a few scattered moments when he took the time to wonder why.

Ambition wasn't the issue. Not if ambition equaled the quest for glory and money. Glory had never concerned him, and money had never been a prime motivation. Success perhaps, in that he had always sought then insisted on quality when anything was associated with his name. But it was more a matter of obsession—that was what his writing had been since he'd first put pen to paper.

When a man had one obsession, it was easy to have two. Booth stared at the half-typed page and thought of Ariel.

The doorbell rang twice before he roused himself to answer it. If his work had been flowing at all, he would have ignored it completely. Interruptions, he thought ruefully as he left the littered desk behind, sometimes had their advantages.

"Hi." Ariel smiled at him and kept her hands in her pockets. It was the only way she could keep them from lacing together. "I know I should've called, but I was walking and took the chance that you wouldn't be frantically writing some monumental scene." *You're babbling,* she warned herself and clenched both hands.

"I haven't written a monumental scene in hours." He studied her a moment, perceptive enough to know that beneath the smile and animated voice there was trouble. A week before, perhaps even days before, he'd have made an excuse and shut her out. "Come in."

"I must've caught you at a good time," Ariel commented as she crossed the threshold. "Otherwise you'd've growled at me. Were you working?"

"No, I'd stopped." She looked ready to burst, he mused. The casualness, the glib remarks didn't mask the outpouring of emotion. It showed in her eyes, in her movements. A quick glance showed him that her hands were fists in her pockets. Tension? One didn't associate the word with her. He wanted to touch her, to soothe, and had to remind himself that he didn't need anyone else's problems. "Want a drink?"

"No—yes," she amended. Perhaps it would calm her more than the two-hour walk had done. "Whatever's handy. It's a beautiful day." Ariel paced to the window and found herself reminded too much of standing in Bigby's office. She turned her back on the view. "Warm. Flowers are everywhere. Have you been out?"

"No." He handed her a dry vermouth without offering her a chair. In this mood he knew she'd never sit still.

"Oh, you shouldn't miss it. Perfect days're rare." She drank, then waited for her muscles to loosen. "I was going to walk through the park, then found myself here."

He waited a moment as she stared down into her glass. "Why?"

Slowly, Ariel lifted her eyes to his. "I needed to be with someone—it turned out to be you. Do you mind?"

He should have. God knows he wanted to. "No." Without thinking, Booth took a step closer—physically, emotionally. "Do you want to tell me about it?"

"Yes." The word came out on a sigh. "But I can't." Turning away, she set down her glass. She wasn't going to level. Why had she been so sure she would? "Booth, it isn't often I can't handle things or find myself so scared that running away looks like the best out. When it happens, I need someone."

He was touching her hair before he could stop himself, was turning her to face him before he'd weighed the pros and cons. And he was holding her before either of them could be surprised by the simplicity of it.

Ariel clung as relief flowed over her. He was strong—strong enough to accept her strength and understand the moments of weakness. She needed that very basic human support, without question, without demands. His chest was hard and firm against her. Over her back his hands ran gently. He said nothing. For the first time in hours, Ariel felt her balance return. Kindness gave her hope; she was a woman who'd always been able to survive on that alone.

What's troubling her, Booth wondered. He could feel the panic in the way her hands gripped him. Even when he felt her begin to relax he remembered that first frantic grip. Her work, he thought. Or something more personal? Either way, it had nothing to do with him. And yet... While she was soft and vulnerable in his arms he felt it had everything to do with him.

He should step back. His lips brushed through her hair as he breathed in her fragrance. It was never safe to lower the wall. His lips skimmed along her temple.

"I want to help you." The words ran through his mind and spilled out before he was aware of them.

Ariel's arms tightened around him. That phrase meant more, infinitely more, than I love you. Without knowing it, he'd just given her everything she needed. "You have." She tilted her head back so that she could see his face. "You are."

Lifting a hand, she ran her fingers over the long firm bones in his face, over the taut skin roughened by a day's growth of beard. Love was something that moved in her too strongly to be ignored. She needed to share it, if not verbally, then by touch.

Softly, slowly, she closed the distance and brushed his lips with hers. Her lids lowered, but through her lashes she watched his eyes as he watched hers. The intensity in his never altered. Ariel knew he was absorbing her mood, and testing it.

It was he who shifted the angle, without increasing the pressure. Easily he toyed with her mouth, nipping into the softness of her bottom lip, tracing the shape with just the tip of his tongue until the flutter in her stomach spread to her chest. He needed to draw in the sensation of her as a woman, as an individual. He wanted to know her physically; he needed to understand the subtleties of her mind. As she felt her body give, her mind yield, Ariel wondered how it was he didn't hear the love shouting out of her.

He was struck by the emotion that raced from her. He'd never held a woman capable of such feeling, or one who, by possessing it, demanded it in return. It wasn't a simple matter of response. Even as his senses began to swim, Booth understood that. He wanted to give to her. And though he wanted, he knew he couldn't. Risks were for the foolish, and he couldn't afford to play the fool a second time.

Compassion, however, touched off compassion. If nothing else, he could give her a few hours' relief from whatever plagued her mind. He ran his hands up her arms for the sheer pleasure of it. "How nice a day is it?" he asked.

Ariel smiled. Her fingers were still on his face, her lips only inches from his. "It's spectacular."

"Let's go out." Booth paused only long enough to take her hand before he headed for the door.

"Thank you." Ariel touched her head briefly to his shoulder in one more simple show of affection he wasn't accustomed to. It warmed him—and cautioned him.

"What for?"

"For not asking questions." Ariel stepped into the elevator, leaned back against the wall and sighed.

"I generally stay out of other people's business."

"Do you?" She opened her eyes and the smile lingered. "I don't. I'm an inveterate meddler—most of us are. We all like to get inside other people. You just do it more subtly than most."

Booth shrugged as the elevator reached lobby level. "It's not personal."

Ariel laughed as she stepped out. Swinging her purse over her shoulder, she moved in her habitual quick step. "Oh, yes, it is."

He stopped a moment and met the humor in her eyes. "Yes," he admitted. "It is. But then, as a writer I can observe, dissect, steal other people's thoughts and feelings without having to get involved enough to advise or comfort or even sympathize."

"You're too hard on yourself, Booth," Ariel murmured. "Much too hard."

His brow quirked in puzzlement. Of all the things he'd ever been accused of, that wasn't one of them. "I'm a realist."

"On one level. On another you're a dreamer. All writers are dreamers on some level—the same way all actors are children on one. It has nothing to do with how clever you are, how practical, how smart. It goes with the job." She stepped out into the warmth and the sun. "I like being a child, and you like being a dreamer. You just don't like to admit it."

Annoyance. He should've felt annoyance but felt pleasure instead. As long as he could remember, no one else had ever understood him. As long as he could remember, he'd never cared. "You've convinced yourself you know me very well."

"No, but I've made a few scratches in the surface." She sent him a saucy look. "And you've a very tough surface."

"And yours is very thin." Unexpectedly he cupped her face in his hand for a thorough study. His fingers were firm, as if he expected resistance and would ignore it. "Or seems to be." How could he be sure, he wondered. How could one person ever be sure of another?

Ariel was too used to being examined, and already too used to Booth to be disconcerted. "There's little underneath that doesn't show through."

"Perhaps that's why you're a good actress," he mused. "You absorb the character easily. How much is you, and how much is the role?"

He was far from ready to trust, she realized when he dropped his hand. "I can't answer that. Maybe when the film's over, you'll be able to."

He inclined his head in acknowledgment. It was a good answer—perhaps the best answer. "You wanted to walk in the park."

Ariel tucked her arm companionably through his. "Yeah. I'll buy you an ice cream."

Booth turned his head as they walked. "What flavor?"

"Anything but vanilla," Ariel said expansively. "There's nothing remotely vanilla about today."

She was right, Booth decided. It was a spectacular day. The grass was green, the flowers vivid and pungent. He could smell the park smells. Peanuts and pigeons. Enthusiastic joggers pumped by in colorful sweatbands and running shorts, streaks of sweat down their backs.

Spring would soon give way to early summer. The trees were full, the leaves a hardy shade rather than the tender hue they'd been only weeks before. Shade spread in invitation while the sun baked the benches and paths. He knew Ariel would choose the sun. And he wondered, as he strolled along beside her, why he'd gone so long without seeking it himself.

As Ariel bit into an ice cream confection coated with chocolate and nuts, she thought of Scott. But this time, the apprehension was gone. She'd only needed to lean on someone for a moment, draw on someone else's emotional strength, to have her faith return. Her head was clear again, her nerves gone. With a laugh, she turned into Booth's arms and kissed him hard.

"Ice cream does that to me." She was still laughing as she dropped onto a swing. "And sunshine." She leaned way back and kicked her feet to give herself momentum. The tips of her hair nearly skimmed the ground. It was pale, exquisitely pale in the slanting sun. As it fell back, it left her face unframed and stunning. Her skin was flushed with color as she pushed off again and let herself glide.

"You seem to be an expert." Booth leaned against the frame of the swing as her legs flashed by him.

"Absolutely. Want to join me?"

"I'll just watch."

"It's one of your best things." Ariel threw out her legs again for more height and enjoyed the thrill that swept through her stomach. "When's the last time you were on one of these?"

A memory surged through his mind—of himself at five or six and his primly uniformed, round-faced nanny. She'd pushed him on a swing while he'd squealed and demanded to go higher. At the time he hadn't believed there was any more to life than that rushing pendulum ride. Abruptly, he appreciated Ariel's claim that she enjoyed being a child.

"A hundred years ago," he murmured.

"Too long." Skimming her feet on the ground, she slowed the swing. "Get on with me." She blew the hair out of her eyes and grinned at his blank expression. "You can stand, one foot on either side of me. It's sturdy enough—if you are," she added with just enough of a challenge in the tone to earn a scowl.

"Practicing your psychiatry?"

Her grin only widened. "Is it working?"

She was laughing at him again, and knowing it, Booth took the bait. "Apparently." He stepped behind her to grab the chain with his hands. "How high do you want to go?"

Ariel tipped back her head to give him an upside-down smile. "As high as I can."

"No crying uncle," Booth warned as he began to push her.

"Hah." Ariel tossed back her hair and shifted her grip. "Fat chance, DeWitt."

She felt him jump nimbly onto the swing as they began to fly, then threw her body into it until the rhythm steadied. The sky tilted over her, blue and dusted with clouds. The ground swayed, brown and green. She rested her head against a firm, muscled thigh and let the sensations carry her.

Grass. She could smell it, sun-drenched and trampled, mixed with the dusty scent of dry earth. Children's laughter, cooing pigeons, traffic—Ariel could hear each separate sound individually and as a mixture.

The air tasted of spring—sweet, light. An image of a watermelon ran through her mind. Yes, that was what she thought of as the breeze fluttered over her cheeks. But overall, most of all, it was Booth who played with her senses. It was he she felt firmly against her back, his quiet breathing she heard beneath all the other sounds. She could smell him—salt and soap and tobacco. She had only to shift the angle of her head to see his strong, capable hands around the chain of the child's swing. Ariel closed her eyes and absorbed it all. It was like coming home. Content, she slid her hands higher on the chain so that they brushed his. The contact, warm flesh to warm flesh, was enough.

He'd forgotten what it was like to do something for no reason. And by forgetting it, Booth had forgotten the purity of pleasure. He felt it now, without the intellectual justifications he so often restricted himself with. Because he understood that freedom brought vulnerability, he'd doled it out to himself miserly. Only on those rare occasions when he was completely alone, away from responsibilities and his work, had he allowed his heart and mind to drift. Now, it happened so spontaneously he hardly realized it. Bypassing the dangers of relaxation, Booth enjoyed the ride.

"Higher!" Ariel demanded on a breathless laugh as she leaned into the arch. "Much higher!"

"Much higher and you'll land on your nose."

Her sound of pleasure rippled over the air. "Not me. I land on my feet. Higher, Booth!"

When she turned her head up to laugh into his face, he lost himself in her. Beauty—it was there, but not the cool, distant beauty he saw on camera. Looking at her now, he saw nothing of his Rae, nothing of her Amanda. There was only Ariel. For the first time in longer than he cared to remember, he felt a twinge of hope. It scared the hell out of him.

"Faster!" she shouted, not giving him any time to dwell on what was happening inside him. Her laughter was infectious, as was her enthusiasm. They soared together until his arms ached. When the swing began to slow, she leaped from it and left him wobbling.

"Oh, that was wonderful." Still laughing, Ariel turned in a circle, arms wide. "Now I'm starving. Absolutely starving."

"You just had ice cream." Booth leaped off the swing to find himself breathless and his blood pumping.

"Not good enough." Ariel whirled around to him and linked her hands behind his head. "I need a hot dog—really need a hot dog with everything."

"A hot dog." Because it seemed so natural, he bent

to kiss her. Her mouth was warm, the lips curved. "Do you know what they put in those things?"

"No. And I don't want to. I want to stuff myself with whatever nasty stuff it has in it and feel wonderful."

Booth ran his hands down her sides. "You do feel wonderful."

Her smile changed, softened. "That's about the nicest thing you've ever said to me. Kiss me again, right here, while I'm still flying."

Booth drew her closer as his lips tasted hers. Fleetingly he wondered why the gentle kiss moved him equally as much as the passion had yet somehow differently. He wanted her. And along with her body he wanted that energy, that verve, the *joie de vivre*. He wanted to explore and measure it, and to test it for its genuineness. Booth was still far from sure that anyone in the world he knew could be quite so real. And yet, he was beginning to want to believe it.

Drawing her away he watched her lashes flutter up, her lips curve. But he remembered that sense of panic he'd felt from her when he'd first opened his door. If her emotions were as vibrant as they seemed, she wouldn't be limited to joy and vivacity.

"A hot dog," he repeated and speculated on how much he would learn of her and how long it would take. "It's your stomach, but I'll spring for it."

"I knew you could be a sport, Booth." She slipped her arm around his waist as they walked. "I just might have two."

"Masochistic tendencies run in your family?"

"No, just gluttony. Tell me about yours."

"I don't have masochistic tendencies."

"Your family," she corrected, chuckling. "They must be very proud of you."

His brow lifted while a ghost of a smile played around his mouth. "That depends on your point of view. I was supposed to follow family tradition and go into law. Throughout most of my twenties I was the black sheep."

"Is that so?" Tilting her head, she studied him with fresh interest. "I can't imagine it. I've always had a fondness for black sheep."

"I would've made book on it," Booth said dryly. "But one might say I've been accepted back into the fold in the past few years."

"It was the Pulitzer that did it."

"The Oscar didn't hurt," Booth admitted, seeing the humor in something he'd barely noticed before. "But the Pulitzer had more clout with the DeWitts of Philadelphia."

Ariel scented the hot dog stand and guided him toward it. "You'll be adding an Emmy to the list next year."

He pulled out his wallet as Ariel leaned over the stand and breathed deeply. "You're very confident."

"It's the best way to be. Are you having one?"

The scent was too good to resist. When had he eaten last? What had he eaten? Booth shrugged the thoughts way. "I suppose."

Ariel grinned and held up two fingers to the concessionaire. When hers was in its bun she began to go through the condiments one at a time. "You know, Booth—" she piled on relish "—*The Rebellion* was brilliant, clean, hard-hitting, exquisite characterizations, but it wasn't as entertaining as your *Misty Tuesday.*"

Booth watched her take the first hefty bite. "My purpose in writing isn't always to entertain."

"No, I understand that." Ariel chewed thoughtfully, then accepted the soda Booth offered her. "It's just my personal preference. That's why I'm in the profession. I want to be entertained, and I need to entertain."

He added a conservative line of mustard to his hot dog. "That's why you've been satisfied with daytime drama."

She shot him a look as they began to walk again. "Don't get snide. Quality entertainment's the core of it. If I was handy juggling plates and riding a unicycle, that's what I'd do."

After the first bite, Booth realized the hot dog was the best thing he'd eaten in a week, perhaps in months. "You have a tremendous talent," he told her, but didn't notice the surprised lift of her brow at the ease of the compliment. "It's difficult for me to understand why you aren't doing major films or theater. A series, even a weekly series is dragging, backbreaking work. Being a major character in a show that airs five days a week has to be exhausting, impossible and frustrating."

"Exactly why I do it." She licked mustard from her thumb. "I was raised right here in Manhattan. The pace's in my blood. Have you ever considered why L.A. and New York are on opposite ends of the continent?"

"A lucky geographical accident."

"Fate," Ariel corrected. "Both might be towns where show business is of top importance, but no two cities could have more opposing paces. I'd go crazy in California—mellow isn't my speed. I like doing the soap because it's a daily challenge, it keeps me sharp.

And when there's the time and the opportunity, I like doing things like *Streetcar*. But..." She finished off her hot dog with a sigh. "Doing the same play night after night becomes too easy, and you get too comfortable."

He drank down cola—a flavor he'd nearly forgotten. "You've been playing the same character for five years."

"Not the same thing." She crunched an ice cube and enjoyed the shock of cold. "Soaps're full of surprises. You never know what kind of angle they're going to throw at you to pump up ratings or lead in a fresh story line." She scooted around a middle-aged matron walking a poodle. "Right now Amanda's facing a crumbling marriage and a personal betrayal, the possibility of an abortion and a rekindling of an old affair. Not dull stuff. And though it's top secret, I'll tell you she's going to work with the police on a profile of the Trader's Bend Ripper."

"The what?"

"As in Son of Jack the Ripper," she said mildly. "Her former lover Griff's the number-one suspect."

"Doesn't it ever bother you that so much melodrama goes on in a small town with four or five connecting families?"

She stopped to look at him. "Do you know your Coleridge?"

"Passably."

"'The willing suspension of disbelief.'" Ariel crumbled her napkin, then tossed both it and her empty cup into a trash can. "It's all that's necessary to get along in this world. Believe it might happen, it could happen. Plausibility's all that's necessary. As a writer, you should know that."

"Perhaps I should. I've always leaned more toward reality."

"If it works for you." The lift of her shoulders seemed to indicate that all was accepted. "But sometimes it's easier to believe in coincidence, or magic or simple luck. Straight reality without any detours is a very hard road."

"I've had a few detours," he murmured. It occurred to him that Ariel Kirkwood had already led him off the paved road he'd adhered to for years. Booth began to wonder just where her twisting direction would lead them. Lost in thought, he didn't notice that they were in front of his building until she stopped. His work was waiting, his privacy, his solitude. He wanted none of it.

"Come up with me."

The request was simple, the meaning clear. And her need was huge. Shaking her head, Ariel touched the hair that had fallen over his forehead. "No, it's best that I don't."

He took her hand before she could drop it back to her side. "Why? I want you—you want me."

If it were only so simple, she thought as the desire to love him grew and grew. But she knew, instinctively, that it wouldn't be simple, not for either of them once begun. For him there was too much distrust, for her too many vulnerabilities.

"Yes, I want you." Ariel saw the change in his eyes and knew it would be much more difficult to walk away than to go with him. "And if I came upstairs, we'd make love. Neither of us is ready for that, Booth, not with each other."

"If it's a game you're playing to make me want you more, it's hardly necessary."

She drew her hand from his and stood on her own. "I like to play games," she said quietly. "And I'm very good at most of them. Not this kind."

Pulling out a cigarette, he lit it with a snap of his lighter. "I've no patience for the wine and candlelight routine, Ariel."

He saw the humor light in her eyes and could have cursed her. "How lucky that I don't have a need for them." Putting her hands on his shoulders, she leaned forward and kissed him. "Think of me," she requested and turned quickly to walk away.

As he stared after her, Booth knew he'd think of little else.

Chapter 7

It was going to be hard work, with long days, short nights and constant demands on both the body and the mind. Ariel was going to love every minute of it.

The producers of the soap were cooperating fully with Marshell—the network strategy was to everyone's advantage. The word, the big word, was always *ratings*. But it was Ariel who had to squeeze in the time for both projects, and Ariel who had to learn hundreds of pages of script as Amanda and as Rae.

Under different circumstances they might have simply written around her for a few weeks on "Our Lives, our Loves," but with Amanda and Griff's relationship heating up and the Ripper on the prowl, it wasn't possible. Amanda had a key role in too many vital scenes. So instead, Ariel had to shoot a backbreaking number of those scenes in a short period of time. This would give her three straight weeks to concentrate exclusively on the film. If that project ran behind schedule, she'd have to compensate by dividing her time and energies between Amanda and Rae.

The idea of eighteen-hour days and 5:00 a.m. calls couldn't dull her enthusiasm. The pace, merciless as it was, was almost natural to her in any case. And it helped keep her mind off the custody trial, which was set for the following month.

And there was Booth. Even the idea of working with him excited her. The daily contact would be stimulating. The professional competition and cooperation would keep her sharp. The preproduction stages had shown her that Booth would be as intimately involved with the film as any member of the cast and crew—and that he had unquestioned authority.

Throughout the sometimes hysterical meetings, he'd remained calm and had said little. But when he spoke, he was rarely questioned. It wasn't a matter of arrogance or overbearing, as Ariel saw it. Booth DeWitt simply didn't comment unless he knew he was right.

Perhaps, if it was meant to be, they'd move closer to each other as the film progressed. Emotion. It was what she wanted to give him, and what she needed from him. Time. She knew it was a major factor in whatever happened between them. Trust. This above all was needed—and this, above all, was missing.

There were times during the preproduction stages of the filming that Ariel felt Booth watching her too objectively, and distancing himself from her too successfully.

Ariel found herself at an impasse. The more skillfully she played Rae, the more firmly Booth stepped back from her. She understood it, and was helpless to change it.

The set was elegant, the lighting low and seductive.

Across a small rococo table, Rae and Phil shared lobster bisque and champagne. Ariel's costume was clinging midnight silk. Diamonds and sapphires winked at
her ears and throat. An armed guard in the studio at-
tested to the fact that paste wasn't used on a Marshell
production.

The intimate late-night supper was actually taking
place at 8:00 a.m. in the presence of a full crew. Sipping lukewarm ginger ale from a tulip glass, Ariel gave
a husky laugh and leaned closer to Jack.

She knew what was needed here—sex, raw and
primitive under a thin sheen of sophistication. It would
have to leap onto the screen with a gesture, a look, a
smile, rather than through dialogue. She was playing a
role within a role. Rae was her character, and Rae was
never without a mask. Tonight, she would project a
warmth, a soft femininity that was no more than a facade. It was Ariel's job to show both this, and the skill
with which Rae played the part. If the actress Ariel
portrayed wasn't clever, the impact on the character of
Phil would waver. The connection between the two
was vital. They fed each other, and by doing so, the
entire story.

Rae wanted Phil, and the viewer had to know that
she wanted him physically nearly as much as she
wanted the connections he could bring her professionally. To win him, she had to be what he wanted. Ambition and skill were a deadly combination when added
to beauty. Rae had all three and the capacity to use
them. It was Ariel's job to show the duality of her
nature, but to show it subtly.

The scene would end in the bedroom; that portion
of the film would be shot at a different time. Now, the
tension and the sexuality had to be heightened to a

point where both Phil and the audience were completely seduced.

"Cut!"

Chuck ran a hand over the back of his neck and lapsed into silence. Both the actors and crew recognized the gesture from their director and remained silent and alert. The scene wasn't pleasing him, and he was working out why. Keyed up, Ariel didn't allow the tension to drain out of her. She needed the nerves to maintain the image of Rae. The sight of the ginger ale and the scent of the food in front of her made her stomach roll uneasily. They were already on the fourth take. Objectively, she watched her glass being refilled, her plate replaced. When this was over, she thought, she'd never even look at a glass of ginger ale again.

"Disgusting, isn't it?"

Glancing over, Ariel saw Jack Rohrer grimace at her. She locked Rae in a compartment of her brain before she grinned at him. "I've never wanted a cup of coffee and a bagel so much in my life."

"Please." He leaned back from the table. "Don't mention real food."

"More feline," Chuck said abruptly and focused on Ariel. "That's how I see Rae—a sleek black cat with manicured claws."

Ariel smiled at the image. Yes, that was Rae.

"When you say the line, 'One night won't be enough, you make me greedy,' you should practically purr it."

Ariel nodded while she flexed her hands. Yes, Rae would purr that line, while she calculated every angle. Ariel had a mental image of a cat—glossy, seductive and just this side of evil.

Just before the clapper was struck for the next take,

Ariel caught Booth's eye. He was frowning at her while he stood off camera. Though his hands were casually in his pockets and his expression was still and calm, she sensed the wall of tension around him. Unable to break it down, she used it and the eye contact to pull herself back into character.

As the scene unfolded, she forgot the flat, warm taste of the ginger ale, forgot the intrusion of cameras and crew. Her attention was completely focused on the man across from her, who was no longer a fellow actor but an intended victim. She smiled at something he said, a smile Booth recognized too well. Seductive as black lace, cold as ice. There wasn't a man alive who'd be immune to it.

When she reached the line Chuck had focused on, Ariel paused a beat, dipping her fingertip into Jack's glass, then slowly touched the dampened skin to her mouth, then his. The seductive ad lib had the temperature on the set soaring. Even while he mentally approved the gesture and Ariel's intuition, Booth felt his stomach muscles tighten.

She knew her character, he mused, almost as well as he did himself. So well, it was always an effort to separate them in his mind. This attraction that plagued him—at whom was it directed? That surge of jealousy he felt unexpectedly when the woman on set melted into another man's arms—for whom did he really feel it? He'd entwined reality and fiction so tightly in this script, then had chosen an actress skilled enough to blur those lines. Now, he found himself trapped between fiction and fact. Was the woman he wanted the shadow or the light?

"Cut! Cut and print! Fantastic." Grinning from ear to ear, Chuck walked over and kissed both Ariel and

Jack. "We're lucky the camera didn't overload on that scene."

Jack flashed a white-toothed smile. "You're lucky I didn't. You're damn good." Jack laid a hand on Ariel's shoulder. "So damn good I'm going to have a cup of coffee and call my wife."

"Ten minutes," Chuck announced. "Set up for reaction shots. Booth, what'd you think?"

"Excellent." With his eyes on Ariel, Booth walked toward them. There was nothing of the cat about her now. If anything, she looked a bit weary. He found that while the knot in his stomach had loosened, he had to fight the urge to stroke her cheek. Booth was more accustomed to the first sensation. "You look like you could use some coffee yourself."

"Yeah." Again, Ariel forced herself to lock Rae's personality away. She wanted nothing more than to relax completely, but knew she could only allow herself a few degrees. "You buying?"

Nodding, he led her off set where a catering table was already set up with coffee, doughnuts and danishes. Ariel's stomach revolted at the thought of food, but she took the steaming Styrofoam cup in both hands.

"This schedule's difficult," Booth commented.

"Mmm." She shrugged that off and let the coffee wash away the aftertaste of ginger ale. "No, the schedule's no tighter than the soap's—lighter in some ways. The scene was difficult."

He lifted a brow. "Why?"

The scent of the coffee was real and solid. Ariel could almost forget the spongy food she'd had to nibble on for the past two hours. "Because Phil's smart and cautious—not an easy man to seduce or to fool.

Rae has to do both, and she's in a hurry." She glanced over the rim of her cup. "But then, you know that."

"Yes." He took her wrist before she could drink again. "You look tired."

"Only between takes." She smiled, touched by the reluctant concern. "Don't worry about me, Booth. Frantic's my natural pace."

"There's something else."

She thought of Scott. It's not supposed to show, she reminded herself. The minute you walk into the studio, it's not supposed to show. "You're perceptive," she murmured. "A writer's first tool."

"You're stalling."

Ariel shook her head. If she thought about it now, too deeply, her control would begin to slip. "It's something I have to deal with. It won't interfere with my work."

He took her chin firmly into his hand. "Does anything?"

For the first time, Ariel felt a threat of pure anger run through her. "Don't confuse me with a role, Booth—or another woman." She pushed his hand away, then turning her back on him, walked back onto the set.

The temper pleased him, perhaps because it was easier to trust negative emotions. Leaning back against the wall, Booth made a decision. He was going to have her—tonight. It would ease a portion of the tension in him and alleviate the wondering. Then both of them, in their own way, would have to deal with the consequences.

Ariel found the anger was an advantage. Rae, she mused, was a woman who had anger simmering just below the surface at all times. It added to the discontent, and the ambition. Instead of trying to rid herself of it—something she wasn't certain she could do in any case—Ariel used it to add more depth to an already complicated character. As long as she clung to Rae's mercurial, demanding personality, she didn't feel her own weariness or frustrations.

True, her senses were keen enough so that she knew exactly where Booth was and where his attention was focused even when she was in the middle of a scene. That was something to be dealt with later. The more he pushed at her—mentally, emotionally—the more she was determined to give a stellar performance.

By six and wrap time, Ariel discovered that Rae had drained her. Her body ached from the hours of standing under the lights. Her mind reeled from the repetition of lines, the drawing and releasing of emotions. It was only the first week of filming, and already she felt the strain of the marathon.

Nobody said it'd be easy, Ariel reminded herself as she slipped into her dressing room to change into her street clothes. And it wouldn't be nearly so important if it were. The trouble was, she was beginning to equate her success in the part with her success in her relationship with Booth. If she could pull one off, she could do the same with the other.

Shaking her head, Ariel stripped out of her costume, shedding Rae as eagerly as she did the silk. An idea like that, she reminded herself, had a very large trapdoor. Rae was a part to be acted, no matter how entangled it was with reality. Booth was real life—her life. No matter how willing she was to take risks or accept a challenge, that was something she couldn't afford to forget.

Gratefully, Ariel creamed off her stage make-up and

let her skin breathe. She sat, propping her feet on her dressing table so that the short kimono she wore skimmed her thighs. Taking her time, letting herself come down, she undid the sleek knot the hairdresser had arranged and let her hair fall free. With a contented sigh, Ariel tipped her head back, shut her eyes and fell into a half doze.

That was how Booth found her.

The room was cluttered in her usual fashion so that she seemed to be a single island of calm. The air was assaulted with scents—powder, face cream, the same potpourri just hinting of lilac that she kept at home. The lights around her mirror were glaring. Her breathing was soft and even.

As he shut the door behind him, Booth let his gaze run up the long slender length of her legs, exposed from toe to thigh. The kimono was loosely, almost carelessly knotted, so that it gaped intriguingly down the center of her body nearly to the waist. Her hair fell behind the chair, mussed from her own hands so that the curve of neck and shoulder made an elegant contrast.

Her face seemed a bit pale without the color needed for the camera...fragile. Without it, the faintest of shadows could be seen under her eyes.

Booth wanted almost painfully to possess her, just as she was at that moment. With hardly a thought as to what he was doing, he turned the lock on the door. He sat on the arm of a chair, lit a cigarette and waited.

Ariel woke slowly. She tended to sleep quickly and wake gradually. Even before she'd drifted from that twilight world to consciousness, she knew she was refreshed. The nap had been no more than ten minutes. Any longer and she'd have been groggy, any shorter, tense. With a sigh, she started to stretch. Then she sensed she wasn't alone. Curious, she turned her head and looked at Booth.

"Hello."

He saw no remnants of the anger in her eyes, nor was there any coolness, that sign of resentment, in her voice. Even the weariness he'd sensed in her briefly had vanished. "You didn't sleep long." His cigarette had burned down nearly to the filter without his noticing. He crushed it out. "Though I don't know anyone who could've slept at all in that position."

"For a ten-minute session, I can sleep anywhere." She pointed her toes, tensing all her muscles, then released them. "I had to recharge."

"A decent meal would help."

Ariel put a hand to her stomach. "It wouldn't hurt."

"You barely touched anything at lunch."

It didn't surprise her that he'd noticed, only that he'd commented on it. "Normally I'd have gorged myself. Eating lobster bisque at dawn threw my whole system out of whack. A bagel's more my style. Or a bowl of Krispie Krinkies."

"Of what?"

"Eight essential vitamins," she said with a half grin. Reluctantly, she slid her feet to the floor. The gap in her robe shifted, and absently she tugged at the lapels. "We are wrapped for the day, aren't we? There isn't a problem?"

"We wrapped," he agreed. "And there's a problem."

The brush she'd lifted paused halfway to her hair. "What kind?"

"Personal." He rose and took the brush from her hand. "Every day this week I've watched you, listened to you, smelled you. And every day this week, I've wanted you.'' He took the brush through her hair in one long, smooth stroke while in the lighted mirror, his eyes met hers. When she didn't move, he drew the brush down again, cupping the curve of her shoulder with his free hand. ''You asked me to think of you. I have.''

Too close to the surface, Ariel warned herself. Her emotions were always too close to the surface. There was nothing she could do about it. ''Every day this week,'' she began in a voice that was already husky, ''you've watched me and listened to me be someone else. You might be wanting someone else.''

His eyes remained on hers as he lowered his mouth to her ear. ''I'm not watching anyone else now.''

Her heart lurched. Ariel would have sworn she felt the jerk of movement inside her breast. ''Tomorrow—''

''The hell with tomorrow.'' Booth let the brush drop as he drew her to her feet. ''And yesterday.'' His gaze was intense, a hot, hot green that had her throat going dry. She'd wondered what it would be like if he allowed any emotion freedom. This was his passion, and it was going to sweep her away.

If she hadn't loved him... But, of course, she did. All caution whipped away as her mouth met his. There was a time for thinking, and a time for feeling. There was a time for withholding, and a time for giving freely. There was a time for reason, and a time for romance.

All that Ariel had, all that she felt, thought, wished, went into the touch of mouth to mouth. And as her body followed her heart, she wrapped herself around him and offered unconditionally. She felt the floor tilt and the air freeze before she became lost in her own longings. Her lips parted, inviting; her tongue touched, arousing. Her breath fluttered, answering.

She was firm, as he was, yet softer. Feeling the hard length of man against her, she became completely, utterly feminine. The pleasure was liquid, passing through her as warmed wine. As his grip tightened, she melted further until she was as pliant as any man's fantasy. But she was very real.

He'd never known another woman like her, so utterly free with emotions that flowed and crested until he was drowning in them. Passion had been expected and was there, but... More, infinitely more, was a range of feeling so intense, so sweet, it was irresistible.

As he'd watched her on the set, he'd wanted her. When he'd come into the room to see her sleeping, desire had assaulted him. Now, with her yielding, vibrating with emotions he could hardly name, Booth needed her as he'd never needed anyone. And had never wanted to.

Too late. The thought ran through his mind that it was too late for her—too late for him. Then his hands were buried in her hair, his thoughts a kaleidoscope of sensations.

She smelled faintly of lemon from the cream she'd used on her face, while her hair carried the familiar fragrance of light sexuality. The thin material of her kimono swished as his hands parted it to find her. And she was softer than a dream, but so small he had a moment's fear that he would hurt her. Then her body arched, pressing against his hand so that it was her strength that aroused him. With a sound that was more of surrender than triumph, he buried his face against her throat.

Even while her mind was floating, Ariel knew she had to feel the texture of his flesh against hers. Slowly, her hands ran up his sides, drawing up his sweater. She followed the movement, over his shoulders, until there was nothing barring her exploration—and nothing to stop her sensitized skin from meeting his.

When he drew her down she went willingly. As her back rested against the littered sofa, she cupped her hands behind his head and brought his mouth back to hers. The taste of his passion rippled through her and lit the next spark.

Not so passive now, not so pliant, she moved under him, sending off twinges of excitement to pulse through both of them. The sudden aggression of her lips was welcome. The kiss went on and on, deeper, moister, while two pairs of hands began to test and appreciate.

He could feel the frantic beat of her heart under his palm. When he pressed his lips against her breast, he felt her shudder. The outrageous desire to absorb her ran through him as he began to draw in her variety of tastes, now with his lips, now with the tip of his tongue. Sometimes, some places, it was hot, others sweet, but always it was Ariel.

The lights glared into the room, reflecting from the mirror as he began a thorough, intense journey over her. The curve of her shoulder held fascinations he'd never known before. The skin at the inside of her wrist was so delicate he almost thought he could hear the blood run through the veins. Everywhere he touched, he felt her pulse. She was so giving. That alone was enough to make his head swim.

And as he touched, tasted, took, so did she. If he became more demanding, she responded in kind, keeping pace with him. Or perhaps it was he who kept pace with her. She stroked with those long, elegant fingers so that he knew what it was to be on the verge of madness, and within sight of heaven.

She wanted nothing more than what she could find in him. Touches of tenderness that moved her. Flares of fires that tormented her. His hair brushed over her skin and that alone excited her. Flesh grew damp with passion and the struggle to control—the struggle to prolong. Ariel learned that pleasure alone was a shallow thing; but pleasure, when combined with love, was all.

Together, they understood that there could be no more waiting. The final barriers of clothing were tugged impatiently away. She opened for him. Madness and heaven became one.

Ariel felt as though she could run for miles. Her body was alive with so many sensations. Her mind leaped with them. She lay beneath Booth, tingling with an awareness that radiated down to her toes and fingertips. With her eyes closed, her body still aligned with his, she counted his heartbeats as they thudded against her. In that private, liquid world they'd gone to, Booth hadn't been calm, he hadn't been detached. Letting her lashes flutter up, she smiled. His hand was laced with hers. She wondered if he were aware of it. He'd wanted her. Just her.

Contentment. Was that what he was feeling? Booth lay sated, drained, aware only of Ariel's warm, slim form beneath him. As far as he could remember, he'd never experienced anything remotely like this. Total relaxation...a complete lack of tension. He didn't even have the energy to dissect the feeling, and instead enjoyed it. With a sound of pure pleasure, he turned his face in to her throat. He felt as well as heard her gurgle of laughter.

"Funny?" he murmured.

Ariel ran her hands up the length of his back, then down again to his waist. "I feel good. So good." Her fingertips skimmed over his hips. "So do you."

Shifting slightly, Booth raised himself on one elbow so that he could look at her. Her eyes were laughing. With a fingertip he traced the spot just below her jaw where he'd discovered delectable, sensitive skin. "I still don't know what I'm doing with you."

She brushed the hair from his forehead and watched it fall back again. "Do you always have to have an intellectual reason?"

He frowned, but his fingers spread over her face as if he were blind and memorizing it. "I always have."

She wanted to sigh but smiled instead. Taking his face in her hands, Ariel brought him down for a hard kiss. "I defy the intellect."

That made him laugh, and because he was off balance, she was able to roll him over. With her body slanted across his, she stretched and nuzzled into his shoulder. Booth felt the crinkle of paper and the rumple of cloth beneath him. "What am I lying on?"

"Mmmm. This and that."

Arching, he pulled a crumpled pamphlet from under his left hip. "Anyone ever mention that you're sloppy?"

"From time to time."

Absently, Booth glanced at the pamphlet about the plight of baby seals before he dropped it to the floor. He tugged at another paper stuck to his right shoulder.

A halfway house for battered wives. Curiosity piqued, he twisted a bit and found another. ASPCA literature.

"Ariel, what is all this?"

She gave his shoulder a last nibble before she rested her cheek on it. He held several wrinkled leaflets. "I suppose you might call it my hobby."

"Hobby?" He put his free hand under her chin to lift it. "Which one?"

"All of them."

"All?" Booth looked at the leaflets in his hand again and wondered how many others were squashed beneath him. "You mean you're actively involved in all these organizations?"

"Yeah. More or less."

"Ariel, no one person would have the time."

"Oh, no." She shifted, folding her arms across his chest for support. "That's a cop-out. You make time." She tilted her head toward the papers he held. "Those baby seals, do you know what's done to them, how it's done?"

"Yes, but—"

"And those abused women. Most of them come into that shelter without any self-esteem, without any emotional or financial support. Then there's—"

"Wait a minute." He let the papers slide to the floor so he could take her shoulders. How slim they were, he realized abruptly. And how easily she could make him forget just how delicately she was formed. "I understand all that, but how can you be involved in all these causes, run your life and pursue your career?"

She smiled. "There're twenty-four hours in every day. I don't like to waste any of them."

Seeing that she was perfectly serious, Booth shook his head. "You're a remarkable woman."

"No." Ariel bent her head and kissed his chin. It dipped slightly in the center—not quite a cleft. "I just have a lot of energy. I need to put it somewhere."

"You could put all of it into furthering your career," he pointed out. "You'd be top box office within six months. There'd be no question of your success."

"Maybe. But I wouldn't be happy with it."

"Why?"

It was back; she felt it. The doubts, the distrust. With a sigh, Ariel sat up. In silence, she picked up her kimono and pulled it on. How quickly warmth could turn to chill. "Because I need more."

Dissatisfied, Booth took her arm. "More what?"

"More everything!" she said with a sudden passion that stunned him. "I need to know I've done my best, and not just in one area of my life. Do you really think I'm so limited?"

The fire in her eyes intrigued him. "I believe what I said indicated your lack of limitations."

"Professionally," she snapped. "I'm a person first. I need to know I touched someone, helped somehow." She dragged both hands through her hair in frustration. "I need to know I cared. Success isn't just a little gold statue for my trophy case, Booth." Whirling, she yanked open the door of her closet and pulled out her street clothes.

As Booth sat up, the papers beneath him rustled. "You're angry."

"Yes, yes, yes!" With her back to him, Ariel wriggled into her briefs. In the mirror, Booth could see the reflected temper on her face.

"Why?"

"Your favorite question." Ariel flung the kimono to the floor, then dragged a short-sleeved sweatshirt over her head. "Well, I'll give you the answer, and you're not going to like it. You still equate me with her." She flung the words at him; as they hit, he too began to dress. "Still," she continued, "even after what just happened between us, you still measure me by her."

"Maybe." He rose and drew his sweater over his head. "Maybe I do."

Ariel stared at him a moment, then stepped into her jeans. "It hurts."

Booth stood very still as the two words sliced into him. He hadn't expected them—their simplicity, their honesty. He hadn't expected his own reaction to them. "I'm sorry," he murmured.

Stepping closer, he touched her arm and waited for her to look up at him. The hurt was in her eyes, and he knew it was the second time he'd put it there. "I've never been a particularly fair man, Ariel."

"No," she agreed. "But it's hard for me to believe that someone so intelligent could be so narrow-minded."

He waited for his own anger to rise, and when it didn't, shook his head. "Maybe it's simplest to say you weren't in my plans."

"I think that's clear." Turning away, she began to brush her hair methodically. Hurt pulsed from her still, laced with anger. It never occurred to her to rely on pride and conceal them both. "I told you before that I tend to rush into things. I also understand that not everyone keeps the same pace. But I'd think by this time you'd see that I'm not the character you created— or the woman who inspired her."

"Ariel." She stiffened when he took her shoulders. He could see her fingers flex on the brush handle. "Ariel," he said again and lowered his brow to the top of her head. Why did he want so much what he'd cut himself off from? "I'll hurt you again," he said quietly. "I'm bound to hurt you if I continue to see you."

Her body relaxed on a sigh. Why was she fighting the inevitable? "Yes, I know."

"And knowing that, knowing what you could do to my own life, I don't want to stop seeing you."

She reached up to cover the hand on her shoulder with her own. "But you don't know why."

"No, I don't know why."

Ariel turned in his arms and held him. For a moment they stood close, her head on his shoulder, his hands at her waist. "Buy me dinner," she requested, then tipped back her head and smiled at him. "I'm starving. I want to be with you. Those are two definite facts. We'll just take the rest as it comes."

He'd been right to call her remarkable, Booth thought. He pressed his lips to her brow. "All right. What would you like to eat?"

"Pizza with mushrooms," she answered immediately. "And a cheap bottle of Chianti."

"Pizza."

"A huge one—with mushrooms."

With a half laugh he tightened his hold. He was no longer sure he could let go. "It sounds like a good start."

Chapter 8

At 7:00 a.m., Ariel sat in a make-up chair, with a huge white drop cloth covering her costume, going over her lines while a short, fussy-handed man with thinning hair slanted blusher over her cheekbones. She could hear, but paid no attention to, the buzz of activity around her. Someone shouted for gel for the lights. A coil of cable was dropped to the floor with a thud. Ariel continued to read.

The upcoming scene was a difficult one, with something perilously close to a soliloquy in the middle. If she didn't get the rhythm just right, the pitch perfect, the entire mood would be spoiled.

And her own mood wasn't helping her concentration.

She'd had another lovely Sunday with Scott, which had ended with a tense and tearful departure. Though she'd long ago resigned herself to the fact that she was a creature of emotional highs and lows, Ariel couldn't rid herself of the despondency or the nagging sense of guilt.

Scott had clung to her, with great, silent tears running down his cheeks, when she'd returned him to the Andersons' home in Larchmont. It was the first time in all the months since his parents' death that he'd created a scene at the end of their weekly visit. The Andersons had met his tears with grim, tight-lipped impatience while both had cast accusing glares at Ariel.

After she'd soothed him, Ariel had wondered all during the lengthy train ride home if she'd unconsciously brought on the scene. By wanting him so badly, was she encouraging him to want her? Did she spoil him? Was she overcompensating because of her love for his father and her pain in the loss?

She'd spent a sleepless night over it, and the questions had built and pressed on her. But there'd been no firm answers in the morning. Within a few weeks, she'd have to live with the decision of a judge who would see Scott as a minor rather than as a little boy who liked to play pretend games. Could a judge, however experienced, however fair, see the heart of a child? It was one more question that kept her awake at night.

Now, Ariel knew she had to put her personal business aside. Her part in the film was more than a job; it was a responsibility. Both the cast and the crew depended on her to do her best. Her name on the contract guaranteed she would give all her skill. And, she reminded herself as she rubbed an aching temple, worrying wasn't going to help Scott.

"My dear, if you continue to fidget, you'll spoil what I've already done."

Bringing herself back, Ariel smiled at the make-up man. "Sorry, Harry. Am I beautiful?"

"Almost exquisite." He pursed his lips as he touched up her brows. The natural arch, he thought with professional admiration, needed very little assistance from him. "For this scene, you should look like Dresden. Just a little more here...." Ariel sat obediently while he smoothed more color into her lips. "And I'll have to insist that there be no more frowning. You'll spoil my work."

Surprised, Ariel met his eyes. She'd been sure she'd had her expression, if not her thoughts, under control. Foolish, she decided, then reminded herself that problems were to be left on the other side of the studio door. That was the first rule of showmanship.

"No more frowns," she promised. "I can't be responsible for spoiling a masterpiece."

"Well, nothing changes. Still cramming before zero hour."

"Stella!" Ariel glanced up and broke into the first true smile of the day. "What're you doing here?"

"Taking a busman's holiday." Stella dropped into the chair beside Ariel, pulling up her legs, then folding them under her. "I used your name—and some charm," she added with a sweep of her lashes, "to get in. You don't mind if I watch the morning's shooting, do you?"

"Of course not. How're things at Trader's Bend?"

"Heating up, love, heating up." With a wicked smile, Stella tossed her thick mane of hair behind her shoulder. "Now that Cameron's trying to blackmail Vikki over her gambling debts, and the Ripper's claimed his third victim, *and* Amanda and Griff are starting to simmer, they can't keep up with the mail or the phone calls. Rumor is *Tube* wants to do a two-part spread on the cast. That's big time."

Ariel's brow quirked. "Cover story?"

"That's what I hear through the grapevine. Hey, I got stopped in the market the other day. A woman named Ethel Bitterman gave me a lecture on moral standing and family loyalty over the cucumbers."

Laughing, Ariel drew off her protective drape to reveal a frothy, raspberry-colored sundress. This was what she'd needed, she realized. That sense of camaraderie and family. "I've missed you, Stella."

"Me too. But tell me...." Stella's gaze skimmed up the dress that, while demure and feminine, reeked of sex. "How does it feel to be playing the bad girl for a change?"

Ariel's eyes lit up. "It's wonderful, but it's tough. It's the toughest part I've ever played."

Stella smiled and buffed her nails on her sleeve. "You always claimed I had all the fun."

"I might've been right," Ariel countered. "And I may've oversimplified. But I don't remember ever working harder than this."

Stella rested her chin on her hand. "Why?"

"I guess because Rae's always playing a part. It's like trying to get inside a half dozen personalities and make them one person."

"And you're eating it up," Stella observed.

"I guess I am." With a quick laugh she settled back. "Yeah, I am. One day I'll feel absolutely drained, and the next so wired..." She shrugged and set her script aside. If she didn't know her lines by now, she never would. "In any case, I know if I have a choice when this is over, I'd like to do a comedy. A Judy Holliday type. Something full of fun and wackiness."

"What about Jack Rohrer?" Stella dug in her purse and found a dietary lemon drop. "What's he like to work with?"

"I like him." Ariel smiled ruefully. "But he doesn't make it a picnic. He's a perfectionist—like everyone else on this film."

"And the illustrious Booth DeWitt?"

"Watches everything," Ariel murmured.

"Including you." Moving only her eyes, Stella changed the focus of her attention. "At least he has been for the past ten minutes."

Ariel didn't have to turn her head. She already knew. In her mind's eye she could see him, standing a bit apart from the grips and gaffers as they checked the lighting and the set. He'd remove himself from the activity so as not to interfere with the flow, but his presence would be felt by everyone. And that presence alone would make everyone just tense enough to be sharp.

She knew he'd be watching her, half wary, half accepting. More than anything else, she wanted to merge the two into trust. And trust into love.

Booth watched her laugh at something Stella said. He watched the animated hand movements, the slight tilt of her head that meant she was avidly interested. Then again, Ariel rarely did anything that wasn't done avidly. Whatever had been clouding her mood when she'd come in earlier had been smoothed over. As he remembered the trouble in her eyes, Booth wondered what problem plagued her and why, when she seemed so willing to share everything, she was unwilling to share that.

Lighting a cigarette, Booth told himself he should be grateful she kept it to herself. Why should he want to be involved? He knew very well that one of the quickest ways to become vulnerable to someone else was to become concerned with their problems.

Beside him a stagehand thoroughly sprayed an elegant arrangement of fresh flowers. The lighting director called for a final check on the candlepower. A mike boom was lowered into place. Booth wondered what Ariel had done over the weekend.

He'd wanted to spend it with her, but she'd put him off and he hadn't insisted. He wouldn't box her in, because by doing so he set limits on himself. That was a trap he wouldn't fall into. But he remembered the utter peace he'd felt lying with her in her dressing room after passion was spent.

He couldn't say she was a calming influence—too much energy crackled from her. Yet she had a talent for soothing the tension from his mind.

He wanted to talk to her again. He wanted to touch her again. He wanted to make love with her again. And he wanted to escape from his own needs.

"Places!" The assistant director called out as he paced the set, rechecking the blocking.

Booth leaned back against the wall, his thumbs hooked absently in his pockets. It never occurred to him, as it often had to Ariel, how seldom he sat.

They would shoot a section of an extensive scene that morning. The other parts would be filmed later on the lawns of a Long Island estate. The elegant lawn party they'd shoot on location was to be Rae's first full-scale attempt at entertaining since marrying Phil. And afterward, indoors and in private, would come their first full-scale argument.

She looked like something made of spun-sugar icing. Her words were as vicious as snake venom. And all the while, with the fury and the poison oozing from her, she hadn't a hair out of place. The fragile color in her cheeks never fluctuated. It was Ariel's job to keep the character cold-blooded, and the words smoldering.

She knew it was all in the eyes. Rae's gestures were a facade. Her smile was a lie. Both the ice and the fire had to come from the eyes. The scene had to be underplayed, understated from her end. It was a constant strain to keep her own emotions from bubbling out. If *she* were to fight with words, she'd shout them, hurl them—and fling off the ones tossed back at her. Rae drawled them, almost lazily. And Ariel ached.

This was Booth's life, she thought. Or a mirror image of what had been his life. This was his pain, his mistakes, his misery. She was caught up in it. If she hurt, how did he feel watching?

Rae gave Phil a bored look as he grabbed both her arms.

"I won't have it," he raged at her, eyes blazing while hers remained cool as a lake.

"Won't have it?" Rae repeated, transmitting utter disdain with the tone, with the movement of an eyebrow. "What is it you won't have?"

"I will not have you raying the pole." Jack closed his eyes and made a gargling sound.

"Raying the pole?" Ariel repeated. "Having a little trouble with your tongue?"

She felt the tension snap as the scene was cut, but wasn't certain if she was grateful or not. She wanted this one over.

"Playing the role," Jack enunciated carefully. "I will not have you *playing* the *role*. I got it." He held up both hands, mocking himself and his flubbed line.

"Fine, as long as you understand that I can and will ray the pole whenever I choose."

He grinned at Ariel. "Smart mouth."

She patted his cheek. "Aw, yours'll wise up, Jack. Give yourself a chance."

"Places. Take it from the entrance."

For the third time that morning, Ariel swung through the French doors with her skirts billowing behind her.

They moved through the scene again, immersing themselves in the characters even with the starts and stops and changes of camera angles.

To end the scene, Rae was to laugh, take the glass of Scotch from Phil's hand, sip, then toss the contents into his face. Caught up in character, Ariel took the glass, tasted the warm, weak tea, then with an icy smile, poured the contents over the elegant floral arrangement. Without missing a beat in the change of staging, Jack ripped the glass out of her hand and hurled it across the room.

"Cut!"

Snapping back, Ariel stared at her director. "Oh, God, Chuck, I don't know where that came from. I'm sorry." With a hand pressed to her brow, she looked down at the now drenched mixture of fragile hothouse blooms.

"No, no. Damn!" Laughing, he gave her a bear hug. "That was perfect. Better than perfect. I wish I'd thought of it myself." He laughed again and squeezed Ariel until she thought her bones might crack. "She'd have done that. She *would* have done just that." With his arm slung around Ariel's shoulder, Chuck turned to Booth. "Booth?"

"Yes." Without moving, Booth indicated a nod. "Leave it as it stands." He pinned Ariel with cool, green eyes. He should have written it that way, he realized. Throwing a drink in Phil's face was too obvious for Rae. Even too human. "You seem to know her better than I do now."

She let out an uneven breath, giving Chuck's hand a squeeze before she walked toward Booth. "Is that a compliment?"

"An observation. They're setting up for the close-ups," he murmured, then brought his attention back to her. "I won't give you carte blanche, Ariel, but I'm willing to feed you quite a bit of rope in your characterization. And obviously so is Chuck. You understand Rae."

She could have been amused or annoyed. As always when she had a choice, Ariel chose amusement. "Booth, if I were playing a mushroom, I'd understand that mushroom. It's my job."

He smiled because she made it easy. "I believe you would."

"Didn't you catch the commercial where I played the ripe, juicy plum?"

"Must've been out of town."

"It was a classic. Over and above my shower scene for Fresh Wave shampoo—though, of course, sensuality was the basis in both spots."

"I want to come home with you tonight," he said quietly. "I want to stay with you tonight."

"Oh." When would she get used to the simple ways he had of saying monumental things?

"And when we're alone," Booth murmured as he watched the pulse in her throat begin to flutter, "I want to take off your clothes, little by little, so that I can touch every inch of you. Then I want to watch your face while we make love."

"Ariel, let's get these close-ups!"

"What?" A bit dazed, she mumbled the word while she continued to stare at Booth. Already she could feel his hands on her, taste his breath as it mixed with her own.

"They can have your face—for now," Booth told her, more aroused by her reaction to his words than he would have thought possible. "Tonight, it's mine."

"Ariel!"

Flung back to the present, she turned to go back to the set. With a look that was amused and puzzled, she glanced back over her shoulder. "You're not predictable, Booth."

"Is that a compliment?" he countered.

She grinned. "My very best one."

Hour after hour, line after line, scene after scene, the morning progressed. Though the film was naturally shot out of sequence, Ariel could feel it beginning to jell. Because it was television, the pace was fast. Her pace. Because it was DeWitt and Marshell, the expectations were high. As were hers.

You sweltered under the lights, changed moods, costumes, were powdered, dusted and glossed. Again and again. You sat and waited during scene changes or equipment malfunctions. And somewhere between the tension and the tedium was your vocation.

Ariel understood all that, and she wanted all of that. She never lost the basic pleasure in performing, even after ten retakes of a scene where Rae rode an exercise bike while discussing a new script with her agent.

Muscles aching, she eased herself off the bike and dabbed at the sweat, which didn't have to be simulated, on her face.

"Poor baby." Stella grinned as a stagehand offered

Ariel a towel. "Just remember, Ariel, we never work you this hard on 'Our Lives.'"

"Rae *would* have to be a fitness fanatic," she muttered, stretching her shoulders. "Body conscious. I'm conscious now." With a little moan, Ariel bent to ease a cramp in her leg. "Conscious of every muscle in my body that hasn't been used in five years."

"It's a wrap." Chuck gave her a companionable slap on the flank as he passed. "Go soak in a hot tub."

Ariel barely suppressed a less kind suggestion. She slung the towel over her shoulder, gripped both damp ends and stuck out her tongue.

"You never did have any respect for directors," Stella commented. "Come on, kid, I'll keep you company while you change. Then I've got a hot date."

"Oh, really?"

"Yeah. My new dentist. I went in for a checkup and ended up having a discussion on dental hygiene over linguine."

"Good God." Not bothering to hide a grin, Ariel pushed open her dressing-room door. "He works fast."

"Uh-uh, I do." With a laugh that held both pleasure and nerves, Stella walked into the room. "Oh, Ariel, he's so sweet—so serious about his work. And..." Stella broke off and dropped onto Ariel's cluttered sofa. "I remember something you said a few weeks ago about love—it being a definite emotion or something." She lifted her hands as if to wave away the exact phrase and grip the essence. "Anyway, I haven't come down to earth since I sat in that tilt-back chair and looked up into those baby-blue eyes of his."

"That's nice." For the moment Ariel forgot her sore

muscles and the line of sweat dripping down her back. "That's really nice, Stella."

Stella searched for another lemon drop and found her supply depleted. Knowing Ariel, she walked to the dressing table, pulled open a drawer and succumbed to the stash of candy-coated chocolate. "I heard somewhere that people in love can spot other people in love." She slanted her friend a look as Ariel stripped out of her leotard. "To test a theory, my guess is that you've fallen for Booth DeWitt."

"Right the first time." Ariel pulled on the baggy sweatpants and shirt she'd worn to the studio.

With a frown, Stella crunched candy between her teeth. "You always liked the tough roles."

"I seem to lean toward them."

"How's he feel about you?"

"I don't know." Gratefully, Ariel creamed off the last of her make-up. With a flourish, she dumped one more part of Rae into the waste can. "I don't think he does, either."

"Ariel..." Reluctance to give advice warred with affection and loyalty. "Do you know what you're doing?"

"No," she answered immediately, both brows lifting. "Why would I want to?"

Stella laughed as she headed for the door. "Stupid question. By the way—" she stopped with her hand on the knob "—I just thought I'd mention that you were brilliant today. I've worked with you week after week for five years, and today you blew me away. When this thing hits the screen, you're going to take off so fast even you won't be able to keep up."

Astonished, pleased and, perhaps for the first time,

a bit frightened, Ariel sat on the edge of her dressing table. "Thanks—I think."

"Don't mention it." Slipping into the character of Vikki, Stella blew Ariel a cool kiss. "See you in a couple of weeks, big sister."

For several moments after the door shut, Ariel sat in silence. Did she, when push came to shove, want to take off and take off fast? She remembered that P.B. Marshell had said something similiar to her after her second reading for the part, but Ariel had seen that more as an overall view of the project itself. She knew Stella, and understood that the praise from her had been directed personally and individually. For the first time the ripple effect of the role of Rae struck her fully. However much a cliché it sounded, it could make her a star.

Wearing her baggy sweats, one hip leaning on her jumbled dressing table, Ariel explored the idea.

Money—she shrugged that away. Her upbringing had taught her to view money for what it was, a means to an end. In any case, her financial status for the past three years had been more than adequate for both her needs and her taste.

Fame. She grinned at that. No, she couldn't claim she was immune to fame. It still brought her a thrill to sign her name in an autograph book or talk to a fan. That was something she hoped would never change. But fame had degrees, and with each rise in height, the payment for it became greater. The more fans, the less privacy. That was something she'd have to think about carefully.

Artistic freedom. It was that, Ariel admitted on a deep breath, that was the clincher. To be able to *choose* a part rather than be chosen. Glory and a big bank account were nothing in comparison. If Rae could bring her that...

With a shake of her head, she rose. Daydreaming about the future couldn't change anything. For now, her career, and her life, would simply have to go a day at a time. Still, she was a woman who liked to expect everything. Ariel would much rather be disappointed than pessimistic. She was grinning when she opened the door and nearly collided with Booth.

"You look happy," he commented as he took her arms to balance her.

"I am happy." Ariel kissed him hard and firm on the mouth. "It's been a good day."

The kiss, casual as it was, shot straight through him. "You should be exhausted."

"No, you should be exhausted after running the New York Marathon. How do you feel about a giant humburger and a glutton's portion of fries?"

He'd had a quiet restaurant in mind—something French and dimly lit. After a glance at her sweatsuit and glowing face, Booth shook his head. "Sounds perfect. It's your turn to buy."

Ariel tucked her arm through his. "You got it. Do you like banana milk shakes?"

His expression stated his opinion clearly. "I don't believe I've ever had one."

"You're going to love it," Ariel promised.

It wasn't as bad as he'd imagined—and the hamburger had been hefty and satisfying. Dusk was settling over the city when they returned to Ariel's apartment. The moment she opened the door, the kittens dashed for her feet.

"Good grief, you'd think they hadn't been fed in a week." Bending, she scooped up both of them and nuzzled. "Did you miss me, you little pigs, or just your evening meal?"

Before Booth realized what she was up to, Ariel had thrust both kittens into his arms. "Hang on to them for me, will you?" she said easily. "I have to feed Butch too." She sauntered toward the kitchen, with the three-legged Butch waddling behind. Booth was left with two mewing kittens and no choice but to follow. One—Keats or Shelley—climbed onto his shoulder as he went after Ariel.

"I'm surprised you don't have a litter of puppies as well." He lifted a brow as the kitten sniffed at his ear.

Ariel laughed as the kitten batted playfully at Booth's hair. "I would if the landlord wasn't so strict. But I'm working on him. Meanwhile—" she set out three generous bowls of food "—it's chow time."

Chuckling, she took the kitten from Booth's shoulder while the other leaped to the floor. Within seconds all three cats were thoroughly involved. "See?" She brushed a few traces of cat hair from his shirt. "They're no trouble at all, hardly any expense and wonderful companions, especially for someone who works most often at home."

Booth gave her a steady look, cupped her face in his hands, then grinned despite himself. "No."

"No what?"

"No, I don't want a cat."

"Well, you can't have one of mine," she said amiably. "Besides, you look more like the dog type."

"Oh, really?" He slipped his arms around her waist.

"Mmmm. A nice cocker spaniel that would sleep by your fire at night."

"I don't have a fireplace."

"You should have. But until you take care of that,

the puppy could curl right up on a little braided rug by the window.''

He caught her bottom lip between his teeth and nipped lightly. ''No.''

''No one should live alone, Booth. It's depressing.''

He could feel her response in the quickening of her heartbeat, the quiet shudder of breath. ''I'm used to living alone. I like it that way.''

She liked the feel of his roughened cheek against hers. ''You must've had a pet when you were a child,'' Ariel murmured.

Booth remembered the golden Labrador with the lolling tongue that he'd adored—and that he hadn't thought of in years. Oh, no, he thought as he felt himself begin to weaken. She wasn't going to get to him on this. ''As a child, I had the time and the temperament for a pet.'' Slowly, he slipped his hands under her sweatshirt and up her back. ''Now I prefer other ways of spending my free time.''

But she'd laid the groundwork, Ariel thought with a small smile. Advance and retreat was the secret of a successful campaign. ''I have to shower,'' she told him, drawing back far enough to smile again. ''I'm still sticky from that last scene.''

''I enjoyed watching it. You've fascinating thigh muscles, Ariel.''

Amused, she lifted both brows. ''I have *aching* thigh muscles. And I'll tell you something, if I were to ride a bike for the three or four miles I did today, it wouldn't be anchored to the floor.''

''No.'' He gathered her hair in his hand to draw her head back. ''You wouldn't be content to stay in the same place.'' He touched his mouth teasingly to hers, retreating when she would have deepened the touch to a kiss. "I'll wash your back."

Thrills raced up her spine as if he already were. "Hmmm, what a nice idea. I suppose I should warn you," she continued as they walked out of the kitchen, "I like the water in my shower hot—very hot."

When they stepped into the bathroom, he slipped his hands under the baggy sweatshirt. She was slim and warm beneath. "Don't you think I can take it?"

"I figure you're pretty tough." Eyes laughing up at him, Ariel began to unbutton his shirt. "For a screenwriter."

In one surprising move, Booth whipped the sweatshirt over her head and bit down on her shoulder. "I'd say you're pretty soft." He ran his hands down her rib cage, then banded her waist. "For an actress."

"Touché," Ariel murmured breathlessly as he tugged loose the drawstring of her pants.

"I like to feel you," he said, stroking his hands over her as she continued to undress him. "Though there isn't much of you. An elegant little body. Long boned, hipless." His hands journeyed down her back, and farther. "Very smooth."

By the time they were both naked, Ariel was shivering. But not from cold. Drawing away, she turned the taps. Water rushed from the shower head, striking porcelain and steaming toward the ceiling. Stepping in, Ariel closed her eyes to let her body soak up the heat and the sensuality.

That was one of the things that continued to fascinate him about her—her capacity for experiencing. Nothing was ever ordinary to her, Booth decided as he stepped behind her and drew the curtain closed. She wouldn't know the meaning of boredom. Everything she did or thought was unique, and being unique, exciting.

As the water coursed over them both, he wrapped his arms around her and drew her back against his chest. This was affection, he realized, the sort he'd felt very rarely in his life. Yet he felt it for her.

Ariel lifted her face to the spray. So many sensations buffeted her at that moment, she couldn't keep up. So she stopped trying. It was enough to be close, to be held. And to love. Perhaps some people needed more—security, words, promises. Perhaps one day, she would too. But now, just for now, she had all she wanted. Turning, she caught Booth close and fastened her mouth to his.

Passion flared in her quickly this time, as if it had been waiting for hours, days. Maybe years. It built so fast that the kiss alone had her gasping for air and fretting for more. Without being aware of it, she stood on her toes so that the curve of their bodies would be aligned. With desperate fingers, she combed through his hair and gripped, as if he might try to break away. But his arms were tight around her, and his mouth was as seeking as hers.

Reeling toward the crest, Ariel clung, and Ariel offered.

God, he'd never known anyone so giving. As he drank in all the flavors of her mouth, Booth wondered if it were possible for a woman to be so confident, so comfortable with herself that she could be this generous. Without any hesitation, her body was there for him. Her mind was tuned to him. Instinctively, Booth knew she thought more of his needs, his pleasures, than her own. And by doing so, she touched off a long dormant tenderness.

"Ariel..." Murmuring her name, he ran kisses over her face, which the water made incredibly soft, incredibly sweet. "You make me want things I'd forgotten— and almost believe in them again."

"Don't think." She rubbed her lips over his to soothe, to entice. "This time don't think at all."

But he would, Booth told himself. Or he'd take her too quickly, and perhaps too roughly. This time, he'd give her back a portion of what she'd already given him. Cupping the soap in his hand, he ran it over her back. He thought he heard her purr like one of her cats. It made him smile.

Her senses began to sharpen. She could hear the hiss of the spray as it struck tile, and feel the steam as it billowed in puffy clouds. Soapy hands slid over her— slick, soft, sensitive. His flesh was wet and warm where her mouth pressed. Through half-closed eyes she could see the lather cling to her, then him, before it was sluiced away.

His hand moved once between their slippery bodies to find her—stunningly—so that she cried out in surprise and rippling pleasure. Then it journeyed elsewhere while his lips traced hot and damp over her shoulder. The tang of citrus from the soap made her head reel.

"Do they still ache?" Booth asked her as his fingers kneaded the backs of her thighs.

"What?" Floating, Ariel leaned against him, her arms curved over his back, her hands firm on his shoulders. Water struck her back in soft, hissing spurts, then seemed to slither away. "No, no, nothing aches now."

With a laugh, Booth dipped his tongue into her ear and felt her shiver. "Your hair goes to gold when it's wet."

She smelled the shampoo, felt its cool touch on her scalp before he began to massage. Nothing, Ariel thought, had ever aroused her more.

Slowly, lingeringly, he washed her hair while the frothy bubbles of shampoo ran down his arms. The scent was familiar to him now, that fresh, inviting fragrance that caught at him every time he was near her. He enjoyed the intimacy of having the scent spill over him and cling—to her skin, to his. Shifting his weight, he moved them both under the gush of the shower so that water and lather raced down their bodies and away.

And while they stood, hot and wet and entangled, he slipped into her. It seemed natural, as if he'd been her lover for years. It was thrilling, as though he'd never touched her before.

He felt Ariel's nails dig into his shoulders, heard her moan of surrender and demand. He took her there, with more care than he'd ever shown a woman. And he felt a rush of freedom.

Chapter 9

Ariel rode a roller coaster for two weeks. Her time with Booth seemed like a ride with dips and curves and speed and surprises. Of course, she'd always loved them—the faster and wilder the better.

She'd been right when she'd told Booth he was unpredictable. Neither was he a simple man to deal with. Ariel decided she wanted it no other way.

There were times he was incredibly tender, showing her flashes of romance and affection that she'd never expected from him. A box of wildflowers delivered before an early studio call. A rainy-day picnic in his apartment with champagne in paper cups while thunder raged.

Then there were the times he pulled away, drew into himself so intensely that she couldn't reach him. And when she knew, instinctively, not to try.

The anger and impatience in him were ingrained. Perhaps it was that, contrasting with the glimpses of humor and gentleness, that had caused her to lose her heart. It was the whole man she loved, no matter how difficult. And it was the whole man she wanted to belong to. This man—brooding, angry, reluctantly sweet—was the man she'd been waiting for.

As the film progressed, their relationship grew closer, despite Booth's occasional stretches of isolation. Closer, yes, but without the simplicity she looked for. For love, in Ariel's mind, was a simple thing.

If he was resisting love, so much the better, Ariel told herself. When he accepted it—she wouldn't allow herself to doubt he would—it would be that much stronger. For she needed absolute love, the unconditional giving of heart and mind. She could wait a little longer to have it all.

If she had one regret, it was that she wasn't free to confide in him about Scott. The closer the trial came, the more she felt the need to talk to Booth about it, seek comfort, gain reassurance. Though it was tempting, Ariel never even considered it. This problem was hers, and hers alone. As Scott was hers to protect and defend.

When she thought of the future, it was still in sections. Booth, Scott, her career. She needed her own brand of absolute faith to believe that they'd all come together in the end.

After a long, hectic morning, Ariel considered the lengthy delay anticipated because of equipment breakdown a reward. It was the first time in weeks she'd be able to watch "Our Lives, Our Loves," and catch up on Amanda's life with the people of Trader's Bend.

"You're not really going to watch television for the next hour," Booth protested as Ariel pulled him down the corridor.

"Yes, I am. It's like visiting home." She shook the bag of pretzels in her hand. "And I've got provisions."

"When they get the sound board fixed, you're going to have a hell of an afternoon ahead of you." He kneaded her shoulder as they walked. Though it didn't often show, he'd seen brief glimpses of strain in her eyes, isolated moments when she looked a bit lost. "You'd be better off putting your feet up and catching a nap."

"I never nap." When she pushed open her dressing room door, she upended a stack of magazines. Hardly sparing them a glance, she walked over to the small portable television set in the corner.

"I seem to recall coming in here one day and finding you with your feet up on the table and your eyes closed."

"That's different." She fiddled with a dial until she was satisfied with the color. "That was recharging. I'm not ready for recharging, Booth." Eyes wide and excited, she whirled around. "It's really going well, isn't it? I can feel it. Even after all these weeks, the edge is still on. That's a sure sign we're doing something special."

"I was a bit leery about doing a film for television." He took a few pamphlets from the sofa and dropped them onto a table. "Not anymore. Yes, it's going to be very special." He held out a hand to her. "You're very special."

As always, the subtle unexpected statement went straight to her heart. Ariel took the offered hand and brought it to her lips. "I'm going to enjoy watching you accept that Emmy."

He lifted a brow. "And what about yours?"

"Maybe," she said and laughed. "Just maybe." The

lead-in music for the soap distracted her. "Ah, here we go. Back to Trader's Bend." Dropping onto the sofa, she pulled Booth with her. After ripping open the bag of pretzels, Ariel became totally absorbed.

She didn't watch as an actress or as a critic, but as a viewer. Relaxing her mind, she let herself become caught up in the connecting plot lines and problems. Even when she saw herself on the screen, she didn't look for flaws or perfection. She didn't consider she was looking at Ariel, but at Amanda.

"Don't tell me what I want," Amanda told Griff in a low, vibrating voice. "You have no business offering me unsolicited advice on my life, much less coming into my house uninvited."

"Now, you look." Griff took her arm when she would have turned away. "You're pushing yourself right to the edge. I can see it."

"I'm doing my job," she corrected coolly. "Why don't you concentrate on yours and leave me alone?"

"Leaving you alone's the last thing I'm going to do." As the camera zoomed in, the viewer was witness to his struggle for control. When Griff continued, his voice was calmer but edged with his familiar passion. "Dammit, Mandy, you're almost as close to this Ripper thing as the cops. You know better than to stay in this house by yourself. If you won't let me help you, at least go stay with your parents for a while."

"With my parents." Her composure began to crack as she dragged a hand through her hair. "Stay with my parents, while Vikki's there? Just how much do you think I can take?"

"All right, all right." Frustrated, he tried to draw her against him, only to have her jerk away. "Mandy, please, I'm worried about you."

"Don't be. And if you really want to help, leave me alone. I need to go over the psychiatric profile before I meet with Lieutenant Reiffler in the morning."

Fisted hands were shoved in his pockets. "Okay, look, I'll sleep down here on the couch. I swear I won't touch you. I just can't leave you out here alone."

"I don't want you here!" she shouted, losing her tenuous grip on control. "I don't want anyone, can't you understand that? Can't you understand that I need to be alone?"

He stared at her while she fought back tears, shoulders heaving. "I love you, Mandy," he said so quietly it could barely be heard. But his eyes had already said it.

As the camera zoomed in on her, a single tear spilled out and rolled down Amanda's cheek. "No," she whispered, turning away. But Griff's arms came around her, drawing her back against him.

"Yes, you know I do. There's never been anyone for me but you. It killed me when you left me, Mandy. I need you in my life. I need what we'd planned to have together. We've got a second chance. All we have to do is take it."

Staring into nowhere, Amanda pressed a hand to her stomach where she knew Cameron's baby was sleeping—a baby Griff would never accept, and one she had to. "No, there aren't any second chances, Griff. Please leave me alone."

"We belong together," he murmured, burying his face in her hair. "Oh, God, Mandy, we've always belonged together."

For his sake, for her own, she had to make him leave. Pain flashed into her eyes before she controlled her expression. "You're wrong," she said flatly. "That was yesterday. Today I don't want you to touch me."

"I can't crawl anymore." Ripping himself away from her, Griff headed for the door. "I won't crawl anymore."

As the door slammed behind him, Amanda slumped down on the couch. Curling on her side, she buried her face in a pillow and wept. The camera panned slowly to the window to show a shadowy silhouette behind the closed curtains.

"Well, well," Booth murmured at the commercial break. "The lady has her problems."

"And then some." Ariel stretched and leaned back against the cushions. "That's the thing about soaps— one problem gets resolved and three more crop up."

"So, is she going to give Griff a break and take him back?"

Ariel grinned at the casualness of the question. He really wants to know, she mused, pleased. "Tune in tomorrow."

His eyes narrowed. "You know the story line."

"My lips are sealed," she said primly.

"Really?" Booth caught her chin in his hand. "Let's see." He pressed his to them firmly, and though hers curved, they remained shut. Challenged, he shifted closer and his fingers spread over her jawline, lightly stroking. With the barest of touches, he traced the shape of her mouth, wetting her lips, using no pressure. When he nibbled at one corner, then the other, he felt the telltale melting of her bones, heard the quiet sigh. Effortlessly, his tongue slipped between her lips to tease hers.

"Cheat," Ariel managed.

"Yeah." God, she made him feel so good. He'd

almost stopped wondering how long it would last. The end, what he considered the inevitable end to what they brought each other, was becoming more blurred every day. "I've never believed in playing fair."

"No?" Her sudden aggression caught him off balance. Before he knew it, Booth was on his back, with her body pressed into his. "In that case, no holds barred."

The greedy kiss left him stunned, so that by the time he'd gripped some control again, she'd unbuttoned his shirt for her seeking hands. "Ariel..." Half amused, half protesting, he took her wrist, but her free hand skimmed down the center of his body to spread over his stomach.

Amusement, protests, reason, slipped away.

"I never get enough of you." He gripped her hair, destroying the sleek knot the hairdresser had tended so carefully hours before.

"I plan to see that you don't." With quick, open-mouthed kisses she moved over his shoulder, drawing away the shirt as she went.

She took him over hills and into valleys with such speed and fury he could only follow. For as long as he could remember, Booth had led in every aspect of his life—not trusting enough to let another guide. But now he could barely keep pace with her. The energy, the verve he'd so long admired in her was in complete control. As he was swept along, Booth wondered why it was suddenly so easy to break yet another rule. Then, as she had once requested, he didn't think at all.

Feelings. Ariel drew them in as they radiated from him. This was what she'd been so patiently, so desperately waiting for. Emotions were finally overtaking him. As they merged with her own, she felt the bond, the link, and nearly wept with the wonder of it.

He loves me, she thought. Maybe he doesn't know it yet, maybe he won't for days and weeks to come. But it's there. The urge to weep altered to an urge to laugh. And it was with laughter and with joy that she took him into her.

Winded, Booth lay still while Ariel curled like a cat on his chest. "Was all that just to keep me from learning the story line?"

Her chuckle was muffled against his skin. "There're no lengths I won't go to to protect security." She snuggled against him. "No sacrifice too great."

"With that in mind, I think I'll ask about the identity of the Ripper—tonight." Drawing her up, he examined her. The silk blouse she'd been wearing was unbuttoned and trailing over one shoulder. The thin slacks lay in a heap on the floor. Her hair was a provocative tangle. "You're going to catch hell from wardrobe and make-up."

"It was worth it." Straightening her blouse, Ariel began to do up the buttons. "I'll tell them I took a nap."

With a laugh, he sat up and tugged on her tumbled hair. "There's no mistaking what you've been up to. Your eyes always give you away."

"Do they?" Carefully, she stepped into her slacks. "I wonder." Absently smoothing out the creases, she turned to him. "You haven't seen it in all these weeks." As she watched, his brows drew together. "You're a perceptive man, and I've never had a strong talent or a strong desire to hide my feelings." She smiled as he continued to frown at her. "I love you."

His face, his body—Ariel thought even his mind—

went very still. He said nothing. "Booth, you don't have to look as though I've just pulled a gun on you." Stepping closer, she touched the back of her hand to his cheek. "Taking love's easy—giving it's a bit harder, for some people anyway. Please, take it as it's offered. It's free."

He wasn't at all certain what he was feeling—only that he'd never felt anything like it before. The very novelty made him wary. "It's not wise to give things away, Ariel, especially to someone who isn't ready for them."

"And holding on to something when it needs to be given's even more foolish. Booth, can't you trust me even now, just enough to accept my feelings?"

"I don't know," he murmured. As he rose, conflicting emotions, conflicting desires tore at him. He wanted to distance himself as quickly and as completely as possible. He wanted to hold her and never let go. Panic—he felt the stab of it. Pleasure, the sweetness of it.

"They're there whether you can or can't. I've never been good at controlling my emotions, Booth. I'm not sorry for it."

Before he could speak there was a brisk knock on the door. "Ariel, you're needed on the set in fifteen minutes."

"Thank you."

He had to think, Booth told himself. Be logical.... Be careful. "I'll send the hairdresser in."

"Okay." She smiled, and it almost reached her eyes. When he'd gone, Ariel stared at her reflection in the mirror. The lights around it were dull and dark. "So who expected it'd be easy?" she asked herself.

In just under fifteen minutes, Ariel walked back to-

ward the set. She looked every bit as cool and as sleek
as she had when she'd walked off over an hour before.
Despite Booth's reaction, which she'd half expected,
she felt lighter, easier, after telling Booth of her feelings. It was, after all, merely stating aloud what was,
sharing what couldn't be changed. As a general rule,
Ariel considered concealments a waste of time, and
consequences a by-product of living. Her gait was free
and easy as she crossed the studio.

She knew something was happening before she saw
the thicket of people or heard the excited voices. Tension in the air. She felt it and thought instantly of
Booth. But it wasn't Booth she saw when she passed
the false wall of the living-room set.

Elizabeth Hunter.

Elegance. Ice. Smooth, smooth femininity. Outrageous beauty. Ariel saw her laugh lightly and lift a
slender cigarette to her lips. She posed effortlessly, as
if the cameras were on and focused on her. Her hair
shimmered, pale, frosty. Her skin was so exquisite it
might have been carved from marble.

On the screen, she was larger than life, desirable,
unattainable. Ariel saw little difference in the flesh.
There couldn't be a man alive who wouldn't dream of
peeling off that layer of frost and finding something
molten and wild inside. If she were truly like Rae,
Ariel thought, that man—any man—would be disappointed. Curious, she walked closer.

"Pat, how could I stay away?" Liz lifted one grace-
ful hand and touched Marshell's check. A fantasy of
diamonds and sapphires winked on her ring finger.
"After all, one might say I have a—vested interest in
this film." The provocative pout—a Hunter trade-

mark—touched her mouth. "Don't tell me you're going to chase me away."

"Of course not, Liz." Marshell looked uncomfortable and resigned. "None of us knew you were in town."

"I just wrapped the Simmeon film in Greece." She drew on the slender cigarette again and carelessly flicked ashes on the floor. "I flew right in." She shot a look over Marshell's shoulder. Not hostile, not grim, but simply predatory. It was then Ariel saw Booth.

He stood slightly apart from the circle of people around Liz, as if he again sought distance without wholly removing himself. He met the look his ex-wife sent him without a flicker of expression. Even if Ariel had chosen to intrude, she doubted if she could have gauged his thoughts.

"I wasn't allowed to read the screenplay." Liz continued to talk to Marshell though her eyes remained on Booth. "But little dribbles leaked through to me. I must say, I'm fascinated. And a bit miffed that you didn't ask me to do the film."

Marshell's eyes hardened, but he stuck with diplomacy. "You were unavailable, Liz."

"And inappropriate," Booth added mildly.

"Ah, Booth, always the clever last word." Liz blew smoke in his direction and smiled.

It was a smile Ariel recognized. She'd seen it on the screen in countless Hunter movies. She'd mimicked it herself as Rae. It was the smile a witch wore before she cut the wings off a bat. Without realizing it, Ariel moved forward in direct defense of Booth. Liz's gaze shifted and locked.

It wasn't a pleasant survey. Again, not hostile but simply and essentially cold. Ariel studied Liz in turn

and absorbed impressions. She was left with a sensation of emptiness. And what she felt was pity.

"Well..." Liz held out her cigarette for disposal. A
small woman with a wrinkled face plucked it from her
fingers. "It's easy to deduce that this is Rae."

"No." Unconsciously, Ariel smiled with the same
cold glitter as Liz. "I'm Ariel Kirkwood. Rae's a character."

"Indeed." The haughty lift of brow had been used
in a dozen scenes. "I always try to absorb the character
I portray."

"And it works brilliantly for you," Ariel acknowledged with complete sincerity. "I limit that to when
the lights are on, Miss Hunter."

Only the barest flicker in her eyes betrayed annoyance. "Would I have seen you do anything else,
dear?"

There was no mistaking the patronizing tone. Again,
Ariel felt a flash of sympathy. "Possibly."

He didn't like seeing them together. No, Booth
thought violently, by God, he didn't. It had given him
a wave of sheer pleasure to see Liz again and feel
nothing. Absolutely nothing. No anger, no frustration.
Not even disgust. The lack of feeling had been like a
balm. Until Ariel had come on set.

Face-to-face, they could have been sisters. The resemblance was heightened by the fact that Ariel's hair,
make-up and wardrobe were styled to Liz's taste. He
saw too many similarities. And as he looked closer,
too many contrasts. Booth wasn't sure which annoyed
him more.

No matter how she was dressed, warmth flowed
from Ariel. The inner softness edged through. He could
feel the emotion from her even three feet away. And

he saw...pity? Yes, it was pity in her eyes. Directed at Liz. Booth lit a cigarette with a jerk of his wrist. God, he'd rid himself of one and was being reeled in by another. Standing there, he could feel the quicksand sucking at his legs. Was there any closer analogy for love?

"Let's get started," he ordered briefly. Liz shot him another look.

"Don't let me hold things up. I'll stay out of the way." She glided to the edge of the set, sat in a director's chair and crossed her legs. A burly man, the small woman, and what was hardly more than a boy settled behind her.

The audience had Ariel's adrenaline pumping. The scene they were to shoot was the same one she'd auditioned with. More than any other, Ariel felt it encapsulated Rae's personality, her motives, her essence. She didn't think Liz Hunter would enjoy it, but...Ariel felt she'd be able to gauge just how successful her performance was by Liz's reaction to it.

With a faintly bored expression on her face, Liz sat back and watched the scene unfold. The dialogue was not precisely a verbatim account of what had occurred between her and Booth years before, but she recognized the tenor. Damn him, she thought with a flicker of anger that showed nowhere on her sculpted face. Damn him for his memory and his talent. So this was his revenge.

While she hoped the film fell flat, she was too shrewd to believe it would. She could shrug that off. Liz was clever enough, experienced enough to make the film work for her rather than against her. With the right angle, she could get miles and miles of publicity from Booth's work. That balanced things...to a point.

She was a woman of few emotions, but the most finely tuned of these was jealousy. It was this that ate at her as she sat, silent, watching. Ariel Kirkwood, she thought as one rose-tipped nail began to tap on the arm of the chair. Liz was vain enough to consider herself more beautiful, but there was no denying the difference in age. Years were something that haunted her.

And talent. Her teeth scraped against each other because she wanted to scream. Her own skill, the accolades and awards she'd received for it were never enough. Especially when she was faced with a beautiful, younger woman of equal ability. Damn them both. Her finger began to tap harder, staccato. The young man put a soothing hand on her shoulder and was shrugged away.

Liz could taste the envy that edged toward fury. The part should have been hers, she thought as her lips tightened. If she had played Rae, she'd have added a dozen dimensions to the part—such as it was. She had more talent in the palm of her hand than this Ariel Kirkwood had in her whole body. More beauty, more fame, more sexuality. Her head began to pound as she watched Ariel skillfully weave sex and ice into the scene.

Then her eyes met Booth's, and she nearly choked on an oath. He was laughing at her, Liz realized. Laughing, though his mouth was sober and his expression calm. He'd pay for that, she told herself as her lids lowered fractionally. For that and for everything else. She'd see that he and this no-talent actress from nowhere both paid.

Booth knew his ex-wife well enough to know what was going on in her mind. It should have pleased him;

perhaps it would have only a few weeks before. Now, it did little more than slightly disgust him.

Shifting his gaze from her, he focused his attention on Ariel. Of all the scenes in the screenplay, this was the hardest for him. He'd crystallized himself too well as Phil in these few sharp, hard lines. And his Rae was too real here. Ariel made her too real, he thought as he wished for a cigarette. In this short, seven-minute scene, which would take much, much longer to complete, it was almost impossible to separate Ariel from Rae—and Rae from Liz.

Ariel had said she loved him. Fighting discomfort that was laced with panic, Booth watched her. Was it possible? Once before he'd believed a woman who'd whispered those words to him. But Ariel...there was no one and nothing quite like Ariel.

Did he love her? Once before he'd believed himself in love. But whatever emotion it had been, it hadn't been love. And it had been smeared with a fascination for great beauty, great talent, cool, cool sex. No, he didn't understand love—if it existed in the way he believed Ariel thought of it. No, he didn't understand it, and he told himself he didn't want it. What he wanted was his privacy, his peace.

And while he stood there, watching his own scene being painstakingly reproduced on film, he had neither.

"Cut. Cut and print." Chuck ran a hand along the back of his neck to ease the tension. "Hell of a job." Letting out a long breath, he walked toward Ariel and Jack. "Hell of a job, both of you. We'll wrap for today. Nothing's going to top that."

Relieved, Ariel let her stomach relax, muscle by muscle. She glanced over idly at the sound of quiet applause.

Liz rose gracefully from her chair. "Marvelous job." She gave Jack her dazzling, practiced smile before she turned to Ariel. "You have potential, dear," Liz told her. "I'm sure this part will open a few doors for you."

Ariel recognized the swipe and took it on the chin. "Thank you, Liz." Deliberately, she drew the pins from her hair and let it fall free. She wanted badly to shed Rae. "It's a challenging part."

"You did your best with it." Smiling, Liz touched her lightly on the shoulder.

I must've been on the money, Ariel thought and grinned. *I must've been right on the money.*

Liz wanted to rip the thick, tumbled hair out by the roots. She turned to Marshell. "Pat, I'd love to have dinner. We've a lot to catch up on." She slipped her arm through his and patted his hand. "My treat, darling."

Mentally swearing, Marshell acquiesced. The best way to get her out without a scene was simply to get her out. "My pleasure, Liz. Chuck, I'll want a look at the dailies first thing in the morning."

"Oh, by the way." Liz paused beside Booth. "I really don't think this little film will do much harm to your career, darling." With an icy laugh she skimmed a finger down his shirt. "And I must say, I'm rather flattered, all in all. No hard feelings, Booth."

He looked down at the beautiful, heartless smile. "No feelings, Liz. No feelings at all."

Her fingers tightened briefly on Marshell's arm before she swept away. "Oh, Pat, I must tell you about this marvelous young actor I met in Athens...."

"Exit stage left," Jack murmured, then shrugged when Ariel raised a brow at him. "Must still be functioning as Phil. But let me tell you, that's one lady I wouldn't turn my back on.''

"She's rather sad," Ariel said half to herself.

Jack gave a snort of laughter. "She's a tarantula." With another snort he cupped a hand on Ariel's shoulder. "Let me tell you something, kid. I've been in the business a lot of years, worked with lots of actresses. You're first class. And that just gripped her cookies.''

"And that's sad," Ariel repeated.

"Better put a layer of something over that compassion, babe," he warned. "You'll get burned." Giving her shoulder a last squeeze, he walked off the set.

Gratefully, Ariel dropped into a chair. The lights were off now, the temperature cooling. Most of the stagehands were gone, except for three who huddled in a corner discussing a poker game. Tipping her head back, she waited as Booth approached.

"That was a tough one," she commented. "How do you feel?"

"I'm fine. You?"

"A little drained. I've only a few scenes left, none of them on this scale. Next week, I'll be back to Amanda.''

"How do you feel about that?"

"The people on the soap are like family. I miss them.''

"Children leave home," he reminded her.

"I know. So will I when the time's right."

"We both know you won't be signing another contract with the soap." He drew out a cigarette, lighting it automatically, drawing in smoke without tasting it. "Whether you're ready to admit it or not."

Feeling his tension, she tensed in turn. "You're mixing us again," she said quietly. "Just how much longer is it going to take you to see me for who I am, without the shadows?''

''I know who you are,'' Booth corrected. ''I'm not sure what to do about it.''

She rose. Maybe it was the lingering strain from the scene, or perhaps her sadness from watching Liz Hunter suffer in her own way. ''I'll tell you what you don't want,'' she said with an edge to her voice he hadn't heard before. ''You don't want me to love you. You don't want the responsibility of my emotions or of your own.''

He could deal with this, Booth thought as he took another drag. A fight was something he could handle effortlessly. ''Maybe I don't. I told you what I thought right up front.''

''So you did.'' With a half laugh, she turned away. ''Funny that you're the one who's always preaching change at me, and you're the one so unable to do so yourself. Let me tell you something, Booth.'' She whirled back, vibrantly glowing Ariel. ''My feelings are mine. You can't dictate them to me. The only thing it's possible for you to do is dictate to yourself.''

''It isn't a matter of dictating.'' He found he didn't want the cigarette after all. It tasted foul. Booth left it smoldering, half-crushed, in an ashtray. ''It's a matter of not being able to give you what you want.''

''I haven't asked you for anything.''

''You don't have to ask.'' He was angry, really angry, without being aware when he'd crossed the line. ''You've pulled at me from the start—pulled at things I want left alone. I made a commitment once, I'll be damned if I'll do it again. I don't want to change my life-style. I don't want—''

''To risk failure again,'' Ariel finished.

His eyes blazed at her, but his voice was very, very calm. "You're going to have to learn to watch your step, Ariel. Fragile bones are easily broken."

"And they mend." Abruptly, she was too weary to argue, too weary to think. "You'll have to work out your own solution, Booth. The same as I'll work out mine. I'm not sorry I love you, or that I've told you. But I am sorry that you can't accept a gift."

When he'd watched her walk away, Booth slipped his hands in his pockets and stared at the darkened set. No, he couldn't accept it. Yet he felt as though he'd just tossed away something he'd searched for all of his life.

Chapter 10

The water was a bit choppy. Small whitecaps bounced up, were swallowed, then bounced back again. Directly overhead the sky was a hard diamond blue, but to the east, dark clouds were boiling and building. There was the threat of rain in the wind that blew in from the Atlantic. Booth estimated he had two hours before the storm caught up with him—an hour before he'd be forced to tack to shore to avoid it.

And on shore the heat would be staggering, the humidity thick enough to slice. On the water, the breeze smelled of summer and salt and storms. He could taste it as it whipped by him and billowed his sail. Exhilaration—he knew it for the sensation that could clear the mind and chill the skin. Holding lightly to the rigging, he let the wind take him.

Booth wore nothing but cutoffs and deck shoes. He hadn't bothered to shave for two days. His eyes had grown accustomed to squinting against the sun reflecting off the water, and his hands to the feel of rough rope against the palm. Both were harsh, both were challenging.

Exhilaration? This time it hadn't come with the force he'd expected. For days he'd sailed as long as the sun and the weather allowed. He'd worked at night until his mind was drained.

Escape? Was that a better word for what he'd come for? Perhaps, Booth mused as he sailed over the choppy water. Lifting a beer to his lips he let the taste race over his tongue. Perhaps he was escaping, but he was no longer needed on the set, and he had finally had to admit that he couldn't work in the city. He needed a few days away from the filming, from the pressure to produce, from his own standards of perfection.

That was all a lie.

None of those things had driven him out of Manhattan and onto Long Island. He'd needed to get away from Ariel—from what Ariel was doing to him. And perhaps most of all from his feelings for her. Yet the miles didn't erase her from his thoughts. It took no effort to think of her, and every effort not to. Though she haunted him, Booth was certain he'd been right to come away. If thinking of her ate at him, seeing her, touching her would have driven him mad.

He didn't want her love, he told himself savagely. He couldn't—wouldn't—be responsible for the range of emotions Ariel was capable of. Booth took another long pull from the beer can, then scowled at the water. He wasn't capable of loving her in return. He didn't possess those kinds of feelings. Whatever emotions he had were directed exclusively toward his work. He'd promised himself that. Inside, in the compartment that held the brighter feelings one person had for another, he was empty. He was void.

He ached for her—body, mind, soul.

Damn her, he thought as he jerked at the rigging. Damn her for pulling at him, for crowding him...for asking nothing of him. If she'd asked, demanded, pleaded, he could have refused. It was so simple to say no to an obligation. All she did was give until he was so full of her, he was losing himself.

He'd work, Booth told himself as he began to tack methodically back toward shore. The boat bucked beneath him as the wind kicked up. Adjusting the sails, he concentrated on the pure physicality of the task. Use your muscles, your back, not your brain. Don't think, he warned himself, until it's time to write again.

He'd bury himself in work for the rest of the afternoon. He'd pour himself into his writing through the evening, late into the night, until his mind was too jumbled to think of anything—anyone. He'd stay away from her physically until he could stay away from her mentally. Then he'd go back to New York and pick up his life as he'd left it. Before Ariel.

Thunder rumbled ominously as he docked the boat.

Ariel watched the lightning snake across the sky and burst. The night sky was like a dark mirror abruptly cracked then made whole again. Still no rain. The heat storm had been threatening all evening, building up in the east and traveling toward Manhattan. She'd looked forward to it. Wearing a long shirt and nothing else, she stood at the window to watch it come.

Earlier, her neighbors had been sitting on their stoops, fanning and sweating and complaining of the heat. She didn't mind it. Before the night was over the rain would wash away the stickiness. But at the moment, though her thin shirt was clinging damply to her back and thighs, she enjoyed the enervating quality of the heat, and the violence in the sky.

The storm was coming from the east, she thought again. Perhaps Booth was already watching the rain she still anticipated. She wondered if he was working, oblivious to the booming thunder. Or if, like her, he stood and watched the fury in the sky. She wondered when he'd come back—to her.

He would, Ariel affirmed staunchly. She only hoped he'd come back with an easy mind. She'd thrown him a curve. With a half smile, Ariel felt the first rippling breeze pass through the screen and over her skin. She wasn't sorry, though his reaction had hurt, then angered her. That was over. Perhaps, for a moment, she'd forgotten that to Booth love wasn't the open-ended gift it was to her. He'd see the restrictions, the risks, the pains.

The pains, she thought, resting her palms on the windowsill. Why was she always so surprised to find out she could hurt just as intensely as she could be happy? She wanted him—physically, but he was miles from her reach—emotionally, but he'd distanced himself from her feelings.

She hadn't been surprised when Booth had absented himself from the last few days of shooting. All the key scenes had been done. Nor was she surprised when Marshell had mentioned idly that Booth had gone to his secluded Long Island home to write and to sail. She missed him, she felt the emptiness; but Ariel was too independent to mourn the loss of him for a few days. He needed his solitude. A part of her understood that, enough to keep her from misery.

Hadn't she herself painted almost through the night after Liz Hunter had visited the set?

Ariel glanced around at the frantic canvas slashed with cobalt and scarlets. It wasn't a painting she'd keep in the living room for long. Too angry, too disturbing. As soon as she'd fully coped with those feelings, she'd stick the canvas in a closet.

Everyone had his or her own means of dealing with the darker emotions. Booth's was to draw into himself; hers was to let them lash out. Either way, any way, the resolution would come. She had only to hang on a little while longer.

And so she told herself when she thought of Scott. The hearing would begin at the end of the week. That, too, would be resolved, but Ariel refused to look at any more than one solution. Scott had to come to her. The doubts she'd once harbored about her right to claim him, his need to be with her, were gone. As time went on, he became more and more unhappy with the Andersons. His visits were punctuated by desperate hugs, and more and more by pleas that he be allowed to stay with her.

It wasn't a matter of abuse or neglect. It was a simple matter of love, unconditional love that came naturally from her, and didn't come at all from his grandparents. Whatever hardships she and Scott were facing now would be a thing of the past before long. It was a time to concentrate on whens instead of nows. That was how she got through the slowly moving days between the filming and the hearing. Without Booth.

Ariel closed her eyes as the rain began to gush out of the sky. Oh God, if only the night were over.

The rain was just tapering off as Booth pushed away from his computer. He'd gotten more accomplished than he'd anticipated, but the juices were drying up. He knew better than to push himself when he got to this point. In another hour he'd try again perhaps, or maybe not for a day or two. But it would come back, and the story would flow again.

No, he couldn't write anything now, but it was still this side of midnight and he was restless. The storm had cleared the air, making him wish he were on the water again, under the burgeoning moonlight. He should eat. As he rubbed the stiffness from his neck, he remembered he hadn't bothered with dinner. A meal and an early night.

As he walked through the house into the kitchen, silence drummed around him. Strange, he'd never noticed just how thick silence could be, just how empty a house could be when it had only one occupant. And stranger still, how only a few months before he'd have appreciated both, even expected both. Again, before Ariel. His life seemed to have come down to two stages. Before Ariel and after Ariel. It wasn't an easy admission for a man to make.

Booth pulled a tray of cold cuts out of the refrigerator without any real interest. Mechanically, he fixed a sandwich, found a ripe peach and poured a glass of milk. The solitary meal had never seemed less appealing—so much so he considered tipping the entire mess down the sink.

Shaking off the feeling, he carried it into his bedroom and set the plate on the dresser. What he needed was some noise, he decided. Something to occupy his mind without straining the brain. Booth switched on the television, then flipped the channel selector without any particular goal in mind.

Normally he would have bypassed the late-night talk

show in favor of an old movie. When Liz's laughter flowed out at him, he paused. He might still have passed it by, but his curiosity was piqued. Thinking it might be an interesting diversion, Booth picked up his plate, set it on the bedside table and stretched out.

He'd been on the show himself a number of times. Though he wasn't overly fond of the format or the exposure, he knew the game well enough to understand the need to reach the public through the form. The show was popular, slickly run, and the host knew his trade. With boyish charm he could draw the unexpected out of celebrities and keep the audience from turning the channel or just flicking off the switch.

"Of course I was terribly excited to film on location in Greece, Bob." Liz leaned just a bit closer to her host while her ice-blue gown glistened coolly in the lights. "And working with Ross Simmeon was a tremendous experience."

"Didn't I hear you and Simmeon had a feud going?" Robert MacAllister tossed off the question with a grin. It said, come on, relax, you can tell me. It was a well-practiced weapon.

"A feud?" Liz fluttered her lashes ingenuously. She was much too sharp to be caught in that trap. She crossed her legs so that the gown shimmered over her body. "Why, no. I can't imagine where anyone would get that idea."

"It must have something to do with the three days you refused to come on set." With a little deprecating shrug, MacAllister leaned back in his chair. "A disagreement over the number of lines in a key scene."

"That's nonsense." *Damn Simmeon and all the rumormongers.* "I'd had too much sun. My physician put me on medication for a couple of days and recommended a rest.'' She glittered a smile right back at him. ''Of course there were a few tense moments, as there will be on any major film, but I'd work with Ross tomorrow....'' or the devil himself, her tone seemed to say. ''If the right script came along.''

''So, what're you up to now, Liz? You've had an unbroken string of successes. It must be getting tough to find just the right property.''

''It's always hard to put together the right touch of magic.'' She gestured gracefully so that the ring on her hand caught the light and glittered. ''The right script, the right director, the right leading man. I've been so lucky—particularly since *To Meet at Midnight*.''

Booth set his half-eaten sandwich aside and nearly laughed. *He'd* written it for her and had made her a major star. Top box office. Luck had had nothing to do with it.

''Your Oscar-winning performance,'' Bob acknowledged. ''And of course a brilliant screenplay.'' He sent her an off-center smile. ''You'd agree with that?''

It was the opening she'd been waiting for. And maneuvering toward. ''Oh, yes. Booth DeWitt is possibly—no, assuredly—the finest screenwriter of the eighties. Regardless of our, well, personal problems, we've always respected each other professionally.''

''I know all about personal problems,'' Bob said ruefully and got the laugh. His three marriages had been well publicized. And so had his alimony figures. ''How do you feel about his latest work?''

''Oh.'' Liz smiled and let one hand flutter to her throat before it fell into her lap. ''I don't suppose the content's much of a secret, is it?''

Again the expected laugh, a bit more restrained.

''I'm sure Booth's script is wonderful, they all are.

If it's, ah, one-sided," she said carefully, "it's only natural. From what I'm told it's common for a writer to reflect some parts of his personal life...and in his own way," she added. "As a matter of fact, I visited the set just last week. Pat Marshell's producing, you know, and Chuck Tyler's directing."

"But..." Bob prompted, noting her obvious reluctance.

"As I said, it's so difficult to find that right brand of magic." She tossed out the first seeds with a smile. "And Booth's never done anything for the small screen before. A difficult transition for anyone."

"Jack Rohrer's starring." Obligingly, Bob fed her the next line.

"Yes, excellent casting there. I thought Jack was absolutely brilliant in *Of Two Minds*. That was a script he could really sink his teeth into."

"But this one..."

"Well, I happen to be a big Jack Rohrer fan," Liz said, apparently sidestepping the question. "I doubt there's any part he can't find some meat on."

"And his costar?" Bob folded his hands on his desk. Liz was out for the jugular, he decided. It wouldn't hurt his ratings.

"The female lead's a lovely girl. I can't quite think of her name, but I believe she has a part on a soap opera. Booth often likes to experiment rather than to go with experienced actors."

"As he did with you."

Her eyes narrowed fractionally. She didn't quite like that tone, or that direction. "You could put it that way." The haughtiness in her voice indicated otherwise. "But really, when one has the production rate this project has, one should shoot for the best talent available. Naturally, that's a personal opinion. I've always thought actors should pay their dues—God knows, I paid mine—rather than be cast in a major production because of a...shall we say personal whim?''

"Do you think Booth DeWitt has a personal whim going with Ariel Kirkwood? That's her name, isn't it?"

"Why, yes, I think it is. As to the other, I could hardly say." She smiled again, charmingly. "Especially on the air, Bob."

"Her physical resemblance to you is striking."

"Really?" Liz's eyes frosted. "I much prefer being one of a kind, though of course it's flattering to have someone attempt to emulate me. Naturally, I wish the girl the best of luck."

"That's gracious of you, Liz, particularly since the plot line's rumored to be less than kind to the character that some say mirrors you."

"Those that know me will pay little attention to a slanted view, Bob. All in all, I'll be fascinated to see the finished product." The statement was laced with boredom, almost as if she'd yawned. "That is, of course, if it's ever actually aired."

"Ever aired? You see some problem there?"

"Nothing I can talk about," she said with obvious reluctance. "But you and I know how many things can happen between filming and airing, Bob."

"No plans to sue, huh, Liz?"

She laughed, but it came off hollow. "That would give the film entirely too much importance."

Bob mugged at the camera. "Well, with that we'll take a little break here. When we come back, James R. Lemont will be joining us to tell us about his new book, *Hollywood Secrets*. We know about those too, don't we, Liz?'' After his wink, the screen switched to the first commercial.

Leaning back against the pillows, his meal forgotten, Booth drew on his cigarette and sent the smoke to the ceiling. He was angry. He could feel it in the hard knot in his stomach. The swipes she'd taken at the film hadn't even been subtle, he reflected. Oh, perhaps she'd fool a certain percentage of people, but no one remotely connected with the business, and no one with any perception. She'd done her best to toss a few poison darts and had ended up, in Booth's opinion, by making a fool of herself.

But he was angry. And the anger, he discovered, came from the slices she'd taken at Ariel. Quite deliberate, quite calculated, and unfortunately for Liz, quite obvious. She was a cat, and normally a clever one. Jealousy was essentially the only thing that could make her lose that edge.

Naturally she'd be jealous of Ariel, Booth mused. Of anyone young, beautiful and talented. Add that to the bile she'd have to swallow over the film itself, and Liz would be as close to a rage as her limited range of emotions would allow. And this was her way of paying back.

Rising, Booth slammed off the set before he paced the room. She'd bring up the film—and Ariel—in every interview she gave, at every party she attended, in the hope to sabotage both. Of course, she wouldn't do any appreciable damage, but knowing that didn't ease his temper. No one had the right to take potshots at Ariel, and the fact that they were being taken through him, because of him, made it worse.

He could, if he chose, book himself on the circuit

to promote the film and to counter Liz's campaign. That would only add fuel to the fire. He knew the best way to make the storm Liz was trying to brew fizzle was to keep silent. Frustrated, he walked to the window. He could hear the water from there. Just barely. He wondered if Ariel had watched the late-night talk show. And how she was dealing with it.

Stretched out in the hammock, plumped by pillows, with a bowl of fresh popcorn resting on her stomach, Ariel listened to Liz Hunter. Her brow lifted once as a reference was made to herself. Ariel crunched on popcorn and smiled as Robert MacAllister reminded Liz that *the girl's* name was Ariel Kirkwood.

Poor Liz, she thought. She was only making it worse for herself. Perhaps because Ariel had been inside Rae's skin for so long, she noticed small things. The tapping of a fingertip on the arm of the chair, the brief tightening of the lips, the flash in the eyes that was a bit of anger, a bit of desperation. The more Liz talked, the shakier her support became.

She'd have been much better off if she'd said nothing, Ariel mused. A no-comment, a shrug of that haughty shoulder. Miscalculation, Ariel thought with a sigh. A foolish one.

I can't hurt her. Ariel shifted her gaze from the screen to the ceiling. No one can take her talent away from her. A pity she doesn't realize that. It's Booth she really wants to hurt, Ariel decided. She'd want to make him pay for using Rae to strip off a few masks. Yet didn't Liz realize he was just as bitterly honest with his own character?

Ariel glanced back at the television screen as Liz's face dominated the screen. There was a line of dissatisfaction between her brows, very faint. Ariel wondered if she were the only one who noticed it, because she was so intimately involved. I know you, Ariel told the image on the screen, I know you inside and out. And that made her swallow hard. It was just a little scary.

Ariel lay back, tuning out the sound of the set and tuning back into the rain. It was nearly over, only a patter now against the windowpane. Booth had probably seen it, she decided. And if he hadn't caught the show, he'd know of the content very soon. He'd be angry. Ariel could almost see his hard-eyed, grimmouthed reaction. She herself had been fighting an edge of temper that threatened to dominate her other feelings.

Anger was useless; she wished she could tell him. He had to know that he'd opened the door for this when he'd written the script. She'd opened it a bit further when she'd taken the part. She hoped, when he'd calmed, that he'd see Liz Hunter had done the film more good than harm.

When the phone rang, Ariel leaned over. Years of experience kept her balanced rather than tumbling out of the hammock and onto the floor. Swinging a bit dangerously, she gripped the phone and hauled it up to her. "Hello."

"That witch."

With a half laugh, Ariel lay back on the pillows. "Hi, Stella."

"Did you catch the MacAllister show?"

"Yeah, I've got it on."

"Listen, Ariel, she's making a joke out of herself. Anyone with two brain cells will see that."

"Then why're you angry?"

She could hear Stella take a deep breath. "I've been sitting here listening to that woman talk—wishing you the *best* of luck." Stella muttered something under her breath, then began to talk so fast the words tumbled into each other. "The best of luck my foot. She'd like to see you drop off the face of the earth. She'd like to stick a knife in you."

"A nail file, maybe."

"How can you joke about it?" Stella demanded.

Because if I don't I might just start screaming. "How can you take it so seriously?" Ariel said instead.

"Listen, Ariel..." Stella's voice was barely controlled. "I know that kind of woman; I've been playing the type for the past five years. There's nothing she wouldn't do, nothing, if she thought she could get to you. Dammit, you trust everyone."

"Some less than others." Though the concern and the loyalty touched her, she laughed. "Stella, I'm not a complete fool."

"You're not a fool at all," Stella shot back, outraged. "But you're naive. You actually believe the kid who stops you on the street asking for a donation is really collecting for a foundling home."

"He might be," Ariel mumbled. "Besides, what does that have to do with—"

"Everything!" Stella cut her off with something close to a roar. "I care about you. I worry about you every time I think about you walking blithely down the street without a thought to the crazies in the world."

"Come on, Stella, if I thought about it too much I'd never go out at all."

"Well think about this: Liz Hunter's a powerful,

vindictive woman who'd like to ruin you. You watch your back, Ariel.''

Who'd know that better than I? Ariel thought with a quick shudder. I've been playing her character for weeks. ''If I promise, will you stop worrying?''

''No.'' Slightly mollified, Stella sighed. ''Promise anyway.''

''You got it. Are you calm now?''

Stella made a quiet sound in her throat. ''I don't understand why you're not angry.''

''Why should I be when you're doing it for me—and so well?''

Stella heaved a long breath. ''Good night, Ariel.''

''Night, Stella... Thanks.''

Ariel replaced the receiver and swung gently to and fro in the hammock. As she stared up at the ceiling, she marveled over how fortunate she was. Friendship was a precious thing. To have someone ready to leap to your defense, claws bared, was a comforting sensation. She had friends like that, and a job that paid her well for doing what she would gleefully have done for nothing. She had the unquestioning love of a little boy, and God willing, would have him to care for within a few weeks. She had so much.

As Ariel lay back, struggling to count her blessings, she thought of Booth. And ached for him.

Two days later, Ariel received a surprise visit. It was her first free day since resuming her role of Amanda. She was spending it doing something she rarely started, and more rarely finished. Housecleaning.

In tattered shorts and a halter, she sat on her windowsill two stories up, and leaning out, washed the outside of her windows. The volume on her radio was turned up so that the sinuous violins of *Scheherazade* all but shook the panes. Occasionally someone from the neighborhood would shout up at her. Ariel would stop working—something that took no effort at all— and shout back down.

The important thing was to keep busy, to keep occupied. If she gave herself more than a brief moment of spare time, time to think, she might go mad. The next day marked the beginning of the custody hearing. And a full two weeks since she'd last seen Booth. Ariel polished window glass until it shone.

She felt something like an itch between the shoulder blades, like a fingertip on the back of the neck. Twisting her head, she looked down and saw Booth on the sidewalk below. Relief came in waves. Even if she'd tried, even if she'd thought to try, she couldn't have stopped the smile that illuminated her whole face.

"Hi."

Looking up at her, he felt a need so great it buckled his knees. "What the hell are you doing?"

"Washing the windows."

"You could break your neck."

"No, I'm anchored." One of the kittens brushed against her ankles so that she jolted and braced herself with her knees. "Are you coming up?"

"Yeah." Without another word, he disappeared from view.

As he climbed the stairs Booth reminded himself of his promise. He wasn't going to touch her—not once. He would say what he'd come to say, do what he'd come to do, then leave. He wouldn't touch her and start that endless cycle of longings and desires and dreams all over again. Over the past two weeks he'd purged himself of her.

As he reached the landing he nearly believed it. Then she opened the door.

She still held a damp rag in one hand. She wore no makeup; the flush of color in her cheeks came from pleasure and exertion. Her hair was scooped back and tied with a bit of yarn. The scent of ammonia was strong.

His fingers itched for just one touch, just one. Booth curled them into his palms and stuck them in his pockets.

"It's good to see you." Ariel leaned against the door and studied him. People didn't change in two weeks, she reminded herself as she compared every angle and plane in his face with the memory she'd been carrying with her. He looked the same, a bit browner perhaps from the sun, but the same. Love washed over her.

"You've been sailing."

"Yes, quite a bit."

"It's good for you. I can see it." She stepped back, knowing from the tense way he was standing that he wouldn't accept her hand if she offered. "Come in."

He stepped into chaos. When Ariel cleaned, it was from the bottom up and nothing was safe. Drawers had been turned out, tables cleared off. Furniture and windows gleamed. There wasn't a clear place to stand, much less sit.

"Sorry," she said as she followed his survey. "I'm a bit behind on my spring cleaning." The pressure in her chest was increasing with every second they stood beside each other, and miles apart. "Want a drink?"

"No, nothing. I'll make this quick because you're busy." He'd make it quick because it hurt, physically, painfully, not to touch what he still wanted...and to still want what he'd convinced himself he couldn't have.

"I'm assuming you saw the MacAllister show the other night."

"That's old news," Ariel countered. She sat on the hammock, legs dangling free, fingers locked tightly.

With his hands still in his pockets, Booth rocked back on his heels. "How'd you feel about it?"

With a shrug, Ariel crossed her ankles. "She took a couple stabs at the film, but—"

"She took a couple stabs at you," he corrected. His voice had tightened, his eyes narrowed.

Gauging his mood, Ariel decided to play it light. She smiled. "I'm not bleeding."

Booth frowned at her a moment, then judged she was a great deal less concerned than he. That was something he had to change. "She hasn't stopped there, Ariel." He walked closer, the better to study her face, the better to perhaps catch the drift of her scent. "She had quite a little session with the producer of your show, then with a few network executives."

"With my producer?" Puzzled, she tilted her head and tried to reason it out. "Why?"

"She wants them to fire you—or, ah, to let your contract lapse."

Stunned, she said nothing. But her face went pale. The rag slipped silently from her hand to the floor.

"She'd agree to do a series of guest spots for the show, if you were no longer on it. Your producer politely turned her down. So she went upstairs."

Ariel swallowed the panic. All she could think, all that drummed in her mind was, *not now, not during the hearing.* She needed the stability of that contract for Scott. "And?"

He hadn't expected this white-lipped, wide-eyed reaction. A woman with her temperament should have been angry, angry enough to rage, throw things, explode. He could even have understood amusement, a burst of laughter, a shake of the head and a shrug. She was confident enough for that. He'd thought she was. What he saw in her eyes was basic fear.

"Ariel, just how important do you think you are to the show?"

She found she had to swallow before she could form the first word. "Amanda's a popular character. I get the lion's share of mail, a lot of it addressed to Amanda rather than me. In my last contract, my scale was upgraded with the minimum amount of negotiation." She swallowed again and gripped her hands together. That was all very logical, all very practical. She wanted to scream. "Anyone can be replaced. On a soap, that's the number-one rule. Are they going to let me go?"

"No." Frowning at her, he stepped closer. "I'm surprised you'd think they would. You're already their biggest reason for the ratings lead. And with the film due in the fall, the show's bound to cash in on it. In a strictly practical way of thinking, you—day after day—are worth a great deal more to the network than Liz in a one-shot deal." When Ariel let out a long breath he had to fight the urge to take her into his arms. "Does the show mean that much to you?"

"Yes, it means that much to me."

"Why?"

"It's my show," she said simply. "My character." As the panic faded, the anger seeped in. "If I leave it, it'll be because it's what I want, or because I'm not good enough anymore." Giving in to rage she plucked up a little yellow vase from the table beside her and flung it and the baby's breath it held at the wall. Glass shattered, flowers spilled. "I've given five years of my life to that show." As her breathing calmed again, she stared at the shards of vase and broken blooms. "It's important to me," she continued, looking back up at Booth. "At the moment, for a lot of reasons, it's essential." Ariel gripped the side of the hammock and struggled to relax. "How did you hear about this?"

"From Pat. There's been quite a meeting of the minds as concerns you. We decided you should hear about this latest move privately."

"I appreciate it." The anger was fading. Relief made her light-headed. "Well, I'm sorry she feels so pressured that she'd try to do me out of a job, but I imagine she'll back off now."

"You're smarter than that."

"There's nothing she can do to me, not really. And every time she tries, she only makes it worse for herself." Slowly, deliberately, she relaxed her hands. "Every interview she gives is free publicity for the film."

"If there's any way she can hurt you, she will. I should've thought of that before I cast you as Rae."

Smiling, Ariel lifted her hands to his arms. "Are you worried about me? I'd like you to be...just a little."

He should have backed off right then. But he needed, badly needed to absorb that contact. Just her hands on his arms. If he were careful, very careful, it might be enough. "Whatever trouble she causes you I'm responsible for."

"That's a remarkably ridiculous statement—arrogant, egotistical." She grinned. "And exactly like you. I've missed you, Booth. I've missed everything about you."

She was drawing him closer, but more, she was drawing him in. Even as her hand reached for his face, he was lowering his mouth to hers. And the first taste was enough to make him forget every promise he'd made during this absence.

Ariel moaned as her lips met his. It seemed she'd been waiting for years to feel that melting thrill again. More. The greed flashed through her. She pulled him down so that the hammock swayed under their combined weight.

There was no gentleness in either of them now. Impatience shimmered. Without words they told each other to hurry—hurry and touch me; it's been too long. And as clothes were tugged away and flesh met flesh, they both took hungrily from the other.

The movement of the hammock was like the sea, and he felt the freedom. There was freedom simply in being near her again. And from freedom sprang the madness. He couldn't stop his hands from racing over her. He couldn't prevent his mouth from trying to devour every inch. He was starving for her and no longer cared that he had vowed to abstain. Her skin flowed warm and soft under his hands. Her mouth was hot and silky. The generosity he could never quite measure simply poured from her.

She'd stopped thinking the moment he'd kissed her again. Ariel didn't need the intellect now, only the senses. She could taste the salt on his skin as they clung together in the moist heat of the afternoon; the dark male flavor along his throat enticed her back, again and again. There was a fury of desire in him, more than she'd ever known in him before. It made her skin tremble to be wanted with such savagery.

But with the trembling came a mirroring desire in herself. The top of the hammock scraped against her back as his body pressed against hers. For one isolated moment, she thought she could feel the individual strands, then that sensation faded into another.

His hands were in her hair, holding her head back so that he could plunder her mouth. She heard his breath shudder, and saw, as her lashes fluttered up, that he was watching her. Always watching.

His eyes stayed open and on hers when he plunged into her. He wanted to see her, needed to know that her need for him was as great as his for her. And he could see it—in the trembling mouth. His name came from there in a breathy whisper. In the stunned pleasure in her eyes. He could bring her that. He could bring her that, Booth thought as he buried his face in her hair. He wanted to bring her everything.

"Ariel..." In the last sane corner of his mind he knew they were both near the edge. He took her face in his hands and crushed his mouth to hers so that they crested, swallowing each other's cry of pleasure.

The movement of the hammock eased, soothing now, like a cradle. They were wrapped together, facing, with her head in the curve of his shoulder. Their bodies were damp from the heat in the air, and from the heat within. A length of her hair fell over her and onto his chest.

"I thought of you," Booth murmured. His eyes were closed. His heartbeat was slowing, but the arms around her didn't loosen. "I could never stop thinking about you."

Ariel's eyes were open, and she smiled. She'd needed no other words but those. "Sleep with me awhile." Turning her head she kissed his shoulder before settling again. "Just for a little while."

For days and nights she'd thought only of tomorrows. The time had come again think only of now. Long after he slept, she lay awake, feeling the hammock move gently.

Chapter 11

Ariel sat on a small wooden bench outside the court-room. It was a busy hallway with people coming and going, but no one paid much attention to a solitary woman in a cream-colored suit who stared straight ahead.

The first day of the hearing was over, and she felt a curious mixture of relief and tension. It had begun; there was no going back. A door opened down the hall, and a flood of people poured out. She'd never felt more alone in her life.

Bigby had outlined it for her. There'd been no surprises. Despite the legal jargon, the first day had dealt basically with establishing the groundwork. Still, to Ariel's mind the preliminary questions had been terribly cut-and-dried. But the wheels had begun to turn, and now that they had, maybe the pace would pick up.

Just let it be over with quickly, she thought and closed her eyes briefly. *Just let it be done.* The tension came from the thought of tomorrow. The relief came from the absolute certainty that she was doing the right thing.

Bigby came out of the courtroom with his slim briefcase in his hand. With his other, he reached out to her. "Let me buy you a drink."

Ariel smiled, linking her hand with his as she rose. "Deal. But make it coffee."

"You did well in there today."

"I didn't do much of anything."

He started to speak, then changed his mind. Maybe it was best not to point out how much she'd done by simply being. Her freshness, the concern in her eyes, the tone of her voice—all of that had been a vital contrast to the stiff backs and stone faces of the Andersons. A judge in a custody suit, a good one, was influenced by more than facts and figures.

"Just keep doing it," he advised, then gave her hand a squeeze as they walked down the hall. Neither of them noticed the dark-suited man in horn rims who followed. "Tell me how the rest of your life's going," he requested. In his unobtrusive way, Bigby guided her through the doors as he guided her thoughts. "It isn't every day I represent a rising celebrity."

She laughed even as the first wave of heat rose off the sidewalk and struck her. New York in midsummer was hot and humid and sweaty. "Is that what I am?"

"Your picture was in *Tube*—and your name was brought up on the MacAllister show." He grinned as she arched a brow. "I'm impressed."

"Read *Tube*, do you, Charlie?" He was trying to keep her calm, she realized. And he was doing it expertly. She slid a companionable arm through his. "I have to admit, the publicity isn't going to hurt the soap, the film or me.''

''In that order?''

Ariel smiled and shrugged. ''Depends on my mood.'' No, she wasn't without ambition. The *Tube* spread had given her a great deal of self-satisfaction. ''It's been a long time between shampoo commercials, and I won't be sorry if I don't have to stand, lathered up, for three hours again any time soon.''

They entered a coffee shop where the temperature dropped by twenty-five degrees. Ariel gave a quick shiver and a sigh of relief. ''So professionally, everything's rolling along?'' Charlie asked.

''No complaints.'' Ariel slipped into the little vinyl booth and pushed off her shoes. ''They're casting for *Chapter Two* next week. I haven't done live theater in too long.''

Bigby clucked his tongue as he picked up a menu. The man in the dark suit took the booth behind them, settling with his back to Ariel's. ''You don't sit still, do you?''

''Not any longer than I can help it. I have good feelings about the custody suit, maybe because I'm on a professional roll. It's all going to work out, Charlie. I'm going to have Scott with me, and Booth's film's going to be a smash.''

He eyed her over his glasses, then grinned. ''The power of positive thinking.''

''If it works.'' She leaned her elbows on the table, then rested her chin on her fists. ''All my life I've been moving toward certain goals, without really understanding that I was setting them for myself. They're almost within reach.''

Bigby glanced up at the waitress before he turned back to Ariel. "How about some pie with the coffee."

"You twisted my arm. Blueberry." She touched the tip of her tongue to her lip because she could almost taste it.

"Two of each," Bigby told the waitress. "Speaking of Booth DeWitt..." he went on.

"Were we?"

He caught the gleam of amusement in Ariel's eye. "I think you mentioned him to me a few weeks ago. A man who didn't think much of relationships or actresses?"

"You've quite a memory—and very sharp deductive skills."

"It was easy enough to put two and two together, particularly after Liz Hunter's performance on the MacAllister show the other night."

"Performance?" Ariel repeated with a half smile.

"An actor can usually see through another, I'd think. A lawyer's got a lot of actor in him." He paused and folded his hands on the chipped Formica much as he did on his desk. "She put DeWitt through the wringer a couple of years ago."

"They damaged each other. You know, sometimes I think people can be attracted to the specific persons who are the worst for them."

"Is that from personal experience?"

Her eyes became very sober, her mouth very soft. "Booth is right for me. In a lot of ways he'll make my life difficult, but he's right for me."

"What makes you so sure."

"I'm in love with him." When the pie was brought over, Ariel ignored the coffee and concentrated on it. "Bless you, Charlie," she said after the first bite.

He lifted a brow at the sliver of pie she was in raptures over. "You're easily impressed."

"Cynic. Eat it."

He picked up a fork and polished it absently with a paper napkin. "At the risk of putting my foot in it, DeWitt isn't the type of man I'd've matched you with."

Ariel swallowed the next mouthful. "Oh?"

"He's very intense, serious-minded. His scripts have certainly indicated that. And you're..."

"Flaky?" she suggested, breaking off the next piece of pie.

"No." Bigby opened one of the little plastic containers of cream that were heaped in a bowl on the table. "You're anything but that. But you're full of life—the joy of it. It's not that you don't face the hard side when it comes up, but you don't look for it. It seems to me DeWitt does."

"Maybe—maybe he expects it. If you expect it and it happens, you aren't as staggered by it. For some people, it's a defensive move." A small frown creased her brow before she smoothed it away. "I think Booth and I can learn a lot from each other."

"And what does Booth think—or am I out of line?"

"You're not out of line, Charlie," she said absently as she remembered how grim Booth had been when he'd come to her door, how intensely he'd made love to her. He'd relaxed, degree by slow degree. Then he'd slept, with his arms tightly around her, as if he'd just needed to hold on. To her, she'd wondered, or to the peace? Perhaps it didn't matter. "It's hard for Booth," she murmured. "He wanted to be left alone, wanted his life to go on a certain way. I've interfered with that. He needs more time, more space."

"And what do you need?"

She looked over and saw her answer hadn't pleased him. *He's thinking of me,* Ariel realized, touched. Reaching over, she laid a hand on his. "I love him, Charlie. That's enough, for now. I do know it's not enough for always, but people can't put a control switch on emotions. I can't," she corrected.

"Does that mean he can?"

"To a certain extent." Ariel opened her mouth again, then shook her head. "No, I don't want to change him, even in that way. Not change. I need the balance he brings me, and I need to be able to lighten some of those shadows he carries around. It's the same with Scott, in a way. I need the stability he brings to my life—the way Scott, maybe children in general, can center it. Basically, I have an outrageous need to be needed."

"Have you told Booth about Scott? About the custody hearing?"

"No." Ariel stirred sugar into her coffee but didn't drink it. "It doesn't seem fair to saddle him with a problem that was already in full swing when we met. Instinct tells me to handle it myself, then when it's resolved, to tell Booth in my own way."

"He might not like it," Bigby pointed out. "The one thing Ford brought up in our last meeting that I have to agree with is that some men can't or won't be responsible for another man's child."

Ariel shook her head. "I don't believe that of Booth. But if it's true, it's something I'll have to deal with."

"If you did have to make a choice?"

She said nothing at first, as she dealt with the ache even the possibility brought her. "When you make a choice between two people you love," Ariel said qui-

etly, "you choose the one who needs you the most."
She lifted her eyes again. "Scott's only a child, Charlie."

He leaned across to pat her hand. "I just wanted to
hear you say it. To be completely unprofessional
again," he said with a grin, "there isn't a man in the
world who'd turn down either you or Scott."

"That's why I'm crazy about you." She paused a
moment, then touched her fork to her tongue. "Charlie,
would you think I was really a hedonist if I ordered
another piece of this pie?"

"Yes."

"Good." Ariel lifted a hand and gestured for the
waitress. "Once in a while I just have to be decadent."

Amanda's life was a pressure cooker. As she went
over the pacing of her lines one last time, Ariel decided
she was grateful for the tension. It helped her deal with
reality just a little better. She'd spent the morning in
court, and the following day she was scheduled to take
the stand. That was one part she couldn't rehearse for.
But the good feeling she'd experienced the first day of
the hearing hadn't faded, nor had her optimism. It was
poor Amanda, Ariel mused, who'd continue to have
problems that would never completely be resolved.
That was life in a soap opera.

The rest of the cast had yet to return from the lunch
break. Ariel sat alone in the studio—lounged, that is,
on the rumpled bed she would rise from when Amanda
was awakened by the sound of breaking glass. Alone
and defenseless, she'd face the Trader's Bend Ripper.
She'd have only her wits and professional skill to protect her from a psychotic killer.

Already in costume, a plain nightshirt in periwinkle-blue, she continued to murmur her lines out loud while doing a few lazy leg lifts. She'd had some vague twinges of guilt about the second piece of blueberry pie.

"Well, well, so this is the lightning pace of daytime television."

Immersed in the gripping scene between Amanda and a psychopath, Ariel dropped the script and gasped. The pages fluttered back down to her stomach while her hand flew to her throat. "Good God, Booth. I hope you're up on your CPR, because my heart just stopped."

"I'll get it started again." Placing a hand on either side of her head, he leaned down and kissed her— softly, slowly, thoroughly. As surprised by the texture of the kiss as she'd been by his sudden appearance, Ariel lay still and absorbed. She knew only that something was different; but with her mind spinning and her blood pumping she couldn't grab on to it.

He knew. As he eased down to sit on the bed and prolonged the kiss, Booth understood precisely what was different. He loved her. He'd awakened alone in his own bed that morning, reaching for her. He'd read something foolish in the paper and had automatically thought how she'd have laughed. He'd seen a young girl with a balloon giggling as she'd dragged her mother toward the park. And he'd thought of Ariel.

And thinking of her, he'd seen that the sky was beautiful and blue, that the city was frantic and full of surprises, that life was a joy. How foolish he'd been to resist her, and all she offered.

She was his second chance.... No, if he were honest, he'd admit that Ariel was his first chance at real happiness—complete happiness. He was no longer going to allow memories of ugliness to bar him from that, or from her.

"How's your heart rate?" he murmured.

Ariel let out a long breath, let her eyes open slowly. "You can cancel the ambulance."

He glanced at the tumbled bed, then down her very sedate, very appealing costume. "Were you having a nap?"

"I," she countered primly, "was working. The rest of the cast is at lunch, I wasn't due in till one." She pushed at the hair that fell dark and disordered over his brow. No tension, she thought immediately, and smiled. "What're you doing here? You're usually knee-deep in brilliant phrases this time of day."

"I wanted to see you."

"That's nice." Sitting up, she threw her arms around his neck. "That's very nice."

It would take so little, Booth mused as he held her close. What would her reaction be when he told her that he'd stopped resisting, and that nothing had ever made him happier than having her in his life? Tonight, he thought, nuzzling into her neck. Tonight when they were alone, when there was no one to disturb them, he'd tell her. And he'd ask her.

"Can you stay awhile?" Ariel didn't know why she felt so wonderful, nor did she want to explore the reasons.

"I'll stay until you wrap, then I'm going to steal you and take you home with me."

She laughed, and as she shifted her weight, the script crumpled beneath her.

"Your lines," Booth warned.

"I know them. This—" she flung back her head so

that her eyes glittered ''—is a climactic scene full of danger and drama.''

He looked back at the bed. ''And sex?''

''No!'' Shoving him away she scrambled onto her knees. ''Amanda's tossing and turning in bed, her dreams were disturbed. Fade out—soft focus—she's wandering through a mist, lost, alone. She hears footsteps behind her. Close-up. Fear. And then...'' While her voice took on a dramatic pitch, she tossed her hair behind her back. ''Up ahead, she sees a figure in the fog.'' Ariel lifted a hand as if to brush away a curtain of mist. ''Should she run toward it—away from it? The footsteps behind her come faster, her breathing quickens. A sliver of moonlight—pale, eerie—cuts through. It's Griff up ahead holding out a hand to her, calling her name in an echoing, disembodied voice. He loves her, she wants to go to him. But the footsteps are closing in. And as she begins to run, there's the sharp, cruel glimmer of a knife.''

Ariel grabbed both of his shoulders then did a mock faint into his lap. Booth grinned. A quick tug of her hair had her eyes opening. ''And then?''

''The man wants more.'' Scrambling up again, Ariel pushed the script aside. ''The scream's caught in her throat, and before she can free it, there's a crash, a splinter of glass. Amanda jerks up in bed, her face glistening with sweat, her breath heaving.'' When she demonstrated, Booth wondered if she knew just how clever she was. ''Did she dream it, or did she really hear it? Frightened, but impatient with herself, she gets out of bed.''

Swinging her feet to the floor, Ariel got out of bed, frowning at the door as Amanda would do, absently pushing back her hair and reached for the low light beside the bed. "Perhaps it was the wind," she continued. "Perhaps it was the dream, but she knows she'll never get back to sleep unless she takes a look. Music builds—lots of bass—as she opens the bedroom door. Cut to commercial."

"Come on, Ariel." Exasperated, he grabbed her hand and pulled her back toward the bed.

Obligingly she circled his neck with her arms as she stood in front of him. "Now you'll learn the best way to keep that shine on your no-wax floor."

He pinched her, hard. "It's the Ripper."

"Maybe," she said with a flutter of her lashes. "Maybe not."

"It's the Ripper," he said decisively. "And our intrepid Amanda goes downstairs. How does she get out of being victim number five?"

"Six," Ariel corrected. "The saying goes—that's for me to know and you to find out." With a jerk of his wrist, he'd whipped her around so that she tumbled into his lap, laughing. "Go ahead, torture me, do your worst. I'll never talk." Linking her hands around his neck, she looked up at him and smiled. And she was so beautiful, so full of life at its best that she took his breath away.

"I love you, Ariel."

He felt the fingers at his neck go limp, saw the smile fade, her eyes widen. Inside, Ariel felt as though someone had just cut off the flow of blood from her heart. "That's a tough way to find out a plot line," she managed after a moment. She would have sat up if she'd had the strength to resist the gentle pressure of his hand on her shoulder.

"I love you, Ariel," he repeated, forgetting all his plans for telling her with finesse and with intimacy. "I think I always have. I know I always will.'' He cupped her face in his hand as her eyes filled. ''You're everything I've ever wanted and was afraid to hope for. Stay with me.'' He touched his lips to hers and felt the tremor. ''Marry me.''

When he would have drawn back, she clutched at his shirt. Burying her face in his shoulder she took a deep breath. ''Be sure,'' she whispered. ''Booth, be absolutely sure because I'll never give you a moment's peace. I'll never let you get away. Before you ask me again, remember that. I don't believe in mutual disagreements or irreconcilable differences. With me, it's forever, Booth. It's for always.''

He forced her head back. In his eyes she saw the fire and the passion. And the love. ''You're damn right.'' Her breathless laugh was muffled against his mouth. ''I want to get married quickly.'' He punctuated the words with another kiss. ''And quietly. Just how soon can they shoot around Amanda so we can have more than a weekend honeymoon?''

Ariel hadn't known anyone could outpace her. Now, her thoughts jumbled as she struggled to keep up. Marriage—he was already talking of marriage and honeymoons. ''Well, I, let's see... After Griff saves Amanda from the Ripper, she loses the baby and goes into a coma. The hospital scenes could be—''

''Ahah.'' With a self-satisfied smile, Booth kissed her nose. ''So Griff saves her from the Ripper, which removes him from the list of suspects.''

Ariel's eyes narrowed. ''You rat.''

''Just be glad I'm not a spy for another network. You're a pushover.''

''I'll show you a pushover,'' Ariel claimed, and overbalanced him so that he landed on his back. He loved her. The thought brought on such giddiness, she collapsed against him, laughing. Before he could retaliate, they heard someone rushing up the stairs.

"Ariel! Ariel, you'd better take a look at—" Stella skidded to a halt when she saw Ariel and Booth laughing and half-lying on the bed. She whipped the paper she held behind her back and swore under her breath. "Whoops!" With the aid of an embarrassed smile she called on all her skill to keep either of them from noticing that she felt slightly ill inside and desperately worried. "Well, I'd've knocked if you'd bothered to close the door." She gestured with her free hand toward the false wall. "Suppose I go out and come in again?" *Right after I burn this paper,* she thought grimly, and grinning, backed up.

"Don't go." Ariel struggled all the way up, but kept one hand tucked into Booth's. "I'm about to bestow a singularly great honor on you." She squeezed Booth's fingers. "My sister, however rotten, should be the first to know."

"By all means."

"Stella..." Ariel stopped because she caught a glimpse of something in her friend's eyes. A glimpse was enough. "What is it?"

"Nothing. I remembered I have to talk to Neal about something, that's all. Look, I'd better catch him before he—"

But Ariel was already rising from the bed. "What was it you wanted me to see, Stella?"

"Oh, nothing." There was a warning, a deliberate one, in her eyes. "It can wait."

Unsmiling, Ariel held out her hand, palm up.

Stella's fingers curled tighter around the paper. "Ariel, it's not a good time. I think you'd better—"

"I think I'd better see it now."

"Dammit." With a glance over Ariel's shoulder at Booth, Stella passed her the paper.

Celebrity Explorer, Ariel noted with a slight flicker of annoyance. As tabloids went it was bottom of the barrel. Half-amused, she glanced over the exploitive headlines. "Really, Stella, if this is the best you can do for lunchtime reading, I'm disillusioned." Absently, she turned it over and scanned under the fold. From behind her Booth saw the tension shoot into her body.

SOAP OPERA QUEEN'S DESPERATE BATTLE
FOR LOVE CHILD

Below the bold print headline was a grainy picture of Ariel sitting on the grass in Central Park with Scott's face caught in her hands. In one part of her mind she remembered that frozen moment from their last Sunday afternoon. As she stared at it, appalled, sickened, she didn't hear Booth rise and come to her.

Something slammed into his stomach—not a hammer but a fist that thrust then ground deep. Even the poor quality of the photo didn't disguise the stunning resemblance between Ariel and the child that laughed into her face. There was no mistaking the tie of blood. As the headline shouted out at him, Booth wanted to murder.

"Just want the hell is this?"

Shaken, Ariel looked up. Scott was not to see it, she thought over and over. This was not to touch him. How? How had it leaked? The Andersons? No, she rejected that thought instantly. They wanted publicity less than she did.

The picture...who'd taken it? Someone had followed her, she decided. Someone had followed her and found out about Scott, the custody hearing. Then they'd twisted it into an ugly headline and an exploitive article. But who...?

Liz Hunter. Ariel's fingers tightened on the newspaper. Of course, it had to be. There were few women who knew better than Ariel what that type of person was capable of. Liz hadn't been able to get to her professionally, so she'd taken the next step.

"Ariel, I asked you what the hell this is."

Ariel focused on Booth abruptly. *Oh God,* she thought, *now I have to work my way through the ugliness before I can explain.* Already, she saw the anger, the distrust. "I'd like to talk to you privately," she said calmly enough. "Down in my dressing room."

As Ariel turned to go, Stella reached out, then dropped her hand helplessly back to her side. "Ariel, I'm sorry."

She only shook her head. "No, it's all right. We'll talk later."

As they wound their way through the studio, down the corridors, she tried to think logically. All she could see was that nasty headline and grainy picture. When she walked into the dressing room she went directly to the coffeepot, needing to do something with her hands. She heard the door close and the lock click.

"This isn't the way I wanted to handle this, Booth." She pulled in a deep breath as she fumbled with the coffee. "I didn't expect any publicity...I've been so careful."

"Yes, careful." He jammed his hands into his pockets.

She pressed her lips together as the tone of his voice pricked along her skin. "I know you must have questions. If I...."

"Yes, I have questions." He snatched the paper

from her dressing table. He, too, needed to occupy his hands. "Are you involved in a custody suit?"

"Yes."

He felt the grinding in his stomach again. "So much for trust."

"No, Booth." She whirled around, then stopped as a hundred conflicting emotions, a hundred opposing answers hammered at her. Would this be the time of choice? Would she have to choose after all, when she almost had everything she needed? "Please, let me explain. Let me think how to explain."

"You're involved in a custody suit." He remembered those brief flashes of strain he'd seen in her from time to time. He wanted to tear the paper to shreds. "You have this child, and you didn't tell me. What does that say about trust?"

Confused, she dragged a hand through her hair. "Booth, I was already deeply involved in this before we even met. I couldn't drag you into it."

Bitterness seeped into him. Booth hated to taste it...again. "Oh, I see. You were already involved, so it was none of my business. It appears that you have two separate standards for your trust, Ariel. The one for yourself, and the one for everyone else."

"That's not true," she began, then fumbled to a halt. Was it? "I don't mean for it to be." Her voice began to shake, then her hands. "Booth, I've been frightened. Part of the fear was that something would leak out. The most important thing to me was that none of this touch Scott."

He waited, trying to be impassive as she brushed away the first tear. "That's the boy's name?"

"Yes. He's only four years old."

He turned away because the grief on her face was destroying him. "And his father?"

"His father's name was Jeremy. He's dead."

Booth didn't ask if she'd loved him. He didn't have to. She'd loved another man, he thought. Had borne another man's child. Could he deal with that, accept it? Resting his palms on her dressing table he let the emotion run through him. Yes, he thought so. It didn't change her, or him. And yet...and yet she hadn't told him. It was that that brought the change.

"Who has the boy now?" he asked stiffly.

"His grandparents. He's not...he's not happy with them. He needs me, Booth, and I need him. I need both of you. Please..." Her voice lowered to a whisper. "Don't ask me to choose. I love you. I love you so much but he's just a little boy."

"Choose?" Booth flicked on his lighter, then tossed it onto her cluttered dressing table as he took the first drag from his cigarette. "Dammit, Ariel, just how insensitive do you think I am?"

She waited until she could control the throb of her heart at the base of her throat. "Would you take both of us?"

Booth blew out smoke. Fury was just below the surface. "You kept it from me. That's the issue now. I could hardly turn away from a child that's part of you."

She reached for him. "Booth—"

"You kept it from me," he repeated, watching her hand drop away. "Why?"

"Please understand, if I kept it from you it was only because I wanted to protect him. He's had a difficult time already, and I was afraid that if I talked about the hearing to anyone, anyone at all, there was a risk of something like that.'' She gestured to the paper, then turned away.

"There's nothing you don't know about my life, Ariel. I can't help but resent that there was something so vital to yours that you kept from me. All this time, almost from the first minute, you've asked me to trust you. Now that I've given that to you, I find you haven't trusted me.''

"I put Scott first. He needed someone to put him first.''

"I might be able to understand that, if you could explain to me why you ever gave him up.''

"Gave him up?'' Ariel stared, but tears blurred her vision. "I don't know what you mean.''

"I thought I knew you!'' Booth exploded. "I believed that, and believing it fell in love with you when I'd sworn I'd never get emotionally involved again. How could you give up your child? How could you have a child and say nothing to me?''

"Give up my child?'' she repeated dumbly. "But no, no! It's nothing like that.''

"Dammit, Ariel, you've let someone else raise your child. And now that you want him back, now that you're involved in something as serious as a custody battle, you do it alone. How could you love me, how could you preach trust at me and say nothing?''

"I was afraid to tell you or anyone. You don't understand how it might affect Scott if he knew—''

"Or how it might affect you?'' He swung his arm toward the discarded paper.

Ariel sucked in her breath and barely controlled a raging denial. Perhaps she'd deserved that. "My concern was for Scott,'' she said evenly. "A custody suit would hardly damage my reputation. Any more than an illegitimate child would—though he's not my child. Jeremy was my brother.''

It was Booth's turn to stare. Nothing made sense. Underlying his confusion was the thought that tears didn't belong in Ariel's eyes. Her eyes were for laughter. "The boy's your nephew?"

"Jeremy and his wife died late last winter." She couldn't go to him now; she could see he wasn't ready. And neither was she. "His grandparents, the Andersons, were appointed guardians. He's not happy with them."

Not her child, Booth thought again, but her brother's child. He waited to gauge his own reaction and found he was still hurt, still angry. Whether the boy was her son or not hadn't been the issue. She'd blocked that part of her life from him.

"I think," Booth said slowly, "that you'd better start at the beginning."

Ariel opened her mouth, but before she could speak, someone pounded on her door. "Phone for you, Ariel, in Neal's office. Urgent."

Banking back frustration, she left the room, heading for Neal's office. So much to explain, she thought. To Booth and to herself. She rubbed her temple with two fingers as she picked up the phone. "Hello."

"Ms. Kirkwood."

"Yes, this is Ariel Kirkwood." Her frown deepened. "Mr. Anderson?"

"Scott's missing."

Chapter 12

She said nothing. Only seconds passed, but a hundred thoughts raced through her mind, tumbling over each other one at a time so that none was clear. Every nerve in her stomach froze. Vaguely she felt the ache in her hand where she gripped the receiver.

"Ms. Kirkwood, I said that Scott is missing."

"Missing?" she repeated in a whisper. The word itself brought up too many visions. Terrifying ones. She wanted to panic, but forced herself, by digging her nails into her palm, to talk, and to listen carefully. But even the whisper she forced out shook. "How long?"

"Apparently since around eleven o'clock. My wife thought he was next door, playing with a neighbor's child. When she called him home for lunch, she learned he'd never been there."

Eleven... With a sick kind of dread Ariel looked at her watch. It was nearly two. Three hours. Where could a small boy go in three hours? Anywhere. It was an eternity. "You've called the police?"

"Of course." His voice was brisk but through it ran a thread of fear Ariel was too dazed to hear. "The neighborhood's been searched, people questioned. Everything possible's being done."

Everything possible? What did that mean? She repeated the phrase over in her mind, but it still didn't make sense. "Yes, of course." She heard her own words come hollowly through the rushing noise in her head. "I'll be there right away."

"No, the police suggest that you go home and stay there, in case Scott contacts you."

Home, she thought. They wanted her to go home and do nothing while Scott was missing. "I want to come. I could be there in thirty minutes." The whisper shattered into a desperate plea. "I could help look for him. I could—"

"Ms. Kirkwood," Anderson cut her off, then breathed deeply before he continued. "Scott's an intelligent boy. He knows where you live, he knows your phone number. At a time like this it's best to admit that it's you he wants to be with. If he—if it's possible for him to contact anyone, it would be you. Please, go home. If he's found here, I'll call you immediately."

The single phrase ran through her mind three times. *If it's possible for him to contact anyone...*

"All right. I'll go home. I'll wait there." Dazed, she stared at the phone, not even aware that she'd replaced the receiver herself. Marveling that she could walk at all, she moved to the door.

Of course she could walk, Ariel told herself as she pressed a hand to the wall for support. She could function—she had to function. Scott was going to want her when he was found. He'd be full of stories and adventures—especially if he had the chance to ride in a police car. He'd want to tell her about all of it. The phone would probably be ringing when she opened her front door. He'd probably just been daydreaming and wandered a few blocks away, that was all. They'd be calling, so she should get home quickly. Her legs felt like rubber and would hardly move at all.

Booth was brooding at the picture of Ariel and Scott when he heard the door open. He turned, the paper still in his hand, but the questions that had been pressing at him faded the moment he saw her. Her skin was like parchment. He'd never seen her eyes look vacant, nor had he expected to.

"Ariel..." He was crossing to her before he'd finished speaking her name. "What is it?"

"Booth." She put her hand on his chest. Warm, solid. She could feel the beat of his heart. No, none of it was a dream. Or a nightmare. "Scott's missing. They don't know where he is. He's missing."

He took a firm hold on her shoulders. "How long, Ariel?"

"Three hours." The first wave of fear rammed through the shock. "Oh God, no one's seen him in three hours. Nobody knows where he is!"

He only tightened his hold on her shoulders when her body began to shake. "The police?"

"Yes, yes, they're looking." Her fingers curled, digging at his shirt. "They don't want me to come, they want me to go home and wait in case he...Booth."

"I'll take you home." He brushed the hair away from her face. His touch, his voice, was meant to soothe. "We'll go home and wait for the call. They're going to find him, Ariel. Little boys wander off all the time.''

"Yes.'' She grabbed on to that, and to his hand. Of course that was true. Didn't she have to watch him like a hawk when they went to the park or the zoo? "Scott daydreams a lot. He could've just walked farther than he should. They're going to call me—I should be home.''

"I'm going to take you.'' Booth kept hold of her as she took a disoriented study of the room. "You change, and I'll let them know you can't tape this afternoon.''

"Change?'' Puzzled she looked down and saw she still wore Amanda's night shirt. "All right, I'll hurry. They could call any minute.''

She tried to hurry, but her fingers kept fumbling with the most basic task. She needed her jeans, but her mind seemed to fade in and out as she pulled them on. Then her fingers slid over the snap. She tried to think logically but the pounding at the side of her head made it impossible. Holding off the nausea helped. It gave her something tangible to concentrate on while she fought with the laces of her shoes.

Booth was back within moments. When she turned to look at him he could feel her panic. "Ready?''

"Yes.'' She nodded and walked out with him, one foot in front of the other, while images of Scott, lost, frightened, streamed through her head. Or worse, much worse—Scott getting into a car with a stranger, a stranger whose face was only a shadow. She wanted to scream. She climbed into a cab.

Booth took her icy hand in his. "Ariel, it isn't like you to anticipate the worst. Think.'' He put his other hand over hers and tried to warm it. "There're a hun-

dred harmless reasons for his being out of touch for a
few hours. He might've found a dog, or chased a ball.
He might've found some fascinating rock and taken it
to a secret place to study it.''

''Yes.'' She tried to picture those things. It would
be typical of Scott. The image of the car and the
stranger kept intruding. He had no basic fear of people,
something she'd always admired in him. Now it filled
her with fear. Turning her face in to Booth's shoulder
she tried to convince herself that the phone would be
ringing when she opened the front door.

When the cab stopped, she jerked upright and scrambled for the handle. She was dashing up the steps before Booth had paid the driver.

Silence. It greeted her like an accusation. Ariel
stared at the phone and willed it to ring. When she
looked at her watch, she saw it had been less than thirty
minutes since Anderson's call. Not enough time, she
told herself as she began to pace. *Too much time.* Too
much time for a little boy to be alone.

Do something! The words ran through her mind as
she struggled to find something solid to grip on to.
She'd always been able to do something in any situation. There were answers, and if not answers, choices.
But to wait. To have no answer, no choice but to wait...
She heard the door close and turned. Her hands lifted,
then fell helplessly.

''Booth. Oh God, I don't know what to do. There
must be something—anything.''

Without a word he crossed to her, wrapped his arms
around her and let her cling to him. Strange that it
would have taken this—something so frightening for
her—to make him realize she needed him every bit as
much as he needed her. Whatever doubts he'd had, and

whatever anger had lingered that she'd kept part of her life from him, dropped away. Love was simpler than he'd ever imagined.

"Sit down, Ariel." As he spoke, he eased her toward a chair. "I'm going to fix you a drink."

"No, I—"

"Sit down," he repeated with a firmness he knew she needed. "I'll make coffee, or I'll see about getting you a sedative."

"I don't need a sedative."

He nodded, rewarded by the sharp, quick answer. If she was angry, just a little angry, she wouldn't fall apart. "Then I'll make coffee."

The moment he went into the kitchen she was up again. Sitting was impossible, calm out of the question. She should never have agreed to come back and wait, Ariel told herself. She should have insisted on going out and looking for Scott herself. It was useless here— she was useless here. But if he called and she wasn't there to answer... Oh, God. She pressed her hands to her face and tried not to crumble. What time was it?

This time when she looked at her watch she felt the first hysterical sob build.

"Ariel." Booth carried two cups of coffee, hot and strong. He watched as she shuddered, swallowing sobs, but the tears ran freely.

"Booth, where could he be? He's hardly more than a baby. He doesn't have any fear of strangers. It's my fault because—"

"Stop." He said the word softly, but it had the effect of cutting off the rapidly tumbling words. He held out the cup, waiting for her to take it in both hands. It shook, nearly spilling the coffee over the rim. As it depleted, she sat again. "Tell me about him."

For a moment she stared at the coffee, as if she had no idea what it was or how she'd come to be holding it. "He's four...almost five. He wants a wagon, a yellow one, for his birthday. He likes to pretend." Lifting the cup, she swallowed coffee, and as it scalded her mouth, she calmed a bit. "Scott has a wonderful imagination. You can give him a cardboard box and he'll see a spaceship, a submarine, an Egyptian tomb. Really see it, do you know what I mean?"

"Yes." He laid a hand on hers as he sat beside her.

"When Jeremy and Barbara died, he was so lost. They were beautiful together, the three of them. So happy."

Her eyes were drawn to the boxing gloves that hung behind the door. Jeremy's gloves. They'd be Scott's one day. Something ripped inside her stomach. Ariel began to talk faster. "He's a lot like his father, the same charm and curiosity. The Andersons, Barbara's parents, never approved of Jeremy. They didn't want Barbara to marry him, and rarely saw her after she did. After...after the accident, they were appointed Scott's guardians. I wanted him, but it seemed natural that he go with them. A house, a yard, a family. But..." Breaking off, she cast a desperate look at the phone.

"But?" Booth prompted.

"They just aren't capable of understanding the kind of person Scott is. He'll pretend he's an archeologist and dig a hole in their yard."

"That might annoy anyone," Booth said and drew a wan smile from her.

"But he wouldn't dig up the yard if he had a sand dump and someone told him it could be a desert. Instead, he's punished for his imagination rather than having it redirected."

"So you decided to fight for him."

"Yes." Ariel moistened her lips. Had she waited too long? "Even if that were all, I might not have started proceedings. They don't love him." Her eyes shimmered as she looked up again. "They just feel responsible for him. I can't bear thinking he could grow up without all the love he should have."

Where is he, where is he, where is he?

"He won't." Booth drew her against him to kiss the tears at the corners of her eyes. "After you get custody, we'll see that he doesn't."

Cautiously, she pulled back, though her fingers were still tight on his shoulders. "We?"

Booth lifted a brow. "Is Scott part of your life?"

"Yes, he—"

"Then he's part of mine."

Her mouth trembled open twice before she could speak. "No questions?"

"I've wasted a lot of time with questions. Sometimes there's no need for them." He pressed her fingers to his lips. "I love you."

"Booth, I'm so afraid." Her head dropped against him. The dam burst.

He let her weep, those harsh sobs that were edged with grief and fear. He let her hold on and pull out whatever strength she could find in him. He lived by words, but knew when clever phrases were of no use. So in silence, Booth held her.

Crying would help, he thought, smoothing her hair. It would allow her to give in to fear without putting a name on it. While she was vulnerable to tears, it was he who willed the phone to ring. And he was denied.

The passion exhausted her. Ariel lay against Booth, light-headed, disoriented, only aware of that hollow ache inside that meant something vital was wrong. Her mind groped for the reason. *Scott.* He was missing. The phone hadn't rung. He was still missing.

"Time," she murmured, staring over his shoulder at the phone through eyes that were swollen and abused by tears. "What time is it now?"

"It's nearly four," he answered, hating to tell her, hating the convulsive jerk he felt because her body was pressed so close to his. There were a dozen things he could say to offer comfort. All useless. "I'll make more coffee."

At the knock on the door, she looked around listlessly. She wanted no company now. Ignoring the knock, she turned her back to the door. It was the phone that was important. "I'll get the coffee." Forcing herself to move, she rose. "I don't want to see anyone, please."

"I'll send them away." Booth walked to the door, already prepared to position himself in front of it to shield her. When he opened it, he saw a young woman wearing a bandanna and paint-smeared overalls. Then he saw the boy.

"Excuse me. This little boy was wandering a couple blocks from here. He gave this address. I wonder if—"

"Who are you?" Scott demanded of Booth. "This is Ariel's house."

"I'm Booth. Ariel's been waiting for you, Scott."

Scott grinned, showing small white teeth. Baby teeth, Booth realized. He's hardly more than a baby. "I would've been here sooner, but I got a little lost. Bobbi was painting her porch and said she'd walk me over."

Booth laid a hand on Scott's head and felt the softness of hair—like Ariel's. "We're very grateful to you, Miss..."

"Freeman, Bobbi Freeman." She grinned and jerked her head toward Scott. "No trouble. He might've lost his way a bit, but he sure knows what he wants. It seems to be Ariel and a peanut butter sandwich. Well, hey, I've got to get back to my porch. See you later, Scott."

"Bye, Bobbi." He yawned hugely. "Is Ariel home now?"

"I'll get her." Leaving Scott to climb onto the hammock, Booth walked toward the kitchen. He stopped Ariel in the doorway then took the two cups from her hands. "There's someone here to see you."

She shut her eyes. "Oh, please, Booth. Not now."

"I don't think he'll take no for an answer."

Something in his tone had her opening her eyes again, had her heart drumming against her ribs. Skirting passed him, she hurried into the living room. A small blond boy swung happily in her hammock with two kittens in his lap. "Oh, God, Scott!"

His arms were already reaching for her as she dashed across the room and yanked him against her. Warmth. She could feel the warmth of his small body and moaned from the joy of it. His rumpled hair brushed against her face. She could smell the faintest memory of soap from his morning wash, mixed with the sweat of the day and the gumdrops he was forever secreting in his pockets. Weeping, laughing, she sank to the floor holding him.

"Scott, oh, Scott. You're not hurt?" The quick fear struck at her again and she pulled him away to examine his face, his hands, his arms. "Are you hurt anywhere?"

"Uh-uh." A bit miffed at the question, Scott squirmed. "I didn't see Butch yet. Where's Butch?"

"How did you get here?" Ariel grabbed him again and gave in to the need to kiss his face—the rounded cheeks, the straight little nose, the small mouth. "Scott, where've you been?"

"On the train." His whole face lit. "I rode on the train all by myself. For a surprise."

"You..." Incredulous, Ariel stared at him. "You came from your grandparents', all alone?"

"I saved up my money." With no little pride he reached in his pocket and pulled out what he had left—a few pennies, two quarters and some gumdrops. "I walked to the station, but it took lots longer than a cab does. It isn't as far in a cab," he decided with a small boy's logic. "And I paid for the ticket all by myself—just like you showed me. I'm hungry, Ariel."

"In a minute." Appalled at the idea of his traveling alone and defenseless, she took both his arms. "You walked all the way to the train station, then rode the train here?"

"And I only got a little bit lost once, when Bobbi helped me. And I was hardly scared at all." His lip trembled. Screwing up his face, he buried it against her. "I wasn't."

All the things that might have happened to him flashed hideously through her mind. Ariel tightened her hold and thanked God. "Of course you weren't," she murmured, struggling to hold on to her emotions until she'd both schooled and scolded. "You're so brave, and so smart to remember the way. But Scott—" she tilted his face to hers "—it was wrong for you to come here all alone."

"But I wanted to see you."

"I know, and I always want to see you." Again she kissed him, just to feel the warmth of his cheek. "But you left without telling your grandparents, and they're so worried. And I've been worried," she added, brushing the hair from his temple. "You have to promise you won't ever do it again."

"I don't want to do it again." With his mouth trembling again, he rubbed his fists against his eyes. "It took a long time and I got hungry, and then I got lost and my legs were so tired. But I wasn't scared."

"It's all right now, baby." Still holding him, she rose. "We'll fix you something to eat, then you can rest in the hammock. Okay?"

Scott sniffled, snuggling closer. "Can I have peanut butter?"

"Absolutely." Booth came back into the room and watched as both heads turned toward him. He might be her own child, he thought, wonderingly. Surprised, he felt a yearning to hold the boy himself. "I just saw a peanut butter sandwich in the kitchen. I think it's yours."

"Okay!" Scott scrambled out of Ariel's arms and bounced away.

Getting unsteadily to her feet, Ariel pressed the heel of her hand to her brow. "I could skin him alive. Oh, Booth," she whispered as she felt his arms go around her. "Isn't he wonderful?"

By dusk, Scott was asleep, with a tattered stuffed dog that had been his father's gripped in one hand. The three-legged Butch kept guard on the pillow beside him. Ariel sat on the sofa next to Booth and faced Scott's grandfather. Coffee grew cold on the table between them. As always, Mr. Anderson sat erect; his clothes were impeccable. But there was a weariness in his eyes Ariel had never seen before.

"Anything might've happened to the boy on a jaunt like that."

"I know." Ariel slipped her hand into Booth's, grateful for the support. "I've made him promise he won't ever do anything like it again. You and your wife must've been sick with worry. I'm sorry, Mr. Anderson. I feel partially to blame because I've let Scott buy the train tickets before."

He shook his head, not speaking for a moment. "An intrepid boy," he managed at length. "Sharp enough to know which train to take, when to get off." His eyes focused on Ariel's again. "He wanted badly to be with you."

Normally the statement would have warmed her. Now, it tightened the already sensitive muscles of her stomach. "Yes. Children often don't understand the consequences of their actions, Mr. Anderson. Scott only thought about coming, not about the hours of panic in between or about the dangers. He was tired and frightened when he got here. I hope you won't punish him too severely."

Anderson took a deep breath and rested a hand on either thigh. "I realized something today, Ms. Kirkwood. I resent that boy."

"Oh, no, Mr. Anderson—"

"Please, let me finish. I resent him, and I don't like knowing that about myself." His voice was clipped, unapologetic and, Ariel realized, old. Not so much in years, she thought, but in attitude. "And more, I've realized that his presence in the house is a constant strain on my wife. He's a reminder of something we lost. I'm not going to justify my feelings to you," he added briskly. "The boy is my grandchild, and therefore, I'm responsible for him. However, I'm an old man, and not inclined to change. I don't want the boy, and you do." He rose while Ariel could only stare at him. "I'll notify my attorney of my feelings on the matter."

"Mr. Anderson." Shaken, Ariel rose. "You know I want Scott, but—"

"I don't, Ms. Kirkwood." With his shoulders straight, Anderson gave her a level look. "It's as basic as that."

And as sad. "I'm sorry" was all she could say.

With a nod only, he left.

"How," Ariel began after a stretch of silence, "could anyone feel that way about a child?"

"About the child?" Booth countered. "Or about themselves?"

She turned to him, puzzled only for a moment. "Yes, that's it, isn't it?"

"I'm an expert on the subject. The difference is—" he drew her down to him again, circling her with his arm so that her head rested against his shoulder "—someone pushed her way into my life and made me see it."

"Is that what I did?" She laughed, riding the next curve on the roller coaster the day had been. Scott was sleeping on her bed, with kittens curled at his feet. He could stay there now. No more tearful goodbyes. "Pushed my way into your life?"

"You can be very tenacious." He gave her hair a sharp tug then captured her mouth as she gasped. "Thank God."

"Should I warn you that once I push my way in, I won't ever get out?"

"No." He shifted so that she could sit across his lap, and he could watch her face. "Let me find out for myself."

"It won't be easy for you, you know."

"What?"

"Dealing with me if you decide to marry me."

His brow rose, and unable to resist, she traced it with a fingertip. "If?"

"I'm giving you your last chance for escape." Half serious, Ariel pressed her palm to his cheek. "I do most things on impulse—eating, spending, sleeping. I much prefer living in chaos to living in order. The fact is I can't function in order at all. I'll get you involved, one way or the other, in any number of organizations."

"That one remains to be seen," Booth muttered.

Ariel only smiled. "I haven't scared you off yet?"

"No." He kissed her, and as the shadows in the room lengthened, neither of them noticed. "And you won't. I can also be tenacious."

"Remember, you'll be taking on a four-year-old child. An active one."

"You've a poor opinion of my stamina."

"Oh, no." This time when she laughed, it held a husky quality. "I'll drive you crazy with my disorganization."

"As long as you stay out of my office," he countered, "you can turn everything else into a building lot."

She tightened her arms around his neck and clung for a moment. He meant it, she told herself, giddy. He meant it all. She had Booth, and Scott. And with them, her life was taking the next turning point. She could hardly wait to find what waited around the corner.

"I'll spoil Scott," she murmured into Booth's neck. "And the rest of our children."

He drew her back slowly, a half smile on his mouth. "How many is implied by *the rest?*"

Her laughter was free and breezy. "Pick a number."

* * * * *

LONE STAR
LSCC
COUNTRY CLUB
EST. 1923

Where Texas society reigns supreme—and appearances are *everything.*

On sale...